Mother Lode

Carol A Sheldon

To Leslie
Carol Sheldon

You can reach the author at www.carolsheldon.com

Published by Houghton

This is a work of fiction. Any resemblance to persons living or dead is purely coincidental.

Historical fiction, Psychological Mystery, Upper Peninsula
of Michigan, Copper mining, Keweenaw

ISBN: 0-6154-4686-8
ISBN-13: 9780615446868

In the middle of the journey of our lives
I came to myself in a dark wood where
the true way was lost to me.
— Dante, 'The Inferno'

Dedication

MOTHER LODE is dedicated to Crys Rourke, whose love of this book and willingness to proof and edit my manuscript at each of its incarnations kept me inspired and moving forward.

Acknowledgements

Others who gave me invaluable help in this long journey are Vicki Weiland, without whose enthusiasm, encouragement, plugs and pitches, I might never have brought this book to print. I thank Joy Stewart and my sister Marilyn Bentley, whose keen eyes found many typos. And Stuart Chappell and Steve Olian, who in addition to giving me their unfailing support, taught me enough about Poker to write that turn-of-events chapter. My brother, David Sheldon's tough love made me rethink some of my story choices. The organization which gave me priceless help and guidance is he Bay Area Independent Publishing Association.

PART I
1900

chapter I

THE BLIZZARD WAS obliterating the road. With the snow already a foot deep, and no town lights in sight, it was almost impossible for Jorie to steer a steady course with the buggy. He brushed his lashes for the hundredth time.

The sun had disappeared over the horizon of Michigan's Upper Peninsula, leaving the sky dark, but not yet black. With no lantern, Jorie knew he'd be lost in this white oblivion if he didn't see some sign of civilization soon. One wrong move and the gelding could slip into a ditch and break a leg. Aiming for a mid-point between the trees on either side of the road was the best he could do.

I need to get to the sheriff's. I need to get there soon, or I'll never get there at all.

Like silent, moving pictures in a kinetoscope, the snow made its presence devoid of sound. Autumn leaves, still blushing red, commingled with the falling snow.

Recent memory bubbled up. *Take my arm, Mother, and you won't slip.* A gust of wind, spinning the snow into a vortex around him brought him back sharply. He must keep his wits about him if he was to get out of this alive; he dare not spend a moment on what lay behind. Not now.

But for the plaintive cry of a wolf, the night fell into a terrible silence. The lap robe did little to comfort him, as spasms of cold ricocheted through his body.

Where was he, how far from Hancock? Had he passed the big turn in the road yet? The otherworldliness of the situation left him without feeling for time or place.

Finally, downdrafts of smoke from the towering stack of the Keweenaw Mining Company reached his nostrils. He was nearing town! Tears of relief turned icy before they'd run their course. Acrid odors of blasting powder filtered downwind from the smelting plant. Soon the exhaust of the Portage Copper Mining Company joined that of the Keweenaw, its fiery red glow throwing sparks from her lofty chimney. At last he'd reached Hancock!

Alone he crossed the silent streets of town. As the sight of gas streetlamps beckoned him, he felt the loosening of his muscles; his hands relaxed their grip on the reins. Then his stomach balled into an even tighter knot: In only minutes, he'd have to inform the sheriff. About his mother.

Peering through the tumbling snow at rows of ghostly houses, he wasn't sure which house belonged to the sheriff. He couldn't tell one from another.

He drew up to one that might be the Fosters', tied up the gelding and opened the gate. Trudging through the ever-rising snow took every last bit of energy. Was this even the right house? White against white. But as he got closer he could see it had two gables, and a porch across the front. It looked like the right place. At least there was a light on in the window.

He was so stiff with cold when he reached the door, he could barely grasp the knocker.

Cora Foster peered out into the blizzard. "Who is it?"

"J—Jorie."

The rounded woman stood back staring at the white apparition before her, blowing wisps of faded brown hair from her face. At last she found her voice. "Jorie Radcliff! What are you doing out in such a misery?"

"I need to see—"

"Come in, come in." She stood back in amazement. "Just look at you, like a ghost from the other side! Lordy, I hardly know you."

She brought him in and closed the door. Unmindful of the snow he was bringing in, Jorie followed her dumbly into the parlor, where Mrs. Foster seated him by the fire and draped an afghan over his knees.

She poked at the coals, and added more wood. "Who'd have thought, such a storm, and it not even November?" she said, although October snowfalls in these parts were not unusual.

Waves of heat bathed him in warmth. Pain replaced numbness as he began to thaw, and a terrible quaking shook his whole body.

Jorie pushed his painful thoughts aside, focused on the sounds: the rasp of metal against metal, the fall of cinders, and the thud of new wood placed on the grate. Cora Foster was making up the fire. He had been in this home many times; he would be all right now.

From the kitchen, he heard, "Who is it, Cora?"

"It's the Radcliff boy, Earl."

Jorie heard the sheriff's chair pushed back from the kitchen table. Mr. Foster came into the parlor, a large blue napkin tucked under his chin and extending over his broad chest. Earl Foster was a barrel-chested man, not tall, but making up for it in strength. With a mustache that complimented a full head of brown hair, Sheriff Foster was noticeable if not handsome. He was proud of his mustache and spent considerable time keeping it properly pruned. Not an ostentatious one, like the judge his poker buddy had, which curled at the ends and extended beyond the parameters of his face. Earl Foster's was modest, befitting his station, which the sheriff believed gave him more visibility. With visibility came authority, he believed. Or at least the feeling that it did, which in itself was worth something.

"What brings you here, lad?" Earl Foster pulled off his bib, wiped it roughly across his mouth.

Whether it was his chattering teeth or the emotional shock, Jorie could barely speak.

"In the forest..." He couldn't finish.

"What about the forest?"

It seemed that Mr. Foster was looming over him like Goliath. Jorie stared at the man's trousers and noticed that a button on his fly was missing.

"It started sn-owing."

"Yes?"

"Let the lad catch his breath, Earl. He's half froze. I'll fix something to warm him up."

Mrs. Foster disappeared into the kitchen, beckoning her husband to follow.

As he sat alone, scenes in the snow played around the edges of Jorie's mind, but he couldn't keep them in focus. He descended into a kind of mental numbness, only to be startled back to the present, as Mrs. Foster placed a tray on his lap. When he finished the fish chowder, the chill began to wear off. He put his spoon down and let his lids fall.

Mrs. Foster collected the bowl, and Mr. Foster returned to the room and sat down.

"Start at the beginning and tell me what happened."

Jorie opened his eyes. Mr. Foster's eyebrows caught and held his attention. He'd known they were bushy, but he'd never noticed before that the left one had several hairs an inch long curling up toward his brow.

"What happened in the forest?"

Jorie forced his thoughts to go where they least wanted to be. "It started out a sunny day. I took my m-mother..."

"Your *mother*? Where *is* she?"

Jorie wet his lips. "I took her for a ride in the buggy, and a walk in the woods."

"In this storm? What the hell did you do that for?" The sheriff was on his feet again.

"It was sunny. It wasn't snowing when we started out!" Jorie buried his head in his hands.

Earl Foster let out a long breath.

"It was sunny, and then it started..."

The sheriff was pacing. And he was scratching a sore spot on his arm. If only he'd stay put, Jorie figured he could get his thoughts corralled.

"It started snowing hard. It turned into a blizzard, and we got lost. She, she kept slipping in the snow." His voice dropped to a whisper. "Then she fell—"

Earl Foster leaned closer. "How's that? I didn't hear you."

"She fell—her ankle. She couldn't walk."

It was difficult to keep focused. He was listening to the pendulum and the cinders falling. Anything, to avoid remembering. But he had to remember. He had to tell Mr. Foster.

"She told me to find the trail and come back for her." There was a catch in his breath. "I tried to make her comfortable."

"Go on."

Jorie swallowed a few times. Earl Foster was looking very agitated, blotting a little blood from the sore he'd been scratching.

"I, I left her." He clamped his mouth shut hard to stop the quivering of his lips. Finally, he continued. "And tried to find my way out. By the time I got back to the road, I was losing the light. I was afraid I'd never find her. I didn't even have a lantern."

"You didn't have one in the buggy?"

"No, sir." Jorie hung his head.

"Why not?"

"I, I didn't expect to be out after dark."

"What did you do then?"

"When?"

"When you found the road, but had no lamp!" The sheriff was losing patience.

"Oh." Squinting painfully Jorie tried to remember. "I started down the road, trying to find a house. I ran into a fellow in a wagon. I asked him if he'd help me. He had a lantern, and the two of us backtracked down the trail."

"The trail you'd just come off of."

"Yes, sir. But the snow had already covered my footprints. We searched for about an hour. It was getting dark." Jorie's voice broke.

"The man said he had to be getting home, and I'd better follow him out of the woods."

"So you left her there." The sheriff took a deep breath. "And she's still there."

Jorie was shaking. Tears were running down his face and he couldn't stop them. "I couldn't help her. I told her I'd come back for her. I didn't see how I could help her by staying. I had to find someone—I" He swallowed. "Can you do something, Mr. Foster?"

"We'll get to that." The sheriff paced again before sitting down. "Let me get this straight. You took your mother for a scenic walk in the forest with a blizzard on the way?"

"It was beautiful when we started out."

"What time was that?"

"Around noon."

"I thought you were working at the newspaper."

"I set type, midnight to eight."

"You didn't hear any forecast about the storm?"

"No, sir."

"What was the man's name—the man with the lantern?"

"I don't know."

"Where'd he live?"

"He didn't say. We just tried to find my m-mother."

"Why didn't you carry her out with you? She can't weigh more than a hundred ten pounds."

"We were lost. I had to find the trail first. Then I was going to—"

"Come back and get her, yes."

Jorie nodded.

"Had it started to snow when you went for your walk?"

"No, sir." Why did the sheriff keep asking the same questions?

Earl poked around on his desk for his writing tablet, fussed with the nib of his pen. Finally he said, "October 22, 1900." He looked up. "Is that right, Jorie?"

"I don't know. I think so, sir."

He wrote down the date. "Catherine—what was her middle name? Some goddess or other."

"Isis. She uses her maiden name now."

"MacGaurin."

"Yes, sir."

Earl Foster wrote her full name on the paper. "Catherine Isis MacGaurin Radcliff. Do you know her age? Thirty-five, is it?"

"Thirty-six." Dimly Jorie wondered how Mr. Foster knew so much about his mother.

"And how old are you, Jorie?"

"I just turned eighteen."

"When was that?"

"Two weeks ago."

The sheriff picked some fuzz off the nib of his pen. "Didn't I hear you moved out of the house awhile back, after a rough patch with your mother?"

"Yes, for about a month."

"When you had that scuffle with her in your sister's room?"

God, had she told him about that? He wiped the perspiration with his sleeve. "Yes, sir."

"Why did you move back?"

"My sister—Eliza, needed me. She's only four."

Jorie watched the sheriff snap a rubber band on his wrist. "What did you do last night?"

"We played Flinch."

"Who did?"

"My mother and I, after Eliza went to bed."

"Did you have any arguments?"

"No, sir."

"After the game, what happened?"

"My mother turned in."

"And what did you do?"

"I took a walk down by the lake."

"What for?"

"I just wanted to think."

"What about?"

Jorie turned toward the window, listening to the scraping of the frozen birch tree branch as it clawed the window pane.

"I can't remember."

"Where's your sister now?"

"Oh, my God!"

He hadn't thought about Eliza since he'd left home with his mother.

"She's with the neighbors. I'm supposed to pick her up at suppertime."

"Why wasn't she included on this outing?"

"She was playing with her friend. Mother said to leave her there 'til we got home."

Jorie's eye caught the grandfather clock. The movement and sound of Mr. Foster's chair, he noticed, was almost but not quite synchronized with the pendulum. If he could just get them together, or stay with the pendulum.

"Can you do something, Mr. Foster? Send some men to find her?"

"In this blizzard? It would take hours to get up there, and even with lanterns, finding her in the dark when you're not even sure where you left her—" The sheriff paused. "I'm sorry, son. We'll send a search party out in the morning."

There was something ominously final about that statement. There was no way she could survive the night, with temperatures plummeting below freezing.

Pictures started playing in Jorie's head in jerky slow motion, like the ones in the penny arcade. He and his mother were walking through the woods and the snow was coming down in huge unstoppable flakes. It rose to their knees, then up to their necks. They tried to swim through it, but soon it was burying them both in its cold, merciless resolve. They lay clutching each other beneath it, looking up through the small air space their breath had reclaimed from the snow.

No, no! It wasn't like that, he knew it wasn't.

At the same time his body was acting up. A tightening feeling in his throat spiraled down to his belly, turned around and spiraled back up, bringing the contents with it.

He dashed for the front door.

Minutes later he stumbled back into the room and collapsed on the floor in a crumpled heap of sobbing flesh. Long tortured wails broke their dam and poured forth in wave after wave of unarticulated grief.

He felt something laid over him, maybe the afghan. The only sound that reached his ears was the steady tock of the pendulum. He deliberately focused on its comforting predictability.

Finally, he heard the sheriff say something about his sister.

"What are you going to do about Eliza?"

He sat up and blew his nose. "I have to get her."

"Will she be in school tomorrow?"

He shook his head. "She's only four." He pulled himself together and got off the floor.

"You'd better make arrangements for her then. Be here by ten. Let's hope the road crew has rolled the road by then. You'll show us where to look."

"Yes, sir."

Jorie's stomach lurched. He knew it was perfectly reasonable for the sheriff to ask him to help in the search, but he hadn't anticipated it.

The thought of coming upon his mother's stiff body brought up more waves of nausea.

chapter 2

EARL FOSTER DRANK his third cup of coffee while he waited for the men he'd rounded up to search for Catherine's body. Kurt Wheeler was coming with his sleigh, and two others would join them. He hadn't slept well last night, couldn't get over what had happened to his old friend. He'd known Catherine since schooldays up in Red Jacket, when the Scottish lass had captured his heart.

Then in Hancock he'd become poker buddies with her husband, Thomas, the engineer for the Portage mine. Catherine had married a widower more than twice her age with two grown sons and a younger one who'd only lived with them a few years. He wasn't sure why, but when the boy was about twelve, he'd been sent away.

Earl remembered how awkward it had been at first to go to the big house on the hill and encounter the girl he'd longed to make his own. As the years passed he became more comfortable with Catherine; when there was an opportunity to talk, it was usually about Jorie. He had watched the boy grow up in that house. On poker nights he remembered the kid asking him riddles until his pa shooed him away.

And the lad had worked for him a couple summers back, gardening. Nice boy. Bright, too.

The last time he'd seen Catherine she was as attractive as ever. Who'd have thought she'd end up this way, dead at thirty-six?

He couldn't help wondering if it was really an accident. No, it couldn't possibly have been otherwise. Still, there were nagging thoughts. There had been serious trouble between the boy and his mother. Catherine had come to him about that, even shown him a bruise on her arm.

"Do you want me to bring him in, Catherine?"

"No. But I want it put down, for the record," she'd said.

And he'd been called to the house once to witness a locked door Jorie had busted down, before he bolted. She'd asked him to wait for Jorie to return, because she was afraid.

"Promise to protect me, Earl," she'd beseeched. "With Thomas gone, I feel so vulnerable."

Whether it was his sense of duty or her imploring green eyes which still mesmerized him, he didn't know. "I'll do what I can."

"He's turned so *violent*," she said.

But this was the same boy who'd nursed an injured wolf back to health when he was twelve. The same young man whose essays and poetry had occasionally graced the pages of *The Copper Country Evening News.*

He slipped a rubber band over his hand. He did some of his best thinking when he snapped it against his wrist.

Jorie and the men arrived more or less on time, and started off in the sleigh. There'd been about a thirteen inch fall, all told. The road workers with their huge rollers and teams of draft horses had not yet compacted the snow on the road leading north. The men in the sleigh found it slow going.

No one else was about, and only the plodding sound of the horses' hooves and their occasional snorts broke the stillness. At least it had stopped snowing; in fact, the sun was out today.

Jorie thought the whole landscape had taken on an ethereal look, as unreal as the previous day's events. Streams had been silenced overnight. Circling wind eddies had made whimsical sculptures of snow banks. Branches heavy with pristine snow caught the sunlight, transforming them into dazzling crystalline figures.

He'd awakened this morning with Eliza jumping on his bed. "Isn't it grand, Jorie, staying all night at Henna's?"

It had taken him a moment to realize where he was and why. Then as yesterday invaded with the full force of another tempest an unvoiced groan descended from his mind to his bowels. He'd brought Eliza to the house of their former housekeeper and nanny the night before. There was nowhere else he would leave her.

He'd had to tell Helena what had happened.

"Oh, Jorie, no! Herself couldn't survive the night in such—" After a pause she asked, "Sweet muther of Christ, is she...*dead*, then?" She clutched her apron with her chapped and chubby hands.

He felt the tears sting his eyes. He could only look away.

"Faith, how could the likes of this have happened?" She crossed herself, then saw the look on his face. "Oh, forgive me, lad, I should'na said nothing 'bout it."

"Can you keep Eliza for awhile?"

"It's blessed, I'd be. Daniel and me will take good care of her."

Jorie was brought back by the sheriff's question.

"Which road was it you turned off on?"

"Tamarack."

He glanced at the other men. No one was talking much. Only Kurt spoke, and mostly to his horses, encouraging them to forge through the snow.

"Getyup, Bess. Getyup, Tess. There you go now. It's not a Sunday outing we're after. Could you make it a bit faster, so's we could get there before the sun sets?"

They turned down Tamarack Road, and Earl Foster was quick to ask, "Where to now, Jorie?"

"We turned in at the old lumbering road."

"Which one?"

"About forty rods on."

There were no wagon tracks to show the way, no sign of human life in the eerie white silence. The only thing he could hear was the pounding of his own heart.

The lumbering road could not be seen, but they turned in where the trees had been felled.

"Where did you stop the buggy, son?" the sheriff wanted to know.

Jorie shook his head. "I don't know for sure. It doesn't look like we were ever here."

"Don't look like nobody was ever here," Kurt agreed.

The occasional absence of trees suggested various trails, leading off in different directions.

"Are you sure this is the right lumbering road?" Earl asked.

"No. But I think it is."

"Did you pass any others before the one you turned off on?"

"I don't think so."

"Well, let's get started."

Earl jumped out of the sleigh, and the others followed.

"Mr. Foster, from wherever I was, I know we started off to the left from the road."

"All right, then," said Earl, "let's all start off this way. You said the trail split?"

"A number of times."

The four of them worked their way through the snow. Only Kurt and Earl had brought snowshoes, although the brush was so overgrown, they found them cumbersome to use.

"You didn't leave any breadcrumbs, Hansel?" Kurt asked.

Jorie looked away. "No, sir."

They came to a split where there were two trails.

"You and Kurt go that way. We'll carry on here."

Jorie followed Earl down the trace. The reprimand of two squirrels disturbed the stillness. Other denizens of the forest peered above their warrens of safety, as the intruders tromped through their habitat.

How different it all looked today. Bright sunshine made the woods appear welcoming, friendly. Chunks of snow fell from the branches of hemlock, as the wind stirred the trees.

Somehow, just maybe she'd managed to survive. It was too soon to give up hope. Perhaps she'd found some sort of shelter, or some kindly soul had found her. He looked for recent footprints, sniffed for chimney smoke. Once, in the distance, he heard the sound of branches breaking underfoot.

"Mother!" he called out.

Earl turned to look at him, but said nothing. The second time Jorie called out the sheriff put a hand on his sleeve. "It's a doe, son. Just a deer."

Nothing looked familiar to Jorie, not the hill they climbed or the split of paths. They turned back, regrouped with the others, and set off in different directions.

"Give a whistle if you find...anything," Earl called after them.

They didn't, and finally gave up on their search for the day, as the spare sun waned. The sheriff decided he'd need more men for the search.

On the way home, Earl said, "You sure you don't know the man's name that helped you? What'd he look like?"

"He was big. Cornish accent."

Cornish. With all the transplanted miners from Cornwall, Earl thought, that narrows it down like saying a man you met in France was French.

They rode in silence the rest of the way, until Earl dropped Jorie off. "You'll have to help us until we find your ma. Be here at nine tomorrow."

"Yes, sir."

Cora didn't allow any form of alcoholic beverage to cross her threshold, and Earl seldom desired it, but after a miserable day searching for the body of his old friend, he decided he was entitled to some refreshment. Besides, he couldn't sit still.

He headed across Franklin and down to Tezcuco Street. This pulsing hub of Hancock sloped steeply down to the long and narrow pollywog-shaped Portage Lake, leading to the shipping and railway companies spawned by the mining business. The larger bulk of the lake lay to the east before it joined Lake Superior. Here, between Hancock and her sister city Houghton, it ran as narrow as a river. Ships plying the Great Lakes would bring in supplies and leave with copper and iron ore along shipping routes from Detroit, Chicago or Duluth.

Along Tezcuco Street a myriad of saloons staked their claims amidst the finest hotel, the busiest Chinese laundries, public bath-houses, banks and barbershops. On this and nearby streets there were saloons for the Irish, the German, the *Cousin Jacks* from Cornwall, the Croatians and almost every nationality in the world.

He passed lampposts bearing the ordinances he'd posted, prohibiting disorderly persons, drunkards, fortune tellers, vagrants, prostitutes. Puppet shows, wire-rope dancing or other idle acts and feats were also forbidden. Already weather-worn by the storm, they needed replacing. The sheriff considered most of these laws a load of bollix, but he didn't write them—only tried to enforce them. It wasn't easy keeping the lid on a mining town. Too many folks in these parts thought they were north of the law, and said as much.

As usual, the blast of the six o'clock quitting whistles at the Keweenaw and Portage Mines signaled the saloon keepers to ready-up for the onslaught of thirsty customers. The pubs were the second shift for the miners and they took it as seriously as the first.

Those who frequented these watering holes had three passions—booze, bawds and brawls—in that order. And here you could learn what had happened *up top* that day. Long after other establishments had buttoned up for the night, gas street lamps lured the working men into the open arms of the saloons. Not that they needed any encouragement.

The Bear Claw was such an establishment. Like many others in most ways, its distinguishing mark was the great bar hand-crafted in Italy a long time ago, and sent all the way to America. The Italian saloons coveted it, but Stout, the owner wouldn't think of selling it. "My Italian sweetheart," he called it.

Miners swarmed in, stamping the snow off their boots, and blowing on their hands. The smells of tobacco mingled with the hard-won sweat from the fiery pits below. The patrons didn't mind. Years of working in the foul-smelling depths, where, like moles, they were accustomed to darkness—the overlay of fog in the saloon, made yellow by the gas lamps and smoke, did nothing to dampen their spirits.

The news that evening caused the din in *The Bear Claw* to rise to an even greater pitch than usual. Everybody in there had something to say.

Stout, the saloon keeper, had made sure to get all the scoop he could while the miners were still below grass. His *congregation*, as he called them, would expect as much.

"What happened to her, Stout?" Red Topper asked.

"Her son took her out to the woods on a joy ride," Flem Crocker said.

Hardy cut in. "He's either plum loony, or he was puttin' his ma away. Ain't that right, Stout?"

"You talk to the sheriff?" Gums asked.

"Nope. Heard all about it from Kurt." Stout spoke with authority as he transferred the dirty glasses from the tub of soapy water to the rinse basin. "He took the kid and a posse out there to find the body this morning."

Stout could afford to be generous with his information and his drafts. The Bear Claw would make a lot of money tonight.

"They find her?"

"Nope."

A hush fell as the door opened and the wind ushered in the sheriff. Heads turned.

Earl mounted a stool. A babble of questions greeted him as Stout placed a whiskey before him.

"Mrs. Radcliff, she's dead?" Red Topper wanted to know.

"Don't see how she could be alive." Earl was sorry he'd come.

"Her son took her out there with a storm comin' in?"

Gums O'Mallory moistened his lips. "And just left her there to freeze to death?"

"What's that look like to you, Sheriff?" Flem Crocker asked.

Earl waved off the questions, and took his drink to a table in the back. And just in time, too, he thought. He wasn't in any mood for the brawling Groden brothers and their lumberjack rabble-rousers. Riding into town, busting up bars and tearing up the place, their cleated boots had left several faces in Copperdom permanently pocked, and more than one young lady a soiled dove. "Butt-cuts of original sin," Earl called them.

Fortunately, they stayed near the front at the bar. But the sheriff had a grandstand seat and could hear the rumble from where he sat.

The Grodens, always sporting for a fight or some way to stir up trouble, stated as fact that Jorie Radcliff had as much as murdered his mother.

"Hey, now, wait a minute. That Radcliff boy is a good kid—"

They quickly stilled the voices of those who defended Jorie or weren't so sure.

In a way it was odd, Earl thought, that there was such a to-do about Catherine Radcliff's death. Plenty of barroom fights, some leading to death, broke out among men who only saw the light of day at night, and the night all day long.

Mine accidents, from explosions and collapses to men falling down mile-deep shafts, had all taken their toll in this community. A woman didn't know when she sent her husband off with his lunch pail if she'd ever see him again. Murder was not that unusual either, in this brawling mining town, where a couple of pints of forty-rod at his favorite saloon was more important than a man's religion. But the thought of a man taking the life of the one who'd given him life was beyond their understanding.

Earl was finishing his drink and about to leave when a young man approached him, pulled up a chair and sat down.

"Walter Radcliff."

Earl appraised the man. "Catherine Radcliff's step-son?"

"Ball in the pocket."

Earl looked for a resemblance between the young man and his father, but couldn't detect any. Must look like his mother. His facial features were unattractive, though he possessed a fine physique. Most miners did, he mused, until the work broke them.

"What can I do for you?"

"I knew there was trouble between Jorie and his ma, so what happened out there in the blizzard—" he tipped his chair back— "Well, there's no great surprise there, is there?"

"You got your mind all made up?"

Walter laughed. "You think it was an *accident*, do you, Sheriff?"

"I'm gathering information about the family," Earl said. "Would you mind stopping by my office tomorrow?"

Walter shook his head. "I'm heading back to Red Jacket in the morning." He surveyed the surroundings. "Strikes me this is as good an office as any."

Radcliff signaled Stout to bring another round to the table and leaned forward. "Watcha wanna know, Sheriff?"

Earl didn't like the man's attitude and he didn't like the venue for this interview, but he remembered something about a bird in hand.

"How old were you when your pa married Miss MacGaurin?"

"'Bout six, I reckon."

"How did you and your step-ma get on?"

"There was no love between us. I won't pretend there was."

"Why is that?"

Earl heard the young man's feet shuffle on the other side of the table.

"She was crazy about her own kid. Didn't want to be bothered with somebody else's brat."

"You must have stored up some resentment about that."

Walter shot his wad of chewing tobacco several feet into the spittoon, looked up with a smile, expecting praise. "Yeah, but I wasn't out in the woods playing 'Hide or Die', was I?"

He took the drink from Stout's hand before it was on the table, and poured it down his throat. "My half brother deliberately left his ma out there in the storm. Some would call that murder, sheriff."

Earl didn't like his cockiness. "What leads you to that conclusion?"

"I saw 'em go—the two of 'em heading into that storm. Only him came back."

"And what grandstand seat did you have to watch these comings and goings?"

"I was over to Peabody's. Could see it all from his front window."

"Anything else?"

"Ain't that enough?"

"What are you doing in Hancock? Heard you worked up in Red Jacket."

"Came down to get the horses. Somebody's gotta take care of them. Jorie 'pears to have taken off."

"Are you or your brothers married?"

"Why do you want to know?"

"We'll be looking for a home for Eliza."

"Who?"

"The deceased's little daughter."

"Oh."

"Her custody is uncertain at this point. The aunt would prefer not—"

"That girl is no kin to me or my brothers."

"Pardon me, but I believe she is your half-sister."

"I don't even know her. And my older brothers barely knew who the *deceased* was. They was all grown by the time I got stuck with a new ma." He chewed on this awhile. "Why can't Jorie take her? Oh, yeah, he's prob'ly going to hang."

Earl shook his head. "Not in this state. Michigan was the first in the union to do away with capital punishment."

"More's the pity." Walter rose. "Well, you think on what I said, Sheriff." He tipped his cap and took his leave.

Earl watched the young man swagger out. Walter's 'proof' wasn't worth a fart in the wind.

He would check on Walter's story, but the only thing it would prove is whether he was the consummate liar Earl conjectured he was.

As he tossed in bed that night, Earl wondered about the man who Jorie said had helped him. He would put something in the paper asking this man to come forth. Seemed a damn shame that Jorie knew neither the name of the man with the lantern nor his whereabouts. And how inconvenient that the falling snow showed no footprints to prove or disprove Jorie's story.

The next day on their way out of town, Earl had the search party stop at Orville Peabody's place on the main road north. Orville lived by himself in an old logger's cabin on the road leading north out of town. Confined to a wheelchair at twenty years old after an accident in the mine, he managed to keep house by himself except for a half-breed who came in once a week to help.

Earl rapped on the door, knocked the snow off his boots and let himself in. Orville looked up from the porridge he was eating.

Earl smiled. Sorry to intrude, sir, and so early."

The wounded veterans of the underground were afforded respect by the community at large, if not by the owners of the mine.

"I like visitors—any time of the day. Watcha got on yer mind, old man? Are you hungry?"

Earl shook his head. "Orville, have you seen anything of Walter Radcliff lately? Has he been by?"

"Yup."

"When was that?"

"He brought over some newspapers, all about his stepmother's death. He seemed quite pleased about it."

"Did you see him the day of the storm?"

"Naw, not 'til the next afternoon. I saw Jorie Radcliff that day, though. Riding north with his ma."

"What was the weather like then?"

"Still sunny. Didn't see him come back, though. In the blizzard I couldn't see that bush by the window."

Volunteers came every day to help with the search, even the coroner, Lester Meisel.

After the fourth day, Earl said to Jorie, "Are you sure it was in *Michigan* you left her?"

But on the fifth, the coroner, with a team of dogs, found the body of Catherine Radcliff lying on her face. Animals had discovered her, torn open her pristine grave of snow. Folding her carefully in a blanket, Lester whistled to the others that the search was over.

When Earl joined him, he shook his head. "We must have walked right by her the first day."

Lester Meisel looked up from the document he'd just signed. "Mrs. Radcliff had a broken ankle, sustained in her fall, I suspect. Apparently, she went willingly with her son."

"What do you make of her lying on her face?"

"Reckon she crawled some from where he left her, trying to save herself." He looked up. "Sad thing, indeed. She died like a wolf cub in the storm, with her back to the wind." He pushed the rug on his pate closer to his left ear.

Lester had a way with words, Earl thought. Some said he should have been a poet.

The coroner capped the ink bottle and blotted the paper. "Here's the certificate."

Earl read it. "Cause of death: Exposure to cold."

"Did you find any bruises or signs of force?"

"Didn't see any." He paused. "It won't be possible to have a viewing of the body, Earl. Animals—"

"That's enough." Earl didn't want to pursue that line. He said only, "Will you be wanting an inquest, Lester?"

"I think we can dispense with that, Sheriff."

Earl Foster dreaded going to the service. He knew he'd be barraged by questions before and after.

He deliberately arrived late. When he entered the Radcliff home he could hear those assembled singing a hymn in the parlor. He winced when he saw that the manner in which it was set up provided no way to slip in inconspicuously. The doorway to the back parlor was at the front of the room where the minister stood.

Earl bowed slightly to the reverend and stood to the side, feeling all eyes upon him. Several more people arrived after he did, and the quartet had to pick up their music stands and move to the next room.

No coffin. A photo of Catherine taken on her wedding day graced a small table with flowers.

Standing at the side of the room gave him a certain advantage. He could see who was there, and recognized most of them. There were his poker buddies—the *Five Aces*, they'd called themselves, when Thomas Radcliffe was one of them. Now they were four, but the name stayed the same." "*Four* aces?" the judge had snorted. "Well, that sounds alltogether too prosaic."

He was here now—George McKinney, and so was Buck Boyce, the prosecuting attorney. But he didn't see Doc Johnson, the other *Ace*. They had met in this house for so many years to play cards, along with Radcliff. He spotted Toby Wilson, the Radcliffs' lawyer. The few he didn't know he supposed were relatives from out of town, or busybodies.

Where was Jorie? Even when he stretched his neck he could see no sign of him.

The pastor, whose job it was to comfort the living and bury the dead, droned on about the rewards in heaven, and then turned his attention to the virtues of the deceased.

"I can only describe the deceased in laudatory terms. There are many here who can testify to the goodness of Mrs. Radcliff. A more upright and charitable soul would be hard to find."

Earl remembered hearing those exact words spoken at other services—all vague generalities. He didn't believe Catherine had attended the Congregational Church in years, doubted this young minister even knew her.

The back parlor, though dusted and aired for special occasions, appeared eternally funereal to Earl. He looked around at the mourners. Any tears? He heard the stifled sobs of a woman in the second row—the housekeeper, he thought. But where was Jorie?

When the service ended, he spotted the smoke haloes coming from the judge's cigar in the next room. George McKinney was one of those folks whom nature had endowed with a perennial red face, always appearing to have just spent a day in the sun. Spared from the labors that aged younger men in the mines, at sixty-eight the judge still possessed a commanding presence and a fine physique. McKinney was well aware of the effect he had on others, and thoroughly enjoyed his standing in the community.

As Earl approached he heard the prosecuting attorney ask the judge, "Going to run for another term, George?"

The judge appeared to be studying his cigar. "Well, you'll be glad to know, I've been thinking of retiring, Buck."

"You can't do that, George—you're an institution!"

"And one that's due for a rest. I guess that opens the gate for you." McKinney turned to wink at Earl.

Buck Boyce pursed his lips and raised an eyebrow as though he hadn't thought of this before.

"Possibly. Possibly, George."

Possibly, indeed! Buck Boyce had been gnawing on that gate for years.

At only forty-seven the prosecuting attorney had already gained in girth what he couldn't attain in stature. But for his featureless face which gave him the undefined look of youth, he appeared to be a much older man. Earl thought him a fop, pulling out his gold watch and chain at any provocation.

Earl spoke to George. "Have you seen Jorie?"

The judge could see over everyone's head. His eyes swept the room. "No, no, I haven't."

Earl wished George would dump his ashes before they dropped to the floor. McKinney was always doing that. There was a crack about how you could always tell where the judge had been—he left a trail of cigar crumbs behind.

As he walked away, George reminded him, "Five Aces tomorrow night."

Earl scanned the remaining first floor rooms, then bounded up the stairs and called. When he got no response he came back, waved off questions and went out on the veranda to look for Jorie.

It was possible he'd gone up in the hills, to his old haunts, but Earl had another thought.

The two-seater privy was built behind the house where the land rose sharply forming the base of the steep hill behind the house.

He knocked. "You in there, Jorie?"

The shuffle of feet was his answer.

"Mind if I join you?"

He heard the occupant fumble with the latch.

With a deep sigh, Earl lowered himself onto the second hole. "I've been waiting to do this all day."

Jorie was silent, elbows on his knees, his head in his hands. A dozen flies, still clinging to life, crawled around them.

Earl swatted at a horse fly landing on his thigh. "Someday they'll invent something to cover up the stink in these places."

When he got no response, he said the obvious. "Didn't see you inside."

"No, sir."

"Any special reason for that?"

"Have to mourn in my own way, not in front of a lot of long-nosers, with their own ideas about why she died."

Earl nodded. "I have to think about that too, Jorie."

"Yeah." The young man lifted his tear stained face.

"Anything more you want to tell me, lad?"

"No, sir."

"Where will you be staying?"

"We'll be at the O'Laertys. Helena offered to take care of Eliza for awhile."

"Then I'll expect to find you there, if I need you."

"Yes, sir."

He gave the sheriff the address.

Earl couldn't get it out of his mind that Jorie must have had some terrible falling out with his mother. Still, he didn't have to resort to murder; he could have just left town. If it was murder, it didn't appear to be a crime of passion. It was well thought out, premeditated.

And that would be the worse for Jorie.

chapter 3

He was awakened at the O'Laerty's by the sound of his sister crying in the next room. He wanted to go to her, but he could already hear Helena's soothing voice comforting the child, singing some Irish ditty. The song seemed to comfort him, too; as long as he could hear the gentle voice of his childhood nanny the world seemed right-side-up.

He'd offered to sleep on the sofa, so Eliza could have the spare room, but Helena had insisted he take it.

"Oh, I couldn't put the wee one in a room by herself. Wakes up cryin', she does, askin' for her ma. And isn't it the deevil's work that such a thing could happen." She wiped her eye with the edge of her apron. "Ours is a big room. We moved the little cot in there, so she could be near us."

Each time Jorie awoke, for the first tiny moment there was peace. Then the awful realization of his mother's death would invade his senses anew, along with a terrible self-loathing. Accident or not, he was responsible.

He'd been dreaming that he'd broken some kind of chalice. He'd found most, but not all of the pieces. A thick malevolent fog would descend, and he couldn't remember what happened that day. Bits and pieces would play at the edge of his mind, but trying to grasp them was like trying to catch a handful of that fog.

Yes, he'd hurried home from work that day. He'd asked Mother to go for a ride in the country—"It's sunny, and probably the last chance we'll have before weather sets in." Eliza was at a friend's, so it was just the two of them.

And then, in the woods the snow had come—more and more of it, until they were lost in a world of whiteness. He remembered the Cornishman with the lantern who'd tried to help him. The lantern, illuminating one tiny speck of this huge and frightening world. It was like trying to find your way out of the blackness of a mine with only the light of one match.

But more he couldn't remember. His fractured memory wouldn't give it up.

Poor Eliza. So young to lose her mama. It was all too horrible.

He helped Helena clear the dishes. But she wouldn't let him do more.

"I'm sure you've your studies to tend to."

"I need to talk to you, Helena."

"Your face is long as a red melon. What is it, lad?"

"It's very kind of you to keep Eliza. And me as well. But I—I don't want you to think I take it for granted."

"Aw, g'wan with you. I love her like my own. You'd have a tough time gettin' her away from me."

He gave her a thin smile. "All right. But perhaps I should move back to the hill—"

"And rattle up there by yerself?"

"It's too much to expect you to keep us both."

"Now will you let me be decidin' how much bother it is? And what about yer poor sister? It's bad enough her losin' her ma. Would you deny her settin' eyes on her beloved bruther, to boot?"

She had a point.

"And Daniel—he's becoming right fond of her. "She's givin' him somethin' to think about besides losin' his job after the accident."

"I could pay you something."

"Oh, go away. You'll save your earnings for going to the college next year."

Eliza wanted her rocking horse.

"I'll get it for you," he said with a resolve he didn't feel. He had no desire to enter the house on the hill, but he would do it for Izzy. Besides there was another task he had to accomplish there—an unsavory one.

After work the next morning he set out with a determined step across Frontage Road by the lake and up the incline. He stopped to stare at the house from a distance. Already it looked forsaken, echoing his own desolation. Sheltered by the grove of pines, the snow still lay about, shrunken and crystallized. Soot from the giant smokestack of the Portage Mine above dotted the surface. It was not the picture of his childhood—sliding down freshly fallen snow, so clean sometimes he'd eat it.

The house with no occupants felt hollow, even from the outside. As though it too had died, left all alone to break down. It had been the finest house on the hill, with a turret, and a grand view across Portage Lake. As a boy, many times he had climbed the hills behind the house all the way to the plateau below the Portage Mine. He could pick wild strawberries as he watched the cargo ships ply the water. Pleasure boats, too.

In the house there were rooms everywhere. He remembered as a child, racing in circles between them, until Pa put a stop to that. A sweeping veranda skirting two sides of the house, sported Concord grape vines growing up the trellis. He quivered, remembering the last time he'd watched his mother suck the sweet flesh from its skin. Looking at the barren vines now, he wondered if they'd ever bear fruit again.

At last Jorie pulled himself from his reverie and strode purposely to the front door. As he let himself in, he was immediately greeted with the raucous strains of *A Hot Time in the Old Town Tonight*. He stepped cautiously into the parlor. He saw no one, but the pianola was playing by itself. The ghoulish sounds followed him as he walked through the rooms. Finding no one on the first floor, he ascended the stairs slowly. He wanted to call out, "Who's here?" but could not sound the words.

Hc glanced in the other rooms, but somehow he knew, chillingly, that the disturbance was coming from his mother's. The door was closed, but he could hear sounds inside. Standing in the hall, he tried to banish the nightmarish thoughts that filled his head.

Finally, he rubbed his sweaty hands against his trousers, grasped the handle and pushed the door open.

Standing at her dresser was his step-brother. What an appalling violation to find Walter in his mother's room! It made his gut twist.

The man was fingering the round blue jar with the silver ballerina on top. "Perty little thing," he said.

Jorie wanted to shout, *Put that down!* but feared Walter would smash it if he knew what love the little Venetian glass evoked.

"What are you doing here?" He watched Walter toss the jar from hand to hand.

"You forget, little brother, this is my father's house."

"My mother—"

"Not no more. She's gone too."

Jorie could feel the sweat run down his back. "You've got your inheritance; you've no business here now."

"Is that right?" A toothpick turned against Walter's lips as he appraised his step-brother. "Just came for the tack and the horses."

"We don't keep them in the house."

Walter nodded, appraising his adversary. "That's a sweet player piana you got down there. A shame to let it go to waste."

"Take what you like from the stable, and leave the house alone."

"Hey, I ain't doin' no harm." Jorie held his breath as Walter lobbed the blue globe in the air, caught it behind his back with the other hand.

"How did you get in here?"

"I got my ways. Don't forget I lived here six long years. I know it like I know what happened out in the woods last week."

"Get out."

Walter tossed the jar on the bed. "I'll follow you down, little brother."

"No, after you."

Walter shrugged, sauntered out of the room and descended the steps two at a time. "Don't 'spect you'll be getting' much chance to enjoy this place." With an ugly grin he turned to the door. "I'll be takin' the horses now."

When Walter was gone, Jorie thought his heart would explode. He strode to the back parlor, pulled the lace curtain back a bit, and wiped enough lamp smoke from the window to see out. Watching his step-brother head toward the stable, he wondered where he'd found the courage to confront his old nemesis.

He had planned to go straight to Eliza's room, but found himself ensnared by the remains of the memorial service. It was all still here! It closed in on him now like a macabre hoax. He hadn't escaped it after all. The sight of all the dead flowers weeping their petals caused him to catch his breath. A wilted rose collapsed across the picture half concealed the small image of his mother. He held the silver frame, staring first at the wedding dress, with its ribbon rosettes and lace, her tiny waist. Only gradually were his hands still enough to allow his eyes to travel upward to her face, to see through the scratched glass, the tin-type still showing her features clearly— bright, expectant eyes, so ready for life.

Shoving the picture in his pocket, he ascended the stairs again. In the almost barren room he found Eliza's rocking horse upended in her closet. Three pale rectangles on the wall replaced the pictures he had painted for her. He felt a stab of pain, but no surprise. He racked his brain wondering why he was not astonished: *What had he known before that was eluding him now? What fugitive thoughts were escaping his memory?*

Returning to his mother's room, he stood in the doorway remembering the many times as a child he'd crawled into bed with her. And the many times in later years he'd hurried past this door.

The things on her dresser were neatly arranged—the ivory comb and brush set her father had given her years ago, including a small receptacle for loose hair. He opened its lid and touched the contents. The auburn strands still gave off the fragrance of lilac.

He could see her pulling the hairs from her brush, winding them around her fingers, and placing them in the receptacle.

The small blue jar lay on the bed where Walter had tossed it. Round as an apple and on its silver lid the ballerina still stood on her toes, one arm reaching to the sky. He picked it up gently and brought it to his face. A flood of memories coursed through him of the times she'd soothed him with its balm. And the best part—the stories from the old country that followed when he was small.

"I'm drowning, I'm drowning! Will no one come tae save me?"

"I'll save ye, Lassie. Just hang on tae my neck and I'll ta'e you to shore." *He fishtailed across the bed.*

"Oh thank ye Seal, ye've saved my life. What can I dae fer ye?"

"You can bide with me, and be me wife!"

"Och I canna marry a seal!" She turned away.

"It's a man ye'll be marryin', not a seal. Look at me now!"

He assumed a strong man pose, and she turned back to him in great surprise.

"Ah, and a bonnie one too. It's a silkie, you are!"

"That I am. Now marry me."

"I cannae marry ye. For I know ye can change back tae a seal as quick as ye changed in tae a man. I've heard 'nuf stories aboot that!"

"I won't go back tae the sea if ye will marry me. I'll stay wit ye, Lassie, and never leave."

"And what will ye do fer me?"

"I'll build ye a manse finer than ye've ever known where just the two of us will live. It's there I'll take care of ye, ever and ever."

Queasiness came over him.

He carried the rocking horse downstairs. The cab he'd hired was due in a few minutes; was there time to accomplish his other mission?

The clip-clop of the driver's horses told him the other task would have to wait.

Eliza was delighted to have the rocking horse back that Jorie had given her for her fourth birthday. Her next request surprised him.

When they'd been with Helena about a week, she said, "Jawie, will you talk French with me?"

Her question made him wince, though he didn't remember why. "I don't know French, Izzy."

"Mummy and I do. I could teach you." She crawled up on his lap.

"I'll read to you."

Half way through the story Eliza asked for the hundredth time, "When's Mummy coming back?"

He closed the book. "I don't know, Izzy."

He couldn't bring himself to tell her the truth. Not yet.

He had trouble keeping his mind on his work. He'd made more mistakes in the past two weeks than he'd made altogether before. His boss called him in.

"I know this is a hard time for you, lad, but we can't have this. Sloppy. Makes the paper look bad."

Jorie nodded. He barely heard the words.

"Are you listening to me?"

"Yes, sir. I'm sorry."

"You'll have to watch your *Ps* and *Qs* if you want to set type for the *Copper Country Evening News*."

He stopped going anywhere except to work, and would leave the house no more than necessary. He fashioned a wooden puppet for Eliza, carving each piece carefully. She squealed with delight, and asked him to make another so they could play *pretend* together. He helped Helena's husband build a cherry china cabinet. He knew Daniel was trying to keep up his spirits by getting a conversation going, but nothing that was said seemed to matter to Jorie, and Daniel soon gave up.

He could put off returning to the hill no longer. There was something up there—something he couldn't risk someone else finding.

This time the house was quiet. Not aired since the day of the snowstorm, a musty smell pervaded it. The sound of scurrying mice reached his ears as he entered his room.

From the back of the closet he pulled out a box of school composition books. Rifling through the pile, he found at last the one he was looking for—the journal of his transgressions and punishment. Presented to him when he was seven, he'd been required to record his misdemeanors in it for years.

Jorie took the book downstairs and put newspaper in the kitchen stove. His hands shook so badly as he lit the match, it was hard to light the paper. As the flame finally rose, he tore the pages from the book, and one by one fed them to the blaze. He sat transfixed, full of anger, remorse and sadness, watching the flames curl and consume the record of his childhood shame.

chapter 4

EARL OWNED A horse, but the gelding was old and full of prejudice. Bigot didn't like to be out after dark. Easily spooked, the white horse always veered away from black horses, especially at night.

Walking to the Five Aces game that night at the judge's house, Earl was consumed with memories about the girl he'd known in school. He'd been crazy for her then, when they'd both lived up in Red Jacket. What a country bumpkin she must have thought him! He, who'd never been outside Michigan's Upper Peninsula, and she, a young lady from Edinburgh, Scotland!

She was fine looking, but it was her mane of red hair and her fiery green eyes that made everybody take notice. Well, that was a long time ago. It was the first year they'd had football at his school, and everybody was keen on it. And then yes, on that one day, the forty yard run all the way down the field with no one even close behind. The whole school was cheering him on. Nothing could stop him from reaching the goal post. Nothing did.

But it hadn't made a bit of difference. Catherine McGaurin was too good for anybody. With a daddy that took her everywhere—to concerts, even to Paris—- What did he have to offer?

He gave in to the itch on his hand. Psoriasis, Dr. Johnson had said. God, it was driving him crazy. Arthur had given him some ointment for it, and for awhile it seemed to help, but then when Catherine died...

He thought about how her life had turned out. And his. Considering her fate, he guessed he'd fared better than she. He pulled his muffler tight around his mouth, as winds whipped up the snow-drifts, blowing the cold, dry stuff into his face, smarting his eyes.

He'd wanted to go out west, latch on to some of that land the government was giving away. Maybe he'd become an officer of the law, and bring order to some lawless town in the west. But then Cora Baker, the girl he was seeing, told him she was pregnant. Well, he did what all honorable men did under such circumstances—he married her. But she lost the baby. Or said she did. He didn't know much about these things, and he believed her.

Cora didn't want to go out west.

There would be other children, he figured. But they hadn't come. That was his biggest regret. He would like to have had children. Still, they'd had a pretty good marriage, good as most, he reckoned.

Judge McKinney's home loomed in front of him. George, the bachelor, accountable to no one, had an enormous antebellum house large enough to hold a family of eight. The games, previously held at Thomas Radcliff's, had shifted to George's.

Iva opened the door, and led him inside. Rumors had circulated about who this mulatto was. Some said she was his daughter, by a woman he'd saved from the slave catchers back in 1855; another version was that Iva was no relation at all; she was his mistress, plain and simple.

The woman led him into the room George McKinney had fashioned into the game room, though you could tell it wasn't designed to be, as Thomas's had been. Rather, it was more of a sun room, with curved bay windows all around the back, overlooking the garden. Still, it served well enough. Except, Earl thought ruefully, it was never warm enough in the winter, which took over about nine months of the year.

The others were already seated. Buck Boyce, the prosecuting attorney, was the youngest member of their band. Buck was so loud-mannered, the sheriff always thought he was making up in volume what he couldn't conjure up in content. And there was the thoughtful, soft-spoken Doctor Arthur Johnson, with his plume of white wavy hair. Earl was glad to be here. He looked forward to these friendly, familiar weekly games with his poker buddies. Maybe this diversion would clear his head.

The pot of money was brought out and set on the floor. Called *Matilda*, the kitty represented the sum total of everyone's winnings over the last ten years. Long ago they'd agreed to pool their spoils for some future project or joint flight of fancy. At first a gag, the longer it remained untouched, the harder it was to disturb. Perhaps they were afraid the spell would be broken if they did, he mused, and the games would end. *Matilda* had grown from a pickle jar to a flower pot to a heavy iron kettle, that had once held enough stew to feed a crew of hungry miners at a boarding house. It was a ritual, bringing it out every time they had a game.

Earl was the first to deal. "Five card draw. Ante up." He placed the deck in front of the prosecuting attorney. "Cut 'em up, Buck."

Buck Boyce, being a small man, was always trying to look taller than he was, Earl mused. Buck wore elevated heels to give him greater stature, and made sure his posture took advantage of every vertebra. There was a bravado about him that Earl thought was a way of making up on the outside for what he didn't feel inside.

When the cards were dealt Buck bet one.

"Arthur?"

"Match," the doctor said.

It wasn't long before the talk turned to the death of Catherine Radcliff. Wife of their friend Thomas, she had for years served refreshments on poker nights.

The judge raised the doctor. "Didn't see you at the funeral, Arthur."

The gentle doctor, now in his seventh decade had been a widower for two years. "I was delivering the Freeman baby. Terrible—about Catherine." He cleared his throat.

"At least when my wife died..." his voice trailed off.

"I'll raise you one, George." Earl pushed his chips to the center.

"Most unfortunate accident," the judge said.

"If it *was* an accident," the prosecuting attorney interjected.

"You're not suggesting, Buck—" The doctor was visibly upset.

"1 don't know. Do you?"

Arthur studied the prosecutor's face. "It's the way your mind works, Buck. Guess it goes with the territory—always suspicioning the worst of everyone."

Buck Boyce smiled. "That's my job."

"Are you in, Buck?" Earl inquired.

"I'm in." He pushed chips to the center.

The others matched.

"How many cards, Buck?"

"Two."

"Arthur?"

The doctor seemed to have trouble focusing. "One," he finally said.

"How's it look so far, Earl? Any chance of foul play?" the judge asked.

Lord, he didn't want to answer that.

"How many, George?"

"Two." The judge's ashes fell to the floor. "You didn't answer my question, Earl."

"And three for me," Earl said. "Too soon to speculate."

"Figured you'd say that. Always play it close to your chest, don't you, boy?"

"You doubt the lad's story, George?" the doctor inquired. "That tender lad who refused to make a butterfly collection because he couldn't kill them?"

Earl scratched his elbow, but Arthur's question to the judge took the limelight off him.

"How do you know that—about the?" McKinney turned back to Arthur.

"He was sick a lot. And his mother kept him out of school one whole term, when scarlet fever was going around. I got to know him pretty well."

"Buck?"

"Fold." The prosecuting attorney rested his hands on his portly belly.

"And I—" The doctor laid down his cards. "I used to stop by on my rounds. He liked to talk about science. Seemed like a lonely kid."

George said, "Three."

Earl knew the judge liked to bluff. "Let's see what you got." He pushed his chips forward.

George had a pair of Jacks, but Earl had three tens, and took the hand.

Boyce shuffled. "Cards are getting gummy. Got any others, George?"

"Nope."

More likely George didn't want to leave the table just now to get them, Earl mused.

"Earl's known Catherine since school days," George informed the prosecutor. "Up in Red Jacket."

Oh, here we go!

"Sweet on her too, weren't you, boy?" George teased, lighting his cigar.

Earl hated to be called *boy*. It rankled him that the judge, whether because of his superior position in society, or the difference in their ages, often treated him like he wasn't grown up yet. He'd always known he hadn't been included in this poker party because of his standing in the community; he was in because he was a damn good player and George McKinney liked a challenge.

Finally, talk about the Radcliffs was dropped as the players turned their attention seriously to poker.

When quitting time came at ten o'clock, Earl fed Matilda more than he had in a year.

"She's getting very fat," he said.

But when he left, the judge quipped, "Good-night, Sherlock. Have fun playing detective."

In the morning Earl decided to make a trip to the *News,* hoping to catch two birds. First he wanted to see Jorie, whose night shift would be finished in about half an hour. Then he'd find the man who did the weather reports there.

He discovered Jorie working in the corner of a large room. On the table before him were wooden boxes divided into tiny compartments, each holding different letters.

Jorie was bent over two boxes picking up the bits of lead. For a moment Earl stood back, mesmerized by the dexterity and speed with which Jorie's hands flew from the boxes to the composing stick on which they were placed. Finally, Jorie looked up. A slight frown crossed his face.

"Good morning, Mr. Foster."

"'Morning, Jorie. "I'd like to get some papers from the house that we'll need in order to settle your mother's estate."

He caught the boy's hesitation. "Can you give me the key, son?"

Jorie dug it from his pocket and handed it to the sheriff. Earl studied his face, looking for signs of something, anything. Except for a kind of melancholy he'd worn since he was about thirteen, Earl could decipher nothing.

"Anything over there I can get for you?"

Jorie paused. "I'd like my mother's rosary, if you can find it."

"Where did she keep it?"

"In her room, I think."

What was Catherine doing with a rosary? The only church he'd known her to attend was the Congregational, and that was a long time ago.

He left Jorie and asked a man in the hall, "Who does the weather report around here?"

"Jack Bickerson."

Earl found the man at his desk, squeezed between two others. It was impossible to have a private conversation here. He leaned over the desk.

"Did you write a forecast of the blizzard last week?"

"Yes, I did."

"Would that have been the day before the blizzard?"

"No, sir. Didn't hear of it until the day it came. Those storms come up so fast over Lake Superior, there's not always warning."

"You get your information from the ships out there?"

"Yes, sir. By Morse Code."

Earl lowered his voice. "Did Jordan Radcliff talk to you that day?"

"Who?"

"Jordan Radcliff."

Earl could feel all neighboring eyes upon him.

"Can't remember."

"I mean did he ask you for a weather report?"

Jack tried to think. "Might have. He did sometimes."

Earl repeated, "He did sometimes."

"Everybody did sometimes."

Toby Wilson's office was two blocks away. Earl decided to ask the Radcliff's lawyer about the wills. There was a sign on the door: "Closed for family emergency." He was informed by the stationer next door that the lawyer had been called away to settle his father's affairs downstate.

The Radcliff place had always seemed a little eerie to Earl, even when he'd gone there regularly to play poker. With its steep gables, lying mostly in the shadow of the pine grove, today it appeared downright spooky.

Inside, the silence was an ominous presence. Maybe it was his imagination, but he felt Catherine's spirit was all about, and he wasn't a man to believe in such things. Probably just some stale perfume playing with his mind. Funny, how a deserted house could cling to something of its dead owner, he mused.

He expected to locate Thomas's will easily enough, and perhaps Catherine's, in the oak roll-top desk. He'd seen Thomas go to it a number of times, knew it was where he kept his important documents. But the papers weren't there. Probably Wilson had them. Their content could be significant.

Now for the rosary. He'd only been to the top of the stairs once, the day of the funeral, and he hadn't taken much notice then. Ascending the steps now, he felt he was pushing through an invisible wall of privacy. The stairs creaked as he climbed them, each with its own particular note.

He saw the little girl's room first. Strange way to decorate a bedroom, he thought—hand-painted peaches and bananas bordering the ceiling. No clothes, not a single toy. Jorie'd probably taken everything over to O'Laerty's.

The only sign of life anywhere were the droppings of mice sprinkled liberally throughout. The visible traps had all been sprung.

He found Catherine's room a picture of femininity. Everything was white, from the window coverings of lace to the quilt on her bed.

He was uncomfortable about going through the dead woman's dresser drawers. It always felt like he was intruding when his job called for this sort of intimate search. When it was someone he'd known it was almost embarrassing.

He found no rosary, only a lot of jewelry. Perhaps Jorie might like something else of his mother's. It might loosen his tongue, even bring on a confession. He put a string of pearls in his pocket.

Farther down the hall he found the boy's room. It certainly had his stamp on it. A bookcase held volumes of poetry, nature and a collection of rocks. One on geology was inscribed by Dr. Johnson, *For my young friend, Jorie Radcliff, with high hopes for his future contributions to science.* It was clear Arthur had an interest in the boy.

He decided to search the closet. On the top shelf Earl found two locked diaries. But the shocker was that toward the back, under a pile of clothes, he found drawings of nudes. The face was unmistakably Jorie's mother. What kind of kid would envision his own mother naked, and affix her likeness to the pornographic outpouring of his imagination?

Earl decided he'd best secure the diaries and drawings in his office. That meant a trip across the bridge to the county courthouse in Houghton.

Battles over where to locate the county seat had been waged more than once: whether to be in Houghton, on one side of the long, narrow lake, or in Hancock on the other. It was a thorn in Earl's side that Houghton had finally won out. This meant he had to trudge back and forth across the bridge from his home in Hancock to Houghton where his office was in the courthouse. And Hancock, after all, had a population of four thousand, several hundred more than Houghton.

Hunkering down in his coat, he was almost knocked down by the winds. Thank God, the old wooden bridge had been replaced by a steel truss. Yet, real or imagined, he could still feel its sway, and the fear that it would collapse beneath him never left.

He kept his mind occupied with the puzzle before him. He knew Thomas's other sons had gotten a chunk of money or stock certificates when they turned eighteen. Thomas Radcliff had made sure his friends knew whenever one of his boys got their 'sizeable sum.' Earl thought he was bragging, a way of letting them know how well he was doing.

Jorie had just turned eighteen, The timing could be relevant: If it was murder, could it have something to do with his inheritance?

But no large amount had been deposited into Jorie's account—he'd checked on that this morning—and none withdrawn from Catherine's. He'd asked if there were other accounts or safe deposit boxes, and inquired of other banks. Nothing. Of course, Jorie could have received stock certificates. Frustrating that Wilson was out of town. He might have some answers.

Earl reached his office, built up the fire in the old, dusty pot-belly, and reached for his leftover coffee. He wondered if Jorie had recorded his feelings toward his mother in his diaries. With luck, he might find the answers to a lot of questions in there. He'd located no keys. Opening the diaries would be no problem, but somehow that seemed a greater breach than using a key. He started snapping the rubber band on his wrist, and took a sip of coffee. "Fly's piss." He tossed the coffee in the spittoon.

His wrist was beginning to sting. Well, no point putting it off any longer. Scratching in his desk, he found an old compass. With its point he picked the clasp which gave easily enough. Now to unlock the contents. He leaned back in his old oak chair, its rusty spring echoing the one in his own spine.

He couldn't believe what he was seeing.

The diaries weren't Jorie's at all. They were Catherine's.

chapter 5

EARL SAT BEFORE the two volumes with sweaty hands. What a violation, to read what was meant for no one except the one who'd penned them. *Why did Jorie have them?*

He let his eyes roam over the yellowed pages, not ready to give meaning to the words. Where had she learned her penmanship? Ah, yes, in Scotland. Well, they had a different hand, all right. The flowery script would make deciphering the words slow going.

She was still in high school then, back in Red Jacket. As was he. They were thinking of changing the name to something more classy, like Calumet, but so far it was still Red Jacket, named for some Native American Chief of the Seneca tribe.

Finally, he focused on the date of the first entry.

Stale cookies kept him going all night, and still he got only part-way through the first diary. He was up to the page where Jorie was about six.

August 1, 1888

Jorie, thank the Lord, is recovering from that dreadful assault on his life three weeks ago. The doctor says his ribs may have been cracked but there's naught to do for it. He is up and playing, although still complaining that his bones hurt.

Thomas still refuses to talk to me. He speaks only of those matters of necessity that involve the household. I have tried on several occasions to converse with him, but he will not have it. Once when I was speaking of Jorie, he looked up from his paper and said, 'My God, woman, Calumet and Hecla have had three fires this year in their shafts, and lost thousands in copper production. The same could happen to us! Do you think I've noth-ing to think about but you and the boy?'

In bed he turns his back to me. Sunday last I fixed him Christmas pudding even though it is nowhere near that time; I was trying to show some kindness, but he ate only one helping and would take none at the next meal.

He ignores Jorie as well, who can't understand why his papa shows no interest in him. Oh, Thomas will correct him—that he'll do. But kind words are few and far between now.

He is after visiting his other sons much of late. If it weren't for my beloved Jorie, surely I would die.

I don't want to be 'a greetin and roarin' as my mother would say, but it is a lonely life I have. At only twenty-three I feel like an old widow.

Assault on Jorie! What in the world was she talking about? What had precipitated Thomas's anger?

He didn't know women put down all their feelings, like that. Just laid bare—things you wouldn't even want yourself to know. He wondered if his wife wrote such things in her diary. "Gott in him-mel," he muttered. Catherine even laid out how she couldn't get her husband to give her a poke. Holy Mackerel, Thomas, were you out of your mind?

In his case, it was often the other way around!

Light from the pale white sun was beginning to work its way into the window, as Earl closed the book and locked both diaries in his desk. The fire had gone out hours ago, leaving him chilled. He pulled up his collar and headed for Mik Dougherty's café.

The leaves were swirling around his feet as fast as the thoughts in his head. Catherine's entries had been sporadic and often lack-ing in context. Well, he couldn't really fault her for that—she was only writing for herself. But it certainly made for confusion, raising more questions than it answered about that family.

He ordered his usual breakfast, but had little appetite for it. Finishing off with his third cup of coffee and still with no sleep, he headed back to the office.

A Mr. Olsen was waiting for him. Quite elderly, his gout forced him to take his seat with care. What hair he had was grey and sparse. "I'm mostly retired now, but I still see a few clients."

"Clients?"

"Law practice over in Dollar Bay."

Slowly the man unfolded a page from the newspaper. "I guess this is two weeks old now, but papers have a way of piling up on me. Just noticed last night this piece about the woman who died in the snowstorm. Name of Radcliff. Survivors include her son Jordan Radcliff."

"That's right."

"This young man came to see me about a week before her death."

That got Earl's attention.

"He wanted to know the procedure for committing someone." He held his fingertips together.

Earl reached for his rubber band.

"Did he say who he wanted to commit?"

"His mother. He seemed very nervous at the time."

Earl swallowed. "What reason did he give for this action?"

"He wouldn't say."

"Anything else?"

"I told him that before anything of the sort could happen there'd have to be a lunacy hearing. He'd need witnesses—a sworn statement from the woman's doctor, and so on."

"Yes?"

"He seemed discouraged. Paid me on the spot and left in a hurry."

Earl rubbed his wrist. He took Olsen's statement and got his address.

"We may need you later. Thank you very much for coming in."

The lawyer rose to his feet in visible pain, and carefully navigating each step, took his leave.

As Earl pondered the significance of this new information, his irate wife sailed in. Cuffing him lightly on the jaw, she cried out,

"I should clobber you, Earl Foster, I was that worried. Where were you last night?"

"Cora." He stared at her.

Was he so consumed with the demise of Catherine he'd forgotten he had a wife at home?

Earl couldn't sleep that night, wondering why Jorie would want to have his mother committed. Was he mentally unbalanced, as his mother had indicated? Was he trying to get her out of the way for some dark reason of his own?

He was driven by the need to discover the truth, and simultaneously repelled to think that his greatest fears could possibly be true.

The next morning he stopped by the *News* again. "I couldn't find the rosary. Thought you might like to have this." He handed Jorie the string of opalescent beads.

"Thanks," was all Jorie said, as he dropped the necklace in his pocket. His face betrayed no emotion.

It was going to take more than a string of beads to crack this boy.

"I want to see you in my office when you finish here," he told Jorie.

The young man sat opposite Earl with the desk between them. "You know a lawyer name of Olsen?"

Jorie frowned. "I'm not sure...the name sounds familiar."

"He says you went to see him. Over in Dollar Bay."

Jorie appeared to be puzzled.

Earl consulted his notes. "October third."

Jorie was silent, his face contorted in pain.

They sat in silence for some time, the sheriff hoping Jorie would open up. Earl waited, studied the stacks of papers on his desk that needed to be filed or disposed of. Some of them had been there so long they were gathering dust.

Finally, he said, "I'll be honest with you, lad. It looks like you took your mother out there to die."

"You think I—" Jorie clutched the edge of the desk. Tiny beads of perspiration burst onto his face, and his Adam's Apple bobbed up and down.

"I don't know, Jorie. But it doesn't look good, doesn't look good at all."

Jorie leaned back and closed his eyes.

"There's too much about this situation that doesn't set right. I'm going to take you into custody 'til you're ready to do some explaining."

The lad blinked, but said nothing. He went without struggle. Maybe a couple of days in the hoosegow would unlock his jaw, Earl mused. He sure couldn't afford to have his prime suspect up and leave town.

The prosecuting attorney would have to submit the petition to the judge for a hearing. He hoped Boyce wouldn't drill him on the particulars. He wasn't at all sure the kid was guilty, and he didn't want this thing blown out of proportion to serve Buck Boyce's political ambitions. Buck would be licking his lips to bring this case to trial for the publicity it would bring him.

The prosecutor was just leaving his office. "Can this wait 'til tomorrow, Earl?"

"I've already got him behind bars."

"All right. Give it here."

That afternoon Toby Wilson came by. He was a man in his fifties, with a pleasant countenance. Earl was glad to see him.

"The stationer said you wanted to see me, Earl. I had business downstate."

"Yes. I've arrested Jordan Radcliff."

"I heard. Under suspicious circumstances, I understand."

"I need to know if young Radcliff got any inheritance, Toby. I know it's privileged, but the boy is under suspicion for murder."

Wilson pursed his lips and rocked back and forth on the new fancy shoes he'd procured in Detroit. He often rocked when he spoke.

"No. To date he hasn't gotten anything. Mind you, he could have. But his mother didn't see fit to open her purse strings."

The next morning Earl got to work early to tackle the diaries. He read the part about the dispute between Thomas and Catherine over Jorie's discipline. Thomas had been so hard on the boy that Catherine had threatened to take Jorie and leave. And all the time Earl had thought their family life was harmonious.

About ten o'clock he'd had enough. He locked the office and headed to Mik's for breakfast.

He caught the headlines at the newspaper stand. The paper Jorie worked for made no mention of the arrest, but their competitor, *The Mining Gazette* reported, "Copper Country Evening News Reporter Held For Matricide!"

Earl strode down Shelden Street with a faster step than usual. He reached Dougherty's just as three of the locals were leaving.

"Whatcha got on that murder case, Sheriff?" One of the Groden Gang said.

"Got him bagged, I hope. Told the wife not to leave the house, just in case," Flem Crocker declared.

Walter had sure spread his rumors far and wide.

"When I know something, the paper will know. And then somebody can read it to you."

"What's gotten into you, Foster? Ain't your missus given you any?"

"Shut your foul mouth, Flem or I'll throw you in the poky with him."

The other two shuffled off.

"Don't get all wrathy, sheriff. We didn't mean nothin'."

Then, he too sauntered off, but not before punctuating his remark with a wad spat within an inch of Earl's boot.

Earl found his customary seat occupied, and chose another as far away from anyone as he could.

When Mik brought him his usual porridge and coffee, Earl countered his "Good morning, Sheriff," with, "I didn't ask for that. I want three eggs, a rasher of bacon and a scone."

Mik looked at him like he was listening to one of the Finns speaking his native tongue, but finally managed, "Yes, sir, we'll get that right up."

That afternoon the judge summoned Earl. He was holding the petition Buck Boyce had passed on to him.

"You think Jorie Radcliff murdered his mother?"

"It's not for me to say, George. But I think there's sufficient reason to have a hearing. You see, he—"

"Don't have time to listen now, Earl." George McKinney clipped the end of his cigar. "That's what hearings are for."

Earl took that for agreement, but bristled that George had once again found reason to school him in his own line of work.

He was never sure when his audience with the judge was over. "If that's settled, then, I'll see you tomorrow night."

"Bring money." George McKinney grinned as he held the light to his cigar.

Earl left, scratching his elbow. He didn't look forward to reading more of the diaries, and he didn't relish his next task either—going down to the jailhouse.

Jorie awoke, sat up abruptly on the edge of his cot. There was that dream again, of walking through the blizzard with his mother, drowning in the snow. *Why were they out in that storm?* He knew at least part of the dream was true. He *had* taken his mother for a ride, and they had walked through the snow in the woods. Yes, he'd reported all that to Mr. Foster.

He was in jail as a possible murder suspect! *Why would he kill his mother? He loved her!* They'd had arguments—mostly about where he was going to college. She wanted him to stay at home and attend the mining college in Houghton; he wanted to go to the University of Michigan in Ann Arbor. And he would, too, as soon as he got the money his father had promised when he turned eighteen.

Mr. Foster said he'd gone to see a lawyer named Olsen. Yes, he remembered that now. But why? There was more, there had to be. Why couldn't he recall? What happened that day in the woods? He willed himself to remember. Yes, some of the fog was clearing.

He'd found a man on the road, and together they went back into the woods with the lantern, looking for her. Yes, he *had* tried to find her, he knew he had!

The jail, mostly housing disorderly drunks from both sides of the lake hadn't been designed with murderers in mind. Probably it wouldn't be too hard to escape, Earl mused.

It was dusk when he descended into the bowels of the court-house. Fetid odors came to him as he took the keys off the peg on the wall—a mixture of urine and cleaning solution. The formula varied from one day to the next, often one defeating the other. Sometimes it was the smell of feces that dominated. Or vomit.

He found Jorie's cell door open, the boy lying on his cot.

"O'Brien, where the hell are you?" he yelled down the hall.

The jail keeper, wounded forty years ago in the civil war, loomed out of the darkness and limped toward the cell.

"Just dumpin' the prisoner's chamber pot, sir."

"The door of his cell is open!"

"I was only gone a minute. He was sleepin'."

"Never leave an occupied cell unlocked."

"No, sir."

Jorie sat up when Earl entered.

"You weren't asleep?"

"No, Mr. Foster."

"Did you know you could have run right out of here?"

"How far would I get?"

Earl straddled the only chair, resting his arms on its back. "Were you thinking of leaving here?"

"No, sir."

"What were you thinking about?"

Jorie's blue eyes pierced Earl's. "Just now? I was watching that spider in the corner there."

The sheriff looked around at the dirty cell. "I could have O'Brien clean this place up for you."

Earl watched a cockroach scuttle across the dark edge of the cell, and disappear into a crack in the wall. The interior partitions of the cells had been plastered and painted light green a long time ago. But years of abuse from enraged and drunken prisoners had left the surface marred and broken, exposing the skeleton of narrow wooden slats of lath. Battles had been lost, nightmares had triumphed here. The ghosts of former inmates marched across Earl's mind.

"You've had some time to think things over, lad. I hope your mind's cleared up."

Earl picked at a sore, waiting for the young man to respond.

Jorie frowned. "How's my little sister?"

"Mrs. O'Laerty is taking fine care of her. Look, I don't like this situation any better than you do. I'll be honest with you. Now if this is true, Jorie, and you cooperate with us, I'll try to get the sentence reduced." He waited.

Jorie looked at the sheriff, then gazed out the window at the lightly falling snow. Finally, he shifted on the cot. "You said I went to see a lawyer."

"Mr. Olsen over at Dollar Bay."

"Did he say why?"

Earl searched the boy's face. *Didn't he know?* "He said you wanted to commit your mother."

"*Commit* her?"

"That's right."

Earl watched the color creep up the side of young Radcliff's neck. He leaned forward. "The hearing's coming up soon. Are you ready to tell me what happened?"

PART II
The years Before

chapter 6

"WHERE DOES PAPA go every day?" Jorie asked as he got ready for bed.

"Tomorrow we'll walk up the hill and I'll show you. Now, what story would you like?"

"The flying horse one, Mummy."

The Greek myth *Pegasus* was his favorite story the summer of his fifth year. For his birthday, Papa had given him the rocking horse he'd spent long evenings working on. Jorie was thrilled. He got both parents to push him on it until he got the hang of rocking it himself. He decided that he liked stories about horses the best, and the Pegasus myth was his favorite.

"I don't think I know that one," his mother teased, as she tucked him in.

"Yes, you do. Peggythis and Belly."

"Oh, *that* one."

Catherine heard her step-son cough in the hallway. Walter frequently hung around the fringe of their story time. She had no quarrel with his listening in the parlor, but bedtime was her special time with her son, the one hour she wanted just for the two of them. Besides, at twelve, she thought Walter too old for such stories; he should be doing his lessons.

"Don't tell the bad part, where Belly loses Peggythis and gets punished because he flew up to the house of the gods, when he wasn't supposed to."

"I won't need to—you just did," she smiled.

Again she heard her step-son cough.

"Walter, go to the kitchen and help Helena with the washing up, there's a good boy."

Catherine held Jorie close, while she spun the tale once more.

When she had finished, Jorie said, "I can call my rocking horse Peggythis."

"That would be a good name."

Jorie yawned. "He's flying, flying way up in the sky, Mummy."

"Yes, Darling."

"The stars are his friends. Here we go, here we go home!"

She lay beside him as he slipped into sleep. How beautiful he was. She fingered his dark curls, imagined she could see the blue of his eyes through the lids.

When she rose to leave the room she could hear Walter scuttling down the stairs.

What a difficult child he was, always hanging in the shadows. She had not been able to trust him since that awful incident in the ice-cream parlor when Jorie was a baby. In the crowded room, the baby carriage had been placed in the corner, where it had been tipped over. Catherine was convinced that Walter had done it, though he wouldn't admit it, nor would Thomas punish him. Later, various unexplained bruises had appeared on Jorie's arms and legs.

She kissed her sleeping child and went downstairs. By the time she reached the kitchen, Walter was busy helping Helena, the Irish housekeeper.

The next day Catherine took the boys for a long walk over the hills behind the house. It was a favorite vantage of Catherine's. More of the lake could be seen from here, as it wound like a silver ribbon around the bend, and Houghton on the far side. But today the spring winds were cold, and they kept their backs to the view as they climbed the sodden hills.

When they reached the plateau at the top she surveyed the dreary landscape. Pulling Jorie's scarf tighter she said, "Look, I want you to see this. Do you know where we are?"

"I don't like it here."

"It's Papa's mine." She pointed to the large stack reaching toward the sky. "That's the chimney, puffing out big clouds of black smoke."

"Like the dragon in the story."

"Do you know that right under our feet there are hundreds of men working deep down in the earth—like little ants?"

"It isn't pretty here, Mummy. Where are the trees?"

For miles around the landscape had been denuded by the voracious appetite of the steam engines. Picked thin were the forests of hemlock, pine, beech and maple that once had graced the land.

"Some are used for fuel to run the engines, and many trees are inside the mine."

"Why?"

"To hold up the walls so they won't cave in and bury the miners."

Walter added his two cents worth, "But there's still cave-ins. Happens all the time. Miners are buried alive and can't get out. Or they get kilt when they set off an explosion."

"Don't frighten him, Walter."

"I wouldn't like to work down there," Jorie said.

A shiver went through her. "No. And you won't. You won't ever have to work in a mine, I promise. That's a horrible way to spend your life—underground."

"My brothers do. They're shaft captains."

"Yes. I know."

"Papa—" Jorie added.

"Papa works in an office on the grass. Way over there where the buildings are. He only goes below once in awhile, to check on things."

"It's pitch black down there," Walter informed.

"Don't they get scared?"

"Some of them do." Catherine said. "They have to go way, way down in the earth."

"The man-car goes straight down to the pits of hell," Walter whooped.

"Walter—"

"They call it that 'cuz it's so hot. Sometimes the miners get pushed off the car, or fall off it. Then they fall and fall a whole mile through a black tunnel! Just like falling out of the sky, only worse, cause it's so dark—"

"Walter, enough!"

"—And at the bottom, they get kilt. My brothers told me. Didn't you know that's how Helena'a husband lost his arm—down there in the pit."

"Walter! I said stop! You'll frighten him."

Walter looked up innocently. "Sorry, ma'am."

In the afternoon, Catherine sat on the sofa with her arm around Jorie, ready to read a story. She looked up as Walter entered the room.

"No, you may not listen today. You disobeyed me, continued to rant on about the mine when I told you not to. Go to the kitchen now and work on your sums.

"Your ma bleeds!" Walter announced with devilish certainty.

"She does not!"

"She does. Want proof?" He backed the younger boy against the wall in the upstairs hallway.

"You're lying. There's nothing wrong with her."

"Wanna bet?"

From behind his back Walter pulled out a soiled rag. He dangled and twirled it in front of the cornered Jorie like a wiggling snake.

"See? See? I told you. It come from between her legs. Her whole insides is bleedin' out. You won't have a ma fer long. Nope, she's gonna die."

"It's not true! She's not dying."

"'Tis so. I found it in her room."

"Did not."

"Did too. There was five of them, all smashed down in a lard pail she hides under her bed. She don't want you to know, see."

"I don't believe you!"

Carol A Sheldon

"Come on, I'll show you the others. It's hard to get the cover off the pail, but I'll do it for you."

"No!" He dashed downstairs, but was afraid to report this news to his mother.

For two days he worried that perhaps it was true. Why else would she bleed? He imagined a constant flow of her life blood leaking out—mostly at night, he supposed—until she was so sick she couldn't get out of bed. And then she'd die, like Grandma.

The horror was too much to bear. He lost his appetite and Catherine thought he was sick.

When she came to his room, she found him curled up in a ball, making a sort of choking noise.

At first he wouldn't tell her why, and squirmed away from her. "I'll get in trouble if I tell."

"Trouble? With Papa?" She forced him to face her.

"No," he cried. "Walter."

"Walter!"

He burst out, "Walter says you're going to die!"

"What?"

"Like his ma did."

"That's a terrible lie. There's not a bit of truth to it. Do I look *ill* to you?"

"No, but..."

"But what?"

It was hard to say. "He showed me a bandage. And there were more he said."

"A bandage? What kind of bandage?"

"There was blood on it."

"He's just trying to frighten you again, my darling. It must have been someone else's, a filthy thing he picked up in the road."

Jorie shook his head, and buried it in his mother's lap.

"What is it? Tell me."

"He said it came from under your bed," he eked out.

Jorie felt her stiffen and push him away. He saw the color first drain from her face, and then come back, darkening to the shade of red plums. He had never seen her so angry.

58

"He is a wicked, wicked boy to fill your head with such frightening falsehoods."

Her hands were tight little fists. A vein on her forehead was sticking out.

Blood comes out of veins. Maybe this one will pop open, and blood will come out of her head too.

"Jorie, look at me."

"Then you don't have bandages under your bed?"

Catherine took a deep breath. "You wouldn't understand, Jorie. But it's nothing to do with dying. It's normal."

Normal. How could bleeding be normal?

Walter was soundly punished.

Three days later, Jorie went out to play. But when it was suppertime, he did not come in.

"Have you seen him, Walter?"

"No, ma'am."

Thomas was not home. She said to Walter, "Help me look for him."

"I'll go this way, and you go that way. All right, ma'am?"

She walked down the hill, as Walter walked up. An hour later, she still hadn't found him. Catherine was at sixes and sevens. She started back up the hill, by a different route, and rounded back to the house to see if he had come home. It was quiet, so she started off again, this time up the hill. A half hour later, Walter called to her.

"The search is over, ma'am. I found him."

"Where?"

"Up in the copse, asleep in the grass."

But Jorie was crying, rubbing his arms.

"What's wrong, Darling?"

He looked at Walter and said nothing.

"Tell me."

It wasn't until she was getting him ready for bed that Jorie relayed how Walter had tied him to a tree, and left him there.

Carol A Sheldon

"Don't let him know I told you, Mummy. He said if I did, next time he'd shove me down the privy hole."

"Oh, good lord."

She held him to her for a few moments, assuring him no such thing would happen.

When she told Thomas later that evening, he was able to get a confession from his older son. Walter was whipped soundly, but Catherine was not satisfied. That night she wrote in her diary:

July 19, 1888

I do not trust Walter. Always I must be on the alert to make certain he does not hurt my Jorie. The lad is dishonest and mean-spirited. He frightens Jorie, and I fear some day may do him real harm. Oh, how I wish he didn't live with us!

Jorie awoke to his brother leaning over him. "Get up."

"What? Why?" he asked still half asleep.

"Come on. Get up." Walter pulled him out of bed.

"Where are we going?"

"You're going in here." He pushed Jorie into the closet. "This is where you'll spend the night, ya hear?"

"You can't do this to me!"

"And if you dare tell yer ma or let out a sound, next time I'll throw ya down the mine shaft, where you'll fall all the way down to hell."

Jorie heard the closet door close and the key turn. In total darkness, he began to cry quietly.

"Please, Walter, let me out."

There was no answer.

"Please!"

Finally realizing there would be no help, Jorie pulled some clothes off the hangers and made a bed for himself on the floor. He woke to the sound of mice scurrying about; fear and cold kept him awake for hours.

Early in the morning, he was startled by the door opening suddenly, blinding him with daylight.

"Get out of there. And 'member, I told you, not a word to yer ma."

60

This time Jorie took the warning to heart.

An urgent knock brought her to the door, where a lad of about fourteen stood. "Would you be Mrs. Radcliff, Ma'am?"

"Yes."

"It's up at the mine, Ma'am. An accident."

"What happened?" Catherine's hand went to her face. "Is my husband hurt?"

"You'd best come up to the agent's office." The boy ran off.

Catherine hesitated. Should she wake Jorie and take him with her on the gelding, or leave him sleeping? The urgency required a swift decision.

She turned to Walter. "You watch your brother, and if there's anything amiss when I come back, I'll take a brush to you myself!"

Saddling up Thomas's horse as quickly as she could, she tore out of the stable, taking the steep road straight up to the Hill.

Walter watched his stepmother disappear in a blur of dust. He crept up the stairs and listened by the room where Jorie was sleeping. Hearing nothing, he opened the door.

"It's time to get up."

Jorie rubbed his eyes. "Where's my mother?"

"She had to go up to the mine. She told me I was in charge."

"What are you going to do?" Jorie sat up, twisted the sheet in his hand.

"Play a game with you. Come on. We'll have a cookie first."

Timorously, Jorie followed Walter downstairs. His mother wouldn't leave him—he knew she wouldn't. "Mummy!" he yelled as loud as he could.

Walter laughed. "I told you she wasn't here." He reached into the cookie jar. "Want one?"

"We're not supposed to."

"Suit yourself." Walter stuffed half of the large oatmeal cookie into his mouth, soon followed by the other.

"Let's go down the cellar. It's cool there, and we can play miners."

"I don't want to."

"How come?"

Jorie twisted his mouth. "You'll tie me up. Or lock me in down there."

"No, I won't. I promise. Cross my heart and hope to die."

Walter grabbed Jorie's hand and led him around the side of the house. "Stop your snivelin', ya big sissy." He lifted the cellar door that lay at an angle against the ground.

"Get in there. I can't hold the door up forever."

"I don't want to."

"It'll be fun. Go on, get in."

"No!"

"Here, I'll help you."

With that Walter pushed Jorie into the cellar. "Down you go, down the shaft." As he let go of the door it slammed shut.

Down the dark hole, falling, falling, falling.

Jorie began to scream.

In a few minutes Walter returned and climbed into the cellar himself. "I'm back. Stop yer bawlin'."

"Let me out, Walter. Let me out!" Jorie cried.

"Don't be skeery. We can pretend we're in a real mine."

"I hurt my knee."

"Miners get hurt all the time. Helena's husband lost his whole arm. Gettin' hurt will make it seem more real."

"Please let me out, Walter," he begged.

When Catherine arrived at the agent's office, Mr. Ahlers and the laborer who'd helped to bring him up top were with her husband. Thomas lay unconscious on a stretcher; a rivulet of blood lay in the crease of his forehead.

Catherine stared in agonizing disbelief. "Is he—dead?"

"No, he's not." Clark Ahlers said. "He'll come around soon."

"Why hasn't the doctor been called?" she snapped.

"If you'll just be patient, Ma'am, the doctor's on his way."

"Get me some soap and water; I'll clean him up myself."

"Your husband will be all right. Just a nasty bump to his head."

"How did this happen?" Catherine knelt beside her husband, studied his wound.

"He went down the mine in the skip and got struck by a loose overhead timber."

"The skip! That's suicide. Why didn't he ride the man-car?"

"The man-car only operates at the beginning and end of the shifts, Mrs. Radcliff. The rest of the time the skips carry the rock up. So if anyone needs to get in or out of the mine they have to use—"

"My God!" Catherine bent over her husband, dabbed her handkerchief on his wound. "Aren't there any safety precautions?"

"Ma'am, a mine's a dangerous place. Your husband knows this." Mr. Ahlers said.

The laborer chipped in, "We lose about a man a week in all manner of accidents."

Mr. Ahlers glared at him.

"They're usually miners though, or trammers," the young man finished lamely.

"The mine should be closed until proper precautions are taken!" Catherine stated.

Mr. Ahlers turned to the laborer. "You can go back to work now."

"We've finished sorting the rocks in the shaft house, sir. Mostly mucking out poor-rock today. Not much copper a'tall."

"There'll be more brought up by now. Go report to your captain."

The laborer left, and Mr. Ahlers turned to Catherine.

"Ma'am, with all respect, the *Portage* has the best safety record in all of Copperdom."

By the time Doctor Carlyle arrived, Thomas had come to.

"You've done a fine job preparing my patient for me," the doctor smiled at her. "I could use a nurse at the company clinic, if you're interested."

Catherine ignored this. She thought he ought to be apologizing for being so late.

Thomas sat up, felt his head gingerly. After getting his bearings, he said, "No need to trouble yourself further, Catherine. Go along home now."

"Not without taking you with me."

"It's only three o'clock."

"Go ahead, Radcliff," Ahlers said. "Your wife is quite right. Go home and take it easy."

They climbed into Thomas's buggy, with the gelding tied to the back.

As Catherine took the reins, she said, "I was very worried, believe you me. What a relief to know that nothing serious happened."

Walter handed Jorie a spade. "We're going to find copper here," he said. "Start working. We'll stope it out, pretend we're diggin' tunnels just like a real mine."

Walter struck the wall several times with the rock. Jorie imitated him, hitting it with his spade.

Walter looked around, saw a wheelbarrow. "Here, we'll use this to haul the rocks."

He brought the oversized barrow to the coal pile. A shaft of light from the dirty window fell upon the boys.

"Come on, fill it with all the rock we busted out today. You have to do that 'cuz you're just a trammer. Trammers don't know how to find the copper—they're just laborers. You have to pick up rock and put it in the barrow, here."

"I don't want to."

"I'm the miner. It's my job to find the veins of copper and choose what to blow up. When I set off the dynamite, there's going to be a big explosion."

"Walter, let's get out now! I want to go home."

"You are home, dummy. Come on. Let's see who can get the most in the barrow."

When it was full, Walter instructed, "Lie down here, next to the coal pile, and check the ceiling for falling rock and cracks."

"No."

"You don't want a cave-in, do you? Buried alive—is that what you want?"

"I'm not the miner—you are," Jorie injected.

Walter spat. "Well then—you be the captain. It's his job to check."

The house was unnaturally quiet. Catherine went to Jorie's room, then called to the boys and got no response.

"Thomas, they're gone! I left Walter in charge of Jorie—something's happened!"

"Perhaps they went to catch polliwogs," Thomas offered. "You go to the creek and I'll see if they're down by the well."

Catherine started in the direction of the creek.

"Oh, my God!" What if Walter had taken Jorie to the lake? As Catherine rounded the house, the open cellar door caught her eye. *Why was it open?*

"Jorie!" she called down the stairs.

There was no answer. As she crept down the steps her mouth went dry and her throat tightened. The sight caused her to gasp. The coal, usually piled high to the window, and restrained at the bottom by a low wooden corral, had overflowed its banks and spilled out on the dirt floor.

"Jorie!" she called. "Walter!"

Still no reply. Her toe caught against a jagged piece of rock in the uneven dirt floor, and sent her sprawling forward on her face. When she was back on her feet, she scurried up the steps and toward the well.

"Thomas! They've been in the cellar playing in the coal," she spat out between gulps for breath. "But they're not there now."

Her eyes widened in fear as a sudden thought crossed her mind. Thomas caught it, and they were off running back to the cellar. They fell on their knees and began raking the coal with their hands, throwing chunks to one side and the other.

A patch of pale blue caught Catherine's eye, and digging more furiously than ever, she uncovered Jorie. He was as black as the substance that covered him.

Lifted from the rubble, he seemed not to be breathing. Catherine held him, pounding him on the back. His head rolled back and he lay still in her arms. At last, as she ran to the house with him, he gasped for air.

Thomas called out for Walter. Had an avalanche of coal buried them both? He fell to his knees again, pushing the coal aside as more cascaded from above. Finally satisfied that Walter was not under the coal, but wanting to make sure he wasn't hiding, Thomas poked his way around other parts of the cellar. In the late afternoon, the light was so scant it was hard to make out shapes. He dared not light a candle amidst the inflammable coal dust in the air. The sudden splintering of glass startled him. Groping in the dark he'd knocked over a bottle of his home-made wine. He stood still and waited in the silence, hearing only the chirp of a lone cricket somewhere in the dark recess.

He was about to leave when a chunk of coal slipping down the pile caused him to look up. Near the top and to the side of the fading shaft of light two eyes gleamed in the darkness. He stepped closer. There, camouflaged by the coal dust that covered him, and crouching like a feral cat, was Walter.

By the time Catherine got him to the house Jorie was crying hysterically, taking in great gulps of air, while his whole body shook. As she held him, he coughed up black phlegm.

Blackened as he was, she couldn't tell what injuries he had, beyond almost suffocating. She could see a trickle of blood drying on a gash on his forehead, and a huge goose egg. She put water on the stove to boil and dragged out the washtub. While she waited for it to heat up, Catherine rocked her son in her arms.

Thomas came in as she was bathing Jorie. "How is he?"

"It's the jerky way he's breathing that bothers me most."

"Any broken bones?"

"I don't know."

Suddenly she looked up. "Where's Walter?" It was the first she'd thought of him.

"On the veranda. He needs a bath too."

"Well, you do it, when I've finished here. Where did you find him?"

"On top of the coal pile."

"He needs to be punished for taking Jorie down there. They both could have been killed in that avalanche of coal."

Finally she took Jorie out of the bath. He wasn't very clean, but the rest would have to wait. She rapped him in a blanket, put iodine on his cuts, and carried him upstairs to bed.

"Don't go, Mummy."

"I won't leave you, Precious."

"It hurts."

"Where?"

"All over." He put his hands on his ribs. "It hurts to breathe."

She tried to rearrange him on a pillow, but it made him cry.

"I'm sorry, Jorie. Whatever made you boys go in the cellar?"

"Walter wanted to play miners."

"You shouldn't have been down there, and you certainly shouldn't have been climbing the coal pile."

"We weren't climbing on it."

"What do you mean?"

"Walter dumped it on me."

Catherine and Thomas stayed up that night talking for hours.

"Walter can't stay with us. He'll have to go away."

"Go where?"

"He should be given over to the care of the Good Will Farm."

"Talk sense, woman."

"They'll be kind to him, I know they will. He can't live here, Thomas. It's out of the question."

"What are you saying? He's my son as much as Jorie is. I will not send him to the Farm."

"He tried to kill Jorie. He lured Jorie into the cellar to carry out his evil plan."

"That's not true!"

"You heard Jorie say it yourself. Walter dumped the wheelbarrow full of coal on him. When he tried to get up Walter pushed him down—"

"They were just playing."

"—And Jorie hit his head on the stone. Then Walter ran to the top of the pile and kicked more coal down on top of him."

"That's sheer speculation."

"How do you think the coal got out of the corral and all over the floor?"

"He might have been trying to scare him, but he wasn't planning to kill him."

"You're blind, Thomas. When we called to him, did he answer? He remained on top of the coal pile while his brother was *dying* under it! That's an admission of guilt, believe you me."

Thomas said nothing. Catherine stared at the wound on her husband's face. The blood had seeped through the bandage, and her heart went out to him, but she had to stay focused.

"And it isn't the first time. Jorie told me that one night Walter locked him in the closet. *All night!* The Lord knows what else he's done. I tell you, Walter is out to do away with Jorie!"

"He's lost his ma. Now you want *me* to abandon him."

"I won't argue any more. I will not risk a repeat occurrence. Either Walter goes or I leave with Jorie."

Catherine held her son that night. Several times he woke crying, sometimes in pain, and sometimes in terror.

In the morning, when Thomas had taken no action, Catherine said, "I am going to see Earl Foster."

"What are you talking about? This is a domestic matter. If you're so sure he did it, I'll give him a whipping."

"A whipping! He tried to murder my son!"

Thomas's hand flashed across Catherine's cheek before he could stop it. It was the first time he'd struck her. She felt the hot burn spread through her face, but refused to let Thomas see her pain. As she started for the door, he rushed to block her exit.

"Sit down, Catherine. Let's discuss this reasonably."

68

"I've done with talking. I will hold firm to my decision on this matter."

Thomas sat down at the table, his head in his hands, while Catherine waited by the door. Finally, he rose, called Walter and left the house.

It was hours before he returned. The suffering of her son served to convince her that she'd done the right thing. Jorie's breathing was shallow and labored. He continued to cough up dark matter, and wanted no food.

Finally the door opened.

"It's done then?" Catherine asked.

He gave a curt nod. "Are you satisfied now?"

"Did you tell Mrs. Lerner what he did?"

"I didn't take him to the Farm. He's with my sister."

Catherine started to say something and changed her mind. Well, what did it matter to her? He was gone, and Jorie was out of harm's way. Walter would never pose a danger to her son again.

Thomas barely spoke to his wife, and the evenings lay heavily between them, with unspoken resentment. In the long silences there was nothing but the ticking of the mantel clock to keep them company, as he read his newspaper and she did her mending. And all the time her mind went back to how she'd gotten into this marriage to begin with.

chapter 7

SIXTEEN YEAR OLD Catherine stayed under the covers as long as she could, ignoring her mother's calls. She would not think about her mother's determination to marry her off. She pulled the covers over her head and thought of her visit to Paris with her father. The realization stung her anew each morning as she awoke: Her father was dead. Pneumonia had taken him quite suddenly several months ago.

It was just last summer they were in Paris. Daddy was going there on business and she had persuaded him to take her along. Early mornings on the ship's deck watching the sunrises while Daddy brushed her long red hair, nights in their narrow bunks so close she could feel his breath.

She lay awake listening to the stories he told—tales of heroism, Greek and Egyptian myths.

"And that explains your middle name, Isis. The goddess possessed all knowledge, beauty and power. And so shall you, my Dearest."

Away from home they could talk about anything. At a sidewalk café on the Champs-Elysees they were having a chocolate.

"Why did you marry mother, Daddy? You appear ill suited to each other."

He looked at her and then away, seeming to watch the endless parade of carriages.

Finally, he said, "I came from a well-positioned family in the old country, and was expected to marry into my own class." He paused, took a sip of his drink. "When I was twenty-four we had a comely servant girl. She offered me her favors, shall we say, and became pregnant with my child."

He paused, finished his drink.

Catherine blushed. "Goodness! What became of her?"

"She was discharged, of course, and I was banished from the family—albeit with a sum of money."

"What did you do?"

"I made this unschooled girl my wife." He paid the bill and stood up, deepening the crooked furrow that ran like a streak of lightning from his hairline to his nose.

Catherine remained glued to her seat. "You don't mean—*Mother?*"

"Yes. She was pretty enough, then. But like a paper fire that first burns brightly, after the sparks died down the marriage turned to ash." He started walking. "You are right: We are not well suited."

Catherine hurried to catch up to him. "And the baby?"

"Your sister, Margaret, so much like your mother."

"Oh, Daddy, how very sad!"

He put his arm around her and guided her across the wide avenue. "But you, Katie, make up for all of that."

Remembering that same night they played out the death scene from *Othello* took her breath away. She bit her lip; she must not think of these things now, for surely tears would overtake her and her mother would make more derisive remarks.

That winter he had taken ill, and in two weeks was dead of pneumonia.

Catherine felt she'd fallen off the edge of the world.

After months of melancholia, she finally roused herself. She remembered all her father had said about courage, and how he'd admired her strong spirit. "You'll be a survivor, Katie. Never let anything best you."

Then for you, Daddy, I will go forward.

Finally, forcing herself to leave her warm covers, she slipped out of bed, punched through the thin layer of ice in her pitcher, and poured the freezing water into her basin. Jumping from one foot to the other, she dashed the icy cloth quickly on her face, around her neck and shoulders, trying to avoid getting her chemise wet. She grabbed the clothes she'd laid out the night before and raced downstairs, to get dressed by the warmth of the kitchen stove. April afternoons were beginning to warm up, but the nights and mornings were still freezing.

While Catherine stood eating her porridge with her backside to the stove, her mother was touting the merits of a suitor.

"I don't want to marry Thomas Radcliff! I don't want to marry at all!"

"Just ye listen tae me, daughter."

"Thomas Radcliff is an old man! He was *father's* friend." She slammed the bowl down on the table.

"He's a well-tae-do widower, Catherine. You'd never be without."

"He has grown sons!"

"And a wee laddie, a needin' a mother."

"You'd have me a step-mother at sixteen?" Catherine shouted.

"Watch yer tongue, miss."

"He must be sixty!"

"Forty-one, and not a day o'er."

"You've already talked to him!"

"He came to me. You coulda do far worse. Thomas Radcliff is Chief Mining Captain for the Portage Mining Company. They 'spect he'll be discoverin' the mother lode of all that copper down below."

"A mole!"

"Och, no. He's a fine office on the grass, Missy. The Portage Mining Company is—"

"Where's that?" Catherine asked impatiently.

"Near Hancock."

"How far from here?"

"Aboot twelve miles, above Portage Lake. It's purty there, 'tis. And the mine's up and coming, believe you me. "

Catherine groaned. "A Cornishman, no doubt—another 'Cousin Jack'. Who ever saw so many immigrants—German, Irish—"

"*Immigrants*, is it? And what do ye think ye are? But no, Mr. Radcliff is American-born. *And* he's the first college engineer any mine in these parts 'as ever 'ad. The other companies still be using Cornish miners for their captains."

"What do I care aboot that?"

"Well, yer living in the 'Copper Country.' That's all you're ever goin' tae hear aboot—minin'. It's the life and blood of the country."

"I hate it here! I want to go back to Scotland. Or Paris."

"They say Mr. Radcliff—"

"Does he *own* the mine?"

"No, the owners own it."

"And who be they?"

"Stockholders, back east, all."

"Then I don't want him."

"Stop yer greetin' and roarin'. He's comin' tae call on ye Sunday next."

"How could ye? Daddy would never have put me through such misery!"

"Hush up aboot yer daddy."

"He's barely cold in his grave and ye'd have me married off—"

"I said hush up aboot him!" Barbara MacGaurin shook her head in disgust. "Yer daddy, always fillin' ye with fancy notions of who y'are! Bletherin' foolishness it was. It's exactly cuz he's gone, it falls tae me tae see ye are ta'en care of."

"I'd rather die!"

In the fall, three weeks after her seventeenth birthday, the wedding day came.

"Ow!" The heat of the curling iron on the back of her neck brought Catherine back to the moment. "Mummy, you're burning me! Will it show?"

"No, yer hollerin' aboot nothin'," her mother replied. "Sit ye still, Catherine. I canna curl yer hair with ye bouncing all aboot. Do you want to look like curly wood shavins are stickin' straight out 'o yer head on yer weddin' day?"

They were in the kitchen by the stove, and Catherine tried to concentrate on giving her mother a hot curling iron in exchange for a cool one, which she replaced on the stove. With great care she could do this without moving any part of her body save her arm.

"Keep turnin' them, so they'll be hot on all sides."

Catherine picked up the ivory looking glass and studied her likeness with objective detachment.

To herself she said, *I am not beautiful. But I cut a fine figure, and Papa would say I am striking.* She held the mirror higher, and raised her gaze to meet it. *I believe my large green eyes are my finest feature.* There was nothing she could do about her freckles. In spite of wearing hats and bonnets meant to keep the sun from her face, there they were. At least a few. She dabbed them with powder.

In spite of herself Catherine was getting excited about her wedding and the prospects of living in a lovely home built just for her on a high hill. Oh, the parties they could have there. She could just see the carriages circling the drive with ladies and gentlemen in their finest stepping out! It was the most magnificent home she'd ever seen.

And the bridegroom. Well, he wasn't such a bad lot after all. Tall and handsome, even though he was more than twice her age, he made a good figure with a well trimmed mustache. He dressed elegantly, with none of the malodorous auras of the working class; her senses did not recoil at his proximity. She knew she could do worse. Their courtship had been short and breathtaking, with jaunts in the countryside and drives to Hancock to see her new home.

Barbara MacGaurin touched a wet finger to the irons, listening for a sizzling sound.

"There, ye see, there's not a hot one among them. Ye've let them all go cold."

She snatched the looking glass from her daughter's hand. Catherine sighed and resumed her task.

As she did, she looked down at her lovely silk and linen underthings. They had been conveyed all the way from Scotland, as such luxuries would be hard to come by in this part of the world.

But they had brought only one wedding gown, and her sister had worn it first.

The dress was lovely, she acknowledged—finer than anything she'd seen in the wilds of the Upper Peninsula. It had delicate lace with rows of ivory ribbon threaded through the neckline and cuffs of the full sleeves, and little pink rosebuds made from even finer ribbon sewn onto the ivory. If only it was new for her!

Catherine sighed. "This is the last time I'm wearing anything of Margaret's. If I must be wed to a man I don't love, at least I'll be rich."

"You mustn't speak o' marriage like it were a bag 'o gold tae dip yer greedy hands in."

"He said he'd take me to Chicago on one of the new clipper ships, with a band and everything."

"Wheesht."

So on this crisp, windy day in September, with the autumn sky a rich deep blue, Catherine and her mother climbed into her brother-in-law's buggy, and set out for the long ride to the little wooden church in Hancock. The inside was adorned with yellow and rust chrysanthemums. How exciting it was, this unfamiliar church all decked out just for her!

After the ceremony there was a supper in the basement social hall, where venison, roasted all afternoon on Carter's spit, was the mainstay of the meal. Spicy hot cider kept the chill at bay. Neighbors brought hot dishes, and there were cakes and every kind of pie for dessert. Thomas had even engaged a quartet for the occasion.

Catherine left her husband's side to speak with her sister. Margaret and her husband were moving to Wisconsin in a fortnight. Well, it was doubtful either would waste much time mourning the loss of the other.

After a brief exchange with her sister, she heard, "Evening, ma'am." and turned to see Thomas Junior and his brother William. "We came to wish you well."

"Why, thank you, lads." Perhaps they were too old to call 'lads'.

How clumsy they looked in their ill-fitting suits and turned up collar points. Tom, a shaft captain at the mine, and William, one of the shift bosses, were not accustomed to dressing up. She thought they looked like country bumpkins, uneducated and unrefined.

"I am so pleased you're able to be here."

They nodded.

"And where is your little brother?"

"Walter's staying with Aunt Alice for a bit," Tom replied. "Pa didn't think he'd take to the wedding."

"How do you mean?"

The older brothers exchanged a quick glance, and Tom cleared his throat. "Well, getting a new ma, and all."

"Ah."

For a few moments no one said anything. Tom kept rubbing one balled up hand with the other, as William twisted his neck like a horse trying to free itself of its bit.

"You must come to call some time," Catherine finally ventured.

"Yes, Ma'am."

For once she was tongue-tied, and so were they. With relief she saw Thomas crossing towards them. He gave his sons a nod, claimed his bride and whisked her to the end of the hall reserved for dancing.

"Oh, Thomas, we could think of nothing to say! They just looked at me like I was some kind of ice-cream to lap up."

"And so you are. I intend to do just that this evening." He nuzzled his nose in her neck.

Catherine giggled, and Thomas swung her across the floor to *The Blue Danube Waltz*. Soon they were joined by other keen dancers for the *Tri-Mountain Two-Step* and the *Stamp Mill Waltz*.

Catherine hadn't had such a fine party since her sister's wedding, but still she was glad when Thomas indicated it was time to leave.

As they approached the carriage, they were greeted by another group of noisy enthusiasts with whistles, bells and saucepans.

"Oh, no!" Catherine moaned, as she heard the first rattle. "A shivaree! They're going to follow us home!"

"Get in."

Catherine spotted someone she knew. "It's Earl Foster! What's he doing in Hancock?"

"You know him?"

"Och! We were in school together!"

"He's probably in love with you," Thomas smiled.

"They've been lying in wait for us! Tell the driver to hurry, Thomas. Let's get away from here."

"First I have to wake him."

Catherine could hardly hear him over the din. "How can he sleep through this noise?"

"I suspect he's been tippling some."

Finally, they were underway, with the noise-makers running alongside, rattling their assorted instruments.

"Can't we go faster, Thomas? And outrun them?"

"It's all harmless fun—a serenade."

"They're making rude noises, Thomas."

"Raspberries." Thomas laughed. "Just ignore them."

With libations in hand, the noise-makers followed the new-lyweds.

"What a bunch of hooligans. It shouldn't be allowed."

"Catherine, relax. You can't change tradition. They're just looking for a bit of fun. It's a wedding, remember?" He smiled and took her in his arms.

"They'll see us!"

"Let them. Give them something to get excited about."

Catherine giggled. Catching sight of the couple through the window provoked louder, more exuberant shouts and catcalls.

Thomas kissed his bride long and hard, as noses pressed and knuckles rapped at the window. Raucous laughter and loud hoots accompanied their glee.

"That's enough," Thomas waved good-bye to them and closed the carriage curtains. "They'll go home now."

The driver snapped his whip and the horse settled into an easy canter, leaving the merry-makers behind. But soon after the bride and groom had reached their bedchamber, the boys had caught up.

Small pebbles pelted the window, and the taunts continued from below.

For the most part Catherine was oblivious to it. The only stimulus she was aware of now was the stir that rose in her body from her husband's touch, a tarantella that had mounted increasingly these last days. *I think I'll like being married.*

"I'll try to be gentle. But it will hurt the first time," he warned her.

She bit her lip. There was an ache inside her she could only look to Thomas to satisfy now.

Two weeks after the wedding, Thomas's sister Alice arrived with six year old Walter, who had been in her charge while the newlyweds became accustomed to each other.

"This is your new mother," the aunt told Walter. The boy frowned, looked at the ground.

"Show some manners, Walter," his father admonished. "Take the lady's hand."

Walter lifted a limp hand, but did not lift his face.

"What class are you in?" Catherine asked.

"Don't go to school yet."

Catherine offered him some cake, which he took outside. Unmannered, unlessoned, and unattractive, he held no appeal for her at all.

"He just lost his ma last year. It will take him some getting used to."

For me, as well. "He'll be going to school this year, won't he?"

"Yes."

In the weeks that followed Catherine tried to make Walter feel comfortable. She could see he was a lonely child, mistrustful. Well, who could blame him; he'd lost his mother so suddenly in a bout of diphtheria. But when her efforts were rebuffed, she grew impatient, complained to her husband.

"He doesn't like me."

"He loved his mother very much."

"Well, I'm not his mother."

"Give him time, Catherine."

She bent her efforts toward her step-son, and gradually, the child began to respond. He stopped banging his head against the wall at night, and began conversing in more than monosyllables.

"Look what I found." He laid a horseshoe on the table.

"Get that rusty thing off my tablecloth. Take it outdoors."

Walter picked up the horseshoe and headed for the door. Catherine, lamenting that she'd spoken so sharply, followed him.

"What do you plan to do with it?"

"Throw it. Want to see me?"

"Yes, all right."

Walter drove a stake into the hard surface of the drive and demonstrated the game to Catherine. Several times he hit the mark on the first try.

"You want to try?" he ventured.

She hesitated.

"Go on, ma'am, have a go at it."

Reluctantly, she took the rusty crescent in her hand.

She was so far off course, Walter laughed, and Catherine turned crimson. Wanting to chide him, or run off, she nevertheless remembered her position and remained still.

"Here, I'll show you," he offered.

She allowed him to instruct her, noticed the action in his wrist. When she tried again, she came much closer. They took turns for some time, Catherine showing some improvement.

"You're better than I am." Catherine brushed her hands off, started back to the house.

"Were you doing your best?"

"Of course I was."

The boy showed a shy smile of pride. Catherine tousled his hair. "You're the winner. There, are you satisfied?"

He slipped his hand gingerly inside hers.

For this, Thomas gave her good marks.

"He needs you, Catherine. He cares for you far more than you realize. You are his mother now, you know."

Her stomach rebelled.

I'm only eleven years older than he! I don't want to be his mother!

How she missed Red Jacket! When they strolled downtown Hancock on a summer Sunday, she'd see girls arm-in-arm with lads their own age. And there she was with a husband more than twice hers.

Still, as Thomas expressed his passion frequently, Catherine responded. Before long she felt the quickening of new life in her belly.

"It's going to be a laddie, sure," the midwife told her.

"How can you tell?"

"It's just the knowin' I have. Ye'll see yersel' when the we'an comes." Her penetrating eyes persuaded Catherine.

"Ye've had no mornin' sickness?"

"Not once."

"Then it's certain to be a laddie. The others, they're not so considerate."

Catherine laughed.

"You're the lucky one," the midwife told her. "He'll be a blessed we'an, never givin' ye a bit o' trouble."

But Catherine's mother wasn't convinced. Down for a visit, she said, "It's bletherin' tales she's tellin' ye. Country folk's superstitions fae the auld country."

"But you're—"

"—fae entirely different parts, daughter. We never believed such foolish cracks in the big city."

It was a sweet and mellow time for Catherine, carrying this child. When she felt the quickening, she held her belly, eagerly awaiting each tiny movement.

"Aye,'tis a laddie. I have the knowing, too," she'd murmur.

On a sunny afternoon in October, Catherine felt labor pains and knew that her time was approaching.

"Fetch the midwife," she told Helena.

"Is it not too soon, mum?"

"No. Hurry!"

The pains started coming quickly, and Catherine, alone in the house, became alarmed. Autumn winds were kicking up, rattling the windows, making her uneasy. Where was the midwife? Had that foolish girl gotten lost? In frustration she got out of bed, walked around the house, periodically doubling over in pain. Why couldn't this have happened at night or on the weekend when Thomas was home?

It would be soon; the pains were one on top of the other now. She went back to bed, and bit down on her pillow each time they came. The Portage whistle blew, signaling the end of the work shift. Maybe Thomas would get there in time.

Then she could feel herself opening; there was no holding back the child. She let out one loud scream as the baby emerged. That was the last she knew.

How long she'd been lying there before the midwife arrived she didn't know. She heard a voice that sounded very far away.

And then: "Dinnae I tell you it would be a laddie?" The midwife handed the baby to his mother. "He's all cleaned up for ye."

"He's alive?"

"Indeed he is. A screamin' he was when I got here, and you looking dead, for all the world. You should have sent for me sooner, lass."

Catherine took the infant to her breast. In such awe of what she had produced, she could say nothing for several moments. Finally, she exclaimed, "What a bonnie wee one he is. He 'near takes my breath away." She stroked the dark ringlets of hair.

The midwife peered at him. "Aye, look at the eyelashes on him. He'll have nae trouble with the lassies!"

"I'm sorry," the flushed Helena was saying. "She wasn't home when I went to call. Sure, and I looked all over for her. Then finally—"

"Shall I be callin' his faither in here?" the midwife asked.

"In a bit. Let me have a few moments alone with my we'an."

The women left. Catherine held her child close, examined his tiny features.

"You are my first-born and my last. You are everything I need in a child, and no other will ever take your place."

"Here be yer man," the midwife announced.

Thomas came in and looked on proudly.

"Catherine, my love, you were very brave to go it alone."

"I didn't have a choice, did I? Isn't he bonnie, Thomas?"

"He's normal? Ten fingers and such?"

She looked again to make sure.

"What shall we call him?" he asked.

"I will call him Jorie, after my father, Jordan."

Thomas leaned down and kissed his wife. "Thank you, my Love, for giving me this son."

Catherine did not feel she had given him anything. She had carried the child and birthed him. He belonged to her.

But she said, "And now we are three."

"Four," he corrected.

chapter 8

AFTER HIS BRUSH with death in the coal cellar, Jorie began having nightmares. Two or three times a week he'd come to his parents' bed. Catherine would pull him toward her, where the comfort of her arms quieted his fears.

One night Thomas half awoke and found Jorie in her arms.

In the morning he asked, "Why does Jorie come to our bed every night?"

"It's not every night, Thomas. When he comes in with us he doesn't wet his bed." As soon as the words were out, she regretted them.

"Wet his bed! How old is he? Six?"

"Not quite."

"What's the matter with him? He used to be dry, didn't he?"

"I think it comes with his nightmares—he can't help it, Thomas. It started after Walter...after the incident in the cellar."

"Can't help it—at six? I'll help it. Where is he?"

Catherine had never seen him like this. She was frightened for her boy.

Thomas found Jorie on the porch sketching an insect. He took a deep breath and sat down beside him.

"What have you there?" he began.

"It's a beetle, Papa. Do you see his thick hard shell and his tiny eyes?"

"Your mother tells me that you still wet the bed."

Jorie froze, felt betrayed.

"Is this true?" Thomas wanted to hear the boy admit it.

"Yes, Papa."

"Why do you do it?"

"It just happens when I'm sleeping."

"Well, you're too big for that and you're going to have to stop it. Do you understand?"

Jorie nodded. "It's called enuresis."

"Enu what!"

"Enuresis. Shall I spell it for you, Papa?"

"No! Just get over it. You will not have any liquids after supper, and make sure to urinate before getting into bed. And when you're sleeping if you feel the urge—you have a chamber pot?"

"Yes."

"Well, use it."

"Yes, Papa."

Thomas started to go, and then turned back to his son. "Where did you learn that word?"

"Mummy taught it to me. That's what the doctor called it."

Jorie wasn't at all sure that he could overcome this shameful habit as easily as his father suggested. That night he stayed awake as long as he could, fearful he would miss the "urge." But eventually he fell asleep, and sometime after that when he rolled over, he knew he was wet.

In the morning his father asked, "Did you stay dry last night?"

"No, sir."

He felt the heat prickling his face, his throat close. He had to get away from here. His mind grabbed on to the sums he was learning. *Three plus four is seven, three plus five is eight.* If he went where the numbers were, maybe he could make this morning disappear. *Three plus seven is ten.*

"Jorie, next time, I'm going to have to punish you. We can't have a big boy like you still wetting your bed. Do you understand?"

Three plus nine is twelve.

"Do you?"

"Yes, Papa."

"Sit down now and eat your breakfast. Sit."

Jorie sat, but could eat nothing, concentrated on the squeaking of his chair, as he gently rocked back and forth, wishing he could fly with Peggythis way up in the sky. Mummy could be Peggythis and he would be Belly. They would ride across the sky and back again. And he would kill the monster.

The next morning Thomas spanked his son.

Catherine reproached Thomas. "Did you have to do that? He was mortified."

"Good. Maybe that will make him stop."

"Thomas, why is this matter so important to you? You aren't the one who has to wash his sheets!"

"Sheets! Hanging out on the line every day telling everyone we have a bed-wetter!"

"Thomas—"

"It's disgraceful. I'll not be humiliated like that!"

"He doesn't do it to humiliate you."

"He is old enough to stop if he wanted to. The boy is defying me."

She choked with anger and bitterness. "It's not fair, Thomas. You're taking it out on Jorie that Walter's gone! You didn't use to treat him so badly."

Thomas slammed his fist down on the table. "By God, woman, I'll not have you judging my actions. It is the *boy's* behavior we're discussing, I'll thank you to remember!"

With that he strode out of the house.

For the rest of the week Catherine managed to avert the bed-wetting by waking Jorie up in time. But one night just as Jorie was climbing back into bed, Thomas was at the doorway.

"Come back to bed, Catherine."

The boy pulled his covers up wondering if his mother would get in trouble.

"Don't go to him," Thomas admonished his wife. "You baby him far too much."

Fearing that her intervention was causing Thomas to take an even harder stand, the next day Catherine told Jorie she couldn't come to his room at night any more.

When he heard her words, Jorie's throat closed. He remembered the baby robins he could see last spring outside his window. Each day he'd watch the mother bring back worms to feed them. Then one day she didn't return. For awhile the babies squawked, but she never came back. The little birds died.

He would just have to stay awake all night. But how?

He decided to sleep on the floor, so he'd wake up if he felt the urge. But the wetting continued and the punishments worsened.

One day Thomas brought out his razor strap. Jorie recited the multiplication tables to escape the staggering pain; he rode high in the sky on Peggythis. When it was over, he lay on his side in the corner.

From his place on the floor Jorie watched a small moth dance against the window pane, trying to find a way out. And he could see a spider in the corner of the ceiling drop, spin, and drop again. Two flies were caught in her web, one still buzzing and wiggling, frantically trying to make its escape. He felt a strange kinship with them, but was too exhausted to figure it out.

When Thomas left for work Catherine tried to take her child's mind off his deep humiliation and the painful punishments by changing the scene.

She sat on his bed and called him to her. "Let's pretend you are a very brave knight. You fought the foe for your queen, and many times you were a hero. But one time there were too many enemies around you. You were knocked from your horse. Your foot got caught in the stirrup, and as the horse raced down the hill you were dragged with it, bumping along the rocky hillside. Finally, the horse stopped, you got untangled, got back on your horse—"

"Peggythis."

"—and returned to the castle. But your bottom was very sore from all that bouncing on the rocks. It was so sore the queen had to rub it with a very special salve."

Jorie looked up.

"On my dresser, Darling, there is a pretty blue jar. Go get it."

"The one with the silver ballerina on top?"

"Yes, Dear. Carry it very carefully. It was a special present from my father."

He ran down the hall to her room, that lovely place that smelled of lavender and lilac.

When he brought the jar to her, she bade him lie across her lap. He could hear her removing the lid, and then she was applying the cream to his burning bottom.

"Mummy, it's so cool. And your hands are so soft."

It became a ritual—after each whipping, Jorie would bring the blue jar. Catherine would rub the cream on his abused skin and tell him a story.

But the whippings were becoming unbearable. Jorie decided he'd have to take a firmer hand with himself. Since none of his other ideas had worked, there was still one more thing he could do. It frightened him, but it was all that was left.

When she was bathing him, Catherine noticed Jorie's penis was bruised and swollen. "Jorie, what is this? What happened to you?"

He burst out crying and would not talk.

"Did Papa do this to you? Answer me!"

Jorie shook his head.

"Did he?"

"No!" Jorie sobbed.

"What happened? How did you injure yourself?"

Jorie pulled away. Finally, she got it out of him that he had wound a piece of yarn around it tightly and tied it so as not to wet.

When she'd gotten the story from him, such a fury mounted in her as she hadn't felt since Walter's attempts on the boy's life. All her damned-up anger at the injustice of Thomas's punishment rose in a torrid swell from her spine upward. This would not, could not continue. That Jorie would feel obliged to resort to such extreme measures to accommodate his father's will was outrageous.

She rocked him in her arms, crying, "Oh, my darling bonnie lad."

Finally, she pushed him up and took his face between her hands. "You must promise me that you'll never do that to yourself again."

"But it's the only way," he cried.

"Jorie, you could really injure yourself. Maybe permanently."

"But I don't know how else to stop!"

For a moment she said nothing. Then she sat straight up. "He won't whip you any more. I promise."

"How can you make him stop, Mummy?"

"I'll find a way."

Although only twenty-four years old, Catherine knew her feminine charms no longer held leverage over Thomas. His smoldering resentment over losing Walter and their continual quarrels regarding Jorie's discipline had risen to such an ascension, that the fire of his passion was all but extinguished. Only occasionally did he require his conjugal rights. She could hardly threaten to deprive him of what he no longer desired.

No, it would have to be something else. Something that would strike at his public face.

She knew that Thomas would be entertaining his poker friends the next evening as he did every Friday night. George McKinney, Arthur Johnson, Buck Boyce and Earl Foster would all be there.

After completing the washing up that evening, she strode purposefully into the dining room, where he sat at the table studying the assays of last month's yield of ore. She did not wait for him to look up.

"If you strike that boy one more time, I will leave you. I will take Jorie and leave your home, Thomas."

He turned to her, stunned. "You can't do that."

"Of course I can."

"I would not support you."

"You forget I have some money of my own."

Thomas laughed. "And how long do you think that would last?"

"If necessary I will go to work."

"Are you trying to undo me, woman? First Walter, now Jorie!"

"It seems to me you are undoing Jorie."

"He needs discipline, Catherine!"

"Not like that."

Thomas took a deep breath. "You cannot take a man's children from him. The law would give him back to me."

The tiniest smile appeared on her face. "Perhaps. But need I point out, Thomas, that in the meantime there would be a great scandal? We shall make our departure tomorrow evening—complete with suitcases."

His mouth fell open. Catherine left the room before he could find words to answer.

The next morning Thomas turned to her. "I have given thought to your remarks. Under one condition I will agree to your request."

For an anguishing moment time seemed to freeze.

"Someone has to discipline the lad," he continued. "If you believe you are up to the task, then I leave it to you. If you are unwilling, unable, or fail in your duty, the responsibility will revert to me."

Catherine could hardly believe what she'd heard.

"All right," she answered. "I'll undertake his discipline."

"Do not misunderstand me. You are soft with the boy. I wager it will be only a short time before the task will fall to me again. I expect an accounting, Catherine, of his infractions and how you have dealt with them. Do you understand?"

"If you think I'm going to beat the boy as you have, you are mistaken. He is a tender lad, and I have never found it necessary to resort to such measures."

"Choose your own methods, but make sure they are effective." He started to leave. With his hand on the doorknob, he turned to her.

"I give you three weeks to stop the bed-wetting."

With that Thomas stomped out of the house. Catherine paced the floor. She felt a thrill of victory, at least for her son, but some doubt as to whether she could meet Thomas's deadline. As for her relation to her husband, no doubt she would incur a debt of consequences. She would not think of that now.

To show Thomas her appreciation she made a peach cobbler for the Five Aces.

As they were leaving that night, Earl Foster said, "Mighty tasty pie, Catherine." He chuckled, "I'd never have thought of having peach pie with beer—leave it to a lady to conjure up such a combination!"

Catherine wasn't sure if he was poking fun at her, or making a crude attempt at a compliment. How strange that Thomas's poker friends were all prominent citizens, all except Sheriff Earl Foster!

Aware of how much comfort she was giving the boy, Catherine wondered if she were in some way prolonging the problem with her ministrations of salve, which he clearly enjoyed.

One day she hit on what she thought might be a solution.

"Jorie, I think we had best turn things around. From now on, Mummy is not going to put the cream on your bottom when you wet the bed. Instead, I'll apply it when you keep dry."

He was confused and disappointed. "When I'm dry?"

"Yes, as kind of a reward. I think that might help you stop wetting sooner. Wouldn't you like that?"

Jorie tried extra hard to keep dry all night. At first the wet nights still outnumbered the dry, but within two weeks he was dry more often than not.

On the first morning he experienced success, he couldn't wait for Papa to leave, and to bring the jar to her.

"I am so proud of you, Jorie," she said unbuttoning the flap of his long underwear and pulling it down. He lay across her knees and she pulled him toward her.

"Mummy, can you do it a long time since I was dry?"

"A little longer." Catherine hummed 'Barbara Allen' as she caressed his bottom with the soothing balm. The jar sat on his bedside table. Catching the morning's light, it created the most wonderful blue, like the sky must be if you could just go up high enough.

To Jorie this elixir felt so much better when his bottom wasn't hurting, he vowed he'd never wet again. How gentle was her touch, how sweet her warm breath on his neck, as he savored every stroke and relaxed into her love. He wiggled his body tighter against hers and closed his eyes, soaking up the delicious mixture of lavender cologne, the sensation of his mother's comforting touch, and the sonorous sounds of the tune she was humming.

"You are my queen."

"And you my knight."

On the eighteenth day of her reign Catherine went to Thomas and announced, "Jorie no longer wets his bed."

If she was expecting surprise or pleasure from Thomas, she got none.

"It's about time," he said, without raising his head from his paper.

chapter 9

CATHERINE COULD NO longer bear her husband's snoring—a whole cacophony of sounds, including intermittent bursts of loud percussion. Her own sleep had been so fitful and interrupted with his odious nocturnal discords, that she thought she could rest more peacefully alone. When she asked him to take another room, he put up no resistance.

Although she received relief from the noise, she had not realized how much she had relied on his body heat to keep her warm. Without him the winter nights seemed unbearably cold. Often when she awoke in the morning, there was frost on the window pane, and snow on the inside sill where it had swept in through the crack.

She did not resist Jorie's forays into her bed at night. His nightmares—always a long and horrible fall down a dark tunnel—drove him to his mother's bed.

One night she knew Thomas had opened the door, making a visit to claim his conjugal rights. Seeing Jorie, he turned and left. At breakfast the next morning, watching his scowl and fearful of repercussions, Catherine anticipated his anger.

She blurted out, "Jorie crawls in with me at night when he gets frightened. Such a baby," she laughed tousling his hair.

Jorie felt the heat creep up his neck and cover his face. Why did she say that? His father was scolding him, but he didn't hear, heard only his mother's shrill laughter, her betrayal of him. He decided he wouldn't go to her, no matter how bad the dreams.

Sitting at the piano for his lesson later that week, she kissed him on the cheek, told him to come to her any night he wanted to.

Unbelieving, he looked at the floor and whispered, "I thought—you told Papa—"

"Never mind what I told Papa. I had to tell him something. It doesn't matter." she tossed it off. "We understand each other, you and I."

"Mummy, I want to learn 'Barbara Allen!'"

Catherine had been teaching him to play since he was four. He would run to the stool, spin it up to raise its height. As she caressed the polished rosewood, she explained that Papa had given it to her on their first anniversary.

"Did it cost a lot of money?"

"I daresay it did. It's made of rosewood. Do you see the beautiful grain in the wood?"

They started playing a simple duet Catherine had made up for them.

Thomas strode into the room. "When are you planning to send that child to school?"

She turned to her son. "Run down the lane and see if the post has come."

When he was gone she said, "He's so sensitive, Thomas. And he's learning to read so well at home, I thought we could delay his formal schooling a bit longer."

"Catherine—"

"He writes beautifully, wonderful stories—all on his own. Would you like him to read them to you?"

"You're making a mama's boy out of him. He should be in school, taking his knocks from the other lads."

"You should see him do his numbers, Thomas. He's very quick. Way ahead of children his age. I'm sure he could best them all in any examination. He'd just be bored at school."

"Did you hear me, woman? Put him in school." Thomas stormed out of the room.

Although the principal first placed him in the beginners' class, by noon it was apparent that he did not belong there, and he was moved to the second grade. In most respects he was well beyond the students of his class, but as he was seven years old, it was decided that's where he would stay.

Jorie didn't care to play ball with the other boys at lunchtime. He was rather reserved and couldn't think of anything much to say to them either, though he longed for companionship of his own age. In the first few weeks he made several attempts to overcome his shyness and get to know the others, but the boys only laughed at him or ignored him altogether.

"Kill a fly and make him cry!" they teased.

"They're just jealous of you, Jorie," Catherine tried to comfort. "They see you know so much more than they. That's all it is."

This did little to console Jorie, but he began raising his hand less when the teacher asked questions. But then the teacher expressed disapproval of him too. Only one or two little girls would play with him, and a dull boy who was no more popular than he.

With Jorie in school now, Catherine realized with acute awareness that she had no real friends. She had been uprooted twice—once from another country, and then from Red Jacket. Since living in Hancock, she'd seldom attended religious services, but on a Saturday in July she went to a jumble sale at a nearby church. Perhaps she'd meet some young people.

Fingering the quilts and cast off toys, Catherine bought Jorie a yo-yo and a hand painted barrel hoop. Laughter brought her attention to two women her age. She walked over to them; soon a third joined, older than the others. When the first two drifted off the third stayed to talk with her. After a time the woman mentioned the D.A.R. meeting coming up.

"Do you belong?"

"No. No, I don't." Catherine didn't want to tell her that she didn't know what the D.A.R. was.

"Well, come along to the meeting this week, see what it's like."

"Thank you."

The woman wrote an address on a piece of paper and handed it to Catherine.

Thursday couldn't come quickly enough. How fortuitous that she'd met this woman. The hostess greeted her pleasantly, and she was offered a cup of tea and a scone. Catherine scanned the room for the woman who had invited her, but failed to see a familiar face. Finally, the chairman asked everyone to be seated and called the meeting to order. She commented on what a good turnout it was, then turned to Catherine.

"Would you please introduce yourself, my dear?"

"I'm Catherine Radcliff."

"And you are being sponsored by whom?"

Catherine felt uncomfortable. "I met a woman at church." She looked frantically around. "But I don't see her here. She, she invited me." Catherine's voice trailed off.

It was the chairman's turn to look uncomfortable.

"What was her name?"

"I don't remember." Catherine could feel the heat rise up her neck and face.

She could hear muffled sounds behind handkerchiefs.

"Did she say she'd sponsor you?"

"She suggested I come today and find out more about it."

"It?"

"The D.A.R." She knew her face was darkening into ever deeper shades of red.

"Do you know what those letters stand for, my dear?"

Catherine felt all eyes upon her. Her discomfort was turning to anger, but she held her head high. Why was this woman testing her, humiliating her in front of a dozen others?

The chairman continued. "We are the Daughters of the American Revolution. To join our ranks you must be able to prove a lineal blood line descent from an ancestor who aided in achieving American independence. You must provide documentation for each statement of birth, marriage, and death. You would start by filling out a pedigree chart."

The woman paused, then probed further. "Can you provide the necessary documentation?"

With a deliberate attempt to display her brogue, Catherine raised her head high. "I came o'er on the *Ivanhoe* fae Scotland six year ago, with my parents. And noobody in my family set foot in America 'afore that."

Perhaps some sympathetic eyes were upon her, but when she added, for no reason she could fathom, "And I be a loyal subject of the Crown," all turned to ice.

The chairman froze, then gathered her composure. "It is exactly to set ourselves apart from the Crown that the *Daughters* was formed."

Catherine rose. "I know you wonta have me, and I dinnae care. I donta wish tae be a member of such a group as yers. Not now ner never."

And with that she set her feet to leave. Her mind was so inflamed she didn't notice she was headed for the kitchen; she had to retrace her steps, walk past all the stunned women again, and take a second leave.

Catherine turned to her son. He loved watching the stars, and they often climbed the hill behind the house to the plateau before the second hill. Here the sky revealed its entire magnificence to them. On moonless nights, when it was hard to follow the path, Catherine carried a lantern to light their way, for these were the best nights to watch the stars.

Wrapped in blankets, and crunching juicy apples, together they looked for constellations. Sometimes Catherine pointed them out to Jorie, often it was the other way around. Having borrowed a book from school which he eagerly devoured, Jorie was now able to locate some of the heavenly bodies himself and point them out to his mother.

He especially liked the Pleiades.

"There are seven sisters. But we can only see six. Did you know that's because one of them hides in shame?"

"No, I didn't," his mother said.

"That's what the book said. Do you know how they got there?"

"Tell me."

"They were sent there to be safe from Orion, who was chasing them."

"I see."

Quiet now but for the chirping of tree frogs, Jorie lay on the grass.

"You can see everything better this way, Mummy. Lie down. You'll see."

Catherine spread her blanket and curled up beside him.

"Do you think stars can talk to us, Mummy?"

"Some people wish upon a star."

"I think they're spirits of the dead, and they can send us messages."

"How do they do that?"

"On invisible paths—starlines."

"Like the Morse Code?" she asked.

"Well, sort of."

"What do they tell you?"

"Different things...Once when Papa was whipping me, they told me to be brave, that it wouldn't last much longer. And it was true! You made him stop."

"Ah."

"They're very wise, Mummy. You have to keep the line straight if you want to hear them. If your starline gets tangled, then the voices get all muddled."

"How do you keep it straight?"

"You have to think very hard, and imagine the white line that goes all the way from them to you. You have to push all your other thoughts out of the way. When it's straight, it shines." He stopped to take a bite of his apple. "When it's tangled, it looks dirty and gray."

"Can you get it untangled?"

"Not always."

Catherine pulled him close to her. She would not destroy his wonderful imagination, would not call it blasphemy, as her mother had done.

"Jorie, I have something to tell you. When your father agreed to stop punishing you, there was another part I didn't tell you."

"Is it bad?" He turned his attention from the stars to his mother.

"He made me promise that I would punish you when necessary."

"Oh."

"You are a good child, but all children must be disciplined. You understand that, don't you?"

"Yes. I'd much rather be punished by you, Mummy. You would never hurt me like Papa does."

"That's true. I think we should practice a little, so that when I really have to spank you, you won't be frightened. Something like our playacting."

"Now? Are you truly going to do it, Mummy?" he whispered.

"Of course, I am!" Her voice was husky. Then softly, "But you know I love you. If I didn't love you, I wouldn't bother about disciplining you. You understand?"

This was a puzzle, but he trusted her. "Yes, Mummy."

She bade him lay over her lap, and caressed his bottom.

"You mustn't tense up. Just relax into it. There, I'll do it lightly." She slapped him gently, as he let go, eased into the soft sting of each slap.

She stopped suddenly, pushed him away. "Now, we can tell Papa you've been properly punished." She smiled at him.

Confused, he nevertheless thought if children had to be punished, he'd much prefer his mother's style.

"Just you and me."

chapter 10

FINALLY, THOMAS AND Catherine began being included in the social life of Hancock. Among their friends were the banker and his wife, Mr. and Mrs. Whyte. Ada Whyte invited Catherine to join *The Ladies' Oratorical and Dramatic Society*. For the first time since she'd lived in Hancock, Catherine felt she belonged. And she took great joy in reciting verse she had learned with her father—everything from Shakespeare's sonnets to the poems of Walt Whitman.

In December Ada invited Catherine to be the lead angel in the Congregational Church pageant. Ada furnished her with a halo and simple white gown which had been used in the past, but Catherine embellished it with gold braid, which crisscrossed beneath her breasts. She purchased special gold-flecked white slippers to complete the outfit.

But on the evening of the performance she couldn't find the slippers. Where had she put them? She took her brown ones.

Thomas drove their little cutter as large flakes fell silently on the fur robe that lay across their laps, and the waxing moon made the snow glitter like jewels.

As she stood at the back of the church, waiting her entrance, she jerked the homey brown slippers off her feet.

I'll go barefoot. Angels don't wear shoes, anyway.

Afterwards, Catherine received several compliments, but a woman named Letitia Redson came up to her and said, "If I'd known you'd nothing for your feet, I'd have loaned you my boots."

Before Catherine could respond, the woman walked away tittering, "Perhaps our angel came from the manger as well."

Climbing into their cutter, Catherine complained to Thomas. "That dreadful woman offered me her Wellingtons!"

"Who?"

"Letitia Redson." Catherine relayed the incident. "She's the same one who sent me to the D.A.R. meeting."

Thomas coughed. "Don't let her spoil it for you. You did look the angel up there."

He was being more pleasant than he'd been for a long time. Perhaps he'd finally forgiven her for sending his son away. The last few months had been a softer time for them. He was even being kind to Jorie.

They continued through the winter night, listening to the crunch of snow beneath the horses' hooves, and the jingle of bells as they passed other sleighs. The snow had stopped falling, and a billion stars looked down on them from above. Catherine held the sleeping Jorie in her arms and leaned against Thomas's shoulder. He held the reins with one hand, pulled her toward him with the other, and tucked the fur lap robe around her.

Catherine let out a long sigh. "Thomas, might we give a holiday dinner party?"

"Splendid, if you're up to all the work."

On the night of the gathering, while the men lingered over their cigars and port, Catherine, with the help of Sarah Beckler, cleared the table and wrapped up the perishables.

"What a tremendous pile of dishes," Sarah said.

"Not to worry. Helena, my housekeeper will see to them in the morning. All we have to do is put this food away."

As Catherine wrapped the meats for the larder, Sarah said, "Thomas is certainly the lucky man to have captured a trophy like you. You're certainly younger and prettier."

"Prettier than whom?"

"Letty, of course."

"I don't understand."

Sarah stopped pouring the cream back into the crock. "Has Thomas said nothing?"

Catherine shook her head.

"He was engaged to Letitia Redson."

Engaged? "I didn't know."

"She's a widow—has a son about the age of Thomas's boy."

"What happened?"

"Well," Sarah hesitated. "It's not for me to say," she added softly.

"Tell me."

"Letty says he jilted her."

"Why would he do that?"

"For you, I imagine."

Catherine blanched, and felt herself color as the heat climbed her neck and throbbed in her cheeks. *Letitia Redson!* That would explain why the woman had been rude to her on every possible occasion!

"In any case they were seeing each other for almost a year. Letitia had every right to expect marriage, I suppose," added Sarah.

Catherine felt betrayed. Why had he never told her? Why had he made her the subject of unsavory gossip?

She went to the parlor to summon the others for Christmas carols. Her eyes sought out Thomas. He was laughing, engaged in conversation with the men, telling some off-color story, she surmised, from the raucous laughter.

She seated herself at the rosewood piano, and the women gathered around. Soon the men joined them, and everyone was caroling the old favorites. Catherine tried to focus on the music, but when she'd look up, there was Thomas, happy, still handsome, giving full voice to old carols.

"Round yon virgin, mother and child,"

How could he look so innocent?

"God rest ye merry gentlemen, let nothing you dismay."

Could anything dismay Thomas tonight? Now he was singing in a lusty voice, his face Christmas red, abetted by the liquor he'd consumed.

When they'd had their fill of singing, Thomas offered more drinks, and people sat together sipping tea or brandy. Catherine watched him in a new light. No longer the poor widower, left with a young child—he was a highly sought-after bachelor, a lady-killer. Staring at him, she found it took all of her effort to focus on her guests. She couldn't wait for them to leave. Now Thomas was smiling at something amusing the surface captain's wife had said.

Why had he never seemed more charming, more desirable?

At last the guests were gone.

"How could you?"

"What are you talking about? Are you going to spoil this lovely evening?"

"Me! You spoiled it. You, you *jilted* Letitia Redson!" Catherine pounded Thomas's chest. "And I had to find out tonight from someone else!"

It was Thomas's turn to pale. He took her by the wrists. "I didn't jilt her, Catherine. We were never engaged."

Catherine pulled away. "*She* thought so, and tells everyone you spurned her. She's been dreadful to me. You knew, and you never told me why!" she screamed at him.

"I didn't see what good it would do to talk about her. I haven't asked you about your former sweethearts."

"I didn't have any!"

"Catherine, I never meant to hide it. It didn't seem important."

"Not important! Everyone knew but me! I've been the laughing stock—"

"You are not the laughing stock. If anything you are the envy—"

"How arrogant you are!"

Thomas took a deep breath, and said quietly, "I promised Letty Redson nothing. We saw each other for awhile. That's all."

"A year!"

"It wasn't that long. I suppose she hoped we'd marry. But I never asked her. I didn't love her." He turned to his wife. "Catherine, I first saw you in your father's house, when you were only fourteen, and I was married to Walter's mother. I had business with your father, and when I went to Red Jacket I looked forward to seeing you. But you were a mere child and I was married."

"You noticed me—at *fourteen?*"

"Yes. When my wife died I started seeing Letty. But I didn't love her. Our boys knew each other at school. That's how it got started." Thomas tried to take her in his arms, but Catherine pulled away.

"Would you have married her if I hadn't agreed to marry you?"

Thomas sighed. "Perhaps. But it doesn't matter now. You did agree."

He pulled her toward him, and this time she allowed him.

"Still, you should have told me. I shouldn't have had to learn something like that from strangers."

"Let's go to bed."

As he began loosening her corset, Catherine sighed. "I feel as though my breasts are being released from prison."

"But they are still captive," Thomas murmured as he cupped one in his hand.

Catherine's fervor was heightened by knowing that another woman had sought her husband. And the thought of Thomas watching her when she was but a girlchild, *wanting* her, allowed her in this moment to once again *become* fourteen, to imagine being taken completely, in all her youth and innocence.

There was something familiar about that dream.

chapter II

OFTEN JORIE WOULD take drawing paper outdoors, sometimes quite far up in the hills. Observing with infinite care, he would draw tiny insects, flowers, butterflies and spiders, but never harm them.

Now that he was almost eight, Catherine bought him a book on wild plants and another with blank pages, in which he could draw pictures.

"This is a beech tree, Mummy. Like the one up on the hill. Did you notice all its eyes and toes?"

Catherine laughed. "They do look like that, don't they?"

"I always feel it's *looking* at me."

Catherine watched with pride. "Why don't you color your pictures, Jorie? They'd be ever so much prettier."

"I don't want to. I like them this way."

"Would you like to write little poems about them?"

It started as a concession to his mother, but he found he quite enjoyed writing verses to accompany the pictures.

His mother was proud of his artistic ability. His father grunted, thinking the lad should take an interest in sports and other activities more befitting his gender. Thomas attempted to teach Jorie to play ball. The child's lack of co-ordination irritated him, but he tried to keep his patience and encourage his son. Several times he noticed Jorie start for the ball, then halt in his tracks.

"Why did you stop?"

Jorie was quite sure his papa would not like the real reason, so he said, "Because I knew I wouldn't be able to get it."

"Well, at least try."

But it became apparent to Thomas that there must be some other excuse, as often with a couple of steps the ball would have been well within reach.

"Run!" Thomas would yell. "Why did you let it go?"

"I couldn't catch it."

"Yes, you could."

The old familiar uneasiness came over Jorie as he tried to find the line between truth and avoiding his father's wrath. At times like these he felt he was walking barefoot on broken glass.

"I—I don't like to kill things," he owned up finally.

"Spiders?" his father asked incredulously.

"It seems everything has a right to live, even if it's small."

"I see. And if a horde of ants invades our house, you would welcome them? Or a wasps' nest in your bedroom? You'd like that?"

Jorie squirmed. "I don't know, sir."

Later Thomas turned on Catherine. "Why do you encourage all this nonsense? He's more squeamish than a girl about bugs!"

"Oh, he's not squeamish, Thomas. Quite the contrary. He likes insects. He studies them." Instantly she knew it was a mistake.

"*Likes?* What are you doing to him?" He started to go, then turned back. "You've made a milk-sop out of him. Disabuse him of this nonsense, Catherine, or I will!"

A week later there was an anthill on the veranda. As he left for work, Thomas instructed Catherine to see that Jorie got rid of it. She closed her eyes, implored the heavens for strength.

"Jorie!" she called.

He came flying down the stairs.

She took his arm and led him out on the verandah, showing him her discovery.

"Get rid of these ants. You must."

Jorie looked up at his mother, blinked, bewildered. He couldn't see what possible harm the small dark mound could do. He did not wish to upset this industrious family.

"But Mummy—"

"Kill them."

"No!"

"Each and every one."

He threw his arms around a post and started bawling.

"Stop that!" she shouted, and pulled him back to the scene. "You will do this!"

He jerked away from her, raced down the steps, and up into the hills. He didn't come home until suppertime. At dinner, his mother said nothing, but Jorie couldn't look at her.

He got ready for bed wondering why butterflies were appreciated and ants were something to be killed. He'd thought perhaps it was because butterflies could fly. But last week when a white moth danced around the lamp, he'd discovered they were no more welcome than the ants.

"Is it because butterflies are prettier?" he'd asked.

"They don't come in the house," she'd said.

Neither had the ants, but he dared say no more.

He could hear her climbing the stairs.

She entered his room. He sat frozen on the edge of the bed.

"You disobeyed me today."

Jorie nodded.

"Sometimes we have to do things we don't want to do. You must learn to do exactly as you're told."

He said nothing.

"Come here, Jorie," she said softly.

He didn't move.

"Perhaps you need encouragement."

Still he said nothing. Suddenly her voice changed, took on an unknown harshness. "Come lie across my lap."

He did as he was told; the throbbing of his heart was so loud he felt certain she could hear it.

"Now tell me what's going to happen to you."

"You're going to spank me."

"Yes. You will learn to obey me perfectly."

A strange mix of fear and excitement washed through him. He felt her undo the buttons on the flap. A prickly heat crawled down his legs.

"You are not to tense up. Do you understand?"

"Yes, Mummy."

She caressed his bottom softly, preparing it for punishment. Gently, she slapped him several times. Then she pushed him off her lap and buttoned his flap.

"Now, are you ready to mind me?"

"Yes. I stayed relaxed, I didn't tense up."

Her voice was normal again. "That's because I didn't hurt you. Don't count on that every time. But if your mind accepts it, your body will open easily to it. Pain doesn't need to cause suffering."

Jorie tried to take this in.

"You must not resist me as you did when your father was so hard on you. We will go slowly. I will never ask more of you than you can accept."

As he stood before her, she clasped his hands in hers. "Your father and I have different views on discipline. I don't believe it improves a child unless he understands and fully accepts his punishment. Do you follow my meaning, Jorie?"

He wasn't sure; his mind was already too crowded to take in more. "I think so."

She brushed a strand of hair from his eyes. "You know I love you very much, don't you?"

"Yes. And I love you."

"Of course you do." She gave him a big hug. "For those who are not loved are not truly disciplined. In that case punishment is only abuse."

"Were you punished when you were little?" he asked.

Catherine sighed and looked away.

"I'm sorry. I shouldn't have asked you that."

"My mother whipped me. But she had little affection for me."

"That's sad, Mummy."

"I don't recall her ever telling me that she loved me."

"Did your Papa ever punish you?"

At first Jorie thought she didn't hear; she had such a faraway look in her eyes.

Finally she said, "Yes, but I knew he loved me."

As she lay beside her sleeping son Catherine let her mind return to the strength of her father's arms as he held her across his lap, to the warmth of his hand as he'd caressed her bare bottom. She could still feel her spine tingle as it once did. The slaps would come, first gently, then hard enough to make her cry. Until, holding her close, he'd explained that in order for her to benefit from her punishment, she must surrender to it willingly in mind and body. He had taught her this, as she was teaching her child.

It had all seemed quite fitting. It was time, Catherine decided, time to start her son's training in earnest.

The next week Catherine unwrapped a package. "I have something for you." She showed him a new notebook like the ones he used at school.

"A copy book?"

"Yes, but this one is for a very special purpose. It is to be your discipline journal, Jorie. In it you are to record each of your transgressions, and the punishment you received."

"*All* of them?"

"Yes. And just as important, you must record the feelings that come up, such as those of appreciation, love and surrender."

"It sounds like homework."

She raised an eyebrow. "And if you feel resentful, you will write that down."

"Will I be punished for that?"

"We will just have to work on removing that feeling."

chapter 12

PORTAGE MINE WAS not the best place to be employed in the spring of eighteen ninety. Many small companies had closed on the Peninsula. The Portage was at risk of following suit. Existing shafts were turning out too high a percentage of poor-rock. But outcroppings of copper on the eastern parcel caused Thomas to believe that site worth exploring. The borings he ordered raised his hopes further.

He approached the agent in charge of the mine. "There are promising veins of pure copper in that conglomerate, Clark. I think we should set our sights there."

"I don't know, Thomas. Sinking new shafts, stoping out drifts, purchasing engines, boilers—very expensive and very risky."

"I know, and more track will have to be laid to carry the rock, but—"

"Beckler thinks the whole idea of a shaft across the road is folly now. Says we ought to go deeper in some of our existing shafts."

"It's not feasible to go any deeper. The machinery, the timbers required—"

Clark Ahlers waved him quiet. "I know, I know."

Thomas dropped his voice. "Possibly, sir, we could find the mother lode on the eastern site."

"What makes you think so?"

"It's the calcite, sir. Always a good sign. As well as the veins of pure copper in that conglomerate."

Ahlers studied Thomas thoughtfully.

"It could save the Portage, sir."

"Or finish it for good." Clark Ahlers took out a cigar, fiddled with the clipping and lighting of it for some time. Finally he said, "Start with an exploratory shaft, then."

Thomas gave his boss a broad smile and started to leave.

"Go ahead, but something bright and shiny had better show up."

The sixty foot shaft was impressive.

Everyone was excited, and all hoped the *Number 9* would put new life in the Portage.

Months were spent sinking the new shaft and blasting horizontally to create long, narrow drifts that would be tunneled into larger areas to be stoped out. All through the shaft and drifts, stulls were erected of huge timbers to support the walls. A modern shafthouse was erected over the collar of the opening. When it was ready, more miners and trammers were hired. Load after load of dynamite was hauled to the new location.

Thomas waited impatiently for reports on the yield. Sometimes the results were good, but on the whole the shaft was barren. He kept praying they'd break through to richer veins.

"Poor-rock—that's all we have, Radcliff." Clark looked very somber. "Your rainbow isn't leading to a pot of copper."

Thomas begged for more time

"One month. If it doesn't improve, we'll have to close it."

Thomas hoped and calculated, inspected the shaft and drifts every week.

In two months time the shaft was shut down. In three months the entire mine closed. Hundreds of miners and trammers were let go. Thomas was dismissed.

"The *Number 9* brought us down," the men said.

"Thomas Radcliff brought us down."

In the weeks that followed, Thomas talked less and less.

One day Catherine said, "Have you heard anything from—"

"No."

"Have you thought of...There are many other mines."

"Do you think anyone would hire me now? Read the newspapers, Catherine. Don't you know what the wags are saying?"

"What do you mean?"

"'*Radcliff Brings The Portage to its Knees*.'"

"Oh, Thomas!" her hand went to her mouth.

The invitations to parties stopped. Thinking she had established a real friendship with Ada Whyte, she sent her a note asking her to come for tea on Friday next. She received a simple reply: "I regret I am unable to accept your hospitality at this time."

A quiet pall settled over the house. Never had she seen her husband like this. Sitting before the window with idle hands, he appeared to be crumbling before her eyes. Weeks passed in this fashion.

"Couldn't you find some other kind of work, Thomas?"

He didn't answer.

"Thomas, I'm talking to you!"

His dull eyes turned from her. Realizing he wasn't likely to come out of it any time soon, Catherine decided she would have to pick up the baton.

She held stock of her own, having inherited half of her father's estate after her mother's death. It was not limited to the Portage Mining Company; in fact most was with the giant of them all—the Calumet and Hecla. She would sell no more than necessary. Knowing little about such things she took a parcel of papers wrapped in black ribbon from an old hat box, and with a new resolve set off one day to see their attorney, Toby Wilson.

Thomas's occasional applications for employment either went unanswered or were turned down. A swift and sure underground network between the mines ensured no one would take a chance on this upstart engineer, under whose tutelage the Portage had foundered.

A long and melancholy winter followed. More and more of the duties Thomas had performed now fell to Catherine. She managed household purchases and kept a careful record of expenditures. She ordered the coal and hired a boy to chop the firewood. She carried in snow to heat on the stove, and firewood to keep it going.

She had thought that in difficult times, at least she and Thomas would have each other. Wasn't that supposed to be the bedrock of marriage? But in addition to remaining distant from her during the day, he had not attempted to be intimate in the bedroom since that awful time when his dreams had collapsed. She decided it was up to her to restore his manhood, even if she had to speak frankly.

"Thomas," she began that night. "I miss you touching me, this long time."

When nothing happened, she bent her face to him and kissed him.

"Please try."

For a few moments he did. Then, "It's no use." He pushed her away gently. "Not now."

Catherine lay on her own side of the bed once more, cold and rejected. But she was not to be so easily defeated, and noting the ill effects this involuntary abstinence had on her temperament, she persisted. Two or three times a week she tried to entice him. One night she sat naked at her dressing table while brushing her long auburn hair. She climbed into bed this way, although she was not in the habit of sleeping unclad except on those rare hot summer nights.

"Put your nightgown on, woman. You'll catch your death of cold."

"I thought you might keep me warm," she said, snuggling up to him. But he ignored her. She grew cold and rose to find her gown.

Still another time, as he lay on his stomach, she straddled him and started massaging his shoulders.

Thomas groaned. "Don't, Catherine."

"It will help relax you. Please don't make me stop," she said, continuing her long strokes down his back. And as she reached his waist, she slid her little body down his legs, so she could rub his buttocks.

"Where did you learn to do that?" he muttered as she continued her ministrations.

"Daddy."

He turned over abruptly, throwing his rider.

"Explain that!"

"I was very young. He taught me how to massage his neck, how to find the muscles that were in knots. He'd sit in the chair, and I'd stand behind him. He said my fingers were so tiny they felt like the work of little elves."

"Oh."

About a mile north of the *Portage* lay the Keweenaw Mining Company. In March, its agent, Burton Haversay, attended a conference in Chicago, in which the advantages of using mining engineers were outlined. Trained in ore extraction and processing, these men could save their companies needless waste. Their superior knowledge of the latest equipment, their in-depth study of geology and the technology needed to safely explore the deeper regions of the earth's crust were all laid out in a convincing manner.

Burton Haversay considered his mine up-and-coming. He decided what he'd learned about the advantages of using trained engineers outweighed the unfortunate circumstances at the *Portage*. When he returned from Chicago he hired Radcliff as chief engineer of the Keweenaw Mining Company.

Thomas arrived home each day, touting the merits of the company he was working for. It was clear that he enjoyed being appreciated again, and even began going out in public.

Catherine was grateful for the comfort their new circumstances provided. But she found it difficult to surrender to Thomas's will. Having had a taste of power, of being head of the household in function if not name, she had discovered this was natural to her. She chafed when she was expected to defer to her husband, who had again claimed the throne.

On warm Sundays he would say, "Catherine, come take a stroll with me this afternoon." But she preferred to go to the cemetery to write. It was the closest thing to a park, possessing lovely trees and shady spots for contemplation. The subject of these walks came up every week.

"Thomas, I've gone with you the last three Sundays. I wish to have some time to myself today."

"As long as the weather holds, I believe your duty is to be seen with me."

"Must we put on a parade each week?"

"Our friends in town, the Whytes—"

"*Friends*? Ada would have nothing to do with me when you were out of work."

"You should be thankful for her amity now."

"I don't care what she thinks!"

"Do you care what I think? I don't understand you. Victoria was so reasonable, so..."

"Obedient?"

"Yes. Is that such a bad thing? You took vows, Catherine—"

"I was seventeen! I am twenty-four now. I have always been willing to listen to reason, when that is what you proffered, Thomas, but no man will instruct me in my duties, or tell me what to believe."

She took Jorie to the cemetery to write.

When she returned home Thomas said, "I've hired a man to paint the exterior of the house next week."

She protested. "But it's the inside that needs—"

"That's enough." He left the room.

That evening as she sat at her dressing table taking the pins from her long hair and shaking it out, Thomas said, "Give me the brush."

Catherine, seated before the mirror, could see him behind her, could feel the anger. Fear and excitement arose in her. She handed it to him and he began the old ritual of brushing her hair. But tonight there was no tenderness in his touch. His strokes were fast and hard. She offered no resistance, bit her lip in silence as he yanked at the snarls.

When he finished he said, "Get into bed."

This too she did without protest, discovering that her wanton body answered his mandate against her will. Familiar responses rose in her legs, flowed into her groin.

In the morning Catherine mused on how much easier everything would be if she could be as compliant out of the bedroom as she was in it. But this state was so contrary to her feelings the rest of the time, it confused her.

As the weeks went on the strain between them was palpable and the attention little, save for the animal passions they played out at night in muted moans. Catherine often thought it was anger, not love, that kindled Thomas's fire, and some dark part of herself that enjoyed these hedonistic scenes with him.

She noticed that whereas at one time her husband's authority had come naturally and without question to him, now it was an ephemeral state, ever requiring shoring up.

"Catherine Dear, don't scrape your chair across the floor when you leave the table."

After a few attempts at false apologies, she decided she would not succumb to this new demeaning status. She tried ignoring him, but he only brought it up again.

"Thomas," she reminded him one evening, "you never found it necessary to school me in the first years of our marriage."

"In that case, my dear, I was remiss in my duties."

"My God, you are pompous!" she retorted.

"You would do well to govern your tongue."

"I will not!"

"I think you had best retire to your room."

"I'll retire when I choose and not a moment before!"

"Then I shall disassociate myself from your society." He left her alone at the table.

chapter 13

RESTLESS AND DISCONTENT, Catherine put her hand to writing verse, as she had before Jorie was born. She sent some of her poems as far away as New York City and Boston, but she had nothing to show for them but a box of rejection notices.

Thomas took less and less interest in the family. When he did talk to her it was all about his work: No one was hiring the Poles, this shaft was closing, that one got flooded in the spring run-off, six men were injured in an explosion last week. But the *Keweenaw* had out-produced the other mines this year—even the mighty *Calumet-Hecla*.

Since his older sons' interests followed his own, they shared their father's life now. Once it was to her that he would pour out his hopes and fears. It was with her he shared his dream of discovering the lode that would make the whole copper country prosperous, and his family in particular. Now he seemed not to need her; she had become a fixture in his life.

In some ways Catherine realized she wanted no more from him than he from her, but she wanted to be wanted, needed by him. She did not fail to see this paradox. Perhaps her imagination did not serve her so well after all. Why couldn't she rein in her desire for love, for physical intimacy? What business had it hanging around like a ghost to haunt and taunt her when there was no prospect for fulfillment? She wished she could find contentment in just raising her child as she supposed other women did.

Catherine recognized a melancholy in herself she knew she had to fight with all her strength, or it would sweep her under. If only Desdemona were still alive. The beautiful mare her father had given her had helped to release some of her pent up feelings. Riding took her out of herself, left her dark demons behind, while she expressed a wildness, an uncensored energy no amount of domestication could tame. She knew that later the demons would find her out, but for the moment she had fashioned a fragile truce with them, allowing her to step out of time and place and lose herself in a world apart.

"Thomas, I want to buy a horse." As he stared at her she added, "I hope you won't fight me on this."

She named the beautiful roan-colored gelding Falstaff. Every day his soft welcoming neigh greeted Catherine in the stable.

One day she took the path up the hill toward the mine and across the fields to the west. New buildings were going up every day, and one of them was the library.

With Jorie in school, Catherine started attending regularly. She'd pore over volumes of poetry and novels, sometimes checking the books out, but often staying at the library to read. In the pleasant surroundings of this new hideaway which held no threat of unwanted intrusion, she could lose herself vicariously in the lives of others.

It was here that she met Chester. Over a period of weeks, nods and smiles gave way to walks on the adjoining grounds. Not long after, they started taking rides across the hills behind the town. She discovered he had been sent there to survey land for the government.

She noticed his tanned skin and healthy appearance. He had deep brown eyes and a great abundance of wavy brown hair, which when it caught the sunlight looked almost blond. She liked the shape of his profile, each aquiline feature clearly defined, reminding her of the statues of Roman soldiers she'd seen. She gauged his age to be about thirty-five.

"Are you here to stay?"

"No, when I complete this job, I'll be sent somewhere else."
He shrugged, smiled down at her.

"You're fortunate to be able to work above ground."

"And what does your husband do, if I may ask?"

She hadn't told him she was married, but she supposed her
ring gave her away.

"He's chief engineer for the Keweenaw Mining Company."

On another day she asked, "How is it that with your work, you
have time to come to the library during the daytime?"

"The first time you saw me was a Saturday, if you recall. After
that, I rearranged my hours. Shall I confess to you that I am now at
the site by dawn, taking advantage of the early daylight, and have
done a day's work by two or three o'clock?"

His openness touched her. She felt a prickly heat creep up her
neck, for surely he'd told her that she was important enough to rearrange his whole schedule!

"I don't mind telling you I am enjoying your company. I
haven't been with young women for some time now."

Young! He thought her still young! Well, she was, after all, only
twenty-six.

"But this town has its share of young women."

"I don't know how to meet them, and I don't care for the company of 'ladies of the night'."

"Do you have a sweetheart back east?"

"Not any more. She got tired of my taking off across the country, and gave her hand to another."

"I'm sorry."

"I doubt if I was ready for marriage five years ago."

He asked her if she liked to bathe.

"If you mean swimming, I haven't been since I was a child."

"Would you like to—at the lake?"

"It's much too cold. It's barely June."

"There's a very small lake on the way to Dollar Bay. It's not so
cold."

She promised to consider it.

"Mummy, you're so happy," Jorie said as they were reading a story that evening.

She hugged him. "Yes, Darling, I am. And with a bright boy like you, why wouldn't I be?"

But she could hardly focus on what he was telling her.

"On the twentieth, Mummy. I can't wait."

"What's on the twentieth, Dear?"

"School's out."

School's out! She hadn't thought about that. Well, thank God for Helena.

"We'll have the whole summer together, Mummy. Just you and me."

"Yes, Dear."

On a warm day in July she met Chester at the library and rode silently toward Dollar Bay. When they reached the shore, her heart was pounding more than ever as they dismounted and tied the horses to a tree. She'd purchased a bathing outfit, and was wearing it under her riding clothes. Still she could not imagine disrobing in front of this man.

He saved her the problem by disappearing for a short time. Catherine quickly removed her outer clothes, and went into the water. She wanted to go as far out as she dared, to avoid the embarrassment of his seeing her in this costume.

She turned and saw him coming toward her, crashing into the water as wildly as a horse. He dove under and came up beside her, shaking his head vigorously to get his hair out of his face. She burst out laughing.

"I'm not that funny, am I?"

"No," she tried to stop laughing. "It's just, I've not seen you this way before."

Through the top of his suit, she could see his nipples, and suddenly wondered if he could see hers. Well, no, the top of her outfit was loose and blousy, thank heavens.

"Can you swim?

"No. It was not a popular pastime in Scotland, and I daresay not here either. I doubt anyone swims in Lake Superior. Even Portage Lake is very cold, I'm told."

She moved her arms back and forth through the water for something to do.

"I would tell you that I was the swimming champion in school, but that would be bragging," he said.

"All right, then, don't tell me, and you won't have that on your conscience!"

"Oh, I've much worse things on my conscience."

He swam in a circle around her for awhile before coming back to her.

When she started shivering he spread a blanket on the ground in the sun. She told him about her son, how bright and inquisitive he was. Chester said he'd like to meet him sometime.

When it was time for her to go he said, "Next time I'll teach you to swim, Katie...Is it all right to call you Katie?"

Katie. Only her father had called her that. It felt strange hearing it from this man she barely knew. She wasn't quite sure she wanted to share it with anyone else, but she found herself nodding.

They started meeting at the lake. He broached the subject of swimming again.

"It's not that hard, truly. I'll teach you to float first. Mostly, it's a matter of trust, of just giving yourself to the water."

He demonstrated. "If you'll allow me, I'll support your back at first, just enough to keep you afloat, while you build your confidence."

She was wary of this new turn, but she agreed.

He led the way to where the water was quite shallow. "See, here you can put your feet safely on the bottom." He stretched his arms out. "Now if you'll just lean back. Remember, just surrender yourself to the water."

Just surrender myself to you, you mean.

Awkwardly, she leaned back against his outstretched arms, and tried to raise her legs. With a few more tries, she was able to stay on her back without doubling up and going down.

"There, now don't you feel more relaxed?"

"Yes." But she felt naked too—exposed, lying before him, as he gazed down at her. She didn't know where to rest her eyes. And she could feel his hands under her, supporting her. She began to have other feelings, too, which caused her concern. She ended the lesson rather abruptly.

At home Helena said, "You've certainly taken to the swimming, haven't you, mum?"

Of course Helena would have noticed the sudden change in her habits, the frequency with which she was away.

"It's a healthy sport."

"Do you meet interesting people there?"

"Sometimes. Did you clean the lamp chimneys?"

"Yes, ma'am, and changed the wicks, too."

More to please Chester than herself, Catherine learned to swim.

The next afternoon he was waiting for her at the hitch where they tied up their horses.

"Let's ride," he said. He did not wait for her to answer nor give her time to dismount. He swung up on his own horse, leading the way, never turning to make certain that she was with him. She followed blindly, outraged at his assumptions, amazed at her own obedience to his will.

He did not take her through town, but cut back through the woods behind the library and up the hill, which overlooked a shallow valley. From there they turned west and rode in silence side by side through fields of timothy and oats. It was unusually warm, a windless day, and Catherine could feel droplets of perspiration on her brow even before he started running his horse. It took her only a second to catch the change, and in a moment she had Falstaff running too, but as hard as she tried, she could not catch up. Finally, in the hollow, she saw him dismount. As she came upon him, he grabbed the reins, brought her horse around and lifted her to the ground.

He took her hand and for a time they walked in silence. Then he turned to her, cupped her face in his hands and pressed his lips to hers. She offered no resistance. It was as though it had been planned, as if she'd always known it would come to this. She felt his hand slide down her back.

In one easy movement, he pulled her to the ground. Suddenly horizontal, she found herself looking up into his face. He had her pinned to the ground, but was studying her face, giving her a chance to catch her breath.

"If you want me to let you go, say it now," he was smiling. "Otherwise, I'll not be responsible for what happens."

She was still breathing heavily, not sure how much to attribute to the hard ride and how much to the man. Her nostrils filled with the sweet smell of alfalfa. She stared at him briefly for a moment, said nothing.

"Then give me your mouth."

She lifted her face to his. His kisses were so soft and gentle for such a long time, Catherine became impatient for something stronger.

"You make me feel like a child—the way I was kissed when I was sixteen," she goaded him.

As she anticipated, her words fired in him a strong response. He sank his hands into her hair and pulled her back to him. He kissed her hard and long, engulfing her in a passion she hadn't felt since the first year of her marriage.

He tongued her neck and the inside of her wrists, bringing her awareness to parts of her body she'd never experienced.

"Still feel like sixteen?"

"No," she murmured.

Then to her disappointment, he stopped, sat up, picked a long stem of grass.

"Were you just teasing me?"

He shook his head.

"Your passions wane quickly."

"They haven't waned at all." He sat still, chewing the grass. "I think we should walk for a spell."

Catherine did not want to, but she pulled herself together, smoothed her hair, as he offered a hand to help her up.

"You're covered with grass."

"Well, you dumped me in a field."

"I did, didn't I? Are you angry with me?"

"For the hay, or the way you treated me?"

"Either. Both."

"I should be. On both counts. What made you think I would..."

She didn't need to finish. "You followed me out of town, didn't you?"

She blushed. "Are you looking for a wanton woman?"

"No." He pulled her to him. "If I thought of you that way, do you think I'd have stopped just now?"

They walked through the field, hand in hand. Finally, they returned to the horses.

"I'd best leave you here. Can you make it back all right?"

"Of course," she answered with all the dignity she could summon.

He turned her around, and she felt his hand brush her shoulders, slide down her back and buttocks as he brushed off the bits of grass. She had all she could do not to turn and throw herself back into his arms.

"Think about what we're doing. I don't need to recite the risks for you."

He helped her mount. "If it pleases you, meet me here tomorrow at three. If you don't come, I'll understand."

She nodded, could barely look at him, raced toward home as fast as she could—away from her shame, her ecstasy. She wished he'd just taken her there in the field before she had to think about it.

That night she tossed in bed; at times so overcome with guilt she decided she would not meet him. The risks of scandal, of losing Jorie—she couldn't bear to think of that.

Then she tried to justify it. It seemed that any kind of romantic life with Thomas was over. And then, out of nowhere Chester Bigelow had appeared. What a fool she'd be to refuse him!

In the morning, she thought, "I've only been playing games with myself. How could I *not* meet him?"

The decision had been made—at least for now. She would not think beyond today.

Three o'clock would never come, it seemed. She busied herself with chores to make the day go faster. She left a bit early to stop and pick up some sweets at the General Store at the bottom of the hill. That would be a way of breaking the ice and put them both at ease.

As she was leaving the shop, Earl Foster entered. Standing in the doorway, he prevented her from making a graceful exit.

"Oh, Catherine," he said, "You're just the person I want to see. I hope you're well. I hope you're feeling better than my wife." He added a nervous chuckle.

Catherine was impatient. *Why now?* It would be rude to push past him.

"Is Mrs. Foster ill?" she managed.

"It started with a summer cold. But she's been running a fever now for three days."

"You should call the doctor."

"Well, that's just it. To tell you the truth, the doctor's medicine isn't helping her."

"I'm sorry, but I—"

"I recall Jorie had something similar and you cured him with herbs you got from an Indian woman."

"Who told you that?"

"Why, you did. Or maybe it was the boy. I don't mean any offense. I was just wondering if I could buy some of those herbs from you; they might help Cora."

"Yes, I could give you some, but—"

"I'd be most grateful. I'll just follow you up the hill, and get them now, if that's all right."

What was she to do? If she told him to come in the evening, and he chatted with Thomas, it might come out that she'd had other business in the afternoon, and Thomas would wonder what was so urgent she couldn't take time to help a friend in need.

"Of course. Yes."

Inside she was seething that this most inconvenient complication had arisen. By the time she'd given him the herbs and explained how to steep them and so on, she'd lost twenty minutes. And she dare not follow him down the hill; she had to wait another ten before leaving the house.

When she was finally free to leave, and had shown some decorum as she rode through town, Catherine raced across the fields as fast as Falstaff would carry her.

As she crested the hill, Chester was nowhere to be seen. She rode to the next field and back again. In the hollow where they'd lain, she could still see the impressions of their bodies, the flattened grass, laughing back at her.

She waited, not wanting to give up. But finally she decided she'd been too late and he had not waited for her. Hot tears stung her cheeks as she started home.

She hadn't realized she was venting her anger out loud as she galloped away from the scene. "Damn, damn, damn!"

She didn't hear hooves catching up to her.

"The damned is here to claim his prize."

She slowed her horse. He hadn't given up after all! He was grinning as he gazed on her tear-streaked face.

"When you weren't here, I waited. Then I thought I might have gotten the time wrong, I went back to clean the place up a bit."

He drew his horse close to hers, reached over for her hand.

"Come, I've something to show you."

She was following him again, and Lord knows where he was leading her this time.

Suddenly he stopped, and pointed to a cabin on a knoll. "That's where I live."

They continued up the hill. As he helped her dismount he said, "It's not much, not what you're used to, but better than the field, I hope. More private, anyway."

He took her hand and led her inside. "I tried to make it as presentable as possible for my lady."

She pulled her hand away. "I'm not your lady!"

"My mistake." He shoved his hands in his pockets.

She turned away from him, looked around the simple dwelling. A bachelor's one-room cabin in the woods. Well, what did she expect? He was a surveyor, used to roughing it. Even in broad day-light it took some adjusting before Catherine could see into the dark recesses of the room. One tiny window covered with a yellowed waxed paper admitted only a modicum of light. He had made a fire in the wood stove in the corner. There was a cot barely wide enough for one in another corner, and a simple table in the middle. A makeshift bookcase had been assembled from rough-hewn planks, the shelves separated by chunks of firewood. To Catherine, only the books made it homey.

She felt like a character in a D.H. Lawrence novel. Upset and out of sorts, she said, "Did you build it?"

"No, it was here—some prospector abandoned it."

"It has a dirt floor," was all she could think to say.

"You don't have to stay."

"I didn't say that!"

Why was it suddenly so unseemly, so awkward and embarrassing? Why did it feel wrong today where it had not yesterday? And why couldn't she say the right things to put them both at ease?

She stood uncomfortably, not knowing whether to run or stay. Her lip started to quiver, and he took her hands in his.

"It's not the cabin," she blurted. "That's not it."

"I know."

"What am I doing here?"

"Do you want to leave?"

"No!"

"Let me make you some tea. I don't have any milk—hope you can drink it plain."

She nodded, watched him as he put an old kettle on the fire.

To put her at ease he started telling her stories of his youth, as a boy on a farm in Pennsylvania, how his pa had died when he was nine, and his mother a year later.

"What did you do?"

"An uncle came to fetch my sister and me and take us back to Boston. I haven't always lived like this," he motioned to the surroundings. "We had an old Victorian house by the sea."

He told her how he loved watching the tall ships come in, being on the docks to help unload the treasures from around the world. How he'd hired on to a lobster boat at thirteen, learned to peg the creatures without being hurt.

Catherine was fascinated with the tales of a life she'd known nothing of. When the tea was finished, she looked at him expectantly.

"I'm feeling better now."

She meant it as an invitation, but he said, "I want you to go home now, Katie. Come back whenever you like."

Embarrassed at being dismissed again, she nevertheless drank up the kindness in his eyes. Well, that would have to do. Perhaps he was right.

She had forgotten all about the sweets.

For two days she forced herself not to go. Let him wonder if she'd ever come. She had been too easy for him. Offered herself to him as a gift and he'd sent her away, unopened!

By the third day she could resist no longer. She crossed the fields at a gallop, but as she neared his cabin, her uncertainty made her slow down. Again doubts filled her mind.

She approached quietly. Nevertheless, he heard, came out to meet her. He helped her from her horse, led her inside. She could smell something good cooking in his pot.

"Are you hungry?"

"No."

He smiled, waiting for her to join him. "The sheets are clean, and the rats only come out at night."

Tentatively, she walked the few paces to join him. He took her hand and led her to the bed. She stood stiffly while he lit a candle.

He raised her head, kissed her forehead, her chin and both cheeks. Then gently, he started unbuttoning her dress—awkwardly, as the buttons were too tiny for his large hands.

"Perhaps you'd better do it," he apologized.

Could anything else happen to discomfit her?

She finished undoing the buttons. He slowly lifted it over her head.

As if he had something precious in his arms, he brought the gown to his face, breathed deeply of its scent. Then carefully, he folded it, and laid it on the chair, making certain it didn't touch the floor. At first embarrassed as he gazed at her, she soon came to realize how much pleasure the sight of her brought him, and allowed herself to enjoy the moment too.

After drinking her in with his eyes, he undid the laces of her undergarment. She was pleased he was in no hurry.

Slowly his eyes shifted from her face to her breasts. He looked at them a long time before touching them. Then with one finger he spiraled from the outer edge of each mound to the nipple.

"Like porcelain," he whispered. "No. Alabaster, with little veins running through."

"I am not made of stone, Chester Bigelow, as you will discover."

As he slowly finished undressing her he treated each garment as though it were a sacred vestment. She had worn her prettiest pantaloons. He touched the violet ribbons laced through the ruffles.

"You're much too fine for these backwoods. How do you abide it here?"

She shook her head, not wanting to talk. Catherine felt his urgency grow and matched it with her own. She must have all of him, feel him envelop her.

"Give me your mouth," he was saying.

Without hesitation she complied, her body once again responding to domination, wanting only to melt into the folds of this man's body. Their fugue built to a crescendo of fire and fury, taking Catherine to places she'd never been. She rode the arc of this magical world, pleasure escalating, until her senses exploded, dissolved, drifted downward as gently as cinders from a blaze.

Neither was in a hurry to speak. At last he said, "You are a volcano of passion. I knew you'd be responsive, but..."

"I've waited a long time."

"I hope you are not spent."

She glanced at him sideways. "There's no fear of that."

They stopped talking, and enjoyed the quiet. Only an occasional crackle from the fire and the sound of their breathing broke the silence.

When she left he said, "Come tomorrow, if you can."

She promised she would try.

But Jorie was sick with another of his bad colds, and Catherine would not leave him. It was almost a week before she returned to the cabin on the knoll.

Chester came out to meet her, his questions pouring out like a fountain.

"I imagined all sorts of things. Next time, please send a message."

"And how discreet would that be? I must say I hadn't a notion you'd be so concerned, Chester Bigelow."

She walked to the stove and sniffed the contents of the pot.

He came up behind her and swept her up in his arms. "Now you're funning with me, lass."

"It's good for you to fret, don't you think?"

"No." He dumped her on the cot, and proceeded to undress her. "I've waited all week for you."

This time there was no slow examination of her clothes or her body. He got her out of them as fast as he could, pushed his own off with careless urgency, and took his place beside her.

"Not so fast, Mr. Bigelow. I think I should have a look at you, as you did me. Let me see. Here we have quite a bit of golden hair upon your chest. Damp, too. I would love to see it glisten in the sunlight, Chester, could we go outside so I can study you?"

"Lass, you are asking for it."

They laughed and he raised her head and kissed her lips hard. He nibbled them so many times, she finally protested.

"You're hurting me."

"That's for being so cheeky."

He pulled her head away from him and looked into her eyes.

"I've a good mind to spank you."

Since she offered no protest, but dared him with her look, he turned her over and started paddling her with his hand. Her squeals were for naught. When he'd given her a half a dozen slaps he turned her back.

She half expected him to apologize for this impetuous behavior, but he did not.

Instead he said, "You deserved that. You are a wild mare in need of taming."

"Do you truly think I'm wild?"

"I do."

"And you would tame me?"

He laughed. "If I thought a few spankings would do that, I wouldn't lift a finger to you."

Catherine tried to carry on at home as normally as possible. Now that school was out, she spent as much time as she could with Jorie in the mornings. They did the shopping together, and as always Catherine was quick to see opportunities to further his education. A ground wasps' nest or a tree splitting a rock—whatever she noticed, they discussed. Soon it was Jorie who was pointing these things out to her.

Once she brought him with her to meet Chester, and the three of them took a picnic lunch to the little lake. Catherine simply explained that Chester was a friend.

"What's the name of your book, lad?" Chester asked.

"*The History of Wolves in North America.*"

"Doesn't look like a child's book. How old are you?"

"Almost eight, sir."

Catherine smiled. "Jorie has quite an affinity for wolves."

"Did you know, sir, that the wolf mates only once, for life? Just like people."

Catherine could not meet her lover's eyes.

She continued to see Chester as often as she could throughout the summer. Sometimes she was consumed by guilt and went out of her way to be nice to Thomas, and other times she felt such a loathing for her husband she could barely endure his presence. He showed no interest in her affairs, nor did he share his private life with her. Often he would leave early in the evening and come in late. Occasionally, he didn't come home at all.

Catherine reasoned that if he could lead a private life and explain nothing to her, she could do the same. Still, she was careful to be home by six when it was time for Helena to leave. Thomas usually came home shortly after.

"Is your husband suspicious?" Chester asked.

"I don't think so. Perhaps he suspects, and doesn't care. Maybe he's afraid if he starts questioning me, I'll question him, so better to leave it alone."

"I wouldn't count on that."

"I'm meant to think he's at his grown son's or over with Alice and Walter, but for all I know he's carrying on with that Redson woman."

"Would that bother you?"

Catherine frowned. "Not if he were discreet."

"Even if he is seeing someone, do not make the mistake of thinking he would abide *your* infidelity."

"Oh! It's all so unfair! If he no longer finds me desirable, he should let me go where I am appreciated."

"Ah, if only it were that simple."

"Do you think I'm horrid?"

His face transformed into a mischievous grin. "Terrible." Then he sobered. "I am hardly the one to give you an objective answer."

"Will you be upset if I tell you that last night he came to me?"

"Yes?"

Catherine cringed. "I had to let him." She waited for some kind of explosion, but he just nodded.

"Well, aren't you going to say something? Aren't you even jealous?"

"He's your husband, Katie."

"Yes. Well, I can tell you I could hardly bear it. I feel clean with you, but with him I feel soiled. Can you understand that, Chester? It's as if I were being unfaithful to *you* to allow him to touch me."

"You must continue to be his wife."

"Oh, Chester, I don't want to!"

"Well, right now, you are mine."

Soon the all-too-short summer was over. Jorie was back in school, and the precious warm days of early fall were upon them. The sky was that deep shade of blue seen only at this time of year. The collage of magentas, oranges and yellows that the maples and birches displayed dared anyone to stay indoors.

On one such afternoon they had gone walking in the woods.

"It must be the light, so low in the southern sky, that gives everything that special patina, don't you agree, Chester?"

He nodded, preoccupied, she thought.

"And creates longer shadows, even in mid-afternoon."

They dismounted, tied the horses, and continued their journey by foot.

"All my senses have been heightened, since I've been with you," Catherine said. "Can you feel the crunch of every twig under your feet? And the smell of wood smoke coming across the valley?" She leaned her head against his shoulder. "I don't want it to ever end."

He stopped, and turned her to face him. "I have something to tell you, Katie."

She had dreaded this moment. "No! I don't want to hear it! Don't say it."

"I must. You knew the day would come."

"You said there was more to do—"

"But I will be finished before the first snows. I've been summoned back east."

"Don't go! Please tell them you won't."

He held her to his breast as Catherine gave vent to her feelings. "I can't let you go," she sobbed.

"Then come with me, Katie."

"Do you mean it?" She studied his face.

"We could make a new life, the two of us, where no one knows us."

"Chester, do you think for a moment I could leave Jorie?"

"Think about it, Catherine. This is not the place for you. I'm offering you a new life."

She was silent.

"It is your choice, Catherine."

chapter 14

FOR DAYS CATHERINE was in a tailspin. She could not imagine leaving Jorie, and she could not imagine letting Chester go without her. He was right; she didn't belong in this God-forsaken country. They could live in Virginia, where it was warm, where they'd make new friends.

Chester coaxed, "Leave Jorie with his father and come away with me. He can't force you to stay."

"I would not be as far as Chicago before I would drown in tears at the thought of leaving my Jorie. I would bring you no joy, being constantly in a state of mourning for my son."

Chester nodded.

"Is there no other way?" she implored.

"I could say that I'd come back some day. But I won't lie to you, Katie. The truth is I have no love for this frigid country. The summer is short and the winter long. I want to go back east, and I would be happy to take you with me." He smoothed her hair. "It is you who will have to decide. You have time; I'm not leaving tomorrow."

"But if you loved me—"

"Don't, Katie."

Sleepless nights continued. One morning she passed St. Joseph's, the Catholic Church in the center of town. A woman was leaving through the large oaken door, and it occurred to Catherine that she could go inside, unseen by anyone she knew. Here, in the stillness of this refuge she could try to massage her thoughts into order.

Quietly, she entered the sanctuary. Immediately she became aware of incense. It took her a moment to get accustomed to the darkness. Tiny candles in little rows flickered in one corner. She saw no one else, walked down the aisle, and slid into a pew. Gradually, she became adjusted to the darkness. A large crucifix stood behind the altar. Her eyes took in a plaster statue of Mary in white and blue, and another statue of Jesus. She spent a long time allowing the sights and smells of this dwelling to permeate her senses.

Catherine hadn't prayed in years, didn't feel comfortable doing so now. But she found that watching the candles flicker in the quiet, darkened sanctuary brought her a feeling of peace. She returned three times that week, and each time felt some of the agitation leave her.

On one of her visits she felt someone slide in beside her. Without lifting her eyes, she could tell by glancing at his lap that he was a priest.

She waited for him to speak.

"I do not wish to intrude," he said, "but I have seen you coming here this week. I am Father Dumas. If you would like to talk to someone, I am available."

"Thank you."

She had not thought to divulge her secret to a single soul, let alone a Catholic priest.

He waited for her to say more. "I'm not Catholic," she added.

"Whatever your faith, you have come here. I am not suggesting confession. I offer my ear should you wish to discuss your problem with someone who can keep a secret."

She hadn't said she had a problem. *But I suppose my very presence here establishes that.*

She shook her head.

He placed his hand over hers. "If you should change your mind, my study is through that archway."

He rose to leave, and Catherine's eyes followed the little man until he disappeared.

She thought about the priest that night and wondered why she'd been in such a hurry to reject his offer. No, she wasn't Catholic, but he knew that. Certainly there was no one else she could turn to.

The next day she knocked timidly at his study door. It was opened by a nun.

"Is Father..." She couldn't even remember his name!

"Father Dumas is not here. Whom shall I say called?"

Catherine shook her head. "He doesn't know my name."

"I expect him back shortly. If you'd like to wait in the sanctuary, I'm sure he won't be long."

"Thank you, Sister."

Catherine became lost in the serenity of the refuge. She didn't know how long she'd been there when she felt the priest's presence beside her.

"Would you like to come to my study?"

"Could we just stay here?" she ventured.

"Of course."

"I don't know where to begin."

"Wherever your thoughts take you."

"I have a most dire decision to make."

She told him about Chester, her marriage, her son, and the terrible choice she had to make. Sometimes the tears she'd been holding back rolled down her face.

He offered no hell and damnation judgments, only gentle promptings when she lost her thoughts. The telling of her story was made easier by the dimness of the church; sitting beside him allowed her not to look at him directly.

"Well, now I've told you everything." She took a deep breath, drawing in the scent from the candle box.

Father Dumas was quiet.

"Aren't you going to tell me what a terrible sinner I am?"

"Do you want me to?"

Catherine was silent.

"Did it help to sort out your feelings? That's what you want, isn't it?"

Catherine sighed.

"Ask God for help. Prayer brings new insights to old questions."

"Then what was the point of telling you everything?" Immediately she regretted her outburst.

"So you could hear the story, untangle it."

Catherine let out a frustrated sigh. "I'm sorry, I'm so confused."

"Pray tonight. Perhaps the answer will come in the form of a dream. If you would like to come back, I'll be here tomorrow, Lady."

Lady! He had called her lady after all she'd revealed to him!

That evening Catherine prayed, or tried to. She had been so removed from this experience that it felt uncomfortable to her. Her dreams were disturbing, and in the morning she could remember nothing.

The next day she reported to Father Dumas.

"Can I tell you a story, Lady?"

"My name is Catherine."

He smiled. "Like the saint."

"There's no comparison."

He brightened. "You are familiar with the saints?"

"Not at all. But I know they wouldn't be called saints if they'd behaved as I have."

"Do you imagine that all the saints start out leading impeccable lives?"

"I don't know."

"Well, I'm sure you know of Mary Magdalene. Jesus saw her love, the beauty of her soul. He did not condemn her."

Catherine glanced sideways at him. For the first time she realized how young he was, perhaps younger than she. It seemed absurd to call him Father. "May I ask *you* a question?"

"Certainly."

She hoped he wouldn't think her too impertinent. "How is it that some people can make a choice to give up all pleasures of...?"

"The flesh?"

She felt herself color. "It is beyond my grasp."

"There is another kind of passion, Catherine, if I may call you by your Christian name. It is a spiritual passion." He chuckled. "And I can tell you, it's more reliable than the physical variety."

"*Spiritual* passion?" To Catherine it was an oxymoron.

"Yes. Once you give it a taste, the soul has a hunger and thirst every bit as persistent as the body's. And the gratification is greater."

"How could that be?"

"I can't describe it adequately; you have to experience it. A feeling of peace and joy transcends all worldly concerns. I can only say that many who have tasted both claim to have reached a state of ecstasy with God that compares to no physical pleasure."

"Ecstasy!" She wondered if the young priest had achieved this.

"Many of the saints reached such a state. Laymen, too."

"How, how did they do this?"

"Some through visions, some through self-sacrifice. Catherine of Sienna, who is your namesake, ate and drank almost nothing in her later years. And when she found she could not keep clean the hairshirt she'd been wearing, she cinched a metal belt under her clothing very tightly."

Catherine was incredulous.

"Though it may sound terrible to you, Catherine of Sienna lived a life of joy!"

She could only shake her head.

"This young woman commanded such respect that even her confessors fell at her feet as disciples. And she had the audience of the pope."

"I can't even imagine—"

"Wait here. I have something for you."

Father Dumas hurried back to his study. *So the saints knew that pain could lead to joy!* Well, she knew a little about that herself!

The priest returned carrying a small book.

"Take this home. I think you will find inspiration in reading it."

"*The Lives of the Saints.*"

"Yes. Right now you are so close to your own dilemma, you cannot see any doorways." He smiled. "I am not suggesting you aim for sainthood, only that you pull back, gain some perspective. Then, perhaps, you will find the answer you seek."

The young priest looked so eager to be helpful Catherine could not refuse him.

"And now if you'll excuse me," he said, "I have another appointment."

Catherine felt no desire to leave. In the dim light of the sanctuary she opened the little volume, noticed the inscription on the frontispiece. "To Francois, affectionately, Carolyn."

Who was Carolyn?

Catherine looked at the Table of Contents. She found Catherine of Sienna on page thirty-two.

An hour later she walked home thinking about this strange Catherine. Perhaps if she gave up the pleasures of the flesh, she could find another kind of joy through strict religious practice.

That evening she devoured the little book. Centuries ago there had been women, like St. Joan and Catherine of Sienna who commanded men of power. This Catherine had told the pope what to do! From where did this power emanate? Was it conviction spawned from a life of devotion and prayer? Were certain individuals pre-destined to lead, including a few women? Incredible that the pope should have given her audience, let alone taken advice from this unlearned young woman!

There was something deliciously secretive and mysterious about going to St. Joseph's. No one she knew attended, and that made it all the more appealing. When she left on Sunday mornings for mass, Thomas assumed she was going to the Congregational Church. Catherine found the service, with the flickering rows of candles, the drone of Latin litany and the shadows all very seductive. As the swinging incense pot, wafting trails of smoke, passed her row, she breathed deeply of its pungent fragrance. Here was a refuge, a true sanctuary, untainted by domestic discord.

Although not a fine stone edifice such as she'd seen in Edinburgh, St. Joseph's had something of the old world about it that she loved. Here she found a way to escape the banal mining town that reminded her of a hastily thrown-together theatrical set, with its high storefronts concealing the smallness behind and within.

For three weeks she struggled with her decision. Sometimes she would try living with a decision to leave Chester and stay with Jorie. During these periods she'd feel a terrible ache, which didn't go away no matter what she did to occupy her mind. Another day she spent hours pretending she was living with Chester in Virginia, where everything was lovely; but the pain she felt at leaving her son, imagining his waving good-bye to her as she left him forever, tore her heart apart. If only she could take Jorie with her, but Chester had not asked, and Thomas would never allow it.

She would wake from dreadful dreams where she knew he was dead! Nothing would do but for her to pad down the hall and peek in his room to make sure he was still breathing.

He is my flesh, my blood. How can I leave him?

Dry leaves scuttled across the wooden sidewalk as Catherine left the church, and a cold wind from the north thoroughly chilled her before she reached home.

"I can't go with Chester. I must give him up."

I will be finished before the first snows. It was time.

She would see Chester tomorrow and tell him. It would take a sheer act of will to hold her resolve.

That evening it seemed that her prayers at last felt genuine. Catherine prayed with fervor unknown to her before. She asked for forgiveness. *Kyrie eleison, Christe eleison, Kyrie eleison.*

She prayed for help in keeping her resolution, and that the sacrifice she was about to make would give her strength.

And please, God, replace the pleasures of the body with a spiritual passion.

A kind of tranquility descended on her. Whether it was simply because she'd finally made a decision, or because her prayers had been answered, she didn't know. But she welcomed it as a balm. *Dona nobis pacem.*

The next afternoon she rode to the cabin on the knoll and watched Chester washing up by the watering trough. The blond, curly hair on his bare chest glistened with droplets of water.

Catherine had never found him more desirable. She waited as he toweled himself dry and approached her, grinning.

"Come inside."

He put his arm on her shoulder and guided her in with his easy authority.

"I'd like some tea."

They sat quietly, sipping the hot drink.

When she was ready she said, "I've made a decision."

He waited for her to continue.

"I can't go with you, Chester." She tried not to look at him. She felt tears straining to overflow their banks.

"I know."

"You *know?*"

"You could never leave your son, little mother," he said gently.

"But, I was *thinking* of it." She buried her face in her hands.

"I am truly sorry that you cannot join me."

He took her hands in his, and Catherine felt the tears she'd been holding back slide down her cheek. "This is the last time I will see you, Chester."

He rose and pulled her to her feet. "Then we must have a magnificent parting."

"No." She hadn't meant to sound so harsh. "It is over," she said softly.

He did not argue.

He held her long and tenderly, but it was she who pulled away and without looking back, took her leave.

Giving Falstaff free rein to carry her homeward, Catherine raced away from the man who had returned to her the joys of youth and love.

She would not go back to the dull life she'd known before she met him; she had found something else. It was still strange and new, but she was determined to mine its mysteries.

She would fashion her new beliefs for Jorie's benefit, too.

"I have made a sacrifice. A great sacrifice," she called to the wind. "I intend to reap its rewards!"

chapter 15

A YEARNING AND terrible longing engulfed her each time she thought of Chester. She must, she would put him out of her mind. It was time to focus on her young son, and bring him into the new teachings.

She told Thomas where she was going to church and that she'd like to take Jorie.

"Just don't imagine you can have him baptized there."

She led him into St. Joseph's and taught him how to dip his fingers in the holy water, and make the sign of the cross.

When they left, she asked Jorie how he felt during the service.

"I liked the smell and the candles. But I didn't understand what the priest was saying."

"We will study together, and you will learn the Latin."

Rigorous study—yes, that would help her to forget!

She began telling Jorie stories about the saints, and the sacrifices they made.

As they were sitting in the parlor one day, Helena came in to add more wood to the fire.

"Never mind. You needn't bother now."

When she had left, Jorie said, "Why didn't you let her tend the fire?"

"It's a sacrifice, Jorie. We needn't *always* be as warm as we like. Do you understand what sacrifice is?"

"You mean punishment?"

"No. Sacrifice is voluntary. Sometimes it takes great discipline."

She told him how Thomas More had worn a hair shirt under his royal robes until the day before he was executed.

"Wouldn't that be very itchy?"

"That's why he did it. Sometimes monks whipped themselves and each other. In some parts of the world they still do."

His little mind was full of questions. "Why would they do that?"

"It's penance, Jorie. It's to cleanse oneself of sin. Others take it further and are able to reach a state of peace, or even ecstasy by doing this."

"What is ecstasy?"

"In this case, a tremendous joy at feeling you are closer to God."

She waited while he chewed over this.

"Are there other kinds of ecstasy?"

"Yes." She felt a stab in her heart, as the familiar yearning came over her.

"Do you make sacrifices?" he asked.

"I made one very big one for you."

"What was it?"

"I can't tell you. But I can let you know about some little ones. Today I will not have lunch. And if I feel rumblings of hunger, it will remind me that I was able to make a holy act of sacrifice."

"I want to do that too. I want to go without my lunch!"

"Are you certain? That means nothing to eat until supper."

"I'm certain."

"Then it will be our secret. It wouldn't truly be a sacrifice if we bragged about it."

The next day she told him she was not having desserts for a week.

After a moment's hesitation, he said, "Then I won't either."

"Good boy."

One day when he asked to go out and play in the snow, she inquired if he wouldn't rather make a sacrifice.

"What would it be?"

"To stay in your room."

"It's cold up there."

"Yes, it is."

"Do I have to?"

"No. Sacrifices are voluntary."

He looked out the window and saw the snow falling softly. "Then I'd rather play in the snow."

"Very well."

But he could see the disappointment on her face. He went outdoors, and slid down the hill a few times, but found no pleasure in it.

The next day he told her he wanted to make a sacrifice. The smile she gave him made anything she'd ask of him worthwhile.

When the sun had finally broken winter's back, the melancholia which had gripped Catherine all winter released its hold, and again she reveled in the precious days of spring, with the scent of arbutus filling the hillsides. Then as spring ripened into summer it became warm enough to venture to her favorite haven.

"Jorie," she called. "It's gorgeous. We can go to the cemetery to write!"

He came flying downstairs with the little notebook she'd given him for drawing and writing.

"No. This time you're to bring your discipline journal. I fear you've fallen behind in recording your transgressions. This will be a good opportunity for you to catch up."

He retraced his steps slowly, returning with the required notebook.

His mother set such a rapid pace as they walked across town, it was difficult to keep up with her. He arrived out of breath and flushed. She put him to writing forthwith, and refused to converse with him until his task was complete.

Even as he wrote, he could feel a prickly heat, for surely when he was finished, in this private place, she would exact his punishment.

When he showed it to her, she nodded her approval and bid him fetch a rose from a nearby bush. "Be sure to get its stem," she added.

Jorie did so, quite certain of the new correction she had in mind for him. When he returned she told him to bare his back and lie over her lap. He heard the snap of the branch as she broke off a piece.

She gave him the flower, freed of its stem. He closed his eyes, taking in the sweet scent of the floribunda, anticipating what she must be planning.

She was transported back to her father and the wild roses in the woods. Daddy found a use for everything.

You know the flowers, Princess. Now you must meet the thorns.

"Listen carefully, Jorie. Each time you feel the thorn, you are to pull off a petal from the rose. When all the petals have been removed your punishment will be complete."

Gently she stroked his back with the stem, allowing the thorns to scratch his back. She paused for him to pull a petal off. Once he caught on to the pattern she'd established, she applied more pressure.

"Keep breathing, Jorie."

Daddy was drawing the thorn across her skin, this time from the base of her neck all the way down her spine.

When it was over she touched her finger to the tiny droplets of blood and showed it to him. "Do you know how much I love you, Precious?"

He watched as she licked blood from her finger. He had been frightened, and the thorns did hurt, but not a lot, so he found it rather exciting, too.

That evening she wrote in her diary:

July 15, 1891

Today as I sat rocking Jorie in the cemetery, I gave thanks to the heavens that I have this soft piece of clay, so fine, yes, like porcelain, and very pliable. Will it hold its shape? But no, I do not wish him to be cast in any final form. Like clay, I can keep him moist, malleable for years to come. I am his potter.

As my father did with me I will take him by the hand and lead him into new pastures.

I have left my mark on him already. He is no sweetheart or husband to forsake me. This is my son! He is mine and I will have him for the rest of my life.

chapter 16

AUTUMN CAME AGAIN all too quickly. Looking up from her sewing, Catherine gazed at Jorie. He was no longer doing his homework, but working on a sketch.

"Show me your drawing, Jorie."

He brought it to her. "It's just a girl at school."

"I have something more appropriate for you to study if you want to learn portrait art."

She brought out a book with pictures of the saints.

"Practice copying these pictures. Then I can see if you are making a true likeness of the features."

He wasn't very interested, but he knew it could improve his skills.

"These aren't photographs, are they?"

"No, they're renderings. That's how artists learn—by copying the masters. Meanwhile, of course, they are developing their own style."

He worked with these pictures for a few weeks, and was surprised one day when his mother said, "How would you like to sketch Mummy?"

"Oh yes! Could I?"

"Perhaps when you get home from school tomorrow."

It was unusually warm for fall. Catherine sat on the swing on the verandah, taking in the fragrance of the Concord grapes on the vines behind her. She had taken extra pains to put her hair right, and apply a little color to her cheeks and lips.

Jorie came running out with his pencils and drawing paper. He sat on the edge of the wicker chair. "This will be fun, Mummy. You look beautiful."

While he sketched, Catherine began to chat. "Did you know that I studied painting when I was a girl?"

"No."

My father encouraged me, but my mother didn't approve."

"Why?"

"She said my work was childish, and Father shouldn't fill my head with foolish notions."

Jorie stopped drawing. "That's sad, Mummy. Did you stop altogether?"

"Yes. But I saved some of my sketches. And I have books with beautiful pictures of paintings by famous artists."

"May I see them?"

"Some day, yes."

When they had finished, she broke off a cluster of the purple fruit.

"One for you," she said squeezing the grape from its skin, "and one for me." In this way they consumed the whole bunch.

She taught him about perspective and proportion, shading and light. Together they devoured the books she brought out of her chest. He learned to look for the focal point and the source of light by studying Rubens, Raphael and Michelangelo. They'd play a guessing game where one of them would open the book at random, cover the artist's name, and the other would try to identify the painter and the picture.

Sometimes she made a test of it. If he got most of the answers right, he could sleep in her bed that night.

Thomas had been out for hours. When he returned, as she passed him in the upstairs hall she caught the unmistakable smell of perfume. Curiosity, more than anything, made her wonder who he was seeing. And although she'd long suspected it, *knowing* he was seeing someone else made her feel totally abandoned. She had lost them all—her father, her lover, and even her husband. Well, she could hardly call the kettle black.

November's dreary landscape with its denuded trees and dark overhanging clouds did nothing to improve her mood the next day. Catherine looked up from her sewing, studied the face of her young son. *He's all I have.*

She looked so forlorn, Jorie said, "What shall we do to cheer you up, Mummy?"

It was Helena's day off; they were alone. "We must think of something new. We have to keep inventing life or it will drown us in banality." She put aside her sewing. "I don't have the temperament for the God-forsaken towns it's been my destiny to live in here. I should be in Paris. Or Rome."

Her thoughts carried her back to the summer in Paris with Daddy. In a shop on St. Mark's Square he'd taken her into a glassblower's shop. Here she'd fallen in love with a small glass globe, its silver lid topped with a ballerina.

"May I have it? Oh, please, Daddy!"

"If that's what your heart desires, Katie. Yes, We shall keep our balm in it."

In Paris they stayed in the home of his friend. During the day they took in the wonderful sights and smells of the city; in the evenings he took her to the ballet or opera. One day he bought a beautiful lace handkerchief. With a look that both excited and frightened her, he told her he had a very special purpose in mind for it, and he would keep it until then. Though they spent the rest of the day in galleries and shops, she barely remembered anything until they were back in their room.

Tonight we have la maison all to ourselves, mon cher. We're going to play 'Othello.'

Catherine brought herself back to the present and looked at her son.

Jorie watched the change in his mother. First, it was as though a mask descended over her face, tightening her lips, narrowing her eyes. Then her posture changed—more erect. By the time she spoke he had already anticipated the change in her voice.

"Jorie, get your scarf."

Fetching the dark blue muffler she'd knit for him he wondered in joyful dread what lay in store. He knew better than to ask.

They were in the kitchen. "I'm going to blindfold you. Then you will open your mouth when I tell you to. You will accept whatever is put into it. Do you understand?"

He was breathless. "Yes."

She pulled on the ends of the itchy wool fabric tightly. "You mustn't be able to see. Do you trust me? Are you willing to accept whatever I choose for you to ingest?"

"Yes," he murmured.

"That's right. You will be given various substances which you will identify and describe. Now then, stand still and wait for me."

He could hear her moving about the kitchen, fetching the things she meant for him to taste. In this state he heard creaks in the wooden floor he'd never noticed before. The smell of wool socks drying near the stove reached his nostrils. He felt slightly dizzy as he listened to the sounds she made: a dish being set on the table, a jar being unscrewed.

"As you experience each taste, I want you to find the words to describe it. Experience each item slowly, with your tongue, your teeth, your whole mouth. Then the words. But first the experience. Now I would like you to put your hands behind your back."

She didn't tie them, but somehow he felt even more helpless.

"I am not asking that you *enjoy* every taste. It matters not whether you like the things placed in your mouth, only that you report your preferences along with a full description of what you're tasting."

He heard a loud pop, almost an explosion that made him jump. Then he realized it was only the wet wood in the stove—a sound he'd heard a thousand times before.

"You will swallow when I tell you to and not before. You are to spit nothing out. Is all this clear?"

"Yes," he murmured.

"Yes, *Ma'am*," she corrected. "Open your mouth."

He did, but nothing was put into it. Confused, after a few seconds he closed it.

He felt a sharp slap on his face.

"Did I tell you to close your mouth?"

"No. No, Ma'am."

"Open your mouth."

He did so, and this time he felt something cool put inside.

"Now chew it. Slowly."

He felt its rubbery smoothness. It was only a piece of hard-boiled egg. He didn't know what he was expecting, but suddenly he felt great relief.

"Do not gulp it down, nor chew it with haste. Be ready to describe the exact textures and tastes."

He chewed it very slowly, couldn't talk with his mouth full, forgot and swallowed it.

Another slap.

He could feel his face redden. "I'm sorry. I forgot."

"Describe what you tasted."

"It was egg."

"Yes?"

"It was cool and hard—"

"Hard?"

"I mean, well, it's not soft like applesauce," he stammered.

"Think of a more appropriate word than hard. It is not hard like a stone, is it?"

"No."

"Then what word does describe its texture?"

"I don't know."

"You disappoint me, Jorie. The word you want is *firm*. Now, did it all taste the same to you?"

"No. The white part was smooth and rubbery, and the yellow part wasn't."

"Let's hope you do better on the next. If you're going to be a writer you must learn to describe things not only accurately, but in fresh and original ways."

He could hear her unwrapping paper. Then the familiar unpleasant odor assailed his nostrils before anything reached his mouth. Limburger cheese. She knew he hated it! The offensive smell had often caused him to leave the room. Now she was making him *eat* it.

He opened his mouth obediently, and let it lie on his tongue, leaving it open to avoid breathing through his nostrils as much as possible.

"Close your mouth. Breathe deeply. Now, note the smell *objectively.*"

He let his mind leave this scene, employed his old habit. *Nine times seven is sixty-three. Nine times four is thirty-six.*

"Chew it, *slowly,*" she was saying. "And do not swallow until I tell you to."

"Eight times seven is fifty-six."

It seemed forever before she said, "Swallow it."

He started retching.

"Stay with it, meet the fear, Jorie, and overcome it. How will you conquer the big fears in life if you can't overcome a simple aversion to cheese?"

He brought himself back. With sheer will power he kept his stomach from erupting.

He forced himself to swallow, not at all certain it would stay down.

"I said describe it!"

How could he describe it without putting his attention on it?

"It tasted...awful."

"Such paucity of vocabulary you have."

The room was too warm. He felt he was cooking.

"It has a strong odor."

"Like?"

"Like nothing else. I can't think of anything else that smells like it. Except..."

"Yes?"

"Vomit."

"Texture?"

"Something like egg—the white part. A bit rubbery, but not as firm."

He started retching again.

"Keep it down, Jorie. Discipline yourself. Keep it down."

He took deep breaths through his mouth, tried to imagine lying under the stars, breathing in the heavenly scent of the lilies of the valley.

"Your father is right; you need toughening up. Would you prefer his methods?"

"No," he gasped. Finally, he was quite sure he had his stomach under control.

"There, what I want you to remember, Lad, is that you overcame a fear, an aversion. You wanted to run, to throw up. But you didn't. You disciplined your body. Not unlike sacrifice and penance. Of that you can be proud."

When the tasting was over, she removed the scarf.

"I am teaching you obedience, Jorie. We will sometimes use games to learn our lessons."

After that she cuddled him. "I wouldn't bother with all this if I didn't love you so."

What she said was confusing. He wanted to think about this some more, but she was talking about something else.

"Now Mummy wants you to make a sacrifice for love for her, if you're willing. Oh, don't look so frightened. Just a little sacrifice."

"What is it?"

"I'd like you to go to bed now, without supper."

He was disappointed. He had supposed it would be something grand, worthy of a knight. "At four o'clock?"

"Yes. Many saints fasted for a very long time as a discipline, or as an expression of their passion for our Lord."

"Oh."

"I'm only suggesting you give up one meal, and go to bed early to reflect on the sacrifice you are making out of love for your mother. Do you think you can do that? You don't have to."

He felt her warm breath caress his cheek, her hand stroke his back.

"Only if you want to, Darling. Do you love me?"

"Yes."

She squeezed his hand. "*Sacrifice* comes from the same Latin root as *sacred*. It's a holy thing if done with the proper attitude. Pure surrender, bearing no resentment."

Again he was confused, but there was something exciting about it. "I'll do it."

She kissed him on the forehead and led him upstairs. As she was leaving the room, she turned back to him. "There's one more thing. The next time Limburger cheese is offered at the table, you're to eat it, surrender to it completely."

When she left him, Catherine went to her own room and lay on her bed. Here she revived the Othello experience. She had summoned it often enough that it was as vivid as the night it had originally happened. She and Daddy had read the great plays, and sometimes in their walks at home they had improvised scenes from them. But tonight, in Paris, would be different, he'd said. Tonight they would play the death scene with costumes and properties.

It seemed Daddy watched her all through their quiet supper of leftovers. She was thankful he said little, as she was so excited she was afraid her voice would fail her.

He caught her mood, as he always did. "Anticipation is ninety percent of joy," he smiled.

After a quiet supper of leftovers he produced costumes. Where he'd procured them she had no idea, but he told her to change into the pale blue velvet gown he handed her.

Her father presented himself dressed as Othello. Catherine had no idea that a costume such as this could evoke such emotion. Already she was agitated, but stimulated, too.

When it came time to show her the handkerchief, claiming it as proof of her infidelity, his anger rose to such a pitch that while she knew he was acting, Catherine became frightened. Despite her insistence that she'd done no wrong, he bade her go to her chamber, get into her nightgown and wait for him. With her head and heart throbbing, she climbed to her room. She knelt, saying the prayers of Desdemona, then composed herself in bed, lying against the soft whiteness of the down pillows.

She heard him climbing the stairs, a pause outside her room, and then the door opening. She was shaking as he came to her side and asked if she'd made her confession to God. With tears coursing his cheeks, he held her face in his large hands and told her how beautiful she was, how innocent she looked.

Then quickly he dropped her head, grabbing her shoulders. "But you have betrayed me. You must die!" A large tear fell to her cheek.

Despite her desperate pleas, he'd covered her face with a pillow. Panic set in, as Catherine fought to free herself. She feared her father had gone as mad as Othello.

But in a moment he removed the pillow, and bent to kiss her forehead.

You were wonderful, dear Catherine. You played your part exactly right. Now I must resuscitate you, my lovely Princess.

He put his mouth to hers, and she responded. Then he pressed the handkerchief against her hand.

"You will keep this as a souvenir of our evening.

It was an extraordinary summer: her father's touching, then withholding, touching and withholding, her passions rising in a bacchanal of desire. But though she had begged him, he would not take her maidenhood. All summer she had known the bittersweet taste of that longing. There was nothing she wouldn't do for Daddy.

Sometime, when he was older, she would make Jorie desire her. There was no power like that of withheld favors.

For now they would play other kinds of games.

Thomas finished his lunch with pear and cheese, and looked up at Jorie. The lad had actually eaten the Limburger!

"Did you enjoy it?" his father asked.

"No, sir."

"Then why'd you eat it?"

"I thought I'd try it."

"He's been trained, Thomas. He will do as he is told. Even eat Limburger," she boasted lightly.

"Humph."

Jorie colored. Why did she do this? Just when he thought they had a secret she spoiled it.

"You see, Thomas, I am not without my ways of disciplining the boy."

"How old are you now, lad?"

"Ten, sir."

"I won't be home for dinner," Thomas announced. "It's Walter's birthday. I'm taking him and Alice to the new restaurant on Quincy to celebrate."

Catherine nodded.

"Being his eighteenth, he's getting his sizeable sum to invest. Good training—giving youths money to invest before they start frittering it away."

He turned to Jorie. "If you keep your nose clean, you'll get a sizeable sum on your eighteenth birthday."

"Yes, sir. Is that money?"

Thomas laughed. "Yes, and a good deal of it. Money and stocks."

Jorie was happy to think his father might hold him with the same regard as his other sons. He'd never been sure about that.

After Thomas left Catherine decided it was a good time to deepen Jorie's understanding of sacrifice. Again, she asked him to forfeit supper and go up to bed. She lay on his bed with him, holding him against her.

"Sacrifice is one of the openings to a life within a life. Many accept their circumstances at face value, and look no further. You are a lad living in a mining town. Are you willing to let that be *all there is?*"

"No."

"You are meant for more than that. You are sensitive and imaginative. I want to help you find the path to all kinds of experiences, regardless of your geographical circumstances. Sacrifice is one such passageway. Are you ready to go on the adventure?"

"I think so."

"There can be great richness if you are willing to plumb its depths. Your half brothers are miners of base metal. But we will turn the base metal of our existence into gold! Not in that underworld of theirs, but *within*! For only in the *inner* world will you find relief from the outer."

Jorie's young mind spun round grasping fragments of this new information.

"How else do you suppose your mother has survived this dreary God-forsaken land?"

"I'll do it, Mummy. I want to go on this adventure with you."

"You and I will travel inside a *Golden Bubble*!"

"Oh, Mummy, yes!"

She smoothed the damp curls lying flat against his brow. "Just the two of us. Our secret."

He kissed her. "Our secret."

"Being alone tonight will be good for you. So much to think about, you need time to digest it all. So I'll bid you good-night."

She closed the door softly.

With only the tumble of his thoughts for company, his confused, yet exciting feelings presented him with much to chew on. What was the *Golden Bubble*? He heard the grandfather clock strike mid-night before he finished his ponderings. Only then did sweet surrender envelop him and bring him sleep.

Shortly he was awakened by inebriated voices coming from downstairs. He pulled the covers up, tried to disappear. Then he heard footsteps stomping up the stairs.

"Jorie," the voice boomed. "I've come to see you!"

There was no doubt who it was. Walter pushed open the door and lunged into the room.

"Don'tcha know me, little brother?" he bellowed, the smell of liquor preceding him.

"Watcha all covered up for? You ain't scared, are you?" He yanked the covers down.

"Stand up. Let's see how tall y'are."

Jorie froze.

"What's the matter with you? Got no legs?" With one arm he jerked the younger boy out of bed and stood him on his feet.

Lighter footsteps were running toward the door.

"Get out!" Walter bellowed, slamming the door in Catherine's face.

Jorie could hear her as she bolted down the stairs crying, "Thomas, come up here—get Walter out of Jorie's room!"

But Thomas, too, was deep into his cups, and had passed out in his chair.

"Hey, kid, you don't need to wait no longer to taste the fine nectar of liquor. I'm treatin' you tonight."

Walter staggered, groping for something in his jacket. Grasping a flask he finally managed to unseat its cork.

"What are you going to do?" Jorie stammered.

"Help you grow up, you little sod."

At that, Walter took Jorie by the hair, pulled his head back and poured the whiskey down the boy's throat. When Jorie closed his mouth Walter kept on pouring, right into his nostrils. Jorie finally pulled away, sputtering and choking.

"Go on, cry, you little faggot. I've finished your initiation."

He shoved Jorie back on the bed, and turned to leave. In the hall he encountered his step-mother with a fire iron. As he grasped her wrists forcefully she winced, at which he displayed great pleasure. As he increased the pressure Catherine cried out, until finally she was forced to drop the weapon.

"Don't worry, I'm leavin.'" He pushed her against the wall, picked up the fire iron and made his descent.

Catherine tore down the steps after him. "Don't you ever enter this house again!" she called after him as he slammed the door shut.

She bolted it and tried to rouse Thomas. It seemed futile. She kicked him in the shins several times before he stirred.

"Let me sleep, Catherine."

Finally, she gave up, went upstairs crying and crawled in bed with Jorie. In the morning Thomas would know her wrath.

Portage Hill was a mile from Hancock, and the Radcliff home had no immediate neighbors, except a Finnish family, the Kukkonens, who had a modest bungalow nearby. Mr. Kukkonen worked in town as assistant to a blacksmith. People often dropped their laundry off there, and each evening he brought it home for his wife to wash and iron. They had two children, but Jorie was not allowed to play with them.

"Why not?"

"Because they are Finns. You come from better stock."

"Stock?"

"Jorie, don't exasperate me. You are of Scottish descent. The copper country is made up of a band of international ruffians, all inferior to the British, but none so much as the Finns."

"I don't understand."

"That's enough."

Possessing neither skill in sport nor easy banter in conversation, Jorie had not been popular at school. The only boy who had befriended him was a new student, Frederick.

Jorie admired the mild manner and intelligence of this solitary youth. Often they talked in the school yard about nature and the books they liked. There was a friendly competition between them. During spelling bees Jorie and Frederick were always the last two left standing. Frederick had collected stamps from around the world, and brought his collection to show Jorie.

"I trade stamps with one man in Peru and another in South Africa. These are my favorites."

Frederick was impressed with Jorie's ability to draw, and asked him to bring more of his work from home.

Jorie spoke of him enthusiastically to his mother, and one day Catherine suggested he bring the boy home to meet her.

On the day he arrived, Catherine served them fresh raspberry pie, and engaged the lad in conversation. He was well versed in many subjects, and at ease talking with adults. Catherine, at her most charming, easily disarmed young Frederick, drawing him out on several subjects. He even told her of his desire to go to the University downstate.

"It's grand there, ma'am, with professors in every subject you can imagine."

"But that must be a long way off," she said. You're how old? Twelve?"

"Thirteen, ma'am."

"And my Jorie is eleven."

Jorie took Frederick upstairs and showed him his drawings and read him a few poems. The boy appreciated Jorie's work and promised to bring his own sketches over some day. Jorie couldn't remember a happier afternoon. He was sure the visit had gone well.

After dinner that evening, Catherine kept Jorie at the table. Tumbling over his words of affection for the lad, Jorie turned to his mother.

"Wasn't it grand, Mum? You liked him too, didn't you? I could tell by the way you laughed and chatted with him."

She took his hands. "What I'm going to say will be hard for you, Darling, and you must be very brave."

He looked up, concerned. "What is it?"

"I don't want you to make a friend of Frederick."

"But why?"

"He isn't right for you, Darling."

"But I like him. And he likes me!"

"You have to trust me on this."

She saw the tears well in his eyes.

"He's too old for you."

"Only two years." He pulled his hands away.

"You see, Jorie, you and I cannot travel in our *Golden Bubble* if it's contaminated by outside influences. We must keep it clean, uncluttered."

"He's a very clever chap, with interesting ideas."

"That would only confuse you, Jorie."

"Oh, Mummy, please. He could be my friend."

"Isn't Mummy your friend? Aren't I enough for you?"

He swallowed. "The other chaps have friends at school."

"And you may too. But not Frederick. Find a younger lad, who can look up to *you*."

She gently removed the napkin he was twisting in his hands.

"I know it isn't easy, but it would be a sacrifice, Jorie. You can do that for me, can't you? I've made a tremendous sacrifice for you."

He started to ask what it was again, but she put a finger over his lips.

"You must not ask. All I can tell you is that I gave up a friend who was far dearer to me than Frederick to you. I did this so that you and I could stay together. I know the pain of that kind of sacrifice, and yours will not go unappreciated." She kissed his brow.

He thought about all she'd done for him—the trips up the hill to look at the stars when he knew she was tired, the times she'd told him stories from the old country and the love that was lavished on him in so many ways.

He said nothing.

"Good lad." She pressed him to her. "I know this is difficult. But when sacrifice is made for love, it's beautiful, remember? Love has its own reward."

He nodded absently, trying not to focus on her words and what they meant.

"If you meet it with surrender, rather than resistance, you will be at peace with it. Do you remember how to make your mind go to a state of surrender?"

"I think so."

"It takes practice, Jorie. You must use diligence and vigilance to keep it there."

She offered him another piece of pie, but Jorie had no appetite for food.

chapter 17

THE NEXT YEAR something started happening between his legs. It was pleasant in the strangest way, and when he reached down to touch himself, he discovered it was hard. He wasn't at all sure it was normal.

For the next few nights he was afraid to go to his mother. As close as they were he knew she wouldn't understand what was happening, and it might worry her. He had awakened twice with something wet and sticky between his legs on his long underwear. If only he could ask Frederick about it, but they were not so close any more. There was no one to tell. He lived in a confusing state of excitement and fear.

After a week his mother bade him to her bed again. As soon as he lay beside her, he felt the stiffness. She pulled him to her and ran her hand through his curls. In a few moments he sucked in his breath, and pulled away from her.

"Tell me what's troubling you," she cooed, pulling him back to her. "Tell me."

"Nothing." Why did she have to know?

"You wouldn't lie to your mummy, would you?"

He squirmed away from her.

"Something's wrong, isn't it?"

He wished he hadn't brought his candle in to the room; he felt the single flame light up the whole room, distort his face, magnify his shame. Shadows danced on the ceiling, on the bed, mocking him.

She pulled him back to her, touched his skin lightly. He felt her hand slide past his genitals in a quick brush. He held his breath.

"It's all right, Jorie. It's...natural."

A long silence followed, while he tried to take this in.

"You mean it's supposed to get that way?"

"I wouldn't say 'supposed to.' But it can happen to boys who are growing up."

So there was nothing wrong with him, and she *did* understand. He should have known. Although embarrassed, he was much relieved.

She turned to him, in that way that was beginning to make him uncomfortable. "Only twelve years old, and already you are growing into manhood. My little boy, my darling, where did the time go? It is too soon, too soon for you to grow up."

She hugged him tightly, and then the feeling got stronger and he didn't know what to do. Hoping she wouldn't notice, he slid one hand downward.

"No, Jorie, you mustn't play with it."

She gathered his hands in hers. "That's wrong, and God could punish you for it. Just lie here quietly with me." She rocked him gently. "You must confess to me each time the hardness or the wetness comes."

He started to object, but she was saying, "If we are to create our fragile bubble together, then you must keep no secrets from me."

He had little success with the mental diversions she had suggested, but learned that if he threw his covers off and lay there in the frigid room, he would lose that strange compelling desire that made him want to rub himself. He thought if he could fall asleep that way, the mess wouldn't come. But he couldn't stand the cold for long, and cursed himself for being a coward, as he pulled the quilt up. What if his father were to find out? He trembled to think. Could he trust his mother not to tell him? It was all so much like the time he'd tried to stop wetting the bed. Again, his attempts to control his own body seemed hopeless.

His mother was pleased that he was working at his problem, but then would grow sad and somewhat detached when he confessed his failures. She gave him prayers of penance to say, and told him to ask God for help with this new challenge. She said nothing of chastisement, but finally, the fear of losing her love drove him to request punishment.

She was delighted that he wanted atonement; it always brought him back to her. Afterwards she'd draw him to her, assure him of her love. Often with tears flowing down her cheeks, she would express appreciation for his devotion to her and to God.

But he didn't feel clean because he knew the feeling would come back; he knew he wanted it to.

Nevertheless he renewed his efforts, even bringing in handfuls of snow from the ledge to place between his legs. The sense of having let her down was excruciating. And God, too. But it was his mother he most wanted to please, and he didn't know how.

One night the feeling was so strong he couldn't resist rubbing himself, and as he continued, the sensation, rising to its peak was so wild and wonderful that he didn't try to prevent it. After that he found it harder and harder to refrain.

He stopped making his confessions. Sometimes he resisted the urge because he felt guilty, but just as often he gave in to it. The guilt from not being honest with his mother was as bad as the guilt for having committed the sin. But the thrill he felt while he was engaged in the act transported him beyond anything he'd known. It was the closest he'd come to the feeling of rapture that she'd said the saints had, which he hadn't been able to feel in a religious way at all.

One day she said, "Do I understand by your silence that your sexual arousal has decreased, or perhaps disappeared altogether?"

Jorie drove his hands in his pockets, felt the flush expose him.

"Since you have come to confess neither your failure to resist temptation, nor those times when you triumphed over it, I should assume, I suppose, that you no longer are subject to such arousal?"

He noted the bite of sarcasm in her voice. Looking at the floor, he shook his head.

"Look at me! Are you studying the pattern in the carpet?"

He raised his head, but did not meet her eyes.

"Well, what have you to say?"

"Both."

"Both what? Don't prevaricate with me. Form a sentence and make yourself understood."

"There have been times when I gave in to it, and times when I didn't."

"Gave in to what? Be specific."

"You *know!*"

Why did she torture him so?

She was silent for a few moments.

"Why haven't you told me?"

Did he have to explain? He wondered if other boys had to confess this sort of thing to their parents. He doubted it.

"It's embarrassing. Whether I do it or not, it's embarrassing to tell you."

She took his hand. "Mortification is a very old tool of purification. It is also a tool to use in deciding your course of action. If you are discomfited in telling me when you have relieved yourself, doesn't that very fact suggest something to you?"

"But I'm embarrassed either way!"

"We've talked about how sacrifice strengthens your character, its sacred origins and how it is an act of love." She paused. "Do you love me, Jorie?"

"Yes."

He knew what was coming.

Suddenly he was on Peggythis riding high in the sky, riding right through all the constellations, coming to rest near the Seven Sisters. But there were only six. He must find the seventh—the one that was hiding in shame.

"Answer me, Jorie!"

Reluctantly he came back to her.

"I didn't hear what you said."

"Where were you?" But she didn't wait for his reply. "Jorie, in the name of love for your mother, I am asking you not to do this. You must resist these animal urges. If you do not, you are no better than they! God did not give us dominion over them for naught."

He was silent.

"It is a weakness of the flesh," she continued, "and you do not have to give in to it. You can overpower it with self-discipline and the help of God."

She paused. "Do you remember how you learned to overpower your resistance to punishment? Discipline, Jorie. The mind has dominion over the body."

Still he was silent.

"Let us pray together."

She retrieved her Bible, and read a passage about abstaining.

"Get down on your knees, Jorie."

He protested. Catherine said, "Shall I call Helena in to witness?"

"No!"

When they were both kneeling, she closed her eyes.

"Mary, pray for us sinners now and at our hour of death. Blessed is the fruit of thy womb, Jesus, and blessed is the fruit of *my* womb, Jorie. We ask that thou help him in overcoming this temptation of the flesh, so inappropriate at his tender age. Give him the strength to fight off these demons and rise victorious above them. In the name of the Father, the Son and The Holy Ghost. Amen."

"Amen," Jorie mumbled.

"Keep praying, Jorie. Go up to bed now."

He got up slowly, and as he was leaving the room, she called to him, "Do you remember the *Golden Bubble*, Jorie?"

With his back to her he nodded.

"Think about what it's worth to you."

Catherine knew she was gambling with high stakes. She had to rely on the power of her previous teachings, hoping the ground work had been laid carefully and securely enough for him to make the right choice.

Flashes of her own erotic feelings danced before her, confronted her with questions: *What was it that made his behavior so abhorrent to her? Was it the act itself, or Jorie engaged in it?* She pushed the thoughts away. Enough that instinctively she felt it was wrong, that it violated all her sensibilities.

For five days Jorie abstained. But on the sixth night he again sought release, and many nights after that.

It was not as easy to overcome as his mother supposed.

The stable was a place of quiet solitude for Jorie. His chores had taken him there every day to feed and groom the horses and occasionally to clean out the stalls. Although he cared nothing for riding, he enjoyed grooming them and felt great fondness for Falstaff, often talking to him and bringing him apples. Jorie rather liked the odors in the stable—the particular mixture of leather, hay and animal smells. When his work was done he could make himself a comfortable bed of straw and get lost in daydreams. He fancied no one knew he used it as his secret lair. At thirteen he thought he'd reached an unspoken truce with his mother. She no longer made him undergo the painful inquiries into his sexual habits. He wasn't sure if she accepted it, or assumed he no longer indulged.

On one particular warm September afternoon, after finishing the mucking out and replacing the old straw with new, he decided to have a lie-down in his favorite corner. Breaking open a bundle of clean straw, he unraveled it under himself, relaxed in the sweetness of the soft sounds coming from the stalls. The tender breezes and late afternoon sunlight found their way through the door at the far end of the barn.

Soon his hands were fumbling with the buttons on his fly, and within moments he was in an ecstasy which defied obedience to any but the powerful drive within. She had said, *we are not animals, we must govern the body,* but here in this most animal of places he could not help himself, had barely tried to for some time now. Here, by himself, he was able to relegate the guilt to some dark recess of his mind—for at least as long as the rapture lasted.

Carol A Sheldon

Caught in the vortex of carnal pleasure, he did not hear her footsteps or even the welcoming whinny of her horse.

Not until he'd finished did he become aware of his surroundings. Only then did he open his eyes to see her towering over him.

Fear exploded in his belly, but it was his shame that overpowered him.

"Get up!"

He scrambled to his feet, yanking at his pants.

"No. Drop your britches."

With mortifying difficulty he did as he was told, stood there exposed in his mother's presence. For a long time she just looked at him, slowly up and down, while he stood shaking before her. *Had she watched the whole thing? Had she seen his swollen penis, his hand pumping it up and down?* He could not bear to think of it.

Finally she declared, "You must be punished. You know that."

Would she tell Papa? Would the beatings return, worse than before?

She moved a few feet away, pushed aside the straw that covered a large flat stone that had been left in its bed when the ground had been prepared for the stable.

"Come here, Jorie."

He started to pull up his pants so he could navigate the space between himself and the rock.

"No, I told you to leave them down. Get over here."

Barely knowing what he was doing, he obeyed, shuffled toward her.

"Kneel. Kneel on this stone."

What was she going to do? He knelt on the cold stone, feeling its uneven points dig into his knees. He thought his mortification was complete when she made him stand before her with his britches around his ankles, gazing at him. But then he had not anticipated this.

"Put your head and chest down until they touch the ground... Yes. Now push your backside up in the air. Higher...Place your arms out at your sides. Reach, as far as you can."

He waited, eternally, it seemed, knowing she was watching him, taking in every crevice of his shame. How could he ever look at her again? His outstretched hands scratched through the straw; his nails dug into the packed earth beneath.

"You will wait here, in just this position, until I decide what to do with you. It may be some time. I needn't tell you the distress this causes me. It is a *violation*, against God, against *me!* You knew that, and you must atone for it."

She left him then. As he remained in this mode of penance he wept deeply with an anguish he didn't know his soul possessed. When the sobs had finally subsided, and his body ached to collapse on the ground, still he kept his position, not from fear, but contrition. The imprisoned guilt, broken loose from its confinement, came flying out with all its condemnation. He had betrayed the only person in the world who loved him, the only one he loved. Like the prince in the fairy tale, his disloyalty would doom him for all eternity. He could not forgive himself; he could find no peace.

The soft shadows and sunlight of the afternoon had forsaken him. It was dark now, he was shivering from the cold that had descended upon the evening, and still she did not come. Once he awoke suddenly as his exhausted body tumbled to its side. Righting himself quickly, he took stock of his surroundings. He could tell by their breathing that even the horses were asleep. The barn swallows were coming home to roost. Night had fallen.

Focusing on the sounds to keep himself awake, he listened to the owl's soft hoot, its mate's reply. He caught the scuttle of mice running across the dirt floor; from the woods he heard the death cry of a small animal defeated by its captor.

Finally, he noticed a light from a lantern cast its glow in the darkness.

Was it his mother, or had she sent his father?

"Get up now," she said softly.

He felt like an old man trying to rise. His knees didn't seem to work as he broke them open. Finally standing unsteadily, he felt the terrible cramping in his calves, thighs, back and arms. He was afraid he might collapse as he waited further instruction. But anything she would do now would be better than what he'd endured.

"Pull your pants up."

Clumsily he did so.

"Now go to the house and up to bed."

"Aren't you going to punish me?"

"Have you not been punished enough these past hours?"

"Yes, yes I have," he said, buttoning his trousers.

"Then go to bed. We'll say no more tonight."

He was glad she went on ahead of him. She did not see him go down twice on his way to the house.

"Where was Jorie at suppertime?" Thomas asked his wife as she came back to the house.

"He was being punished."

"What did he do to bring on your displeasure?"

"I found him—abusing himself."

"You found him what?"

Catherine reddened. "Pleasuring himself."

Thomas snorted. "Every boy does that."

The casual remark flattened her. She sucked in her breath.

"He had been specifically told not to, that it was a violation against God!"

"That's a lot of bollix, Catherine."

"The Bible—"

"—Would prefer us all to be celibate, but then how would we produce children to glorify God?"

"Surely, you don't mean to say—"

"Glad to hear there's something normal about him."

"Thomas—"

What do you imagine other boys do with their sexual urges? Have you never thought of that?"

"No, I never have. Oh, Blessed Mary!"

He laughed. "Either that, or find a handy ewe."

"Ah! How can you jest so?"

"Not a jest, my dear. Not a jest at all."

"Oh, that is horrible! Disgusting!"

Thomas laughed again as he moved toward her.

"You can't mean to say that it's right for him to handle himself so—that I should tell him to go ahead!"

"Don't tell him anything. Boys do what boys do. Best to turn your back and ignore it."

He laughed. "Put all the fancy dress on us you like, Catherine, we are still animals."

"We are not!"

"We shall see about that, my little ewe."

The conversation had aroused Thomas. He pulled his wife toward him, and said lightly, "Now I'd like a little 'ewe' tonight."

Despite her long hunger, she was offended at this treatment. But he marched her up the stairs to her room, tossed her on her bed, and threw up her skirts.

"Turn over," he commanded.

"Thomas! Are you mad?"

"I see I have to do it for you." He flipped her over, pulling her bloomers down in one swift motion.

"Aw, you've still a beautiful white ass, my dear."

"Stop it!"

He pushed her higher up on the bed. His powerful hands grasped her flesh while he ignored her objections. He squeezed until the protests stopped.

"Wait," he directed.

He left her for a moment, and she was shamed to realize she had not the will to even attempt an escape.

Returning with the blue jar, he put an ample amount of its contents inside her.

"Now if I were truly to take you as a ewe, there'd be no balm to soften the sting of my arrow as it finds its mark. But I still treat you as a lady," he said lightly.

With no further ado he invaded her, ignoring cries of pain which soon evolved into moans of pleasure, as he knew they would.

Abruptly he paused. "You see, my dear, you too are an animal, as I have just proven."

She pushed against him.

"You do grasp my point." He laughed at his pun, as he rammed in deeper.

As she moaned he rode to the finish hard and fast. When he was spent, he rolled off her and lay on the bed apart.

Catherine was angry with him, angrier still with herself. Her body had betrayed her. How could she hope to train Jorie to rule his physical urges if she had no dominion over her own?

He pulled her roughly toward him.

"How's that for lessons? I rest my case."

She tried to pull away.

"Aw, Lass, don't take it all so seriously. Some day I'll take you down to the barn and we'll pretend we're young gypsies a-rollickin' in the hay."

Lying alone later that night she looked at her own blindness. She had to admit that if she had thought about other lads giving themselves relief in this way, it wouldn't have bothered her. She had to ask why, then, was she so upset with Jorie?

Ugly glimpses of her possessiveness came twisting through her mind. Having questioned her own motives, she could not now find the key to stopping them. She didn't want to know more, but still the fact overflowed its banks, flooded her knowing: *Because he's mine.*

She shook with the truth, which was too uncomfortable to countenance, and tried to push it out of her head. She spent a restless night, and by morning knew what she must do.

She went to his room, sat on the side of his bed, her hands in her lap. "Jorie, I have wronged you. In my ignorance I thought I was doing right to insist you not touch yourself. But I do not know as much about such things as your father does. When I told him—"

"You told Papa!"

"He asked me why you were being punished and I had to tell him."

Jorie's heart sank.

"He said, 'All boys do that.'"

Jorie couldn't believe his ears. A great silent sigh of relief flowed from his toes upward through his whole body.

"I don't think that makes it right. I'm sure it's a sin, but perhaps I shouldn't have...You'd better speak to Father Dumas about it." She waited for him to take this in.

Jorie moved his stiff body slightly, swallowed. He'd gone to bed in misery and shame. Exhausted, he'd fallen in and out of a fitful sleep. He'd thought he heard noises coming from his mother's room, but was too weary to give it his attention. In the morning, he'd re-experienced all the shame and pain of the previous night, covered his head with his pillow and tried to find the sweet balm of slumber. But sleep would not return. He had struggled to bend his crippled knees, forced himself to flex them until they would bear his weight when he stood up. But it was extremely painful to walk, and having no wish to go anywhere, he had returned to bed.

When she'd opened the door, he thought there would be more talk of punishment. What he was hearing now astounded him.

Grateful that she'd been brave enough to say she'd erred, he found something frightening about it too. It was as though the lamp that led the way had been extinguished. He had trusted her implicitly, even when he was angry with her. Now he saw her for the first time, not as the idol he worshipped, but *equally fallible,* small and pathetic.

He was quiet for so long, she rose to leave. "I think we'd better stop our...education. For the time, at least. Perhaps I am not a suitable teacher for you."

She waited mournfully for a response, received none and left the room.

A cacophony of voices rang through his head.

She apologized. Forgive her, you dog!

How could she have shamed me so? For something normal?

Is it wrong, or not?

And the biggest one of all, that brought the angry tears: Why did she come back and break the *Golden Bubble?* He didn't see how they could continue their voyage into the inner world now. There was no one at the *helm.*

For days the rain came down unrelentingly. Mirroring Jorie's mood, it made everything muddy, brought a bone-chilling dampness into the house that no fire could temper. It was the ugliest fall he could remember: dark clouds swirled in the angry skies and the merciless winds brought the maple leaves down before their glorious colors had played their hour upon the trees.

His mother carried on with a distant dignity, but there was no closeness between them. The gap between them grew like a great yawning abyss. He realized he'd made an irrevocable choice that day in his room. She had waited, humbled after her confession, and he had not absolved her. She would not come to him now and beg for his understanding. And he could not bring himself to cross the gorge to meet her, though the pain was nigh intolerable.

Even the hills, so healing and peaceful to him were being punished by the gods. Usually, when the waters of heaven were so violently unleashed, the storm lasted only a few hours. Now it seemed the torrents would never end, and Jorie wondered who would build the next ark. Certainly he would not be among the chosen.

He did his chores with alacrity, and sought his own company as quickly as possible. But here he was miserable too. Looking for diversion, he tried to read books he'd once loved. Impatiently, he'd discard them after a chapter or two. Dissatisfied with his drawings, he threw them in the fire. His inner world was shattered; the outer was nothing without her. Again he was walking on broken glass, but this time it was shifting beneath his feet.

When he could stand it no longer, at the end of the most confining week, he put on his oil slicker and forged his way in the dark out into the driving rain, seeking to spill his explosive feelings. Tramping up the hill and slipping in the mud, he was beaten unmercifully by the teeth of the rain that slashed at his face. Reaching the birch copse at last he threw himself down on the ground and wept into the earth. His sobs, absorbed by the storm, made no sound. A feeling of total insignificance overcame him, a tiny speck unnoticed in a vast uncaring universe. When he was spent, he rolled over on his back and let the rain slash at his face. It was the only clean thing in this world.

Exhausted, he rolled over on his face again and fell asleep. He didn't care what happened to him; it was hours later before he awoke from a stupored sleep and dragged himself through the rain back home.

Catherine, believing him to be asleep in his room, had made no search. It was not until the next day when he didn't come down for breakfast that she went up to rouse him and found him feverish. When she saw the heap of wet and muddy things on the floor she surmised where he'd been.

"Good Lord, lad, have you lost your senses? Out in that misery last night to catch your death? How long were you gone?"

Jorie shook his head, tried to say something, gave up.

Seeing his torpor she knew he was ill, his teeth chattering and chills shaking his crumpled body.

She hurried into the kitchen. "Helena, build up the fire, and heat water for a hot bath. Jorie's chilled to the bone."

When all was ready, Catherine helped Jorie down the stairs. He saw the housekeeper.

"I can't go in with *her* there."

It was too late. Helena came to the doorway. "Begod and bejasus, Look at you, with a face like you'd seen the deevil himself. Puts me in mind of—"

"Just pour the water in the tub, Helena."

"Oh, I was just havin' a bit 'o fun, mum."

"Well, now's not the time. Go tend to his room, please."

"Will I be doin' the wash?"

"Just go, Helena."

The woman left and Catherine seated Jorie on a chair, where she proceeded to remove his nightshirt and help him into the steaming water.

The tub being small, she dipped a small blanket in it and wrapped it around his shoulders. When it cooled, she repeated the process.

"Better get out now," she said when the tub water cooled, "before you catch a worse chill."

Helena had removed the muddy clothes and changed his sheets. Catherine helped him back to bed, fearing pneumonia. Retrieving the feather comforter from her own bed, she tucked him in tightly, bringing it up to his chin.

When she'd done with that she prepared him a pot of hot dandelion tea, which she urged him to drink, against his protests.

Not wanting to leave him, she was yet uneasy with conversation, and lapsed into telling him the old silkie stories again. They had a soporific effect, and at last he slept.

Doctor Johnson confirmed he had pneumonia. He prescribed mustard plasters, came daily, checking his fever, supplying remedies, but the best medicine came from the visits themselves. They often lasted an hour or more.

"You can hear the wolves at night, in the winter, howling up in the hills. I think they're very lonely, sir."

"And hungry."

"I found an injured cub once up in the copse. She was shot for the bounty, I'm sure."

"What did you do?"

"I cleaned her wound, and took scraps to her every day. She'd lick my hand. But one day, when I came, she was gone. Probably the bounty hunters had gotten her."

"Animals know better than we when it's time to move on."

"Do you think she might have survived?"

"I think it quite possible."

Jorie tried to swallow, then coughed.

"Is it painful?" the doctor asked.

"Not really. But I can't get it out. It won't blow out or cough up."

"I know exactly what you mean. Well, son, that too shall pass."

"It feels like a snail crawling slowly down my throat."

Doc Johnson chuckled. "You have a way with words, son."

Jorie had worried all week whether he dared broach this most difficult of subjects with the gentle doctor.

"Could you tell me something about—human reproduction?"

"What would you like to know?"

Jorie flushed.

"Where babies come from?" the doctor asked gently.

"No, I know that much. How it all works—the organs and such."

"I'll bring you a book on anatomy. Would you like that?"

Jorie hesitated.

"Was there something specific, son?"

He blurted it out. "Sometimes—it gets *stiff*."

The doctor nodded. "Oh, I see. Yes, yes."

Jorie coughed. "Is it, is it...*natural*?

"Oh, yes. Yes, that comes with adolescence."

Jorie wished the doctor would say more about this, and tell him *what to do about it*, but he just smiled in his understanding way.

"I don't know." Jorie stammered. "I don't know how to say this."

"Just spit it out."

Jorie took a deep breath. "Is it wrong to, to *rub* it?" he turned his flushed face to the seam in the wallpaper he'd begun to pick at.

The doctor took a moment to respond. "People have different views on that subject. Certainly from a medical point of view, there's nothing wrong with it. Despite all the myths abounding, you won't grow hair on your palms, go blind or any other such nonsense."

"But is it *wrong?*"

"*I* don't think so. But everyone would not agree with me."

Their attention was caught by the chatter of jays outside the window. They looked out to see the male chasing the female from the cherry tree to the elm to the pine.

"All part of nature's plan," the doctor smiled.

Jorie took another deep breath. If it were all right with the doctor, then it would be all right with him. The matter was finally settled.

After five long days, the fever broke, and Doctor Johnson said the crisis was over. The visits tapered off, causing Jorie to be almost sad he was getting well. The doctor was the closest thing he had to a friend. Unless you count Ma.

That night Catherine thanked God that he'd been spared. She had not attended St. Joseph's for several weeks. On Sunday she went, but a different priest was officiating. After mass she inquired of the sister.

"Father Dumas isn't with us any longer. He was transferred to Minnesota."

Minnesota! Catherine could hardly believe it.

Without her old friend, she was again a stranger in a foreign land. She stopped going to church. Anyway, hadn't praying to God directly saved her son?

Jorie had not spoken to her much during this time, except to give brief answers, ask for things. Now he was feeling better and watched her as she changed his bed sheets. A feeling of tenderness came over him as pictures of all she'd done for him this week flashed through his mind. How she loved him. Why had it all been spoiled!

She bade him climb back into bed, and he asked her to apply the liniment. Its pungent smell caused his eyes to water, but as he was still deeply congested, he welcomed it as she generously rubbed it on his chest.

"Would you rub it on my legs too? They're aching."

She pulled down the covers, extracted one leg trying to keep the rest of him covered.

"It wouldn't do to let you get cold."

She noticed the brown hairs growing on his legs, glistening with the oil. He was beginning to lose his boyishness and take on the look of a man. She lingered over the first leg longer than she realized, lost in her reverie. Abruptly she pushed it under the covers and withdrew the other. As she did, she noticed a bulge at his groin.

"That's enough, Ma. The other one isn't aching."

But she had it out, and commenced to rub it anyway. Holding his foot, her long strokes went upward from his ankle to his knee. Then pushing her hand up the back of his thigh she heard him moan softly. His eyes were closed. She covered him then, and left the room.

A sense of jubilance filled her. How silly of her to think the reverent obedience of the son who adored her had vanished. What further proof of her power could she ask than what she had just witnessed in his room? If he'd avoided her these past weeks it was because she herself had failed him by abdicating her throne. There must be no crack in the crown.

chapter 18

HE HAD A feeling she was planning one of her games.

"I'll clear the table, Ma," he said rising. "Then I have to study." His chair scraped against the rough wooden boards of the kitchen floor.

"Not so fast," she said softly, wrapping the left-over bread in the paper he'd helped Helena to wax. "You'll lend a hand with the washing up, and then we'll see."

"*We'll see.*" These words, had come to strike apprehension in his young soul. Beads of perspiration broke out on his forehead as he stacked and clattered the dishes. For once he wished his pa was here.

She chided softly, "You're going to break my grandmother's plates, Laddie. We brought them all the way from Scotland, when I was but a girl."

"Sorry," he mumbled, forcing himself to slow down. After all, why was he in a hurry? "I'll wash."

The large pot of water on the wood stove was already boiling when they brought the dishes to the kitchen. There must be sap in the stovewood, as it crackled and spat loudly—echoing the explosions in his chest. He wanted to tell it to hush, not to shout to all the world his fear, his confusion.

With whatever suds her homemade lye soap began, they were soon defeated by the slippery venison fat sliding off the plates. Jorie watched with fascination as each bubble popped, the greasy circles forming around his hands.

"Lad, what are you doing? You forget yourself."

With a quickening of his heart, he came back to the present. She was waiting for more dishes to wipe. Slowly, but not so slow as to cause further comment, he continued washing the dishes, as her hands caressed each cup and plate slowly and lovingly. When the dishes were done, and he feared he was finished, he spotted the pots and pans on the stove.

"I'll pour fresh water for the pots," he told her.

"Let's just let them soak overnight," she cooed. "No hurry about them."

"It's all right," he said with a surge of will. "I don't mind." As he propped the back door open with a piece of firewood, the frigid air swooped in like a bird for the kill. He took the dishpan outside, flung the greasy water over the stoop, watched it turn instantly to ice. Returning, he pushed the sleeves of his woolen shirt and his winter underwear up to his elbows, attacked the pots as though in a duel to the death, determined to undo their dirty, begrimed faces. Somewhere in the distance he thought he heard her say, "That's enough, Jorie. They're only pots." But something made him keep scrubbing, polishing, pouring every ounce of his sap into this task.

It was her hand on his shoulder that finally brought him back. The hair on the back of his neck went up, his hands fell limply down in the warm water.

Slowly he opened the door again. This time he drizzled the tired dishwater, watching the last drops glisten in the moonlight as they fell to the snow, the steam rising in the crisp cold of the northern night. In the distance he could hear the clip-clop of a single horse. Probably Mr. Kukkonen coming home late again. He wished he could run to him, help him carry in the bundles of laundry.

"I better bring in more firewood," he stalled.

"Come in, Jorie." She had done with coaxing.

Slowly he returned, closed the door, placed the dishpan on its nail by the stove.

"Follow me." His mother picked up the kerosene lamp on the kitchen table and led him to the back parlor, closing the curtained French doors behind them. The parlor that was saved for special occasions. The parlor the family rarely saw, and hadn't been in since last Christmas. Despite its fancy rug and stuffed furniture, it was always cold, except for special occasions. Tonight there was no fire, no Christmas tree with brightly lit candles. His heart leaped with apprehension, as the room swallowed him.

He watched the shadows dance crazily across the forbidding room as she carried the single lamp to the table.

"Rub my feet," she commanded softly, wrapping herself in a heavy shawl, and placing her small, voluptuous body on the horse-hair sofa. "I've been on them all day, and Lord knows they ache so. I'm sure you're the perfect one to take that pain away," she crooned.

Jorie slid obediently to the floor and grasped his mother's slender ankle, untying her black high top, loosening the laces slowly. Finally, he slipped the shoe off her tiny foot and began rubbing it gently, the way she'd taught him to.

"Grasp it firmly, Jorie, it won't break!" The tinkle of her laughter echoed through the sparsely furnished room.

She smiled indulgently at him as he tried to take back the hot red blotchy rash he knew was giving him away. He imagined his embarrassment always heightened the pleasure she took in him.

Clumsily he rubbed her feet.

"Not so fast, my Precious. Try using a longer stroke, like this." She demonstrated on his arm, while he tried to keep it from shaking.

He continued a few minutes longer, then started to put her shoes back on.

"No, leave them off, Jorie. Too late for shoes. Run get my slippers, there's a good lad."

He left the room, wishing desperately there were some escape, some way not to return.

"What's taking so long?"

He came slowly down, crouched again before her, ready to wiggle the slippers on to her feet.

"Didn't you notice something, Jorie?" she stopped him.

He hated it when she asked questions like that—making him feel stupid and knowing he was about to be told something he didn't want to know.

"Feel my stocking—the one on my foot. There, a little higher on my ankle. All that time you were feeling your mother's foot, didn't you *notice* anything?"

He could feel the rash popping out again—the prickle and the heat, running down his neck like the hot wine he'd been given at Christmas time.

"What was I supposed to notice?" he mumbled, staring at the floor.

She pulled something out of her pocket and dropped it in his lap.

"What's that?" he muttered.

"Well, pick it up Laddie. What does it feel like?"

Obediently, because he was unable to be otherwise with her, he picked up the object.

"Well?" she coaxed.

"It's a stocking." He had to say it twice because the first time his words carried no sound.

"Now feel its texture, and then feel the one on Mummy's foot, Dear."

He felt a sort of murkiness come over his brain and knew he was making a fool of himself. His mother waited patiently, seeming to enjoy each tortured moment.

Finally, he came back enough to make contact with the thing in his hand.

"This one's rougher. Rougher material."

"Yes. So that means the one on my foot is—?"

"Softer," he felt the idiot, wondering why her dulcet tones confused him so. He watched as their steamy breath met in the space between them and became one.

"And? Feel it, dear. Learn to discriminate between the feel of things. Just as you do between tastes. You must develop an awareness of all senses and be able to detail them; that will serve you greatly as a writer. "

He shuddered, remembering. *Find the words to describe...*He hoped she wouldn't say that now. He had no words to describe what he was feeling, only a chattering of his teeth, and a familiar sensation in his groin. He wanted to run from her, or to be so young he could lose himself in the comfort of her bosom with innocence. But at thirteen he could do neither.

"Touch it, Jorie."

He hesitated.

He put his fingers on her ankle, could feel her pulse beating there, took his hand away.

"Silk it is," she intoned.

He touched it again—first as though it were a hot coal about to sear him, then slowly, mesmerized by his mother's voice, and the smell of her lilac cologne. He lost all sense of time and forgot how cold he was. A sweet surrender began to overtake him as he felt her soft hands on his curls, welcomed her warm breath on his cheek.

And once again, he knew he'd lost to her. Though all she asked of him was to go to sleep contemplating the sense of touch, and how different textures could evoke different sensations.

That winter brought more snowfall than the young folks had ever seen. All over town, people were erecting high wooden sidewalks three feet above the ground between their homes and the road. When it snowed, it could be swept off with a broom.

The streets were rolled, and snowshoes came out of cellars and sheds sooner than usual, to the annoyance of adults and delight of children. With the wind sweeping across the lake, it wasn't unusual for snow banks to get as high as thirty feet. Some families were so snowed in, their only escape was through an upstairs window.

From his bedroom, where he was working on a Christmas present for Ma, Jorie watched the blizzard continue to swirl around the fruit trees in the circle drive; soon they were so white, that as close as they were, he could no longer make them out.

He wondered if they'd have a Christmas tree this year. With the snow so deep, and Christmas only five days away, Jorie didn't see how they could manage a tree. Well, that was all right with him.

He always felt sorry for the poor tree anyway. All dressed up with cookies, candies and candles—but *dead*. Chopped up a few days later for firewood. He'd read about humans being sacrificed in other cultures, and now imagined a person being killed, then propped up and decorated for some peculiar ritual, later to be burned, like the discarded Christmas trees. How uncivilized it all was.

He'd bought his father a new pipe, and he had finished one present for his mother. Every boy in his industrial arts class had made a two and a half foot long wooden fork for turning the clothes in the boiling water on laundry day. His mother's old one was cracked, so it was a good time to replace it.

Now he was working on a diary for her. He knew she wrote regularly, and she'd mentioned that the last was almost full. Larger than the others, with wooden covers, it had yet to be fixed with a strap and clasp. He'd bought fifty pages to put in it, but others could be added. In a couple more hours he'd have it finished.

His mother and Helena had been busy all week making Christmas cookies and candy. Even his father seemed to appreciate the extra efforts and the special foods prepared for the occasion.

He gave the covers a coat of varnish. In the morning he'd give them another coat, and attach the strap. Then it would be finished. To rid the room of varnish fumes, he opened the window a couple of inches and brushed away the snow that had piled up on the outer sill. He sucked in the cold evening air and slipped into bed.

During the night the wind came up and the snow blew in the window. Jorie awoke to the sensation of a fine mist blowing onto his face. The storm was over, and with an almost full moon shining in the clear sky, he could see the dusting of snow covering the floor between the window and his bed.

Sounds came to him from another room, as though someone was being hurt. He lay absolutely still and listened. Another groan and muffled cry.

His mother!

He crept silently down the hall in his white nightshirt. He opened her door softly, but was stopped short by what he saw.

In horror he watched his father grunt and thrash about on top of his mother. She was moaning, gasping.

He wanted to yell out to his father to stop! He must do something to protect her. But he stood frozen in his tracks.

Then he saw his father sink his hands in her long un-pinned hair and pull her head back, causing her to arch her back and cry out.

Suddenly, he sprang to action in a stabbing fit of passion. With no thought for his own safety, he lunged for his father, grabbed him by the shoulder and yanked him off his mother.

Momentarily startled beyond comprehension, with the help of the moonlight streaming through the window, Thomas quickly recognized the ghostly apparition standing over him. He came to a full seething rage, rose from the bed and smacked his son hard across the face with the back of his hand, sending him flying against the wall.

"What the hell do you think you're doing?" he boomed.

Reeling from pain and shock, Jorie could only blink back.

"This is not your room! You are never to come in here! Do you understand?" his father thundered.

Catherine concurred with Thomas. "How could you blunder into your parents' bedroom like a three year old? For God's sake you are thirteen! What in the world were you thinking?"

Dizzily, Jorie staggered back to his bed, where he lay miserably in a curled up heap under all his covers. Although his cheek was radiating shooting pains in all directions, it was his mother's words that hurt the most. Her words and his own self-loathing. He had seen animals fornicate, but there in his mother's sanctuary, he had not imagined his parents capable of such beastly behavior. And she had been in pain...Hadn't she?

How could he have been so far off the mark?

He heard someone coming down the hall, and hoped it was his mother, come to soften her words. But the steps were too heavy. Now he knew it was his father, and freezing in terror, he waited to receive more punishment for his terrible invasion of parental privacy.

But the footsteps passed, and Jorie breathed again. His father would be going back to his own room. Jorie couldn't remember the last time his father had been in his mother's bed. His thoughts were all a jumble. Had his mother actually been *enjoying* it? How dreadful, if that were true, that he'd charged in like a jealous lover, and interrupted something she found pleasure in. *But how could she?*

In the morning the throbbing soreness on his face forced him into consciousness, immediately reviving the memory of last night, invading every sinew in his body with guilt and remorse.

He wondered if he had ever really believed she was being hurt. Maybe he just didn't want his father there with her, doing *that*. He felt betrayed. She'd made him feel he was the special one, and just sometimes she had to say things to keep the waters calm between her and Pa.

A sullen truce fell between Jorie and his parents. On Christmas morn Thomas presented his wife with a new woolen robe, and Catherine gave her husband a vest she'd knitted. Jorie offered his mother the laundry fork he'd made at school, but did not feel inclined to present her with the new diary.

It was a solemn time, with less cheer than Jorie could remember on any previous holiday. Soon Pa left to spend the rest of the day with his other family members.

The holidays offered no relief from chores, especially with Helena given a few days off. When he came downstairs the day after Christmas, half the morning was gone. Even before he got to the kitchen, the smell of steaming wool underwear was the harbinger of wet laundry. Piles of dirty clothes lay about the floor, sorted by color. The clothesline had been strung on its hooks across the kitchen, back and forth, and his mother was stirring the clothes on the stove with the new laundry fork.

She heard him but did not turn to look. She spoke sharply. "As you can see I'm very busy. I haven't time to fix your breakfast now."

"Can I have this bread?"

"Yes. And there's some bacon." She nodded to the warming shelf on the stove.

He ate the bacon and bread, grateful for the laundry that hung between them, obscuring her view of him. She was clearly stewing over something. He had no way of knowing whether it was what he'd done earlier that week, a spat with his father, or something to do with the laundry.

"When's Helena coming back?"

"Not until Thursday, and the clothes won't wait. You'd better get out of that filthy underwear," she spoke sharply. "I need to wash it. Put on something clean."

"Are you angry with me?"

She was silent.

"What did I do now?"

The bubbling of the boiling water on the stove pretty much summed up his mother's mood, he thought.

"Well, don't tell me, then."

Her angry face, haloed by a wreath of steam, appeared suddenly between the shirts she jerked apart. "Don't you talk to me that way, lad."

"Well, if you're going to be cross with me, I ought to at least know why!"

"You ruined things between your Father and me. Is that reason enough?"

So it was that again. "I was trying to protect you from him!" he shouted.

"I didn't need protection!" she shouted back.

"Then what was all that moaning and groaning about?"

"I'll hear no more of your impudence!" she yelled, waving the new laundry fork in his face. For a moment he thought she was going to strike him with it.

Suddenly she saw what she had in her hand, dropped it and disappeared behind the laundry, crying.

He saw the expanding puddles on the floor caused by the dripping laundry. This weekly chore had caused the boards to warp over the years. Jorie fetched the mop, and ducking the clothes, began to clean up the mess.

He had never been able to stand his mother weeping. Pushing through the wet laundry, he went up behind her, put his arms around her, dropped them, put them back on her shoulders. "I'm sorry, Ma."

She stooped down and picked up the laundry fork. "It's beautiful, Jorie. I'm upset, but I shouldn't be taking it out on you."

Jorie thought now would be a good time to give his mother the diary. It might cheer her up.

"I have another present for you, Mum. It wasn't finished on Christmas. I'll just run up and get it."

When he returned she wiped her reddened hands on her apron and looked at the wrapping. "When did you draw this? It's lovely." She was studying the picture he'd wrapped it in—a drawing of the veranda last fall, with the vines laden with grapes in their fullness.

"Aren't you going to open it?"

Slowly she took the paper off, carefully setting it aside.

Jorie watched her reaction. First he heard a little gasp, and then staring at the diary, he saw her start to shake. "Mum, what's the matter?"

She pulled him to her lap like a little boy, hugging him tightly.

"Oh, my Darling. This is the most precious gift I've ever received, because you thought of it and made it yourself."

She freed one hand to caress the book. "It's beautiful, and how long you must have worked on it."

"Why are you crying?"

She buried her head in his shoulder. "I have not been fair to you. The other night...you couldn't have known. I'm just a wicked woman to yell at you so. And now you've given me this."

"It's all right." He tried to stand up, but she was pulling him back.

"I love you, Jorie. You know that, don't you?" She tugged at him.

"Yes. And I love you."

She searched his eyes. "Do you? Do you truly?"

"You know I do."

He had to get away. He stood up before she could stop him, and tried to bring her attention back to the book.

"Do you like what I wrote on the cover?"

"'This diary belongs to Catherine Radcliff, given to her by her son Jorie, December, 1895.' Oh, my precious! I shall treasure it always."

chapter 19

IN THE SPRING Jorie thought his mother seemed happier, but more distant. He had to deal with a strangeness in her for which he had no road map. It often seemed, as it did today, that when he wanted to converse with her he had to bring her back from a faraway place. Then she would smile sweetly at him as if he'd been gone for a long while.

As they were finishing lunch he asked, "Ma, can I take my bicycle down to the shop?"

"Jorie, you're growing so fast!"

He repeated the question. "The rim is crooked. I want to see if they can fix it."

"'May I'," she corrected him.

"Well, may I?"

"Yes, you may. And pick up two pounds of starch while you're in town for your father's shirts, and some lemons, if they have any." She placed a quarter in his hand. "Save a penny or two to buy yourself an ice-cream."

He started to dash out the door.

"Wait. I have something very important to tell you." She motioned for him to sit beside her at the table.

"What is it?" His foot was jerking impatiently.

She didn't answer, brushed some crumbs from the cloth, and seemed to be puzzling over how to begin.

Finally, she said, "This will change our lives, Jorie."

She looked so serious he was suddenly frightened. "Are you going to die?"

Her laughter startled him.

"Heavens, no. At least I don't think so. What made you say that?"

"I don't know."

Finally she said, "Jorie, you know where babies come from, don't you?"

He turned away, so she couldn't see him flush in the dim light. Why was she doing this? "I'm thirteen, for God's sake, Ma."

"You needn't speak to me that way."

He waited for her to continue.

She patted her belly. "A little brother or sister is growing here for you."

His mind went blank with shock, then scrabbled to make sense of this revelation. Was this some kind of new game of hers? He looked at her closely, trying to read her face.

"Are you jesting?"

"Not at all. It's quite true." She watched him. What are you feeling, Jorie?"

He shook his head.

"Well, are you happy about it?"

"I don't know yet. I'm just surprised."

"Yes, I was sure you would be. You're the first I've told, except your Pa, of course."

He thought she looked disappointed that he expressed no joy in her news. He left her as soon as he could. He did not go into town, but up into the hills by the mine. Thoughts tumbled out of his head like the poor-rock he could see in the distance plummeting from the chute. He knew everything would change. *Wasn't she too old to have a baby? Wasn't he enough for her? Was she telling him he'd failed her in some way?*

He refused to release the hot tears.

She was *happy* about this new child.

A deep sense of betrayal engulfed him.

As if to add insult to injury, shortly before school was out in the spring, Catherine told him he had a job for the summer.

She's trying to get rid of me. "What kind of job?"

"Mr. Foster wants someone to work in his vegetable garden."

"The sheriff?"

"Yes. He asked for you."

"Why?"

"He likes you. You can start going over there after school to turn the soil, and then to plant. Mrs. Foster will show you what to do."

She hadn't even asked if he wanted to. But he liked Mr. Foster. Besides, it would help to keep his mind off the change at home.

He found the sheriff easier to talk to than his father. Earl Foster showed him the green worms that plagued the tomatoes, and told him why he wanted the whole garden bordered with marigolds.

"The smell keeps the rodents away."

"Is that true? I'll have to tell my mother, for her garden."

"I doubt your mother would take to learning from me."

Jorie looked up puzzled.

"We were school chums. Classmates, anyway. But she was smarter than me."

Jorie thought the sheriff had more to say, but Mr. Foster turned back to the garden.

On a warm August evening the baby came. Jorie had been sent to fetch the midwife, and this time she arrived in time. Unable to bear the sound of his mother's cries, he went outside. He sat under the apple tree whittling a stick, wondering if she'd have any time for him with a baby to care for.

And then it was a girl! He supposed if it had to be here, he'd rather it was a brother. What would he do with a sister?

In the weeks that followed, it seemed his mother used him just to fetch things.

"Get the baby's bath ready." "Find the clean rags for her bottom."

But the most fascinating part was seeing his mother nurse little Eliza. Those beautiful breasts he'd only imagined before were now being used like a hog's teats. He wondered if he'd been allowed to suck them when he was a baby. He supposed he had, but he couldn't remember. It struck him that that privilege should be reserved for a time when it could be better appreciated.

Oh, what was he thinking!

Then, just when he was ready to leave the room, his mother suddenly dumped the infant in his lap! "Here, hold her, Jorie."

He looked down at this small creature, no heavier than a small cloud, trying to comprehend that she was his sister. He didn't feel anything for her, anything good, that is.

"Ma, she peed on me!"

Catherine laughed, but Jorie didn't think it was funny at all.

"Well, change her."

"Ma!"

"Here, I'll show you."

"Can't Helena do it?"

"She's busy."

He found this an unsavory task, but before long he'd learned to do it as adeptly as the women.

Except for the nursing, he soon discovered that it was he and Helena in whose care the baby was most often given.

chapter 20

IN HIS SOPHOMORE year Jorie had a new teacher. Her name was Caroline O'Dell and it was her first year of teaching. Jorie liked her right off, but something happened in October that endeared her to him for life.

Someone had taken money from Miss O'Dell's purse the day before. She had not discovered it until she got home that evening. The next day she said that if the money was returned, no more would be said about it.

She waited three days and there was no response. That evening she held the class after school.

"No one may leave this room until my money is returned, or a confession is made."

With no other sound to catch the ear, the ticking of the clock seemed ominously loud. The hands marked off the passing of time as each student looked to his mates for signs of culpability.

Finally, an older boy raised his hand.

"I hate to tattle, Miss, but I seen Jorie Radcliff sneak back in the schoolhouse when you was outside with the rest of us."

A hush fell upon the room as all eyes turned to Jorie. He couldn't believe his ears.

"I have asked for a confession, not an accusation," Miss O'Dell said.

"I didn't take it!" Jorie called out. "And I didn't sneak back into the school. I was outside the whole time we were watching the baby snakes by the creek."

"Thank you, Jorie." She turned to the others. "I am still waiting for a confession."

None was forthcoming, and finally Miss O'Dell dismissed the class.

"Jorie, would you stay a moment, please?"

Jorie's face prickled with humiliation as he felt the accusing glances of the departing students. When they were alone, Miss O'Dell sat in a student desk next to his.

"Do you know anything about this, Jorie?"

"No, ma'am." His feet scraped against the warped boards of the floor.

"I want you to know that I don't believe you took the money. I truly don't. And you're not to worry about it."

Jorie looked at her with great relief and gratitude.

"Thank you. Thank you very much, ma'am."

She shifted her weight, and her serious countenance segued easily in to a smile. I've noticed you like to draw, Jorie. Have you been interested in art for a long time?"

He took a deep breath now that the crisis had passed.

"Yes, ma'am, I have."

"I have a beautiful book at home of animal pictures. Most of the animals are from other countries, such as zebras and anteaters. Would you like to see it? You could try copying these photographs if you like, to practice."

"Oh, yes, ma'am, please!"

"Then I shall bring it to class tomorrow."

When they said good-bye Jorie was ecstatic. She believed him about the money, and she was bringing him a prized possession of hers to study.

"You'll never believe it!" he called to his mother when he entered the house. My teacher is wonderful! Shall I tell you what happened?"

He regaled her with the tale.

"She couldn't help but see you're an honest lad."

"She's so fine. I've never known a teacher like her."

"Let's hope she's schooled enough to stay ahead of you, and advance you in Latin and Geometry."

"I think she's very smart."

"Well, we shall see, shan't we?"

True to her word, Miss O'Dell brought the book for Jorie. It was filled with reprints of pictures taken around the world; Jorie had never seen such detailed likenesses of the creatures of the jungle. He stayed in at recess to study the book, and pored over it at lunchtime.

During the next few weeks his skill in drawing improved dramatically. Miss O'Dell asked if she could mount two of his drawings and hang them on the wall. Jorie felt a happy blush cover his face.

When he told his mother, she replied, "It's about time someone noticed your artistic ability. What does she think of your writing?"

"She said I was the only one in the class who knew how to use adverbs properly."

"That's all?"

"Well, she said I write well."

"I should think so."

Catherine added a sprinkling of water to the pie dough she was making and worked it into the flour.

"Is she pretty?" She shaped the dough into a ball and slapped it on the board.

"Oh, yes, Mum. She's very pretty, and she's only nineteen."

"How do you know that?" She punched the dough, flipped it over, punched it again.

"She said so."

"Why would a teacher tell the class her age?"

"She didn't tell the class, just me."

"And how did that come about?" She massaged the dough into a perfect circle with her rolling pin.

"Well, I figured it out. One day she told me she started drawing at my age. And another time she said she'd been drawing for five years, but still wasn't as good as me."

"I see." She tossed the disk into the waiting pan. "When do you have these tête-à-têtes?"

"Usually at lunchtime, when the others go outside."

"And you don't?"

"Not always. I'd rather draw."

"You need exercise too."

The baby was fussing in her kitchen basket.

"Pick her up, Jorie. You can always calm her down."

Jorie took Eliza in his arms, watched her as she reached inquisitively for his face. "I must draw her," he decided, "in all her sweetness."

Jorie and Miss O'Dell continued to converse before and after school, as well as at lunchtime.

One day he forgot his lunch, and Miss O'Dell said, "I'll share mine with you."

"Oh, I couldn't, Miss. I'll be fine."

"No, I won't eat unless you do too," she replied with a twinkle in her eye.

"All right, if you put it that way."

But he wouldn't take more than the apple and one of three small cookies.

At home, his mother pointed to the lunch pail still on the table, and asked, "How did you manage without your noon meal?"

"Miss O'Dell offered to share hers with me."

"And you accepted?"

"Well, she made me."

"*Made* you?"

"She said she wouldn't eat if I didn't."

"Well, I never!"

Although Miss O'Dell usually stayed after school to check papers, as well as do her chores, she suggested one day that if Jorie would wait a bit, she could leave early, and they could walk together until their paths parted. Delighted, Jorie helped her with the chores—drawing water from the well for the drinking bucket, bringing in firewood for the stove and sweeping the floor.

As they walked along the lake road she told him a little about her life, how she had been brought up on a farm near Lake Linden, and had then gone to school for two years in Redridge to get her Life Certificate for teaching. She said she didn't know the Houghton-Hancock area very well yet, but had recently been attending a church, and hoped to become more acquainted with the people.

"Are you married?" he ventured.

"Goodness, no. If I marry, I'll lose my job."

"That doesn't seem fair."

"Well, the school board has its reasons, I suppose."

"Did you ever have a beau?" Jorie wanted to take the words back, but Miss O'Dell didn't seem to mind the question.

"Once. Back home." She looked wistful. "He was an engineer. But when he finished at the university, he took a job in South America, and I, well, I studied to be a teacher."

"You must be lonely, then."

"You know all about that, don't you?" She surprised him.

Well, of course, she must have noticed that he didn't mingle much with the others. Perhaps that's why she'd brought the book, to let him save face by giving him something else to do at lunchtime.

"I'm sorry." She touched his shoulder.

"Oh, no ma'am. It's true, I don't seem to be able to mix with the other lads very well. I'm no good at sports and no one seems to like the things I do. Except," he swallowed, "Frederick."

"I seldom see you together."

"My mother prefers I not associate with him."

He was sure Miss O'Dell saw the twitch in his cheek. "You would have liked him for a friend?"

Jorie lowered his head and nodded. He told her what his mother had asked of him.

"Does she often ask you to make sacrifices?"

Jorie hesitated. Suddenly he was in deeper than he'd realized. He'd already said too much, but he didn't know how to stop.

"Well, sometimes. She believes sacrifice strengthens character, and is an act of love." He hesitated. "Do you believe that, Miss O'Dell?"

She answered slowly. "Sometimes, I suppose, under certain circumstances. What sort of sacrifices does she ask of you?"

"Oh, mostly little things—like going to bed without supper, or sitting for awhile without doing anything—just thinking."

"Thinking? About anything in particular?"

"Yes, she gives me assignments, you could say."

Jorie thought that perhaps Miss O'Dell could see that he was uncomfortable. She said only, "Well, I'm sure she has her reasons."

"Like the school board," he smiled.

They laughed at that, and spontaneously, without knowing why, Jorie hugged Miss O'Dell. Then he was so embarrassed he grabbed his lunch pail and took off.

"What did you and Miss O'Dell talk about today?" Catherine handed him a scone fresh from the oven.

He looked for an escape. "Where's Eliza?"

"I asked you a question."

Jorie scanned his recent conversation quickly. What part of it could he tell her without arousing her ire?

"Not much. She told me she had a beau once, but he went to South America, and she couldn't get married anyway, because the school board didn't allow it."

"I see."

Catherine would bide her time. No point letting Jorie know how upsetting these conversations were to her, how inappropriate for a teacher to take a pupil into her confidence. She would gather more information.

While Jorie was sweeping the classroom floor the next week, Miss O'Dell offered him a chocolate. He shook his head. "I'm not having sweets this week, Miss O'Dell, but thank you very much."

She frowned. "Another sacrifice?"

"Yes, ma'am. But it's not because I did anything wrong. It's not punishment."

"Whose idea was it?"

"My mother's. But I didn't have to. I never have to—it's up to me."

"Do you always follow her wishes in this regard?"

"No. But we get along better when I do."

Miss O'Dell nodded.

"She says it helps to keep our bond strong."

Suddenly Miss O'Dell changed the subject. "Are you planning to go on to college?"

"I'd like to."

"I think it would be splendid if you could go to the University of Michigan. Have you heard of it?"

"Yes." He got excited. "That's where Frederick wants to go! It's downstate near Detroit, isn't it?"

"Ann Arbor, yes. I wanted very much to go there, as my beau was there. They have several different colleges—everything from Law School to the College of Literature, Science and Arts."

"They allow women?"

"They do now, since 1870. But I didn't have the money. I have dreamed of it often—the great variety of studies, the grand buildings, standing as silent sentries to higher education."

Miss O'Dell seemed far away and Jorie waited patiently for her to come back. When she did, she seemed embarrassed, and Jorie felt sad to think she'd been denied something she wanted so badly.

She pulled herself together. "Forgive me, I do tend to romanticize it."

"No, it's all right. I want to know all about it. Please."

"There's a very large square, with a diagonal walk running from one corner to the other. Almost all the buildings are on the perimeter of this square. No runaway horses to watch out for. Very pastoral, with a few sheep grazing, I'm told. I can picture it all in my mind."

Jorie wondered how she knew so much.

"My friend wrote letters for a time, describing the campus to me. I think it must be beautiful. Oh, Jorie, you should go!"

The subject of Women's Suffrage was a hot topic all across the nation, with raging debates and impassioned speakers extolling the woes or blessings of women getting the vote. Beginning in the eighties, it would fire up, then die down, and every now and then burst into emotional flames again. Miss O'Dell led a discussion in her classroom, and encouraged everyone to study both sides of the issue, and speak their mind on the subject.

After school one day she told Jorie that *The Copper Country Evening News* had announced they would be accepting essays addressing the question.

"I think you could write a compelling essay."

"For the newspaper?" He was astounded. "Is this a student project?"

"No, mostly adults will be submitting, I should imagine. But there's nothing said to disqualify students."

He thought about it that night, and looked at the paper to see what he could find out. He read some old papers to get filled in on the subject. He could see the issue met with much resistance from a large portion of the male population. It evoked such questions as, were women truly equal to men? Since it was in their very nature to be soft, receptive, and skilled in the domestic arts, was it fair to expect them to grasp the complexities of politics? If women were expected to strain their minds regarding politics, what implications did this have toward other areas of their lives? What price would marital harmony pay for propagating such ideas? Some said women would vote as their husbands directed in any case, so didn't that put married men at an advantage, giving them in effect, two votes?

He asked Miss O'Dell if she knew any more about the matter.

"Women in Michigan have had the right to vote in school elections for some time now. Some say that was a mistake, as it only whets their appetite for more!"

He could see she was getting excited about it. "Do you have a stand on the subject?"

She smiled, and he dropped his eyes.

"Well, of course you'd be for it. Probably all women are."

"Would you believe that some are not? They feel the affairs of the world should be left to the men, and the business of the home left to them." She paused. "And how do *you* feel about women getting to vote?"

"I'm definitely in favor of it."

"It's the men who vote now, so they're the ones who need convincing. If you could add your masculine voice to others, it might make a real difference."

Jorie blushed. "I'm only fourteen."

"The paper won't ask for your age."

He spent two evenings writing and re-working his piece. On the third day he presented it to Miss O'Dell after school. She read it through silently, nodding gently as she did. When she'd finished, she looked up.

"It's very good."

"Do you think it's convincing enough to print?"

"You must submit it. You will, won't you?"

She offered to mail it for him, and they waited a week to see what would happen. Finally the essay appeared in the paper, no mention made of Jorie's age, stating simply that it was written by Jordan Radcliff of Hancock, which made him feel very grown up.

He hadn't said anything to his family, but they discovered it on the night it appeared.

His mother was jostling little Eliza on her lap. "It's well written, but why didn't you tell me about it beforehand? I could have helped you with it."

"Miss O'Dell didn't think it needed improvement."

The baby was crying.

"Jorie, you are only fourteen. When you wish to do things that are put before the public, your parents have a right to know. You represent the entire family when you speak out like that. You should have shown it to me first."

"Are you angry with me? I thought you'd be pleased."

Catherine looked at Eliza. "Oh, you are the fussy one." She got up and put her in her basket. "I must get the supper on."

The baby bawled louder than ever. When Jorie picked her up she stopped crying immediately. It pleased him that he was able to calm her so easily.

Later, after reading the evening paper, his father slapped him on the back and said, "Good job, lad. A fine piece of work."

He was so dumbfounded by this praise he stood speechless. But he was proud indeed to have won a point with this hard taskmaster. When Pa smiled, it seemed his head came out of dark clouds.

Jorie wondered if he were in love with his teacher. Sometimes he wished he was as old as she was, and that he could court her. She was too lovely to 'die on the vine', an expression he'd read in a novel.

He was telling her about the hill behind his house one day.

"It's very dark and still, especially when there's no moon—a beautiful place to look at the stars and meteors. And last year it was grand, watching the aurora borealis. All those colors, bursting from the heavens. I tried to capture it on paper. But it's hard to draw light. Did you see it, Miss O'Dell?"

"One night I did, yes."

"Do you have a starline?"

"What do you mean?"

"It's an invisible path that goes from your special star to you. Only sometimes it is visible, if you concentrate very hard you can see it. And messages travel along this line."

"What kind of messages?"

Jorie caught himself. "I shouldn't be telling you all this. I'll get in trouble."

"What kind of trouble?"

"My mother thinks certain things shouldn't go outside the family—most things, actually."

"Will you be asked to make another sacrifice?"

"If she feels I disobeyed, she might punish me."

"How does she punish you, Jorie?"

"It's not always the same. She likes me to think of new ways." Now he knew he'd gone too far. He felt his sphincter muscles contract.

"Do you want to tell me about it?"

He shook his head. "I can't. I'd best be going."

When he reached home his mother was angry. "Where were you all this time? With that teacher, I suppose."

"Yes."

"I don't want you staying after school with her."

"I like to talk to her."

"Why? Most lads are glad to get out of school. It's not natural, hanging on to the teacher like that, after everyone's gone home."

"I don't hang on to her. She likes me, and it's easy to talk to her."

"Did you tell her things you shouldn't? What have you told her?"

"Nothing."

"Tell me." She waited. "I know you tell her things. I'll have none of your mendacity!"

Jorie swallowed, shifted in his chair. "I mentioned my starline."

"Your star—What must she think of you—spouting such gibberish? What else?"

"I told her you were very intelligent and taught me a lot of things."

She was bearing down on him. "Go on. There is no room in the *Golden Bubble* for anything but total veracity."

Jorie listened to the crickets sound their evening song. And then he was riding Peggythis far from home, straight up his starline.

"Don't prevaricate with me!"

Her shrill voice brought him back.

"I told her once about making sacrifices." He saw his mother's eyes widen. "I explained that it builds a strong bond between us."

The words turned to ash in his mouth.

"I see." She fairly hissed. "And did you fail to remember that all of these things are to be discussed solely between you and me? What you have done is pernicious, baneful. You have defiled our *Golden Bubble*!"

He could feel the heat crawl up his neck and a sudden urge to relieve himself.

He watched her trying to contain her anger. "Go to bed, Jorie. Just go to bed."

The letter asking for an appointment had reached the Superintendent, and he had replied that he'd be happy to meet Mrs. Radcliff on Monday next at ten o'clock. On the appointed day, Catherine arrived at his office fifteen minutes early. Dressed in an attractive but modest navy blue suit and wearing no make-up, she thought she looked appropriate for the occasion. She sat in the corridor eagerly awaiting the interview, the letter in her hand.

With the certainty of one who knows the correctness of their mission, she had no cause for apprehension. Besides, she knew by his name this Mr. Ferguson was a Scot, like herself. Finally, the door to the inner office opened, and she was invited in. A rather small man, Catherine noted, remembering with satisfaction that small men are seldom very sure of themselves.

After introductions, she inquired if he knew which clan his people belonged to. He brightened, and she explained that she too, was a Scot, her maiden name being MacGaurin.

He shook her hand heartily, and for a few moments they exchanged stories about the old country, Mr. Ferguson explaining apologetically, that he had never actually been there, his knowledge coming strictly from his forbears.

With the bond of common heritage established, Catherine launched her mission.

"I would like to talk to you about my son's teacher, Miss Caroline O'Dell."

"Oh, yes, our new teacher—very dedicated."

"Verisimilitude." Catherine raised her eyebrow.

"Excuse me?"

"Dedication is the face she would have you see. However, Miss O'Dell oversteps her role as teacher in the following several ways." She handed the letter to Mr. Ferguson.

As Mr. Ferguson read the list of grievances, Catherine recited them.

"She keeps my Jorie after school to help her with her chores so they can walk home together like school chums. She shares intimate details of her life with him, such as her broken engagement, and how if she married, she wouldn't be allowed to teach."

Catherine could see Mr. Ferguson start to work his mouth.

"Your son told you this?"

"He did. He is very open with me. In addition, she inquires into Jorie's home life, prying out of him the most intimate details of our family. I find these conversations totally inappropriate."

"An example, if you please, Mrs. Radcliff."

"She demands to know the exact nature of discipline which he receives at home. This is none of her concern, Mr. Ferguson."

The superintendent gave a noncommittal nod.

"She treats him differently than other students—he's clearly her pet. And she encourages him to covet that which is unobtainable."

"And what is that?"

"She has whetted his appetite for the University of Michigan. I cannot afford to send my son so far from home for his advanced studies. We have a perfectly good college here in Houghton, and he can board at home."

"You refer to The Mining School."

"Yes."

"Perhaps she thought your son's interests lay elsewhere."

"Indeed! But the curriculum is very broad here, I'm told. This arena too, is out of her domain." Catherine took a deep breath and reined in her emotions. "In summary, Mr. Ferguson, Miss O'Dell's behavior is totally improper."

"Well, I shall have a talk with her."

"Mr. Ferguson, it is not a *talk* that I am after. These are grievous charges against her character. When you've read my letter in its entirety, you will see that I do not believe she should be allowed to continue influencing the minds of our young people. I am asking that she be discharged immediately!"

"I understand your position, Mrs. Radcliff. I will bring your letter to the attention of the school board, which meets next Thursday. It will be up to them to make a decision in this matter."

"But they will act on your recommendation, will they not?"

"It is no easy task to find competent teachers willing to brave northern Michigan's winters. Especially on short notice."

"Nevertheless, these are serious charges, which cannot go unattended."

"I will make sure the board understands your grievances." Mr. Ferguson rose.

Catherine put one last effort into her farewell, giving Mr. Ferguson her most captivating smile.

"I'm sure you'll do everything possible to persuade them to our way of thinking."

Miss O'Dell had not looked happy all day. She never smiled at him once, and after school she went straight to grading the math papers.

"Miss O'Dell, is something wrong?" Jorie asked.

"I think you'd best run along home."

"But I'd be happy to sweep the floor before I go."

"That won't be necessary, Jorie."

The teacher continued to study the papers she was grading and didn't look up.

"Did I do something wrong, Miss?" he ventured.

Finally she put down her red pencil and looked into Jorie's puzzled face.

"Has your mother said nothing to you?"

"What do you mean?"

"It is not my place to discuss this with you. You'd best ask your mother."

"About what?"

"That's all I can say. Run along, Jorie." She picked up her red pencil and began making check marks again.

Jorie sped all the way home, flew in the door, and confronted his mother. "What did you say to Miss O'Dell?"

"Close the door and hang up your wraps. Then you may speak to me courteously."

When he was seated he asked again.

"I said nothing to Miss O'Dell. I spoke with Mr. Ferguson, the superintendent."

Jorie paled. "Why?"

"Because your teacher's behavior is totally inappropriate and I have asked for her removal."

Jorie jumped up. "You're trying to get her fired?"

"If that's the word you choose to use."

"It's not fair! She's the best teacher I ever had!"

"I can't agree with you. She's a meddler, Jorie."

"I like her! She's my friend."

"That is part of the problem. She is supposed to be your teacher, not your chum. The two don't mix."

"I don't see why."

"I have said all I have to say. We will know in a few days whether the school board will take action to dismiss her."

Jorie was miserable. After school the next day he tried to apologize to Miss O'Dell for getting her into trouble.

"It's not your fault, Jorie. You mustn't blame yourself."

He bit his lip to stop the quivering.

"Whether or not I'm dismissed, we cannot continue our private talks. You do see that, don't you?"

"Yes." He knew his chin was quivering. "No, I wouldn't want to get you into more trouble."

He started to leave. "Just to say, ma'am, you're the best teacher I ever had, and I'm awfully grateful for everything you've done for me. Whatever happens, I'll never forget you."

He rushed out the door, unable to hold the tears back any longer.

He thrashed in his bed at night, going over and over the way he'd contributed to the predicament Miss O'Dell was in now. He'd told Ma everything, well almost. She'd said he had to—it was part of the covenant they had. Well, damn the *Golden Bubble*. He was sorry he hadn't been loyal to Miss O'Dell.

Carol A Sheldon

He prayed hard for three days that they wouldn't let her go. There'd be an awful hole in his life even if they let her stay, but he'd feel worse if she couldn't keep her job.

On Friday morning, after sleeping little the night before, he approached her before the others came in.

"I can't help it, Miss O'Dell, but I have to know. Does your being here mean they didn't let you go?"

She shook her head. "I don't know yet. I expect to hear sometime today. And even if they decide to let me go, they may want me to stay until they find a replacement."

About mid-morning someone came into the classroom and handed Miss O'Dell a letter. The teacher looked nervous, but laid it aside. At lunchtime, while the others were eating she opened it.

Jorie watched her carefully. When she'd finished, she cast her eyes toward him. He thought she smiled, but he wasn't sure what it meant. He dare not ask her again.

During math in the afternoon his attention wandered. Suddenly he heard her say to the class, "In the spring I will teach you more about geometry. But for now, that's all."

He jerked up and caught her eye. He was certain the remark was made to set his mind at ease. So she hadn't been fired! He wanted to jump up in his seat.

"Well, I'm sure it's only because they couldn't find a replacement for her," his mother said later.

He didn't care what the reason was. He'd won one victory over his mother.

Still, he was downhearted. He imagined he felt like someone who'd lost their sweetheart. She wasn't that much older than he. How humiliating it must have been for her to face the school board. How awful, in her first year, to be made to feel as though she'd done such wrong. He imagined her as very lonely, with no one befriending her at all.

He tried to be as cheerful as he could in class to buck up her spirits, and they still had little talks as she made her rounds among the students. She'd quiz him on material she'd assigned and give him ideas for further study. She was always pleasant and he was grateful for her smiles.

But the special after-school times were gone forever.

In the early spring there was an outbreak of scarlet fever in town, and three of Miss O'Dell's students came down with it.

"Jorie, I'm taking you out of school for the remainder of the term," his mother said. "It's not worth the risk. I will tutor you at home in those subjects—"

"You can't do that!"

"I can and I have."

"I'm going to speak to Pa!"

"Your father supports my decision."

Jorie stewed all evening, and by bedtime had made up his mind. In the morning he was dressed and out of the house before his mother was down. In the dim light he walked to school and waited in the cold, sunless morn for Miss O'Dell to come and unlock the schoolhouse.

When at last she did, he followed her inside.

"Jorie, what are you doing here?"

"I'm not dropping out, Miss O'Dell; I'm going to stay the course."

"I'm afraid I can't let you. I have a letter from your mother."

Jorie's heart sank.

"I cannot disregard it. It's a parent's prerogative, in cases like this. Surely you understand."

Jorie felt angry and miserable, but he managed to say, "I wouldn't want to get you in any more trouble."

He turned to leave.

"Wait," she called. He watched as she carefully chose a number of books. "Take these with you. I know you'll put them to good use."

He managed to say, 'Thank you.'

Their eyes locked for a moment; then he turned and walked away.

He had lost the battle, after all. Ma knew that in the fall Miss O'Dell wouldn't be his teacher. For his last two years, he'd have Mr. Smythe.

Catherine tutored him in Latin and Literature, while Pa instructed him in geology and mathematics. Jorie remained distant with his mother, and Catherine wrote in her diary: *He'll get over it. Puppy love. And he should thank me for saving his life—he'd be the first to succumb, so prone to illness is he.*

But when weeks passed, and he still had little appetite for conversation, she became concerned. He spent long hours in his room alone with his books or his writing.

A month later when Dr. Johnson came, Catherine said, "And to what do we owe the pleasure of your company, Arthur?"

"I've come to see the boy."

"I'm not sick, Doctor" Jorie said.

"Thank God for that."

They went in the parlor, and the doctor showed him the books he'd brought.

Jorie was delighted. "Look at this one—*The Origin of the Species* by Charles Darwin."

"I think you'll enjoy that."

"Oh, yes, sir."

Arthur started making it a practice to stop by once a week, to talk to the boy and bring him books.

chapter 21

FROM DOWN THE hall Catherine could hear little Eliza crying. She lay in bed luxuriating in the knowledge she didn't have to get up. Thank God for Helena. Catherine had discovered she didn't have the enthusiasm or energy she thought she'd have for a baby. Well, the child was here now, and Helena seemed to derive great pleasure in caring for her.

In a moment, she could hear Helena cooing to the baby, and the crying stopped. Catherine stretched, feeling the sinewy tightness of her thighs as she did so. Her hands found her buttocks and realized they were tight and shapely too. At thirty-two, she was still in fine shape. And her face had not suffered the ravages of time that many her age had. She'd always been careful to wear a sunbonnet when in the garden.

Her mind turned to thoughts about Jorie that had been troubling her. He'd been so difficult to reach since she'd taken him out of school. She realized she was paying a heavy price for the course she'd taken.

She must think of something to bring him back to her.

Perhaps he'd open up more if she altered the curriculum. She decided this would be a good time to further his education in art.

In her closet she found her old art books. She could feel the flush on her cheeks as an idea came to her. She tried to sweep it from her mind. When it stubbornly refused to budge, she accepted it, prepared the groundwork.

She took down the books and decided which pictures she'd use. She called Jorie downstairs, and told him she wanted to review some of the art they'd studied.

"Eliza's crying," he said.

"Helena will see to her."

She sat on the sofa, motioning him to sit beside her. Then she opened to the large book.

She spent little time in the review, as she didn't want to lose his attention.

"Now I'm going to show you some work using modèles nus."

She let a page fall open to a nude by Rubens, watched Jorie to catch his reaction. She saw him swallow twice, move closer to the picture. The she asked, "What are you thinking?"

What was he supposed to say? "I dunno."

"Well, do you like it?"

He tried to stay on safe ground. "She's kind of fat."

Catherine laughed. Jorie tried to remember and apply some of the principles he'd learned before, things his mother would expect to hear. "The artist used pink, white and blue to create almost translucent skin tones."

She smiled. "Très bon. Anything else?"

"A boy in our class drew a picture of a naked girl and the teacher caught him. I thought he'd be punished, but all Miss O'Dell said—"

He stopped short. He hadn't wanted to mention her name in his mother's presence ever again.

"What did she say?"

"That it was dirty and he was not to draw girls like that," he mumbled. Then he pointed to the picture in the book. "Is this dirty?"

"No. This work is created by one of the masters. You see the lines of the body and how the artist has carefully arranged them to form the focal point of his composition. Notice the contrast between the very whiteness of her skin and the somber background. Many factors go into creating a work of art, such as this."

"Do you mean it's all right to draw bare naked people?"

Catherine winced. "Let's call them nudes. Under certain circumstances it's all right. God created our bodies and he was the greatest artist of all. We should not be ashamed of them. Our bodies are beautiful and meant to be appreciated. But if one uses them in drawing or any other way simply to titillate the senses, then it is not art. It is something coarse, lewd."

"Oh."

"In what sense do you think the boy at school was drawing the nude?"

"Lewd, I think."

The next day Catherine told her son that she had another book of drawings and paintings she hadn't shown him before.

"They're all nudes," she confided.

He sucked in his breath. "But they're not lewd?"

"No, they're not. I didn't think you were mature enough before to understand the difference, but perhaps you are now. Would you like to see them?"

He could only nod.

"Wait here."

Catherine retrieved the secret book, unwrapping the yellowed newspaper that concealed its contents. If Arthur Johnson could teach her son anatomy from a scientific point of view, she could instruct him from an artistic one.

"Where did you get it?"

"It was a gift from my father. Like all of my art books, he gave it to me when I was able to properly appreciate it."

Still holding it closed, she looked at Jorie. "You must promise not to laugh, or get silly about this. If you do, we shall have to put it away. Art is something to be appreciated and studied seriously like any other subject."

He nodded.

She opened the book to a page with a buxom nude. Catherine watched her son's expression, gauging the effect the picture had on him.

"What is your response to this composition?"

His response was in his groin, but he tried to focus on the meaning of her question.

"Uh, there's not as much contrast in the background as the other one."

"Anything else?"

He was still angry with her for taking him out of school, but he couldn't afford to let those feelings deny him the feast of these wonderful pictures. He tried to remember what she'd said about lines. "The lines make good curves—in her body."

"I think you mean the artist has drawn her body in such a way that her curves make good lines in the composition."

"Aye, that's it." In a moment he added, "May I hold the book?"

She laid it reverently across his lap.

"That darkness in the corner—what's that for?" he said to distract her from the real reason for holding the book.

"You bring up an important point. With art, light is everything. Where do you think it's coming from in this picture?"

"From the window?"

"Very good. Now do you see that with the tub there, the light can't go through it? It creates a shadow. That's why this corner is dark."

"Oh," he said, starting to turn the page. He was eager to discover the other treasures this volume offered.

"Not so fast," she said, holding the page down. "You can't discover all there is to know about a work of art in a couple of minutes. We'll save the others for another day."

He was disappointed; he'd have liked to devour every tasty morsel in one wonderfully satisfying meal, but he dared not complain.

"What else do you observe about this painting?" she was asking.

"He wanted to say, "She has lovely tits," but he knew his mother wouldn't like that, so he said, "Her hair is dark like the corner of the picture."

"Excellent! You observe how those dark tones resonate with each other. You remember that from the other books, don't you? In a way, these dark areas *speak* to each other."

He didn't know what she meant by that, but he wasn't interested in her hair that much, anyway.

She continued to admire the work. "And doesn't she have comely breasts, Jorie?"

He sucked in his breath knowing he was blushing and the bulge in his pants was growing. "Yes," he muttered.

For days they studied the book of nudes. Like some extravagant and delicious sweet, she allowed only one at a time.

"I want you to have a full appreciation of the female form, and the reverence these artists have shown for it in their works. The women's bodies are not all alike, as I'm sure you have noticed."

"Some are fat."

"Rubenesque is a kinder word. Figure is a matter of fashion just as clothes are."

"Did artists get real women to pose for them or did they just imagine them?"

"Real women, if they could afford to. Most of them were models who did this for a living. Unless they were friends of the artist."

"Isn't that dirty?"

"Oh, I suppose in provincial Michigan it would be considered so, but not in Paris. Most of the great artists of that period lived in one part of that great city where they could discuss their work over a meal and a bottle of wine with other artists. The models lived nearby, so they could get work. Sometimes the model was the artist's lover."

Jorie swallowed. He couldn't imagine such a grand life.

She watched him carefully. "Perhaps someday you would like the experience of drawing a nude."

"Yes." He knew he'd said it, but no voice came forth.

"I didn't hear you."

"Yes." It seemed he had to exert a great deal of effort to make the smallest sound, and then only part of the word was audible.

Carol A Sheldon

Three days later he summoned the courage to ask if she knew anyone who might be willing to pose for him.

"Oh, non, Jorie. Pas dans cette ville provinciale."

She let another week pass before venturing, "Jorie, if it's truly important to you, perhaps we could work something out."

"What do you mean?"

"You mustn't breathe a word of this to anyone, whether you like the idea or not. Is that understood?"

"Yes." He held his breath.

"I'm not sure, but just perhaps you and I could work together. As your mother I would certainly not pose for you in the usual manner, standing naked before you. That wouldn't be right. But perhaps if we could think of a way to do it *indirectement*."

"You mean the mirror?"

"No. That would provide me no screen of privacy at all."

Jorie looked puzzled. "Then how can we do it?"

"Well, perhaps we can't. Unless you can find a *solution*."

The next day he said, "I have it—I could draw your reflection!"

"How would you do that?"

"I'd sit on a chair facing the window, at an angle, and you could stand *behind* me. I would draw your reflection in the candlelight. That way I wouldn't see you...exactly."

"You're very clever, Jorie, to think of that."

He frowned. "But it would have to be night. And the curtain would have to be open with light in the room!"

"Yes, you're right. No, we couldn't do that," she sighed.

Jorie's thoughts were still spinning.

"But one of your bedroom windows backs up directly to the hill, where nobody ever goes, so it would be safe to leave the curtain open there."

"Perhaps."

"Would that work?"

She hesitated. "It's a very serious thing. I don't know if you're grown-up enough, Jorie. And I'm truly not the right person. If only there were modeling classes in town, as in the big cities."

218

"I won't tell anyone. I will consider it a sacred privilege and a gift from you toward my art education."

She smiled. "That's nicely put, but I will have to give it careful consideration."

Suddenly Jorie thought of another obstacle. "Pa! "

"We would have to wait until he's out some evening."

Several days passed. Pa was out very late one night and not home at all the next. Still she didn't speak of it.

But a week later his father's sister was suffering with a bout of influenza, and Thomas announced that he would see her through it. He left with a small valise.

If she doesn't say something now, she never will.

All day Jorie waited, employing every nervous habit he had to keep the suspense at bay.

At supper time she said, "On the matter of which we spoke earlier—are you certain you want to proceed?"

"Oh, yes, Mum."

Again she hesitated.

"You are not to turn around when I'm undressed. Agreed?"

He was afraid his voice would break if he spoke; he nodded.

"Wait until Eliza is asleep tonight, then come to my room."

He could hardly contain his excitement. He knew he had to be very grown-up about this or she would get angry and send him away. He would wear his baggy pants, which were actually too big for him, to avoid embarrassment.

When the appointed time finally arrived, he approached her door, pressing his ear to it to determine if he could hear any noises from within. Detecting none, he finally knocked.

She took so long to respond, he was about to leave. But here she was smiling, beckoning him to come in.

He wanted to run away. *How crazy! I've waited all day for this!* He stood there, speechless. Already feeling the flush on his cheeks he knew he couldn't bear to look at her even with her clothes on.

Seeming to sense his fears she said, "Well, come in lad. I won't bite you."

He forced himself to enter, hoping she couldn't hear his heart beating, his groin throbbing.

He'd forgotten to wear the baggy pants!

"Sit down," she directed him with an encouraging smile.

He knew what to expect, so he took the hardback chair facing the window at an angle, and opened his sketch book. He could hear her behind him, undressing. Somehow he'd expected she'd be ready, wearing her dressing gown, but she had greeted him fully clothed, and now was taking ever so long to get out of her clothing. The thought of those mysterious petticoats, garters and bodices further excited his senses.

He heard something snap and thought it must be the elastic garter. Then out of the corner of his eye, he could see she had lifted her leg onto the bed and was slowly rolling down her stocking. Just that knowing aroused him. He stared at the pattern of pale roses on the wallpaper and tried to pay her no heed. Finally she stepped behind him, framing herself in the window.

Jorie drew in his breath. Although he could see only her re-flection—and had to strain to see that in the dim light—he thought she was a goddess, more beautiful than he'd ever imagined. Forget-ting she was waiting, he stared for some time. How thrilling it was. He was glad for the privacy this strange arrangement provided him.

"Begin, Jorie. We've only a few moments."

He pulled himself together and quickly made a few strokes on the paper. The lines seemed all wrong and didn't do her justice. He tried to erase, but in his nervousness, he'd been using so much pres-sure with the pencil that the erasures caused the paper to smudge and tear. He turned to a fresh sheet and started again.

"Two more minutes. That's all I give can you. I'm very cold, and there's always the chance that your father may come home."

He was more anxious than ever now.

"Finish up. Don't worry about how good it is. This is your first time."

In a few more moments she stepped out of the frame. He looked at the window but she was gone. Currents of frustration coursed through his body. It had ended all too quickly.

When she was robed, she said he could turn around.

"Well, let's see what you have." She sat on her bed, indicating he should sit beside her.

"Please, I don't want to show you. It's not like you at all. You're beautiful, and this is ugly."

She smiled. You were no doubt nervous, Love. Don't be so hard on yourself. Let's have a look." She held out her hand for the paper. Shamefaced he gave it to her. He'd drawn her torso too large for the paper, leaving no room for her feet.

He held his breath while she studied his efforts seriously. "You must learn to make a few light sweeping strokes quickly that will generally outline the subject. You can fill them in later. That way, you don't waste a lot of time on a drawing that will never fit on the page."

She turned the paper sideways, and back again. "In terms of composition it isn't very interesting, but that's not your fault. You see the vertical lines of my body? And the vertical lines of the window frame? They're parallel, and that doesn't make for a very appealing composition. Perhaps next time I could give you a pose that wouldn't parallel the `frame.'"

He barely understood what she was talking about. He only knew she'd taken his efforts seriously, and her comments had been kind.

She rose, and he knew he was being dismissed.

"One more thing, Jorie. You are not, ever, to discuss these drawings or show them to anyone. People would misunderstand us completely."

He nodded. "Yes, ma'am."

"These rendezvous will be part of our *Golden Bubble*, a space where you and I alone may tread."

She enfolded him in her arms then. Sucking in the sweet scent of her perfume, he wished that all the clocks in the world would stand still.

As soon as he was under the covers, his hand found his throbbing penis. He lay awake that night reliving what had transpired. How grateful he was that she hadn't made fun of his paltry efforts, had refrained from commenting on the poor likeness. How understanding she'd been. And there would be more times like tonight.

No doubt you were nervous. That was putting it gently!

He couldn't wait to have another go at this new project. But he dared not broach the subject himself for fear his mother would think him too eager, would suspect his motives. In the nights, he saw her over and over in his mind—the lovely curve of her bottom as it disappeared into the shadows. He would try to capture that the next time. But maybe she'd changed her mind; maybe there wouldn't be a next time. Two days passed.

Finally, she came to him.

"Would you like to have another art lesson tonight?"

"Oh, yes, please!"

"Well then, suppose you come to my room tonight at nine o'clock."

"Yes." He tried to sound more grown up than he felt.

The hours passed slowly. He took out the pencils, and practiced from memory what he had seen before. How to get the shoulder—he couldn't remember that part at all. His efforts made her look like a wrestler! He would have to pay more attention tonight. If he did poorly again he feared she'd be disappointed, declare him an unworthy student. And where was the source of light? He'd have to put that in the picture. What little illumination there was came from her left, he remembered, from the candle on her table.

Still, his mind wandered from the serious task before him to the unadorned figure of his mother. What if she were to turn, come through the glass? Escape the dark branches that tapped at the window, reminding him of the barrier of separation. Fanciful scenes played in his mind, while his body ached for release. But he would not give in to it, not yet.

When the hour finally arrived, he gathered his drawing materials and walked toward her room. His knock was so soft he was sure she hadn't heard it, and knocked again.

"I heard you the first time. You mustn't be impatient."

As she undressed slowly behind him he tried to will himself to dispel his sexual feelings, tried to force his thoughts to turn to other matters—anything. The soapy dishwater came to mind, but then he saw it sliding down her back. He was pouring it over her and they were both laughing. He thought about the stars, but she was sitting beside him on the hill, cradling his head in her lap. His body was not the least obedient. Again he could feel the throbbing. At least this time, he'd remembered to wear the baggy trousers.

He heard the rustling of her petticoat and his attention was brought to the nearness of her. He would like to take a closer look at those secret garments.

"Are we ready?" The question came so close to his ear, he jerked to attention, felt her warm breath stirring the little hairs on the back of his neck.

He could only nod.

As he raised his head, she was turning around behind him, and he thought he'd burst. She had her back to him, the reflection of her beautiful round bottom cheeks three feet in front of him! And the real ones were right behind him! At the same time the most delicious fragrance greeted his nostrils. He wanted to go to her, be swallowed by her, or at least lie down and comfort himself.

"I promised you a new pose," she was saying. Her arms were raised high above her head, and a hip thrown slightly to one side. He stared at the marvel before him. His eyes followed the superb curve down her arms, turning inward toward her body as far as her waist, then out again where her hip thrust out, and finally back to center at her feet.

"Think of it as *Woman Stretching Upon Rising*. That will give you some context. Now get started. I can't maintain this pose for long, so you will have to work quickly."

He tried to see her as an artist would.

"Draw my arms first; I can't hold them up much longer."

Forcing himself to put pencil to paper, he did as she told him.

"At least you won't have to work with all parallel lines this time."

He could hear the first drops of rain on the window. She lowered her arms.

"Please don't leave," he implored.

She was still holding her position. "A few more minutes, but you won't be able to see in the rain."

"Yes, I will."

He was squinting, hurrying to get more of her on paper. Already the picture in the glass was a wavy blur, her features distorted. Again he'd drawn her too low on the page. He'd forgotten what she'd said about that. He sighed in frustration.

So bent on fixing his mistakes, he did not see her leave the frame. When he looked at the window, like an apparition, she had disappeared.

"I'm not finished!" he wailed, whirling to face her before he thought. Too late he jerked his head back to center.

Thrusting her robe in front of her she rasped, "You have broken our agreement. Leave me!"

In despair Jorie left the room, barely able to contain the stinging tears until he was out of her sight. Reeling with disbelief, he stumbled down the hall. Standing at his own window he watched the rain sliding down the windowpane mirror the tears running down his face. The thunder in the distance seemed to generate within his own wretched belly. And in the lightning he saw an angry god hurling thunderbolts.

How could all that had been so precious to him be dashed in one careless moment?

When sleep finally came, in dreams they were walking in the wood, but he could only see one side of her; her far side was in the shadows. It seemed she was being sucked into the darkness, devoured by it, until only a sliver of her remained shining in the moonlight. Frightened, he put his arms around her to assure himself that she was still there, but nothing remained of her but a tiny silver thread. Then that was gone too.

He awoke in a cold sweat, his pillow soaking wet.

In the hours that followed, sleep did not return. Only the wretched feeling that he had betrayed her trust.

The next day she said nothing, and the strain between them was palpable. But three days later she said pleasantly, "Would you like to give it another go tonight?"

He thought he must be dreaming. "Do you mean it?"

"You must remember the rules."

"I will. I promise!"

"Be sure you do."

The thrill of having another opportunity to capture her likeness was delicious. But even greater was the ecstasy at having his banishment lifted. He would get it right: He would behave properly and focus on getting her whole figure on the paper.

They did the washing up together in silence and Jorie broke a cup. His mother said nothing. Looking up nervously, he received her *forgiveness* smile.

She left the kitchen before he was quite finished, leaving him to wonder if she'd forgotten, or changed her mind. But no, he didn't think so. She'd have said, wouldn't she?

Still, when the time finally came, and he approached her door with his tablet and pencils, he felt more trepidation than before.

The door opened promptly, and with only a glance toward his mother, he took the six steps to the chair.

With his ears tuned to every sound, he could hear the unfastening of the buttons. He hoped she could not hear the pounding of his heart.

Just then the jarring sound of the doorbell jangled through the house.

Every fiber in Jorie's body froze. *Was it Pa? No, he had a key. Why did anyone have to come now!*

"Go answer the door, Jorie." His mother's voice was sharp, husky.

Jorie left the room reluctantly and descended the stairs slowly. Half way down the grating sound of the bell again reached his ears. As he opened the door, he was greeted by the sheriff.

"Hello, lad. Is your mother here?"

"Is anything wrong, Mr. Foster?"

"Hope not. That's what I came to find out. Where's your ma?"

"What do you need her for? She, she's upstairs."

"Well, do you think you could get her for me, Jorie?"

"I guess so."

Just then Catherine appeared in her woolen robe.

"Earl Foster, what brings you here?"

"Well, I know Thomas is away, and I just came by to see if you and the children were all right. Didn't see any lights down here—"

"That's because I went to bed early with a headache."

"Oh, sorry to bother you, Catherine. Just wanted to make sure—"

"Of course. Now if you'll excuse me."

She closed and locked the door, fairly seething with rage. Under her breath she hissed, "If Earl Foster isn't the most incommodious busybody ever! Always showing up at the wrong time!"

She turned to her son. "Go to your room, Jorie. It's over."

"For good?"

"Yes."

chapter 22

THE DAYS WERE joyless. He longed to be back in school again with Miss O'Dell, and the other chaps, however dissimilar they were. When his father returned in three days Jorie was never so glad to see him.

In May Thomas said, "With all this time on your hands, how would you like to come work up at the mine for a spell? Until school starts up in the fall."

"Do you mean it, Pa?"

"You're pretty good with figures."

"Yes, sir."

"Are you fifteen now?"

"Yes. I mean, I will be in the fall."

"Two more years of school?"

"Two more in high school." He wanted to say something about college but Pa was talking about the job.

"The bookkeeper could use some help."

"What does Ma say about it?"

"Haven't talked to her yet."

"Oh."

"You think she'll object?"

Jorie nodded. "Probably."

"Well, I'll speak to her."

Maybe he was imagining it, but it seemed his father was kinder than he used to be. Maybe Pa had noticed that he was growing up and was somebody you could have a conversation with.

After dinner Catherine slammed down the forks she was drying, and addressed her husband. "He will do no such thing! I promised him years ago he'd never have to work in the mine!"

"He'll not be *in* the mine. He'll be in the bookkeeper's office. Be good for him. You don't want him in school—"

"You know why!"

"The lad's got to be doing something. Idle hands all these months."

"We've been working on his studies."

"He needs to apply some of those skills in the real world."

"The risk of scarlet fever is everywhere!"

"We don't have any cases there. That's pretty well blown over now."

"You make it sound like a spring storm. It's taken *lives* in this town, Thomas! Sixteen of them!"

"You can't isolate him forever."

"Must *all* your sons work at the mine?" Catherine tried to compose herself. "Earl Foster could probably use him again this summer in his garden. That's much more suitable to his nature."

"His nature! For God sakes, woman, I'm tired of hearing about his nature. He needs to be around *men*."

"Thomas!"

"When did you plan to cut the cord, Catherine? When did you plan to pull him from your teat?"

In the end, Pa won; Jorie would go to work with his father.

He got up early on his first day and spent considerable time trying to tame the cowlick in his hair. Tiny hairs were appearing on his chin; he'd have to ask Pa if he should start shaving. Pa had told him to wear a clean shirt with a tie and his good brown sweater. When he came downstairs his mother had a hot breakfast ready for them.

Her lips quivered as she said, "I'm sorry you have to go. I tried to convince him—"

"I want to, Ma."

"You *want* to?"

"Yes."

"Whatever for?"

How could he put it? "I need to be *doing* something."

Thomas came down and started talking about the job, sparing Jorie further argument and his mother's injured looks.

The first few days took Jorie more by surprise than he'd expected. He'd never heard so much foul language in his life, and wasn't quite sure what some of it meant. The filthy spittoon was used as a target, and sometimes Jorie had to dodge the bullets. Soon he was goaded into trying this manly custom by the others. After getting sick on his first wad, much to the amusement of the three men in the office, he gave up trying. In addition, the room was so filled with smoke, he had to go outside to get air every hour or so.

He received a new kind of education from the stories they told. The man named Jim Willoughby told the best. One day after Lars Jensen came by to ask about his paycheck Jim started in.

"You heard what happened to Lars and his fiancée?"

"No, what?"

"Tell it, Jim."

"Well, one Sunday afternoon a few years back, he was takin' his sweetheart out for a ride in his buggy, up around the lake, toward Laurium. He started pitchin' her a little woo, spoonin', and meanwhile ignoring the reins. Anyway, his horse, doing what it always did on that particular road, turns into the circular drive of *The Luce Women of Laurium*, and stops at the front entrance!"

Loud guffaws from the men.

Jorie could feel his face color, and pretended to be so deep in his work he didn't hear.

"Now Lars looks up to see why the horse had stopped and saw they were at the Pleasure Palace. "Wonder why the horse turned in here," he says, all innocent. His sweetheart didn't know either, never having been there. He turned the horse around fast just as the Madam Luce come out to greet him, calling him by name. But Lars continues up the road, keeping a tight rein on the old gelding now. For awhile it looked like he was going to get away with it, until the girl up and tells the story at her dinner table that night in front of both her parents and Lars."

There were more guffaws and chortles from the men in the office.

"Fuck, Jim. You're not fibbin'?" one of the men choked.

"It's true," Jim swore, crossing himself, though he was not a Catholic or a member of any other known religion. He raised his voice to imitate the girl and the men laughed again. "'You won't believe what happened this afternoon,' she says to her family. 'For no reason at all Thor, that's Lars's horse, turns in to the drive of this beautiful Southern style mansion, with big white pillars and beautiful red velvet curtains. I think you'd call it an ante-bellum house, Daddy, but I'm not sure about the architecture. The prettiest woman comes out—she's all in red velvet too, and says 'good-afternoon, Lars. Didn't she, Honey? But he didn't even know her, so he just drove off real fast. Now isn't that the strangest thing?'"

The boys couldn't stop laughing and Jim enjoyed how well his little story had come off.

When he could get his laughter under control, the one called Ben gasped, "Did you make this story up, Jim?"

"Not a word. Whole town knows the story."

"What happened then?"

"Well, poor Lars had planned to marry this girl, but that was the end of the romance. Her pa knew all about *The Luce Women of Laurium*. He'd prob'ly had a few pokes there himself."

Jorie wondered if his father had ever been at a bawdy house.

The work presented no challenge. The only difficult part was the many errors he discovered in the books; he wasn't sure whether he should point them out or not.

"Better not," Pa said, looking up from his newspaper. "They'd just think you were a fresh kid, and if you think they're having sport with you now, just imagine what they'd do if you bested them."

Jorie was glad for his Pa's advice, but whenever he could do it without causing a chain reaction, he corrected the figures in the ledger.

Thomas looked at his son, now becoming a young man. "How do you like it there? Different from school, eh?"

"Oh, yes." Jorie nodded his head vigorously.

"Tell me about it."

"They chew a lot, spit a lot, and tell dirty stories."

"You're growing up, son." He returned to his newspaper, then looked up again. "What kind of stories? You got one?"

Jorie colored. "You want me to tell you?"

"Yeah, I could use a good tale."

Jorie started telling him the one about the Pleasure Palace, all the time asking himself why he was doing this. Would Pa get mad at him, or pull him off the job? But he'd started, and he couldn't stop now.

When he finished, he held his breath, but Pa rolled with laughter, and clapped him on the knee.

"Good one, son. That's a good one!"

For a moment Jorie froze, then their eyes met. He started laughing, self-consciously at first, then in full voice with Pa.

Jorie realized that he had just passed some sort of initiation with his pa.

After a few weeks with his new teacher in the fall, Jorie decided Mr. Smythe was neither friend nor foe. He was a hard taskmaster, but for once this gave Jorie an edge. Studying helped to push certain scenes, real and imagined, out of his mind. Besides, he hoped to go to the University, and he knew he'd have to excel if that was ever to happen.

He had two poems published in a nature magazine, and an article in *The Copper Country Evening News.*

One evening his father sat with him in the parlor smoking the pipe Jorie had given him. He tamped the tobacco down.

"I finally got it broke in, son. Fine pipe."

"Thank you, sir."

"You're becoming quite a writer, aren't you?"

Jorie tried to swallow the immense pleasure he felt.

"Have you thought of what you'll want to do when school's out?"

"I have another year to go."

"And then?"

"I don't know, Pa." Why had he said that? "What I mean is—" Oh, God, he wasn't ready for this pitch. "I'd like to go to college." He took a deep breath. "I mean the University."

"In Ann Arbor. That would cost a great deal of money. Room and board on top of tuition."

"Yes, sir."

Just then his mother came into the room. "Eliza's calling for you, Jorie. I can't get her to settle down."

Jorie looked at his father.

"You'd better go."

Damn! What awful timing. Now Pa would tell Ma what they were talking about, and that would be the end of it.

When he came downstairs his mother said, "It's much too soon to be talking about college. That can wait another year."

He looked to his father, but Pa was engrossed in the paper.

No more was said that year about college.

The fall term of his last year went quickly. By spring everyone was already talking about the millennium, even though it was still months away. Grammar school children's visions of what the coming century would bring were drawn on huge pieces of butcher paper and posted in the stores and banks. Adults were publishing stories and articles which prophesied such unbelievable exploits as outer space exploration with the aid of strange new rockets. There were also tales of expeditions deep into the crust of the Earth where communities lived without need of air, water or light. Some of the best-written pieces and some of the most fanciful were published in *The Copper Country Evening News*.

One was Jorie's. He didn't write anything about exploring outer regions. Rather it was about taking care of what we had, protecting it for generations to come. He had read John Muir's essays about preserving more land in the west to be set aside for national parks. Jorie declared himself as being in favor of establishing a national park in the Upper Peninsula of Michigan, at Brockway Mountain.

The piece he wrote was well received, and folks told Thomas Radcliff they thought his boy had a real knack for writing. Thomas passed the compliments along to Jorie. Catherine was proud too, and told him so.

"Now aren't you glad I helped you edit it?" she said. "That part about saving the wolves would have just annoyed people, and then they wouldn't have even read the rest."

He nodded absently.

"There's a fine line, you know, between putting forward fresh ideas, and being so radical you offend people. You can only move the public a little at a time, and you tend to be rather outspoken."

Catherine chopped up the vegetables and meat with a vengeance. It wasn't that she minded making pasties; she could do that in her sleep. She had been sending out her packet of poems for the past year to various publishers, and today had received yet another rejection notice. The poems were beginning to look shabby, worn around the edges, and she would have to painstakingly copy every single one of them again before resubmitting them.

"We find your material unsuitable for our publication," she mimicked as she diced the turnips.

Why was it so hard to be a woman? She was sure that's what it was. In the one way she could express herself as an individual she was thwarted. She could have sent them out with a man's name as George Eliot and George Sands had done, but her poems were obviously written by a woman and she would not betray them by editing, removing the very pearl from the oyster.

What did anyone here actually know about her? Did they have any idea of the yearnings, disappointments, fantasies hidden in her breast? She knew other women had lost children and husbands, but she could find no passion behind their paste-like faces. Perhaps it was just that their masks were so thick she could not see beyond them. Catherine knew she wore a mask too, but if she ever met a like soul, she was sure they would lock eyes and know instantly.

There was no way she could share her work locally. The *Ladies Oratorical and Dramatic Society* would be shocked, outraged at her pieces. Some had been scandalized when she read poems by Walt Whitman.

She finished cutting up the turnips, tossed them in with the other vegetables and beef, and flipped the mixture onto half of each awaiting crust. One for Jorie to take to school the next day, and one for Thomas. In the morning she would heat them on the stove and wrap them in newspaper to keep them warm for their mid-day meal. A convention brought over by the Cornish miners, Catherine found them a godsend.

Her thoughts went back to her poems. Well, if she couldn't make a name for herself in writing, surely Jorie could. It was his last year of school. She could put her energies into his career. He would have her as a mentor and agent, something she had never had. And besides Jorie was a male. That made all the difference. He would just have to stop writing ode-to-an-onion kind of pieces and focus on serious work.

Essays. Yes, that would be it. Suitably masculine. They were very popular these days, and their authors often traveled a circuit, frequently stopping in Houghton and Red Jacket to give talks on their subjects. People like James William Bryant. Even the amusing Mark Twain.

Her son could be a purveyor of ideas; she liked the sound of that. She folded the dough over and pinched the edges of each pasty. With her tutelage there would be no telling how far he would go. Of course he'd attend college. The school of mining across the lake wasn't ideal for his talents, and Catherine winced a bit as she thought about that. But it would give him credentials, and if he had to, he could supplement his writing career as a mining engineer. He'd spoken of the University of Michigan, but she had no intention of losing him to some distant arena. No, the college across the lake would suffice, and he could live at home.

chapter 23

THE POTS ON the stove were boiling, ready for her bath. Helena had stayed home with a toothache, and Catherine was tired from doing her work and preparing supper. A nice hot bath would soothe her aching legs.

She went upstairs and changed into her dressing gown and brought down the towels. When Jorie got home he'd bring the copper tub from the shed and pour the steaming kettles for her bath.

As he walked in the kitchen door, she noticed that at sixteen he was good-looking, with an amazing resemblance to her father. It's not that he always reminded her of him—she could have gotten used to that. It was just when she looked long into his deep blue eyes or he turned his head a certain way that she was taken by such surprise that it caused a quick intake of her breath.

"Frederick's going to the University next fall. He just got his acceptance letter." Jorie's face was flushed.

"You haven't kissed your Mummy."

He gave her a perfunctory peck on the cheek.

"I'm going to have my bath now," she said. "I'm only waiting for you to get it ready for me."

He fetched the copper tub, and set it on the kitchen floor near the stove.

"I want to go to the University, Ma."

"I think it needs wiping out."

"What does?"

"The tub, Jorie. Focus."

He grabbed a rag and ran it around the inside of the tub.

She said, "The water's ready on the stove, you can pour it for me now, if you will."

"Could you just listen to me first, Ma?"

"It won't stay hot forever."

She picked up a kettle and poured it herself. He carried the second and the third, emptying them in her bath.

"Will you get the cold bucket now from the rain barrel?"

"I'd like to apply for admission."

"You didn't answer me, son."

"What did you say?"

"I asked you to fetch the cold water."

He went out through the shed to the rain barrel, dipped a bucket into it, brought it back to the house and set it on the floor.

"I've sent for an application."

"Pour it, Jorie. What are you waiting for?"

"I'm trying to talk to you!"

"Watch your tone of voice. I want to take my bath now."

"Every time I bring it up you change the subject!"

He picked up the bucket, ready to dump the whole thing in the tub.

"Not so fast. Let me test it first." She raised her gown, exposing her leg and swished it with her tiny foot. "All right, a little more. That's enough. It cools off so fast. Now turn around."

She slipped out of her dressing gown and stepped into the tub, as Jorie turned away. Making small whimpering noises, she finally lowered herself into the hot water.

The steam rose in a plume around her. "Hand me the small towel and the pot of soap."

With his back to her he did so. "And scrub my back." She placed the small towel across her chest. "Do I have to tell you everything?" He picked up the brush as he had so many times before, dipped it in the soap, and rubbed it over her back.

"Ouch! Not so hard!"

He threw down the brush in total frustration, kicked a chair over and strode out of the room.

"Jorie, come back here and pick that up!"

Reluctantly, he returned to the kitchen and righted the chair.

"I think you'd best go upstairs until you have that temper under control," she directed.

"That's just what I plan to do."

He picked up his things and stormed up the stairs two at a time. Tossing his books on the floor and himself on the bed, he lay fuming with frustration. Anger and arousal met in a collision of feelings he couldn't sort out. He relieved himself in the only way he knew.

But when it was over, he felt worse than ever. He knew what had incited his desire, knew that all it took was the most fleeting sight of his mother's body, and the picture of her sitting naked in that tub, to bring him to climax. He was filled with self-loathing.

He had to get away from her.

He'd been trying to talk to her about the University for months now, and always she changed the subject. When he brought it up to Pa, he'd said, "Talk to your mother."

The application he'd sent for was waiting for him to fill out. He would have liked her approval, but if she was going to stall like this, he'd send it in anyway, and see what happened.

He took the form from *The Complete Works of William Shakespeare*. Just filling it out made him feel closer to obtaining his goal.

In the morning before school, he took the letter to the post office, stopping at the window to buy a stamp.

Mr. Gilroy unabashedly read the address, and turned to Jorie. "The University, is it? Well, I guess our little college here isn't good enough for you. Winning prizes and all kind of swells your head, I reckon."

Jorie dropped his eyes. Mr. Gilroy's son had not been able to get his essay published in the paper.

The weeks went by slowly as Jorie waited for a response from Ann Arbor. Perhaps they didn't let you know if you were not accepted. Then an awful thought occurred to him. *What if Ma saw the letter and kept it from him?*

"Oh, my God!" he thought. "How will I ever know? I can't accuse her."

Finally, the letter came. He knew his mother was upset about something when he walked in the kitchen. She was looking down at a large manila envelope in her lap. Then she raised her furrowed brow to him.

"Tell me what this is, Jorie."

Had she opened it? His heart was pounding. He wanted to pounce on the letter, but stood paralyzed, in front of her.

"No, I have not opened it. You will please to do so now, and let me know what it says." She handed it to him.

With shaking hands, that were both sweaty and cold, Jorie took the letter from her, and tried to open the envelope carefully. He wanted to savor the delicious anticipation that caused his heart to pound in his ears.

In exasperation, his mother said, "For heaven's sake, son, tear it open."

He didn't want to tear it, not even the envelope. Why couldn't he have this one moment of heightened expectation to himself? Perhaps he'd have laid the letter aside until after dinner. Maybe he'd have taken it to Frederick's to share with him. But here was Ma, demanding *her* satisfaction.

Suddenly, he turned and darted upstairs with the letter. He would not be bullied into having this experience spoiled by her. And if the University rejected him, he would not lay his embarrassment and disappointment bare for her rejoicing.

"Come back, here, Jorie!"

He ignored her, went in his room, and closed the door behind him.

"Jorie, you come back here! You hear me? I said, right now!"

He listened, waiting to see what she would do. She did not follow him up the stairs. He lay down with his hand on the letter under his pillow. He closed his eyes and imagined a letter of acceptance, as he had done over and over before. Then to prepare himself for the worst, he tried to imagine the University had rejected him. There was a sense of dread, but beyond that, he hadn't thought what he'd do.

Finally, unable to bear the suspense any longer, he opened the envelope and removed the letter. His eyes caught the first words, "We are happy to inform you..."

He didn't know what made him do it, but he fell on his knees and gave thanks to God. "I know you are my ally, for in this thing, oh Lord, surely my mother is not. But you have seen fit to guide me in this direction, to help me."

Then he read the complete letter over and over, until he practically had it memorized. There were more papers. And they had included a catalogue of courses. It made him feel as though he was already on his way. He wouldn't think, just yet, about the little paragraph stating that since he would still be under the age of eighteen when the fall term began, it would be necessary for his parent or guardian to file a letter giving consent to his admission.

Sitting over a cup of tea in the kitchen late that evening, she felt the last of the warmth coming from the stove as her mind spiraled inward and downward. Had she pushed him too far demanding that he open the University letter in her presence? Some cliché about honey and vinegar flitted through her mind. Was this letter from the University of Michigan an application, or had he already applied and this a notification of acceptance? It never occurred to her that he would be rejected. If he'd stay in the North Country, she thought he'd be content in the end. But once he left, he'd be lost to her forever. Her job was to keep him home, and keep him content.

Well, the battle wasn't lost yet. The cost would be very dear. If they didn't provide the funds, there was no way he could go, and that would be the end of it. He'd be upset, but he'd get over it. She tried to relax.

She waited until morning, and then got it out of him that it was a letter of acceptance.

"That doesn't mean you're going," she reminded him.

All week Jorie pored over the catalogue from the University. He waited until the weekend for a chance to talk to Pa alone, when

Ma would be gone to do the shopping. On Saturday he could hear
Pa out back chopping firewood. He put on his jacket and went to
help him.

"I'll spell you for awhile, Pa."

"Pick up the other axe."

The duet of their axes, point and counterpoint, rang out
through the spring woods as they worked together splitting the
logs. It felt good to dissipate his energy this way.

When they'd finished Jorie said, "Can I talk to you, Pa?"

"Just let me get a cup of tea."

Jorie waited in the parlor, fearing his mother would return before they had a chance to talk.

Finally Thomas settled himself in his favorite chair, blowing
on his tea. Jorie waited while Pa poured part of the tea into the sau-
cer and back into the cup.

"Your mother doesn't like me to do this," he said sharing his
secret. "What do you have on your mind, son?"

He handed his father the letter from the University.

"What is it?"

"Read it, Pa."

Thomas set his tea down and opened the envelope. Then he
fumbled for his glasses.

"Have you seen them? I always leave them right here on this
table."

Jorie went to the table and felt around on the floor. He was
getting more nervous. Ma had been gone over an hour.

"Here they are."

"I must have knocked them off."

Jorie waited while Pa put his glasses firmly on his face and
adjusted the ear pieces.

Finally, Pa picked up the letter. When he'd finished reading it,
he looked up. He studied his son's face for such a long time Jorie's
agitation mounted.

"This means a lot to you, doesn't it?"

"Yes, Pa."

"Your mother thinks you ought to go across the lake."

"I know, but that's not the right kind of school for me."

His father's eyes fell to reading the letter again.

"Pa, I could show you the catalogue. Just as the word implies, they have courses about everything in the universe! It's quite astounding."

His father was still looking at the letter.

"With all due respect to you, Pa, I've no interest in mining."

"I know that."

Jorie licked his lips. "Can I go—to the University?"

"I can't ignore your mother's views. But if you don't go this fall, you can, of course, when you're eighteen. That's only another year. You'll be getting your sizeable sum then, like your brothers." His father paused, sipped his tea. "If you want to use it for your education that would be fine with me. You've a good mind, and it deserves to be developed."

"Thank you, sir."

Jorie's throat swelled up. His father had given him few words of praise. And the 'sizeable sum'—well, it had been mentioned before, though he hadn't dare count on it.

Still, he wanted to go to the University *now*. He thought he'd suffocate if he had to wait one more year.

"Will you talk to her?"

"You want me to take on your battles? Don't you think I have enough trouble with her on my own?"

Jorie saw a little smile in the corner of his father's mouth.

His father rose to leave, but turned, waving the letter. "Whether you go or not, this acceptance is quite a feather in your cap."

Two days later, Catherine called to him.

"I see you've wound your father around your finger."

Jorie held his breath.

"At sixteen, you're much too young to be thinking about going so far away from home for any reason."

"I'll be seventeen in the fall."

She shook her head. "Go to school here, at least for two years. Like other boys. Then we'll see."

"I don't want to go to the mining school."

"Jorie, it's not only mining and engineering they offer. They have other courses, too, English and Geology and suchlike. We could study together. I'd read the texts too. I promise. And then we could discuss them."

"Ma, no! I want to be with boys my own age—discuss my classes with them."

"We could have soirees, like they have in Paris. That's it! We have a lovely home, and you could invite some of the bright young men to come—maybe every Sunday night. We'd have discussions, then I could serve refreshments and you could even play the piano for them. You would become very popular."

He could see she was getting desperate, but he took a deep breath. "No, Ma, I don't want you to be in my academic discussions, wherever they are."

Catherine blinked. He could hear the catch in her breath. "Well, then, I'll stay in the background, just serve refreshments."

How pathetic she looked. And how he hated hurting her. But he shook his head.

That evening Jorie eavesdropped on a conversation between his parents. From upstairs he thought he'd heard his name, so he crept partly down the stairs, avoiding the part of each step that would herald his presence.

"You made sure to tell me about all his literary accomplishments, my dear. Am I meant to conclude that he belongs in a *mining* school?"

"For two years, Thomas."

"You've molded and shaped a little intellect after your heart, and here he is, too big for his books, wanting the University, if you please."

Jorie thought he heard his mother sniffle. He crept closer.

"And deserving it, too, I might add," Thomas said.

Catherine gasped and shoved her hand in her mouth.

Thomas looked hard at his wife. "You got what you wanted, woman, now be done with your blithering." Thomas tapped his pipe. "You've another child to tend to. Had you forgotten?"

In the end, Pa declared that he could go to Ann Arbor in the fall, and Ma couldn't prevent it.

Leaving home wasn't that easy. His mother's tears were so unbearable he tried to put his attention on little Eliza. But she clung to his neck and cried too. At three she was very attached to Jorie, and he to her. Totally without judgment of him, she was always delighted with whatever games he'd suggest or stories he'd tell. For his part, he thought being with her was like a walk in the garden after leaving a smoky room.

But now that he was on his way, the more miles he could put between himself and his family, the brighter the delights that lay before him. The train rocked back and forth, putting many to sleep. But not Jorie. The University was promise of a new life, and he couldn't be more excited.

He had informed the dean that he would like to live in a boarding house. He was assigned a room on Ann Street, near the campus. Six other students lived and ate in the same house, and although shy and uncomfortable with his peers, he found there was one with whom he could relate quite easily. Lawrence was also from a small town called Paw Paw, and quite bright.

Jorie saw a counselor to discuss the classes he'd be taking, and was pleased to find that although most were required, there were also electives. He had chosen to major in Journalism, but his favorite class was philosophy.

He wrote to his mother:

We are studying Socrates, who believed an unexamined life wasn't worth living, that one should question and be critical of his society, and of himself. Imagine my surprise at reading this, as I first heard much the same from you! This gives me the confidence to continue writing against all I find abhorrent in Society. Although I know you miss me, it is you I can thank for instilling in me the quest for knowledge, the ever-deepening desire to explore what lies beyond the obvious. You would be proud of me, Mother.

Your devoted son, Jorie

Catherine pressed this bitter pill of praise to her heart. Oh, the irony!

He'd never imagined there were so many ideas in the world. And he'd never had so much opportunity for stimulating exchange of thought.

Having felt most of life that he was an aberration of his species, he was now discovering that he was part of a subspecies that actually took pleasure in learning. He remembered the story of the ugly duckling. Although still not comfortable with his peers, he saw the possibility. Perhaps in the spring, when they accepted new members, he might join the debating club.

When her first letter came, he felt his hands shaking as he opened it. He'd thought getting away from home and the discipline of study would erase his attachment to her. But even at this distance, and as much as he loved school, he found that her tentacles still ensnared him. With shame he realized he missed her terribly. The distance helped him to see how strange their bond had been. Well, he'd always known it was *unusual*.

He didn't know what kind of relationships other boys had with their mothers, but he knew it wasn't like his; it just couldn't be. He'd heard some say they were homesick, and maybe that meant they missed their mothers, but he doubted if they missed them in the same way he did. He thought about the training he'd had in discipline and sacrifice, and wondered if others had experienced anything like that. He didn't think so, and sometimes this made him very angry with her. But he knew she loved him, so it was difficult to fault her for the intense feelings he had. No, the problem must lie with him.

The first letters he received from her were so sad that when one came, he would brace himself, scan it quickly, and turn his mind to his studies. But inevitably he would pull it out before turning in for the evening, read it slowly, taking in the breath behind the words.

Pa sent him money each month, and if he was careful there was some left over, which he used to attend the Men's Glee Club and other musical events.

As the holidays neared his mother wrote:

I can hardly wait for you to come home. There will be wonderful activities for the millennium, which you will enjoy. There's to be a sculpture contest on the lake with huge towers of ice to be carved, one for the old century and one the new. Points will be given for speed and artistic achievement. Everyone will be there, watching and cheering on their team. And there will be a parade on New Year's Day that is sure to be jolly. It's almost the Twentieth Century, Jorie! Can you believe it? I count the days until your return.

But Jorie asked permission to stay in Ann Arbor over the holidays. The semester wouldn't be over until the end of January. He wrote that he had a paper to prepare for his philosophy class, due when the holiday ended.

He tried not to think of the real reason.

Pa wrote that he didn't have to come home and was proud that he was leaning into the wheel so hard. Ma objected, but on the whole took it rather stoically, he thought. Maybe she's getting used to it. She went on to tell him of the wonderful gala they were going to up in Red Jacket.

To assuage my disappointment in your not coming home, or perhaps for letting you go so far away in the first place, your father is making an extra effort to be kind to me. We will take the train up with other members of his men's club and their wives. There will be a lavish dinner, followed by dancing to an orchestra. Everyone will be dressed in their finest and your father gave me money to purchase a new gown and shoes for the occasion. It won't replace your absence, Dear, but it is something to look forward to.

He felt very grateful that his father was taking up some of the slack.

On Christmas Eve Jorie went caroling with a group of local students who were staying in town. Like something out of a picture book, huge gentle snowflakes fell slowly as they sang their way through the lamp-lit streets. It was almost warm compared to the Upper Peninsula.

One of the *town boys*, another science major and his lab partner in zoology, invited him to his home for Christmas dinner. When Alan's mother discovered that Jorie could play the piano, she laughed, "Well, now, you must sing for your supper!"

Jorie broke out in a sweat when the telegram came.

"Father dying. Come home."

It was the last day of the year, the century. At all the stops along the way, banners flowed from the little train stations. "Welcome, Twentieth Century!" "Here's to Progress!" The excitement in the air was everywhere. People bustled on to the trains with bundles of food, on their way to nearby relatives, with whom to share the occasion.

But for Jorie, the trip home was an interminable ordeal of guilt. He should have gone home for the holidays. If he'd been there, he would have had a chance to see Pa before he took sick. He prayed he wouldn't be too late.

Maybe he wasn't dying at all. Jorie didn't even know what was wrong with him, and Ma was prone to exaggerating. Perhaps it was just Ma's way to get him home.

His mind traveled back through the years. Scenes from the past played on the stage of his mind. How he'd hated and feared his father when he was small. And for years how little they'd communicated. Only recently there had been a breakthrough, and they'd begun to soften toward each other.

He'd never bothered to wonder what his father's dreams and disappointments were. Was he grief stricken when his first wife died? How must Pa have felt about sending Walter away? He hadn't seen his half-brother since the night Walter had poured liquor down his throat. If Pa was in the hospital, he supposed he'd be seeing Walter now.

Thoughts continued to race through his mind as the hours dragged on. He forced his mind back to school. Damn! He should have brought his books home, and the paper he was working on. In such a hurry to catch the train, he'd stuffed only a few clothes in his satchel and run down State Street toward the depot. He sank back in his seat in frustration. He'd have a lot of catching up to do when he got back.

By the time he neared Hancock, it was dark. Candles flickered in windows; he could see lights across the frozen lake. As the cab's tired horse trudged its way up the lane, Jorie's heart went to his throat, fearing he'd be too late. But even before they reached the house, he could see that no one was home. He had the cab take him to the hospital.

Strong smells of ether and ammonia stung his nostrils as he entered the building. Farther down the hall, his mother ran to him, threw her arms about him and began sobbing.

"You're here at last!"

"What's wrong with Pa?"

"He's had a stroke. He's unconscious."

"Where is he?"

She motioned toward the room.

He pushed past her and went to his father's bed. Pa was making strange gurgling sounds. How old he looked!

Finally, Jorie turned, aware that others were behind him.

Three men stood near the doorway, caps in hand. None of them were recognizable to Jorie.

One spoke. "Guess you're Jorie. I'm Tom and this is William here."

Jorie looked at the third. "Walter?"

The young man turned away.

This was not the time to get reacquainted. Jorie turned back to his father, *their* father. What a strange feeling—these men he didn't know at all, having the same Pa.

When he went back in the hall his mother was crying.

"You didn't even say 'hello' to your mama."

He put his arm around her and walked her down the hall, away from the others. "Tell me what happened."

"We were coming back from the gala, on the train. I'd gone to the Ladies and stopped to talk to a woman I knew in another car. Someone came to get me. Oh, Jorie, it was awful! And to think I wasn't there when it happened."

"He hasn't been conscious at all?"

"No." Jorie could see she was trying hard not to cry again. "Arthur says it does not bode well. Even if he were to live..."

She stopped, and Jorie held her, feeling her small frame shake with silent sobs against his chest.

"Where's Eliza?"

"Helena's watching her."

At midnight they finally left the hospital. New Year's Eve. The blaring dissonance of the whistles from the mines and factories proclaimed the beginning of the new millennium. As the sleigh glided across the freshly fallen snow sparkling under the full moon, they heard the revelry in town and across the lake. Driving along the Frontage Road they could see dozens of bonfires on the ice. A potpourri of smells assaulted them—everything from fried fish and stew to some heavy bathtub brew. There were even a few cutters racing in the moonlight. Fireworks lit up the sky, and noisemakers were sounding off in all directions. Every sound and sight from lilting laughter to raucous brawling accosted their senses as they traveled homeward.

So this was the Twentieth Century, the great event the world had awaited. To Jorie, the revelry was mayhem, a bizarre background against which to play his own dark themes.

chapter 24

THREE DAYS LATER, Dr. Johnson came to the house early in the morning. With one look at his careworn face, Catherine burst into tears.

Funeral arrangements were made with Mr. Markel, of Markel and Miller Funeral Parlor. Catherine decided against having the service at the funeral home, nor would Thomas have wanted it in a church. It would be held at home in the back parlor.

Mr. Markel took a good deal of time explaining things to her and helping her choose the coffin. Beyond that she felt he spent an inordinate amount of time comforting her. She wondered if the dapper undertaker were as solicitous with all of his clients.

"This is probably the most difficult time in your life, Mrs. Radcliff. I want you to know that I am here for you, and you can call on me in whatever capacity you find need for assistance," he insinuated.

"Indeed?"

"Yes, ma'am. For instance, like most widows, you may find yourself totally unfamiliar with the financial aspects of life, your husband having seen to all that in the past."

"Oh, no," she answered candidly. "There was a time when I handled our affairs completely."

"I see. I do not wish to press myself on you, but then there is the matter of bereavement counseling. Perhaps you are unaware that funeral directors have much experience in this area. More, I might say, than most clergy, as this is the heart of our work." He patted her hand with his meticulously manicured one. "I can be quite effective in this domain."

"With all your experience."

"Yes, ma'am. And if you are at a loss for any other service you are accustomed to receiving from your husband..."

The tinkle of Catherine's laughter served to silence the ingratiating tones of Mr. Markel for the moment.

When it was time for the service, Eliza begged to go, but she was held back in the care of Helena.

"Come upstairs with me, child. I'll tell you a good tale. Better 'n any you'd be hearin' in there today."

After she'd heard Helena spin a few tales, Eliza fell asleep, and Helena crept downstairs to take her seat in the parlor.

Friends and business associates of Thomas's from Red Jacket, Houghton and Hancock attended.

Catherine held Jorie's arm throughout the service and part of the reception. But toward the end, after receiving condolences from the guests she drifted toward Mr. Markel.

"How good of you to come. I didn't realize your duties extended to attending the service."

"On the contrary, ma'am. I feel it is my responsibility to stay with my client until the final sendoff."

Catherine looked at him in amazement.

"Perhaps that's putting it dramatically, but I don't hold with just selling a casket, and that being the long and short of it."

"I see."

"And on occasion, when I am particularly moved by someone's loss, I go because, well, my heart bids me."

"Pretty speech."

"In this case, I thought, well, you're such a young widow. There's something so very vulnerable about you. If there were anything we'd overlooked, I just wanted to be in the background, in case you should need me."

Catherine concealed her amusement with a delicate cough.

In the short time Jorie'd been gone, changes had been made to the house. There was a new oriental rug in the front room; and the front door, originally all wood, had been replaced by one whose upper portion displayed a beveled leaded glass design. Lavish in color, it sprouted a lovely rose in the center. There was a new carriage, and even a telephone! His father must have been doing very well.

That evening Catherine told Jorie again what a shock Thomas's passing was, how they'd had such a grand time at the ball, how well Thomas looked. Jorie asked if there were anything he could do for her, and she said she'd like to hear him play something on the piano. When the first notes of *Pavane for a Dead Princess* reached her, she stopped him.

"Oh, heavens, Jorie. Play something gay. Cheer me up."

He was taken aback, but he countered with *When the Saints Come Marching In.* For the first time since he'd been home he saw her smile.

Finally, she bade him good-night and went to bed. Jorie stayed downstairs reading for awhile, hoping she'd be asleep when he went up. But he'd no sooner gotten into bed when he heard the door open.

His mother whispered, "I know you can't be sleeping yet."

She crossed the floor and sat on the edge of his bed.

"I can't sleep, Jorie. I don't want to be alone."

"You're shivering."

She nodded. "Let me slide in with you, to keep warm. Just for a little while."

In one swift motion she was under the covers, lying next to him.

His heart leapt. He wasn't sure if it was in fear or exhilaration. Had he ever known the difference?

He willed his physical response to fade.

She started shaking. "Oh, Jorie, hold me. I'm so cold."

He put his arm around her, and she turned to him. "I'm all alone now. I don't know what I'll do."

"You're strong. You'll carry on." How lame that sounded.

"Thank the Lord, you've never known how painful it is to be alone. And you never will, not as long as you have me."

Gradually her shaking stopped. He was about to suggest she go to her own bed, when her slow, deep breathing told him she was asleep.

He held her for some time, but found it impossible to sleep himself. He noticed he had unconsciously adjusted his breathing to match hers as in years before. Quite deliberately he broke his rhythm to counter hers, exhaling as she inhaled.

Memories from years before flooded in, how she'd held and comforted him. The *Golden Bubble*. What a magical paradise it had seemed at the time. Thank God he'd been able to break it, finally, and get away.

Again, he realized he'd fallen into matching his breath to hers.

He couldn't wait to get back to the University.

In the dark week that followed, only the happiness of little Eliza at having her brother home lightened Jorie's heart. The rest of the time he was preoccupied with sadness for the father he'd never tried to reach and for what now could never be. He watched his mother and ached for her, too. Even though his parents hadn't always seen eye to eye, he knew she would miss Pa. Jorie did everything he could to comfort her and ease her burden. But after a week he was getting restless, eager to get back to his studies. Thank God for Helena. He was glad his little sister had this cheery Irish woman to watch over her. As he was finishing his breakfast he told her so.

"So you're planning to go back then, are you? Have you spoke to her 'bout this?"

Jorie shook his head. "No."

"Best you do, lad."

"You think she'll object?"

"Oh, I couldn't say." Helena left the room.

He approached his mother.

"Leave me! What are you talking about?"

"I don't mean tomorrow, Ma. In a few days."

"Oh, no. Oh, no!" She looked frightened.

"What are you saying?" he stammered.

"You can't be thinking that you'd abandon your mama now and go back to that school like nothing happened here!" Tears filled her eyes.

"Ma, I'm sorry Pa died. I've tried to be of help this past week, and I'll stay another if you like, but then I have to go."

"No!" she screamed. "You will not!"

Why hadn't he anticipated this? How could he have been so blind?

"But Pa wanted me to be at the University!"

"Your father up and died leaving me all alone with a baby to take care of!"

A feeling of strangulation came over him. *I can't!*

"Your obligations are *here*! Do I have to tell you that? And believe you me, your pa would have wanted you to show some human kindness and stay to look after your family now!"

"I've got to go back!"

The look in her eyes changed from fear to steely resolution. "You are only seventeen and I forbid it!"

Jorie felt something like a lump of hot coal in his throat.

He grabbed his jacket and muffler and dashed out of the house. Running, sliding down the icy hill, he reached Front Street, raced along the road toward the bridge, abruptly cut down the embankment and jumped onto the ice. He heard it crack, went farther, heedless of the loud booms of fracturing ice and their resounding echoes.

Somehow he made it to the other side, slipped and slid his way up the steep bank on the other side, dashed past the saloons on the outskirts of town, and onto the county road that led west to Redridge, and Lake Superior.

Somewhere, about five miles out of town, the pain in his chest caused him to slow down. Maybe he was having a heart attack. Well, he didn't care. He turned off the road, collapsed in a field, and rolled onto his stomach. He pounded the frozen earth until his fists were as tired as his legs, then flipped over on his back.

He didn't know how much later it was when he was awakened by snowflakes falling on his face. It was dark and he could see no light anywhere. Still, he lay there.

He tried to calm himself. Why was it so terrible to postpone college a year?

If I stay she will swallow me.

Finally, he got up and started back. Oblivious to the total whiteness of his world, he walked about a mile when a man in a wagon approached him going the other way.

"Where ye 'eaded, boy?"

"Hancock."

"You're hafter going the wrong way, son. You won't reach 'ancock that way hin a month of Sundays. I reckon I'd better carry ye. Snow's comin' down good now and yer six or seven miles from town. Get in."

Jorie scarcely cared whether he made it home or not, but climbed into the buckboard and thanked the Cornishman.

"Wasn't but two year ago a man and 'is wife was found froze to death. Up in Red Jacket hit was. Blizzard come on 'em and they got lost between the barn and the 'ouse. Couldn't see a thing. 'E didn't come back, so she went to look for 'im. That's what the deputy figured. They was found ten feet apart, not more'n twenty feet from the 'ouse."

Jorie was silent.

"What be yer name?"

"Radcliff."

"Ah, from up on Portage 'ill."

"Aye."

"Used to work for your Pa. Miner I was. Got too old for that. Now I'm a waggoner. You work for your pa?"

Jorie shook his head.

"It's a load of furniture I'm 'aulin' at the moment." The wind picked up. "Whoa, 'erbert! The tarp's a comin' off."

He stopped the wagon, and for some time the man wrestled with a large piece of canvas, trying to cover everything and get it tied down.

Jorie finally jerked to attention, jumped down and helped him.

When they'd finished, the waggoner tossed him a blanket and they climbed back in.

"Should 'a 'ad this load delivered afore sunset, but my axle froze up hon me. Lost a couple of hours tendin' to hit."

They rode on, the stranger carrying on a one-sided conversation. Most likely he didn't even notice, Jorie thought.

As they neared the bridge in Houghton, Jorie said, "I've probably taken you out of your way. I can walk the rest."

"For certain?"

"Yes. Here's for your troubles." He gave the man a coin.

"I thank ye, sir, I do. An' I 'ope someday ye'll think yer life was worth the savin of hit." He smiled and tipped his hat. "Good-evening to ye."

When he reached home, Jorie found a cold supper on the table, but his mother nowhere in sight. Hoping to avoid another confrontation, he went up the stairs and down the hall as quietly as he could. A numbness came over him, toward his own woes and his mother's. What did anyone's dreams matter? Perhaps it was better to have none. Then there could be no room for disappointment.

He fell asleep determined to lead a life indifferent to events.

It was late morning when he awoke. He scrunched his pillow under his head and went over everything that had happened. Now that he'd had some sleep, maybe his head would clear and he could find a solution.

Obviously, she meant to cut off his funds. Another payment of tuition was due as well as rent for his room. Well, some chaps worked their way through college. He could do that if he had to.

He heard the door open and turned his head to the wall. Would she allow him no privacy at all?

Eliza ran to his bed and jumped up on it.

"Get up, sleepy head! It's twelve o'clock!"

She started tickling him unmercifully.

"All right, all right, Izzy."

He rose and carried her to the hall. "Now you let me get dressed, and I'll be right down."

He realized that almost against his will, he was hungry.

In the kitchen he found cold pancakes that had replaced the cold supper. Without bothering to sit down and butter them, he ate them with his fingers, standing.

His mother came into the kitchen.

"Where are the pancakes?"

"I ate them."

She opened her mouth to say something, thought better of it.

He poured himself a cup of lukewarm tea.

"I can heat it for you."

He shook his head.

"Jorie, sit down, I want to talk to you."

He ignored her.

"Please sit down."

"I can hear you."

He could see she felt at a disadvantage, but he remained standing.

"It's unfortunate our words were unpleasant and overly emotional yesterday. I want you to know that I am not without respect for your sentiments regarding the University."

Had she memorized this little speech? He said nothing.

"But it isn't the end of the world. You can go to college across the lake."

He shook his head.

"Oh, do sit down, Jorie."

He complied, waited. He listened to the wind tormenting the window.

"Do you have anything else to say?" he asked.

She started to whimper. "Please don't make this so hard for me, Jorie. Look at me."

"What do you want, Ma? I'm not going to sit here all day."

"Oh, God, don't talk to me that way! I can't stand it."

She put her head down on the table, and wept bitterly for what seemed a long time. He tried to feel nothing, but already the recently acquired numbness was wearing off.

"You're all I have."

"No. You have Eliza."

She was still sniffling. "You know what I mean. I need a man, a grown-up. Oh, I'm saying it all wrong. I need *you,* Jorie."

He heard the mouse trap go off in the pantry.

"And Eliza needs you." She let out a deep sigh. "She's not very attached to me, Jorie."

She would be if you'd give her the love and attention she deserves.

Eliza came into the room and crawled up on his lap. "Stay, Jawie. Please stay."

"Maybe next year you could go back to Ann Arbor. You'll still only be eighteen. But this year—please try to understand. I've just lost my husband."

She seemed so pathetic, so vulnerable. An intense feeling of remorse filled him at the thought of leaving her alone so soon after her loss.

Eliza cupped his face in her small hands and turned it toward her. "Promise you won't go 'way again?"

That evening at dinner she smiled as he carved the meat. "Do you remember the meaning of 'sacrifice', Jorie?"

Silently he groaned. "Yes."

"Tell Eliza what it means."

He could feel the heat crawl up his neck and face. "It comes from the same word as sacred."

"That's right, Darling. So what you're doing for your sister and your mama is a very sacred thing. Knowing that should make it easier for you."

Somehow it didn't.

The trunk he'd sent for arrived at the train station, and Jorie went down to get it. All his books, papers, clothes—in short, all his dreams were packed inside that chest. He hired a dray to haul it home. The cart, with no sides, required he secure it somehow. Jorie sat on the floor holding the trunk as they jostled along the bumpy road. He put his legs and arms around it to keep it in place, hugging it harder than necessary, trying to believe it was the stinging winds off the lake that were causing his eyes to water.

chapter 25

IT WAS SUNDAY morning; he hadn't had to work Saturday night.

When he came down stairs, his mother asked, "Did you have a good lie-in?"

"I hate type-setting."

"You've only been there two months. You won't be doing that forever," Catherine said as she pulled her apron over her head. She turned around and he tied it for her, as he'd done a thousand times before. She turned and patted his cheek.

"You do well with that job, and they'll see how bright you are and move you up. *The Copper Country Evening News* is a good place for you."

He turned away from her. "It's so boring."

"You could have gone to college across the lake, but oh, no, that wasn't good enough for you." She began humming a little tune.

"I went with the *News* because I thought I could do some *writing.*"

"You will, in time."

"I can't keep my mind on placing those little pieces of lead all night, and when I drift, I make mistakes."

"You have to keep your attention on it, Jorie. You'll never get ahead making gaffes for the whole county to see when they read the paper."

"You talk as if I was going to be there forever. It's just temporary, you know, until I go back to Ann Arbor."

She didn't say anything, just looked up surprised with big, sad eyes.

"The worst of it," he said, "is I can't change a single word, no matter how badly written it is! It's full of overly sentimental editorializing, bad grammar—"

"You better not be showing that attitude at work. Remember your age, and show some respect for your elders." She held up a slice of apple mixed with cinnamon and sugar. "Here." She popped it in his mouth.

He said, "Can you imagine a sentence like this: 'We are informed that Joe Abbot fell down the shaft to a depth of forty feet resulting in a fractured femur of both limbs, also the tibia and fibula of the left limb directly above the ankle and otherwise he was not injured.'"

Catherine laughed.

"Or this: 'Mr. Pollack departed this life after a disabilitating, long and lingering illness, in which his devoted wife stood sentry at his bedside during the whole of these long and tortuous months, ever watching over him, anticipating his every need.'"

Catherine shook her head. "When you are the obituary reporter, I'm sure the notices will ring with—"

"Brevity. I'm going for a walk."

She sighed. "Another walk. Is there a rabbit or fox hole in the whole county you don't know by now?"

His work schedule required that he sleep during the day. On Thursday when he came down stairs at five o'clock his mother was excited.

"What is it?"

"Jorie, I have it! Let's pretend we're having a soiree tonight, like they have in Paris. Un soiree Français. We'll dress just as though we were in a fine salon. You will read some verse to me, I will play the piano for you, then you will play—"

"Oh, Ma." She led him into the dining room. He saw the table, with its fancy cloth, china and candles.

"Remember when you were little, and I taught you how we had to reinvent life in order to survive it? We can do that now, too." She looked up, awaiting his answer. "I want you to be happy here!"

How could he explain that playing dress-up with her would not do the job?

"We'll take turns being the performer and the audience. And a very appreciative listener you'll find in me, Jorie."

"Sounds silly to me."

"It will be very amusing. We'll call it the Thursday Night Musicale, and we can have it every week. Something to look forward to. It will help us get through this dreadful winter."

He saw her hopeful shining eyes. She looked so excited, was trying so hard to raise his spirits.

"Well, if it will please you."

"I've prepared a special meal. Kind of an appreciation dinner, shall we say? Venison with gooseberry sauce, lemon pie with—"

"Ma, you don't have to do all this."

"Oh, but I want to. We both need a lift. Here, Jorie, open the wine, will you? We'll let it set while we get dressed."

Eliza came running up to him in her party dress. "I get to come to the music."

"I've allowed her to join us for the recital part. Then she'll go to bed and we'll dine later. She's had her meal."

He wished Eliza could stay the whole evening. Having her there would make it seem more like a family affair.

Before he could see her, he could hear the rustle of her gown as his mother descended in a shimmering blue taffeta gown. At the bottom of the stairs she did a little twirl to show off her gown. All innocence and expectation, like a school girl waiting to be taken to her first dance.

He tried to dismiss the potpourri of feelings that overcame him—pity, desire, and a growing resentment. "I haven't seen that dress before."

"Your father bought it for me to wear to the gala. He said I looked girlish in it."

She held out her arm, and he escorted her into the front parlor. "You go first, Jorie. I'll be your audience."

She carried a lamp to the piano, took a chair a few feet away from it and waited expectantly.

"What do you want to hear?"

"Surprise me. You decide."

He chose a Chopin nocturne. When he had finished, Catherine clapped enthusiastically. Merci! C'était merveilleux!"

Eliza clapped too.

"Your turn."

He listened to the sonorous tones of Beethoven's *Moonlight Sonata.*

During his Bach cantata, she leaned over his shoulder humming the tune. In a moment she put her hands on his back.

"You're all stiff here, Darling. There should be movement as you play, all across your upper back, not just in your arms." She danced her fingers between his shoulders.

He could feel her warm breath erecting the hair on the back of his neck. He was glad when his number was over.

Although there was a chair placed for her, when her mother was playing, Eliza climbed into Jorie's lap.

"I want to play like that," she whispered.

"Isn't Mummy teaching you?"

"No, she isn't."

"Then I will."

"Promise?"

"Promise."

Catherine stopped, ending with a crashing chord. "I must say the audience is very rude tonight."

"We're sorry," Jorie said.

"We're sorry," Eliza echoed.

Later, when they were eating alone, Catherine said, "Wouldn't it be grand if we could have music while we dined?" She laughed softly. "Minstrels de flânerie, jouant des violons."

Eliza came down stairs in her nightgown and crawled up on Jorie's lap.

"I don't feel well."

"Go back to bed, Eliza," her mother instructed.

"Come tell me a story, Jawie. Please."

"All right."

He started to rise, but Catherine objected. "She has to learn obedience. I told her to go to bed."

Jorie looked at the child. "You go on up like Mummy says, and when I've finished eating I'll come up and tell you *two* stories."

Pacified, Eliza left.

"She can't just come down and interrupt our meal like that and drag you off."

They ate in silence. "I worked so hard to make this a pleasant evening for us, and now it's all spoiled by that selfish child."

Jorie bristled. "I don't think she was being selfish. She doesn't feel well."

"Then the best place for her is in bed!"

The evening ended poorly. Nevertheless, each Thursday evening Catherine had a special dinner waiting in the dining room with her best tablecloth, candles and china.

He spent the night at work doing the same thing he'd been doing every day since he took this job. He picked up tiny pieces of lead with tweezers, whole words for the most common, and individual letters for the rest. Then he set them down carefully in the trays to make words and sentences. He'd learned to do it fairly fast, but his eyes started burning as they did every night, and by the end of his shift he had a headache.

He was about to leave in the morning when Mr. Abbot called him into his office.

"Roger's sick with influenza. I'd like you to cover that anti-union speaker tonight at the Town Hall. Can't promise, but if you do a good job, we'll probably run it tomorrow, and you'll be paid the free-lance rate."

Jorie was exuberant. In the weeks that followed he received two more assignments. But as enjoyable as the reporting was, it did not lessen his desire to return to Ann Arbor.

One evening he wrote to the University for a list of available scholarships, to be sent to him in care of *The Copper Country Evening News*. Even with his 'sizeable sum', whatever that was, he'd have to stretch it out over four years. He did not want to be caught short in the autumn.

When the letter arrived he spent an evening poring over the qualifications for each prize. Some struck him as absurd.

The applicant must be able to prove that he is a direct descendent of Joshua Daniel Abrams of Columbus, Ohio, and be seeking a degree in the field of law.

Another: *The recipient must have spent a minimum of two years in service for the Union in the Civil War, and have in his possession proof of honorable discharge.*

My God, thought Jorie. Eligible applicants would have to be over fifty years old!

But there were some that appeared to be more available, based on merit alone. Since Jorie had not been able to complete even one semester, he would have to rely on his high school records.

He decided to go to the school after work to ask Mr. Smyth if he would write a letter. On his way, the idea of asking Miss O'Dell came into his head. Did he dare?

As he approached her room he began to sweat. Class had been dismissed, and the youngsters, some of whom he recognized, were grabbing their coats and satchels, eager to be done with the school day.

But it was not Miss O'Dell he saw cleaning the blackboard.

"Hi, Jorie." A younger student waved to him.

"Where's Miss O'Dell?"

"She's not here no more."

The boy ran off. Jorie felt his stomach tighten.

He approached the heavy-set woman at the blackboard.

"Excuse me, ma'am, but could you tell me why Miss O'Dell is not here?"

The older woman looked him hard up and down. "Who are you, and what business is it of yours, may I ask?" She pushed a stray strand of grey hair back into her bun.

"I'm sorry. I was her student, Jordan Radcliff. I, I came to see her."

The older woman raised an eyebrow. "So you're Jorie. The one who got her in all the trouble."

The most awful pain was spreading from his throat down to his belly. They'd let her go, after all.

Suddenly the woman laughed. "Your Miss O'Dell has gone and got herself married."

"Married!" he was stunned.

"And moved downstate to Grand Rapids, she has. They dug me out from my grave over in Dollar Bay to take her place 'til they find someone else." She emitted a hearty laugh.

He barely heard anything after 'married.' He knew he had to say something. "That's grand. Thank you, thank you very much, Miss—"

"Billy."

He left in a happy daze. At least *someone's* dreams were coming true. He ran all the way home with a joy he hadn't felt in months, because he loved Miss O'Dell and she deserved to be happy.

The next day he was back again. "Excuse me, Miss—"

"Billy."

"Billy. Would it be possible for you to give me her address? I'd like to write her."

She regarded him for a moment. Then she said, "She'd like to hear from you. I'm sure she would." She rummaged through her desk for a piece of paper.

"Her husband, he's a fine young man. A salesman for a furniture company. Office and school furniture. Up and coming, he is. Did you notice the new desks?"

He had not. He looked now.

Mr. Gillespie—that's *her* name now, too—Mr. Gillespie, convinced the board of education that new desks would improve student performance. Doesn't that beat all? A good salesman, I'd say, wouldn't you?" She gave him a knowing look.

Jorie nodded. "Yes, ma'am."

"So that's how she met him. Him coming in here after school, measuring the room and such. Even measured the students, if you please, to make sure he had the right size desks for them—said that was the first thing a student should have—a desk that fit properly! Anyway, he kept coming back to make sure he got everything right. Leastways, that was his excuse." Miss Billy chortled mightily.

"That's splendid."

Jorie didn't tell his mother anything about the scholarship application. He received letters at the *News* from his philosophy professor and Miss O'Dell stating that their recommendations had been sent to the dean. Miss O'Dell told him she was thrilled that he was planning to attend the University. She also confided that she was expecting a baby in a few months, and that if ever he was near Grand Rapids she'd be most pleased if he were to visit them.

From the University of Michigan's Scholarship Committee, he received the following letter:

"May we express our heartfelt sympathy at the passing of your father. As the sole remaining parent of a minor, your mother has written withdrawing her permission for you to attend the University because you are needed at home. Therefore, any request for financial assistance from the University will have to be deferred until you have reached the age of eighteen. Your application will be held until next year, at which time you should let us know if you are still interested in procuring a scholarship."

Jorie groaned. He talked to Phillip at work. Phillip was the closest thing he had to a friend. Ten years his senior and already possessing stooped shoulders, the soft-spoken man had taken notice of Jorie. Often they ate together.

The next night Jorie complained, "If I wait until I'm old enough to apply, and then have to wait until they act on it, it will probably be the year *after* next before I'd get it, if ever."

"Get out of here while you can. I was set on going below and getting work at *The Detroit Tribune*, but I stayed to support my widowed mother. My older brothers got away, but it looks like I'm stuck for the duration."

"Well, scholarship or not, I'm going down there, toward the end of the summer, get a job, and go back to school. Might have to be part-time, but it will be something."

"What about your ma?"

"She said I could go. She'll be used to being a widow by then."

If he believed it, why did his stomach turn over when he said it?

Now that it was spring, Jorie stayed up to fill his senses with this wonderful season that was the harbinger of the coming summer. He would sleep in late afternoon and evening before going to his midnight shift.

In the warm May afternoon, shadowed snow banks still loomed high, but the hills were finally releasing their keep of water, held frozen so long in winter's clasp. Jorie stopped to listen to the trickle of little rivulets and the rush of broadening streams. Adding to the harmony were the calls of starling and blue jay. He wished it were as easy for him to discharge the frozen, pent up waters of his mind. He leaned against the fence imagining that all his troubles were melting away, joining the bubbling streams, leaving his head free and clear.

Finally, returning home, he went around the back and removed his muddy boots in the shed.

When he entered the kitchen, his mother didn't greet him with the hot chocolate she usually had ready for him. He found her sitting in a chair with her head on the table.

"What's wrong?"

She raised her tear-stained face. "We're done for, Jorie."

"What are you talking about?"

"I've just come from the lawyer's. Your pa's stock—it isn't worth the printer's ink."

She ran her finger back and forth over the words on one of the certificates. "Two of the companies went under." She tossed it in the air. "They don't even *exist* any more."

"What!"

She raised a fistful of wrinkled papers. "You see these bills? All unpaid."

Jorie was incredulous. "Why?"

"There isn't any money!"

Eliza came in and crawled silently up on his lap. Her tear-stained face implored Jorie. "Henna's gone."

Jorie looked to his mother.

"I had to let her go. We can't afford a housekeeper any more."

Eliza buried her head in Jorie's jacket. "I want Henna back."

Jorie added her protest. "She looks after Eliza!"

"*We*'ll have to do that now."

His head reeled with the new information. He sputtered, "But the new buggy, the oriental carpet, why did he buy them?"

"None of them paid for!" She turned away from him, her eyes overflowing with tears.

"How could that have happened?" Jorie struggled to grasp this new information.

"Your father handled the money. He was known as a man of means. He had good credit, but his investments had been failing—"

"Did you know this?"

"I knew some investments had dropped in value, but I had no idea how bad it was. He kept saying that as long as he left his stock intact, it would bounce back."

"But it didn't?"

She shook her head. "He put most of his salary into buying *more* stock, in different companies, hoping to redeem his losses. He was obsessed with the stock market. And buying new things made him feel safe, as though it weren't actually happening." Her lips twitched. "You didn't know your pa, Jorie."

He was silent. He could hardly believe what he was hearing. There was a ringing in his ears that was trying to drown out her words.

She wiped the tears. "Meanwhile, the debts piled up. The creditors were patient, not wanting to converge on a widow, but now they're demanding their money." She choked on the words. "And I don't have it."

Jorie tried to take this in. "He never let on to me he was short."

My God! He gave me money for school when he didn't have it to give!

Carol A Sheldon

He felt his throat swelling up. An old familiar feeling of guilt enveloped him. Maybe all these financial problems caused his stroke, and he had added to the problem by begging to go to the University.

"The Company isn't doing anything for you?"

She shook her head. "Had he lived 'til retirement, they may have given him a small pension. But death benefits for a widow, no."

They were silent while his head reeled with this new state of affairs.

He could hear the robins singing in the trees, and for a moment it was just another spring afternoon. He tried to take himself out of the scene the way he used to but her words pulled him back.

"I could sell my grandmother's china, and some of the furniture, but it wouldn't be enough." She implored him with her eyes. "We'll have to sell the house. That's the only way."

"Sell it! Where would you go?" Some vision of his future was trying to come into focus but he kept pushing it out of reach.

"I don't know. Take rooms in town, I suppose."

"With Eliza? You can't do that!"

His mother turned to him. "What else can we do, Jorie?"

We. She was treating him like he was the man of the family now.

The full implication of this news finally penetrated.

I'll never be able to go back to school. I'll never be able to leave her.

She was staring at him, waiting for his offer to stay and support them, while he sat numbly feeling he'd just consumed a meal of rocks.

He searched feverishly for alternatives, but could find none. He heard the scream inside his head. *What if he just took off and left her to work it out?*

Pictures started rolling in, playing in his head. Like the player piano at the ice-cream parlor, he saw the brass pins with the little square holes turning unstoppably toward their certain end. Pictures of being trapped. The anguished face of a miner caught in a cave-in, squeezed to death by the pressure of rocks, flashed before him. He saw this in some sort of dizzy spin intermingled with flashes of his mother's words, and all the time those little brass pins kept going round and round and wouldn't stop.

Suddenly the front door was before him. He kicked the bottom part again and again. When it refused to budge, he backed up, barreled forward ramming his body against the door. Five, six, eight times he did this before it finally yielded to his will. And as it did, the beveled glass splintered, sending out showers of glittering glass like fireworks.

Heeding neither her screams nor those in his head, he pushed through it, feeling the visceral satisfaction of muscling this barricade, knowing for one brief moment a taste of freedom. He dashed across the veranda, around the house, and up into the familiar hills, where he'd so often sought peace.

As he dashed up the muddy grade, he could see in the distance the towering smokestack discharging its black venom. To Jorie it was the apparition of a giant dragon whom the whole village feared, spewing its poison by day and by night.

I'll never be free. I refuse to live this way!

Before him stood the silhouette of the great shafthouse; its peaked structures, each higher than the last, rose step-like toward the sky. Housing enormous engines, belts and gears, it dominated everything below, standing sovereign over the whole village, and everything beneath it.

Surely a leap from the top would end his misery swiftly.

Jumping first onto a pile of snow-covered timbers near the lowest building, he leaped to the roof of the lowest part. From there, with the aid of the thick rope hanging from the cupola, he continued upwards, scaling the whole series of slippery, steeply pitched roofs, while at each level, melting icicles crashed to the ground.

Reaching the top he teetered on the crest, feeling the pull of the ground below.

I need time to think!

With shaking knees, he lowered his body, straddling the ridge. A downdraft brought the never-ending smoke from the towering chimney to his nostrils. Through the foggy web of ropes imprisoning him, he caught glimpses of the sky. He looked for the Seven

Sisters, which had always comforted, anchored him, somehow. He found them, but his starline was hazy, crooked. He couldn't focus enough to make it straight.

The roaring grind of the shaft belts reminded him of the colony of men working even now below the ground. How fortunate she'd said he was, to escape that fate. So much misery in all those drifts and shafts crawling with life. But did anyone really escape? He had his own dark tunnels, and was as much a prisoner of this community as they. At least a miner could use dynamite—discharge outward what wanted to be released within.

How could he live here, how could he *leave* here—this community she'd taught him to hate, that she wouldn't let him quit.

He threw back his head, spread wide his arms, and howled out his rage.

The shafthouse, with its own dissonance of noise, devoured the impotence of his fury. Even his screams went unheard.

I can't. I can't even do this!

"I don't know what got into him, Earl, to kick the door down like that. All he had to do was unlock it."

Catherine had summoned the sheriff and was relaying the incident over a cup of tea. She looked at the clock ticking away the night. Jorie had not yet come home.

"He's always been such a sensitive boy, thoughtful and caring. Lately, though, he's been acting queerly, so irascible."

"Of course the news about your...financial circumstances must have come as rather a shock."

Catherine nodded. "I think he was hoping to go back to school next year." She turned to Earl. "But considering our reduced circumstances, it's hard to believe he wouldn't *want* to stay and look after us." Despite her shawl she shivered with cold from the wind ushered in by the missing door.

She drained her cup. "And this is the boy who said he'd take care of me forever," she added bitterly.

"I'll talk to him."

She took his hand in hers. "Would you, Earl? He looks up to you, I know he does."

"Perhaps you'd best go up to bed, and leave him to me."

"Thank you. You've no idea how much I appreciate this."

When Jorie returned, the gaping hole where the front door once stood now demanded his attention. He would have to buckle down immediately, fashion a temporary barrier against the cold. It could not even wait until morning. Going round to the shed in back, he picked up what he needed and returned to the veranda.

The sheriff was waiting for him. Neither spoke. Jorie set the lantern down and positioned the first length of pine. Earl picked up a nail and the hammer, and pounded it in place. They worked silently in this fashion until the job was done.

"Thank you, sir."

"Let's go inside."

They walked 'round the house, through the shed into the kitchen.

"Are you going to arrest me, sheriff?"

"Hadn't planned to."

"Isn't that why she called you?"

"No. Let's sit down."

They sat at the kitchen table.

"Your mother's upset. She knows you're disappointed about school and thought—"

"Why did she send for you?"

"I believe she was frightened—by your behavior."

Jorie looked away.

"What did you do when you left here?"

"Ran."

"Where?"

"Up by the mine."

"Why?"

"I don't know. I had to go somewhere."

"What did you do up there?"

"Nothing."

"Look, boy, now that you've had your temper, you do understand that the only sensible course of action, considering the circumstances, is for you to stay at home."

"To support her, you mean." *Ad infinitum.*

"There are hundreds of boys and men around here doing exactly the same, some of 'em not more than fourteen years old. All those miners' widows, most of 'em looked after by their sons. Some grown men have been doing this for years. Can't afford to get married."

Jorie saw blood on his hand, shoved it in his pocket.

"I know about broken dreams, son. Had a few myself. But there's a fresh bloom behind every drooping one. Things will open up for you here, things you haven't even thought of yet. I hear you're doing real well at the paper."

How could he explain that it wasn't just his education that was at stake. It was his *life*. How could he tell the sheriff that he had to get away from *her?* That if he didn't escape soon, the net would so entangle him that it would become impossible.

"You can't just leave her and the child to the poorhouse. You wouldn't want that, would you?"

It was getting hard to breathe.

chapter 26

JORIE TRIED TO keep an ominous reality at bay by imagining it wasn't true. The situation was only temporary, and soon he'd be free to go wherever he wished. But even in his dreams it didn't last. Sometimes she'd find him in another city, envelop them both in the *Golden Bubble*, and bring him home. In the worst nightmares, he'd go back on his own. She'd smile in a strange sort of way, and lead him into her room. He'd crawl in bed beside her and she'd pull him to her bosom the way she did when he was little, but this time he would suffocate. Or she'd tell him to fetch the blue jar, but it was he who was applying the balm to her.

Each week he gave her the money he'd earned, keeping only a small amount for himself. The first allotments went to replace the door. After that he kept handing it over to her for running the household.

"Jorie, you don't know how much this means to me. What you're doing for your mama and sister."

She held her cheek up to be kissed. "I'll save it for you, for college."

He tossed his cap on the hook. "I'm going to go hear Mr. Lewis tonight, and write it up. See if old Abbot will buy it."

"You're such a clever one. You'll get ahead at the *News*. I know you will."

He changed the subject. "New York will begin service on its underground railroad this year."

"The world is advancing so. But Jorie, right *here* this summer, we're going to have the Ringling Brothers Circus! Won't that be exciting?"

"I'll take Eliza."

She picked up an envelope, and pushed it toward him.

"Open it," she said eagerly. "It's from *The Modern Journal of Poetry.*"

He tore open the envelope. "'We are pleased to inform you that we look forward to publishing your poem *The Intruder* in our fall issue. We would like to retain your other poems for future consideration.'"

"There's no check?"

He shook his head. "'We are a small press, unable to offer remuneration except as follows: We will send you five copies of the spring volume when the issue is printed in October.'"

"Still, they accepted it, and maybe they'll print the others later. Don't look so disheartened, dear. You're on your way, and I'll be with you every step!"

He'd been thinking about Pa's 'sizeable sum' all afternoon. He wondered if he dared ask. Well, now was as good a time as any.

"Ma, Pa said I'd get a sum of money when I turn eighteen."

He could see her shoulders droop.

"Did he...did he leave me anything? Or was it part of that worthless stock?"

"That money was not in stock certificates. It is intact, being held for you in trust."

He breathed a silent sigh of relief. "Do you know how much it is?"

"You will find out in the fullness of time."

"I want to know now."

She turned hard to him. "Are you thinking that when you turn eighteen you'll just take that money and run, deserting your mama and sister?"

"No! No, Ma. I feel obliged to support you, if Pa left you nothing. But if I get a scholarship I could go back to the University in the fall, and my inheritance could be used to maintain you and Eliza." He thought this the perfect solution.

She looked up at him in surprise, confusion. Finally, she said, "That's very thoughtful of you. But I don't think it would go very far. We'll talk about it when the time comes."

"How much is it?"

"The terms will be disclosed on your birthday."

"Tell me now!"

"I don't know! You've set my head spinning enough for one night, thank you!"

Surely she knew, but he realized that if she didn't care to divulge it, she wasn't going to.

Jorie started teaching Eliza to play little pieces on the piano. One day she turned to him. "Why doesn't Henna come any more? Doesn't she want to?"

"We don't have the money to pay her, Izzy."

"Can we go see her?"

Jorie made some inquiries and found that the O'Laertys had moved to a better section of town. He was glad at least that their lot had improved.

Three days later, on a lovely June afternoon, he took Izzy to visit Helena. He didn't tell Catherine where he was taking her. He decided to just go, before she could say no.

They took the new trolley as far as it went. That was an exciting treat in itself for the child, who'd never been on one.

The neighborhood was certainly a vast improvement over the squalor of their previous living quarters. A well-kept, modest house stood before them. A colorful garden of bright flowers danced behind the gate.

A woman came rushing out of the house to meet them.

"Jasus, Mary and Joseph, if it isn't m' darlin' Izzy."

Eliza jumped into her arms. "Henna!"

Picking her up and swinging her around, Helena cried, "It's blessed I am to have ye back in my arms, lass. It's sorely missed, you've been."

"Hello, Helena. Hope you don't mind our popping in like this. Eliza's been begging to see you."

"*Mind*, is it? I should think not in a thousand years. Come into the house and have yerself a rest."

While the kettle was on, Jorie asked, "Are you doing all right, Helena?"

"Better than all right." She looked around her. "As you can see."

Jorie didn't understand how this had come to be, but decided it wasn't his place to inquire.

"And what be yerself doin' home from the big college?"

"I'm not going back. Not this year."

Helena pursed her lips. "Is it your ma, then, won't let you go back?"

"She needs me."

"Aye, she always will."

Helena served tea and molasses cookies, and brought Eliza milk. "Come sit on my lap, my darlin' lass. She puts me in mind of an angel in heaven, with her chestnut curls and innocent face."

"Why don't you come to my house, Henna? Don't you love me anymore?"

"Oh, my precious darlin', what put that into yer wee head?" She grasped the child to her bosom. "Of course I love you, and will to the end of time, dear child."

"Then why don't you come?"

Helena held the child away from her and looked straight into her eyes. "Because yer mummy told me not to. And that's the long and short of it."

"Why?"

"I told you, Eliza," Jorie said, "Now hush about it."

Helena looked at the unhappy child. "I'll tell ye a faery tale. Have ye heard the one about the faeries that raised the human child?"

"No. Tell me that one."

When she had finished, Jorie asked, "How's Mr. O'Laerty?"

"Oh, himself's doin' grand. Daniel runs the *Penny Whistle* now, he does, Sean bein' retired."

"I'm glad he was able to find work after...the accident."

"As himself would say, "He's still got his drinking arm," she laughed.

When it was time to go Jorie stood up and thanked Helena for her hospitality.

"So soon? Well, don't make yourself a stranger. Come back and meet my Daniel."

"I will. I promise."

There was a clap of thunder.

"It was so sunny when we came—"

"Aye, the angels 'll be havin' a pee now."

As they ran for the trolley Jorie couldn't get over what a nice house Helena had. But how had she come by it?

He first met Kaarina at the little book store, where she worked as a clerk. Often in the late afternoon, after he'd awakened, Jorie would go for a walk, or peruse a book in this cozy warren where a comfortable chair rested near the fire. He'd been reading about the creation of national parks, and had asked the young woman if she had anything else on this subject. Lately he found himself returning more often, asking her questions and enjoying her conversation. She was a Finnish girl. He knew his mother wouldn't approve, but he refused to let that deter him.

She got off work at six. He'd wanted to ask her out for some time, but he wasn't accustomed to the company of young females. Would he be able to keep up his end of a conversation?

Nevertheless, one day he summoned up the courage to invite her to go for a walk. It was tea time, and he was embarrassed that he had no pocket money. So after a pleasant hour, he said "Good-night," promising to see her again.

The next payday he kept a little more money for himself. His mother stared down at the sum.

"I can't save anything for your future education on this, Jorie."

He wondered if she were saving anything anyway.

"I need some for myself."

He could see she tried to keep it light. "What are you up to?"

"I've met a girl. I'd like to take her out."

"At seventeen? Oh, Jorie." She rubbed his chin. "Barely a whisker, you're still a baby."

He jerked away. "I thought I was the man of the family, breadwinner and such, didn't you say? But when it's convenient for you, I'm a baby!"

She bristled. "Well, we can't afford for you to be courting yet. That's the truth. Some day when you get a by-line at the paper—"

"I've a right to keep some of my own paycheck."

She was quiet for a moment. Then, "As you wish. Of course, it's all yours, Darling."

Since he could find no way to feel good, whatever choice he made, he kept some of the money.

Kaarina agreed to go with him to tea on Thursday. All week Jorie waited impatiently. He remembered her sweet mouth, the way it moved in the most pleasing manner when she spoke. He wondered what it would be like to kiss her. He thought it odd that he knew so much about female bodies but had never actually kissed one. He hoped it wouldn't be long before he had that opportunity.

At about five o'clock he went to the book store and waited for her to get off work. He tried to read, but found himself forever glancing between the clock and her lovely face. She had full red lips, light colored hair, some of which escaped the hairpins and curled around her face.

At six o'clock they walked down the road to the Richmond Tea Room, a modest, but cozy English establishment. He had never been inside, but from the street he thought it looked just the place to take a young lady. To his delight they were seated on a brocade settee near the back of the room. A low table awaited refreshments.

Although he'd noticed girls before, it was the first time he'd been so close to one. He thought it heavenly. He drank up her shy smiles, barely aware of the scone and clotted cream he was consuming.

Suddenly Kaarina's finger was grazing his chin. He jumped.

"Just a bit of cream," she smiled, wiping it off.

The feel of her finger on his chin and the scent of her hand swept through his senses. It was one of the happiest moments he could remember. Long after the scones were finished, they sat and talked. He confided to her his dream of returning to the University; she told him of saving money to go to Suomi, the new Finnish College.

But under all the words, a strong feeling stirred in Jorie. Was he falling in love? Not having any experience with girls his age, he could only hope her smiles meant she felt the same.

Finally, the mistress of the tea room informed them it was closing time. As they sauntered down the street, he reached to take her hand, and she allowed him.

"Where do you live?"

He walked her home. Slowly, in the warm summer evening they ambled past children rolling barrel hoops and playing kick-the-can. Grown-ups, too, were out enjoying the all too short warm season. They lingered along the way, taking in the evening song of the birds and the bouquet of flowering lilacs. He broke off a small blossom from a branch overhanging the walk, and placed it in her hair. It soon fell to the ground but she quickly retrieved it, and for the rest of their walk twirled it in her hand, taking in its fragrance from time to time.

As they neared her home he couldn't decide whether to try to kiss her or not. He was so afraid she wouldn't let him that he decided to savor the sweet flavor of the success he'd had so far, and let the kiss wait for another time.

"Minum kaveri," she said.

"What does that mean?"

She smiled shyly. "It means 'Goodnight, my friend."

He practically ran home, jumping off the ground a few times. "Minum kaveri," he repeated over and over.

It was nine o'clock. On the dining room table, he could see candles in their silver holders burning down to stubs. He'd forgotten all about the Thursday musicale.

Carol A Sheldon

He stood there a moment while familiar feelings of guilt overcame him. It was so still he thought his mother must have gone up
to bed, but suddenly she appeared from the parlor in her dressing
gown. He braced himself for the confrontation.

Instead she said softly, "Did you have a nice evening?"

He wasn't sure he could trust her tone. "Yes. I'm sorry about
tonight. I forgot."

"Are you hungry? There's chicken. I've saved you the bosom—
your favorite."

"No, thank you."

"Let's at least have some wine together. Will you join me?"

She picked up the half empty decanter. After not showing up
for dinner, how could he refuse? She held up the glasses for him to
pour, and led the way to the parlor.

He lit a lamp. "I'm very sorry I missed dinner. It smells wonderful."

"No doubt you were having a wonderful dinner with someone
else."

"Just tea and scones."

"Tell me about her. Is she beautiful and talented? I allow she's
young, of course."

"She's very pretty."

"She'd have to be, and you so handsome. What else?" She
smiled up at him.

"She's very nice."

"Surely you can come up with a more descriptive term than
'nice'," she sneered. "You must have written a 'woeful ballad to your
mistress's eyebrow' by now." She laughed lewdly, then furrowed her
brow. "Was that Keats? No, it was Shakespeare."

He was at a loss for words. Some he'd save for his own reverie,
but did not care to share with her. "She has light brown hair. She's
rather tall."

"And how do you feel about her?"

It just slipped out. "Enraptured."

"Enraptured! By a plain tall girl with brown hair!" She lurched
towards him, but quickly righted herself.

He wished he'd told her nothing. Then he smelled it. She must have been drinking all evening.

"I shouldn't have said that. We are all equal in God's eyes. What's her name?"

He'd been dreading this. "Kaarina Pakkala."

"A Finn!"

"Yes."

"Common as pigs' feet. Oh, Jorie, is that the best you can do?"

He was accustomed to the prejudice. It wasn't just his mother, but a prevailing cancer in the whole community.

"She'll be out beating you with switches in the snow, if you're not careful, after a good warm-up in the sauna!" Her laughter was coarse, lewd.

He wanted to get away from her, to go to his room, and replay every minute of this amazing evening in his mind. He turned to leave.

"Jorie, please." She pitched against a chair.

"I'll help you up to bed now," he said.

She stumbled, but he got her to her room, leaving quickly before more requests were made of him.

Still, from down the hall, he could hear her calling him.

He lay on his bed trying to return to the sweetness of the early part of the evening, pushing his mother's needs out of his mind. Finally, he drifted into a dream where he and Kaarina were getting married. He was watching her dancing eyes as he placed lilacs in her hair; she was wiping cream from his mouth, and licking it off her fingers.

How sweet summer was: Everything tasted better, smelled better. He saw Kaarina as often as he could, and once a week took her on a picnic or to a restaurant. He was careful to be home on Thursday evenings.

One morning at breakfast he asked his mother if Kaarina could join them for their next musicale.

She set the coffee pot down. "Thursdays are *our* evenings. I don't ask for much of your time, and that's all I have to look forward to all week."

"But why couldn't she come too? You might like her."

She turned from the hotcakes she was making. "Do you invite me along when you take her out?"

"I thought you'd like to meet her."

"No, I wouldn't. You're not seriously courting her, are you?"

"I don't know, Ma. But she's grand."

She went back to flipping the hotcakes. He thought he saw her wince.

"You're moving too fast, Jorie. If you get that girl in trouble, you know what's expected of you, don't you?"

Jorie turned crimson.

"You would have to marry her—the first girl you'd ever known. And that would be the end of your education, believe you me! The end of all my dreams for you."

"And what might they be, eh? That I go to the Mining School and spend the rest of my life keeping house with you?"

For a moment he thought she might strike him.

Instead she dumped the hotcakes on his plate. "Please don't ask me to share you on our only evening."

He met Kaarina's parents. Her father spoke very little English, and her mother almost none. Both of them struck him as rather cold and distant. Jorie thought they were as suspicious of him as his mother was of Kaarina.

It was Thursday again, and Jorie headed home with a kind of grim determination to make it a short evening: to plead fatigue, and go up to his room.

He was in for a surprise.

"Darling, you'll never guess what new and wondrous piece of engineering we have acquired!"

"What are you on about now?"

"We'll call it an early birthday present for you. But first, let's don our party clothes, for tonight is indeed a very special evening. Don't peek in the parlor—not yet."

He couldn't remember seeing her so excited.

"Where's Eliza?"

Catherine drew the curtains. "She's been fed and put to bed."

"So early?"

"I've decided to allow her to skip her nap on Thursdays, so she's content to go to bed early."

"I wish you'd let her join us."

"To be frank, Jorie, I need some adult company and entertainment. I think you do, too. We'll take her on a buggy ride Sunday, all right? Now, change your clothes, and then go directly to the dining room—not the parlor."

When he came down, she handed him a bottle of wine.

"It's the last of your father's thimbleberry. Let's enjoy it!"

She lit the candles. The fragrance of lilac coming across the table reminded him of Kaarina.

"Now then, enjoy your wine; I'll be back in a moment."

She hurried off to the parlor.

In a few minutes he heard music!

She returned all excited. "Isn't it wonderful, Jorie? Can you imagine?"

"You didn't, did you?" His heart froze. "You haven't bought a player piano?" He rushed into the parlor. She hurried after him.

He stared at the alien addition to the parlor. "My God, Ma, they cost two hundred fifty dollars, at least!"

"I didn't *buy* it, Dear. Did you notice the dishes? They're not the china you're used to on our special evenings. I traded the china for the pianola."

"You traded it?"

"In a manner of speaking. I sold the china, in order to buy the pianola. I thought we'd get more enjoyment out of the music than the dishes. Don't you agree?"

"I suppose so."

"You didn't even miss them, did you?"

"Didn't the player piano cost a good deal more than you got for your china?"

"Oh, no, Darling—quite the other way. That's how I was able to afford this new dress. That china is from the old country. There was a lot of it, and it is very dear to buy here."

He tried to absorb the news. "Well, if it means so much to you."

"Oh, it has all kinds of possibilities. Different musicians to entertain us as we dine, won't it be splendid? And what's more, we can dance to it!"

"Dance!"

"Don't act like you never heard of it. Of course, dance. I'll teach you how, as my father taught me. I acquired several music rolls with the instrument—some classical, and some popular. Now we won't have to take turns playing for each other; we can both be entertained at once, by the invisible musicians! Won't that be fun?"

He couldn't share her enthusiasm. Was it her net closing in tighter, or the money that felt like strangulation?

"Oh, Jorie, cheer up. Let's enjoy ourselves. Don't make your mummy work so hard to bring a smile to your face."

He forced a smile.

"Now listen to the pianist. Do you know who it is?"

"No."

"It's the famous Paderewski. Did you ever think we'd hear him, almost as though he were right here in our parlor?"

She led him back to the dining room. They spoke little, listening to the melodious tones coming from the other room. He had to admit it was quite remarkable.

After dinner she explained how it worked. "The man who delivered it showed me, and now I'll show you. We can still play this piano manually, and will, Jorie. It's so versatile."

Something was missing. He looked around. "Ma, where's the rosewood?"

"We didn't have room for two pianos, and that was part of the trade."

"You *gave away* the rosewood? The piano I learned to play on?" His voice rose in intensity. "That was a work of art, Ma. This is a piece of—machinery!"

He saw the tears form in her eyes. "I thought it would make you happy." She turned to leave. "You are so difficult to please."

She went up the stairs, leaving the dishes on the table. He was left with his own angry words echoing in his mind and an intense feeling of shame in the way he'd treated her surprise. He decided finally to go to her.

She didn't answer his knock, but the door was ajar. He could see her lying, fully dressed on her bed. He stood in the doorway.

"I'm sorry. I know you were thrilled, and I've spoiled it for you. It's just...I loved that old rosewood. I thought we'd always have it."

Slowly, she turned toward him. "Then it's I who must apologize. I should have consulted you. You are the bread winner. I just wanted to brighten our dreary life. Acknowledge you, Darling, for your sacrifice."

"The evening need not be ruined. Let's go down and listen to some more."

"Truly? Oh, I'm glad you're not still upset. Yes, let's hear another piece." She rose from the bed. "What would you like—a concerto or sonata by Beethoven?"

"You choose."

She inserted a roll of music which had popular dance tunes on it. The first piece was *A Hot Time in the Old Town Tonight*.

"Now this is a change of mood, wouldn't you say?"

They listened to it while Catherine danced to it by herself, spinning around the room, keeping time to the music.

When it was finished she held out her arms. "Come, I'll teach you to dance."

"Oh, Ma, I don't—"

"You must, Dear." She was laughing.

He thought of Kaarina, and how he'd like to take her dancing. Perhaps he'd better learn.

He was seated and she went to him, pulling him up with both hands. "Now. You put one hand, here, around my waist—that's it, and I put my hand on your shoulder. Oh my, you're so tall, Jorie. No, put your left hand out here and I'll hold it with my right. It is you who must lead.

"This is a waltz, *The Sidewalks of New York*. Before we start the music up again, let me teach you the footwork."

She worked with him awhile, going over the steps.

The lessons continued, and not just on Thursday nights, but on other nights as well. Occasionally Eliza was allowed to join them, but never on Thursdays.

"Teach me to dance, Jawie."

Sometimes he'd hold her high and swing her around the room. Other times she made her own little dance steps. Eliza's favorite tune was *Pop Goes the Weasel*. His was *Jeanie with the Light Brown Hair*. Every time he heard it he thought of Kaarina.

"Don't look at your feet, Darling, look at your partner!"

He deliberately didn't hold her close to him.

"Jorie, you really do give yourself away as a beginner, holding me a yard away. It not only looks better, but allows the woman to follow you if you hold her firmly." She glanced at his stricken face. "Now don't look so frightened. I'm not going to bite you."

He held her closer. She looked up at him. Occasionally, he looked down into her upturned face, smiling self-consciously. Finally she rested her head on his chest. At least he didn't have to look at her then, but he knew she must be able to feel his heart beating wildly in his chest. Why did he find her so soft and beautiful? She was his mother, for God's sake!

"Do you know how old I am, Jorie?"

"I hadn't thought about it."

"Take a guess."

He didn't dare. What if he guessed too old?

"Well, I'll tell you this. I was only eighteen when you were born."

"Then you're just twice my age."

He could tell that wasn't what she wanted to hear. "Still only in your thirties," he added. "That's very young." He could see she wanted more. He tried to keep it light. "You look grand, Ma. Now let me concentrate on the steps."

"A pity we can't go to the dance with the band, but we'll just make do with our private soiree, and our very own pianist," she laughed.

Well, he didn't intend to make do. He decided he was confident enough now to suggest to Kaarina that they go dancing.

"Oh, Jorie, I don't know how!" Kaarina brought her hands to her face.

"Then I will teach you."

chapter 27

ONE EVENING, IN the middle of her bedtime story, Eliza said, "Jawie, what are those things waving up there?" She pointed up to the corner. "They're moving."

"Cob webs."

"I don't like them."

A soft summer breeze coming through the open window caused them to billow and flatten. Jorie took a good look around her room. The walls and ceiling were dingy and dirty. He was sure it was the original wall paper, never redecorated as many of the rooms had been. The paper was yellowed, and peeling at the corners.

"Would you like me to get them down for you?"

"Yes."

He fetched a broom and came back to clear them away.

Eliza's fourth birthday was coming up and Jorie decided he'd like to re-paper her room for her.

Catherine said, "We can't afford it. Not with you spending half your earnings gallivanting around town with that tart."

"Stop it! I'll not have you speak that way of her."

"I'll speak of her any way I wish. Whatever charms she has, they're dangerous, Jorie."

"Ma, you don't know her at all. You've no right to speak of her that way!"

"At least you could have picked one of your own kind. Even birds know to find their own feather."

"Are you going to start in on that again?"

He waited for her to simmer down. "I want to do something for Eliza's room. It needs redecorating."

"Then paint it."

He asked Eliza what color she'd like. "Lellow. With 'nanas and peaches on it."

He spent several evenings preparing the room—getting the old paper off, and plastering holes.

When finally the last orange had been painted, Eliza said, "Jawie, it's so pwitty!"

Her exuberance was all the thanks he needed.

Catherine said, "What in the world is that border of fruit doing up there?"

"That's what she wanted."

Catherine shook her head and walked away.

There was something else he wanted to do, and this required a trip to the cellar. Just descending into these depths brought back that dreadful memory of Walter. The late western sun streaked through the one small window, catching in its rays a galaxy of dust particles.

Jorie was looking for his old rocking horse. In the storage corner, cobwebs and coal dust covered everything—an old wicker perambulator, now partially eaten by mice, a barrel of Christmas decorations, bruised lampshades and a broken looking glass. He started moving boxes, crates, and sheets from the mysteries they concealed.

The rocking horse was hiding under an old quilt. He pulled it from its covering, and as he gently moved it back and forth, he recalled his boyish fantasy of riding across the sky until he'd overcome the monster.

He ran his hand over the smooth saddle. How polished it had become from all its rides. He noted the many chips in the paint, even on the left eye, giving it a strange blinded appearance. He hadn't noticed any of this as a child.

As he was leaving with it, his foot caught on a wooden crate. Something about the clatter it made stopped him short. He bent, opened the crate, and found himself staring at his mother's heirloom china. With his heart beating fast, he investigated a second wooden box, and a third. It was the entire set!

I sold the china to get the player piano.

Jorie stood in the cellar, trying to make sense of this discovery. Perhaps there was some explanation for it, but an ominous chill came over him.

That evening he asked Catherine about it.

"I *was* going to sell the china, and I had it all crated up, but when the player piano was delivered, and the man saw our old piano, he said he'd take that instead. He was taken by the rosewood cabinet, you see, and he gave me a bit of money besides."

He waited for her to continue.

"I knew you might be disappointed that our old piano was gone, so I didn't want to mention it right away, before you'd even heard the new one. That's all."

"But why did you cart the china all the way down to the cellar?" How difficult it must have been for her to carry those heavy boxes down the cellar steps by herself!

"I told you, I already had it all crated up to sell, and we really don't need it." She stopped suddenly. "Jorie, I'll not be questioned by you!"

He was silent, but not satisfied. He knew that she'd give no more away no matter how he pressed her.

Since Eliza had chosen a color scheme of yellow and peach he decided to paint the horse with the same colors. As he sanded the worn wood, he thought of his father planning and building it from scratch. He wondered if it gave him the same satisfaction he was getting now by restoring it for his little sister.

On the morning of her birthday, Jorie unveiled his gift to her. He winced when he realized that she probably wasn't really big enough for it, but he might be gone by next year, so this was the time for it.

"Rock me, Jawie, rock me!"

Her joy and cascades of laughter made it all worthwhile, made his sentence to this house bearable for a time.

"What's his name, Jawie?"

"Pegasus."

"Peggythis."

"Kaarina, John Muir is coming here. I'm going to go, and write up a report for the *News*. Will you come with me, Friday evening?"

Jorie spent the whole week in eager anticipation of Friday night. Two wonderful things on the same evening—hearing the famous John Muir and being with his girl.

As they entered the auditorium, he felt a hand on his shoulder. He turned to see the sheriff grinning at him.

"Didn't know you were interested in national parks, Jorie. Or are you here to cover the speech for the newspaper?"

"Both, actually."

They jostled their way in and the three of them sat together. Jorie introduced the sheriff to Kaarina.

"If I didn't have my heart set on going back to Ann Arbor, I'd sure like to go out west and join John Muir," he told them both.

"I had a similar dream once—of going out west," the sheriff confessed.

Jorie glanced quickly at Mr. Foster. For just a moment the curtain had been parted on his life—but just as quickly it closed.

"You have a lot of talent he could use—your knowledge of biology, skills in drawing and writing. That would be a great career for you."

"Maybe after I've finished my schooling." He took in and let out a deep breath. "It's a dream, anyway."

After Mr. Muir's impassioned speech there was such a round of applause Jorie started a standing ovation. Then he nodded goodbye to the sheriff, grabbed Kaarina by the hand, and strode toward the podium, where Mr. Muir was entertaining questions.

When it was his turn, he told John Muir flat out that he was a reporter, but also he would like nothing better than to follow in his footsteps.

"There's always room for young men with your enthusiasm."

As he walked Kaarina home, he said, "I think when I've finished my education, I'll join Mr. Muir out west. By golly, I think I will."

He grabbed Kaarina and pulled her to him.

They walked the rest of the way in silence. He was thinking how he'd like to ask her to go to the University with him, or out west, or anywhere at all they both would like to be. But it was too soon to say any of these things out loud.

He turned to her. "What about you? Are you making any headway in your savings toward Suomi?"

"A little. Dreams can change along the way, though." She looked up at him, her eyes shining in the darkness. "But we should always have at least one, don't you think?"

He squeezed her hand. In the shadow of her side porch, he held her close to him, aware of the pleasant way her body shaped itself next to his. Finally, he kissed her good-night, and raced home, excited about everything.

Life was good, after all.

The next day his mother hinted that it was her birthday. For the first time ever he'd forgotten. Late that afternoon Jorie walked along the wooden sidewalk of Quincy Street where the nice shops were and looked in the jewelry stores. He didn't have a lot to spend, and was surprised by how much everything cost. But he knew she'd felt badly about losing an emerald earring that matched her green outfits. He found a beautiful pair in Diemel's Jewelers.

"These are emeralds, but if that's too rich for your budget, I have something similar in glass."

Although the design was somewhat different, he couldn't tell the difference between the stones. Still, he wouldn't want to tell his mother they were glass, and he wouldn't want to lie, either.

"If you like, I can arrange a payment plan."

"Then I'll take the emeralds."

"Good choice."

It was a beautiful summer day, one so perfect, that in this land folks savored such days, spending as much time outside as possible. Mothers and nannies were wheeling babies in perambulators. He was whistling—happy with the gift he'd bought, reveling in the mellifluous times with Kaarina, and beginning to feel that life was bearable even in the copper country. He didn't know if he'd ever get away, but for now it was all right, and he had the satisfaction of knowing he was doing something for his family. Maybe Kaarina was right—dreams can change. He wondered if she were hinting that hers had, and she might be willing to go away with him.

Just then a familiar laugh caught his attention. Across the street he saw a woman on the arm of a man coming out of the Northwestern Hotel.

Could it be? He stared, trying to get a clear view of the pair without being noticed. Staying on his side of the street, he followed them for two blocks. The man hailed a cab. As they turned toward the carriage in the street, Jorie could see their faces, unmistakably.

It was his mother, with Mr. Markel, the undertaker!

He ran the rest of the way home with his thoughts spinning. Why was she seeing this man? Why hadn't she told him? And what were they doing in a hotel?

She was home before he was, already preparing dinner. When he walked in she greeted him pleasantly.

He asked, "How did you spend your birthday?"

"Much like any other day. I was looking forward to having a nice dinner with you, Dear."

"Wasn't the company of Mr. Markel enough for you?" It just came out.

She stopped stirring the pudding.

"I saw you, coming out of the Northwestern."

She gave him a big, innocent smile. "Mr. Markel invited me for lunch. I thought this might be a good day to take him up on it."

"Then why did you lie?"

"I didn't!"

"You said you spent today much like any other. Do you see him every day at this 'most commodious hotel', as you call it?"

"Jorie!"

"Why didn't you tell me?"

"It wasn't your business. What are you doing—going around town spying on me?"

"No. I was only there because you reminded me it was your birthday. I was buying your birthday present if you must know. Here!" He threw the box at her.

"Good Heavens!"

He grabbed her by the shoulders. "Are you intimate with this man?"

"Let go of me!"

She pulled away from him, rubbing her arm. He realized suddenly what he was doing and raced upstairs. Some weeks before he'd installed a hook and eye on his door, presumably to keep Eliza out when he was sleeping. He used it now and threw himself on the bed.

All of her teachings about honesty came ghost-like to ridicule him for being so naive. What of the *Golden Bubble* now, the sanctity of their relationship built on absolute trust and honesty? It all seemed a charade. With sudden clarity he saw that sacrifice for her wasn't holy at all, but simply an indulgence of her selfish whims.

Feelings of intense jealousy and rage filled him. Why had he stayed home, given up his own life to please her, if all the time her interests lay elsewhere? But why did he care? He knew those were the feelings of a jealous lover, and he had a romance of his own.

He tried to get the picture of his mother in the arms of Mr. Markel out of his mind, but it kept coming back. Maybe they weren't having that kind of relationship, but then what were they doing in the hotel? She'd said lunch, but it was almost four o'clock when they came out.

Realizing how inappropriate his rage and jealousy were, he was filled once more with self-loathing. He thought since he'd been seeing Kaarina that he'd gotten over his feelings toward his mother. He hated her for showing him he had not. Why had she hinted for the damn present! He wished he'd never gone downtown.

Three times she came upstairs and knocked on the door, but he would not let her in. When he rose to go to work, she called to him, but he grabbed his jacket and left.

In the morning when he returned, she was waiting for him in the kitchen.

"Jorie, you can't go on like this."

He stood at the window, watching a cardinal coaxing her little ones to leave the nest.

"Will you look at me?"

"I'm sorry I lost my temper yesterday."

"Yes, you should be."

"I wish I'd saved my money."

"I'm sorry you feel that way."

He turned to her. "Well, it didn't turn out well, did it? Pity you reminded me about your birthday—I could still be ignorant of your *amours*."

"Jorie, it's time you knew, I suppose, that Mr. Markel intends me to be his wife."

"You're going to marry him?"

Jorie's head spun with this new information.

She made her face take on the look of a girlish blush. "He's asked me to," she confided.

"Are you going to?"

"I suppose it would solve a lot of problems," she sighed. "He is not without means."

A hodgepodge of feelings rushed through him.

"Yes," she continued. "I suppose you could say we are engaged."

"When is the wedding?"

"I haven't given him a date. Don't rush me, Jorie."

When he left for Kaarina's that evening, he suddenly felt as though the prison door had been unlocked. He no longer felt duty-bound to stay and support his mother. She was going to be married! He was free, and it was time to get on with his own life.

With a lighter step he jogged the rest of the way to Kaarina's.

Three weeks after the subject had first come up, Kaarina and Jorie were bound for their first dance. There had been no place of privacy for him to teach her any steps, but the pleasure of holding his sweetheart would make up for all of their awkwardness on the dance floor.

"I'm sure a caller will give instructions for the reels. Let's just go."

He whirled her around the room to waltzes, and tried to keep up with the cotillion. As they sipped on lemonade, the announcer was telling them to ready up for the 'Tri-mountain Two-Step'. Jorie'd never seen Kaarina so happy.

Stepping and stomping around the room, Jorie suddenly found himself face to face with Mr. Markel, who didn't appear to recognize him. Jorie caught his breath and looked for his mother. But it was another woman whose hand the undertaker was holding. For the next half hour he kept glancing around, searching for Catherine, but it was clear that Mr. Markel's companion had his complete attention. Although he continued to enjoy holding and dancing with Kaarina, Jorie's mind whirled in confusion. Ma was expecting to marry this man, and here he was, in a public dance hall with another woman!

He felt a constriction in his throat. The road to freedom was disappearing in the dust of the dance floor.

Should he tell her?

"You went *where?*" Catherine bellowed.

"To the dance hall."

"You took that person *to the dance hall?*"

"Ma, I'm trying to tell you I saw Mr. Markel there with another woman. I thought you should know."

"I instruct you in the art of dancing, so we might have a bit of pleasure together in our own home, and you take my gift to go off cavorting with *her!*"

"I appreciate the lessons, but I have a right—"

Her voice was rising to a roar. "You deceived me! I gave you—"

"Don't *bray*, Ma!"

She reached up and slapped him sharply across the face.

He rose to go upstairs. "You don't own me."

On one of his walks, Jorie had discovered just the perfect place to take Kaarina for a secret rendezvous. They planned a picnic, and on a sunny Sunday afternoon they walked along the Frontage Road.

"Where are you taking me, Jorie?"

"You'll see."

"You won't tell me?" she teased.

He put his finger to his lips.

Soon he turned away from the road, and down a path. She followed him. There, between the road and the lake were boulders of sufficient size to shield the couple from the wind, and to give them some privacy. There was a flat area, too, on which they could sit.

"This is perfect, Jorie."

She stood still and looked around her, taking in a deep breath. Jorie watched with pleasure as she let out her breath, closing her eyes and spreading her arms wide. He wanted to take her in his arms right then, but decided not to rush things.

Together they spread the blanket Jorie had brought and then the table cloth Kaarina had, she carefully pulling the corners straight. Whether it was the reflection of the water or just her own natural beauty, Jorie felt her eyes sparkled like the pebbles glistening on the water's edge.

They placed the food from the basket on the cloth, and Kaarina handed him a napkin. Carefully with delicate hands she sliced the cheese. She handed him the knife and he cut large hunks from the freshly baked loaf of bread. She unwrapped the ham, already sliced, and put some on his plate. Although they ate silently, their eyes latched on to each other's frequently, and Jorie was offered a bouquet of smiles. He saw a speck of food on the corner of her mouth. It was his turn to reach across and wipe it from her face. She grabbed his hand in flight.

"What is it?" she asked inquisitively.

"Just a bit of bread."

"Touché," she said, remembering the cream on his mouth. He wiped it off slowly, grazing her lips with his finger.

When they'd finished the ham and cheese, Kaarina unwrapped something else.

"This is piparkakut," she explained.

"And the translation?" Jorie asked.

"Gingerbread biscuit. With molasses and orange peel. But you didn't ask for the recipe," she added laughing at herself.

He bit into one. "Very tasty. Did you make them?"

She nodded, and he ate two more to show his appreciation.

When they had finished their meal, Kaarina was the first to jump up and walk toward the water. There she turned and Jorie could no longer see her as she was hidden by the boulders. He followed her. She did not wait for him, and for a moment he thought perhaps he'd offended her in some way. But he dismissed that thought and jogged to catch up to her. She had found a low, flat boulder that jutted out over the water. Sitting on it, with her knees pulled up to her chin, she patted the warm stone next to her, and Jorie took his place beside her. She was looking out over the water, watching water birds looking for food, and ore boats heading west. He was watching the sun and shadows play on her face and the soft damp hair on her arms glisten in the sunlight.

He was surprised when she flipped over on her stomach and hung her head over the edge of the low precipice. He joined her in this pose. Kaarina pushed her sleeves up and ran her hand through the water. Jorie added his own hand to the water and together they created a little whirlpool. He reached for her hand, and they danced their entwined fingers together through the ripples. He recognized familiar sensations in his body as the heat began to climb his legs.

Suddenly Kaarina turned toward him, her face very near to his and gave him a quick kiss. That was all it took to ignite his courage. He pulled her toward him and kissed her, lightly at first. Then he grasped her tightly and kissed her longer—still softly; he didn't want to hurt her. But when she moved into him, her mouth eager and waiting for his, he thought no one since time began could have felt such bliss. She fulfilled all the promise he'd seen in it the first time he was with her. Her kiss swept away all his fears that the unnatural feelings he had for his mother might make it impossible to respond to another woman. This was wonderful! This was normal. A tremendous joy came over him, and to her amazement, he started laughing. Then he held her very close, savoring the moment for a long time, as she nestled in his arms.

chapter 28

THAT AUGUST EVEN the breeze felt like a blast from a smelting furnace. Jorie'd promised Helena he'd bring Eliza back for another visit, but the real reason he wanted to go was he was hoping Helena would have more information for him. This time he'd sent word so she'd be expecting them.

When they arrived, Helena swung Eliza around as the child squealed with delight. "There's my darlin' girl."

"Daniel's here today. Himself 'll be right pleased to meet you."

Her husband walked down the steps. "So this is the lass you've been weepin' o'er these many months. And here be the lad I been hearin' about for thirty years or more."

"I'm not as old as that," Jorie laughed.

"Don't recall a day as hot as this in ten year, do you? Must be the deevil heatin' up his furnaces to remind us what waits us below."

"Oh, don't be talking," Helena laughed.

"It's a cool drink we'll be needin'. I reckon the lad is old enough to have a draft of cider," said Daniel. He turned to Jorie. "It's not the soft cider you be used to."

Helena left to fix the refreshments, Eliza on her heels.

Daniel turned to Jorie. "Is it still working with the type-setting you're doing, or have you moved up to writing the whole paper now?"

Jorie smiled. "A little of both. I sneak in a piece now and then."

Helena brought in their drinks, and after a bit she gave Daniel a look and a nudge. He drained his glass and said there was something down at the pond he wanted to show Eliza.

Helena and Jorie sat on the porch swing. "I told him you might be wanting a bit of a chat, and would he take the child to see the polliwogs." She dabbed the perspiration on her neck with a large handkerchief. "Has she forgotten me, Jorie, or does she miss me still?"

"She misses you, Helena." He brushed the mosquito buzzing near Helena's neck away.

Tears welled up in the woman's eyes. "I love that little lassie. You too, mind, when you were a little lad. Though in your case you were so filled with your mum's love, there wasn't much space for me in your heart. But poor little Eliza, she was empty, she was, and had all the room in the world for me."

She blew her nose loudly. Jorie felt like doing the same.

"I miss her somethin' fierce. I couldn't have any of my own, not after...I lost the one. Your little sister was the same to me as if I'd borne her."

Jorie let a silence fall between them, while the mosquitoes, as thick in summer as snow in the winter, buzzed around them.

Then he said, "It's a nice home you have here, Helena. I'm glad providence was good to you."

"Providence, is it! Your father, that's who it was."

He didn't think he'd heard right, and stared at her, dumbfounded.

"It's just as amazed we were," she smiled. "Begod and bejasus, we never would have dreamed in a million year, your pa would be so generous."

"I don't understand."

"Nor did we. Shortly after the will was read, we was notified that Mr. Radcliff had left me a tidy bit. 'For her long and faithful service to the family' is what it said."

She looked up with pride. "What do you think of that, lad?"

"Splendid," was all he could say.

"How else did you think we got this place?" She fanned herself with her handkerchief. "It weren't the leprechauns that brought the bag 'o gold, believe you me." She sat rocking, musing.

"Pa lost everything, you know. His stock failed." He hoped to get Helena to open up some more.

"Failed, is it? Like the sun fails to set. No, lad, you got that all wrong. Your father died a rich man, he did."

"My mother, we...we don't have anything, except what I earn. That's why I have to stay home."

"Is it now? Is it indeed?"

He thought she looked angry, dabbing at the perspiration on her forehead.

"You're stayin' home because that's where your ma wants you. And that's the long and short of it, lad."

Something in his mind began to churn. But he said, "Mother took all the stock certificates to the lawyer, and they're worthless."

Helena just shook her head, and watched him carefully. "Maybe you've heard enough for one day."

"No. Go on. Please."

"Well, this much I'll tell you. One day when your ma was out your pa asked me to witness the will he'd written. 'Read it first,' says he to me, 'before you sign it.' 'I can't read, not that kind of fancy language,' says I. 'Then I'll read it to you,' says he, and he did. He said something about feeling bad he hadn't done more for us in our Hour of Need, he did. That was when Daniel lost his arm in the mine, and I was at such sixes and sevens about it, I lost the baby I was carrying. Oh, such a time was that. Anyway, he said he wanted to make it up to us. Saints be with us, you could have blown me over. Of course, I had no idea it would be comin' to us so soon, or so much, God save us all. But it weren't more 'n three weeks later he took sick and died."

"I see," said Jorie. Ugly pieces he didn't want to see were coming together.

"And as for you, lad, I'm sure you know your brothers got a sum when they turned eighteen—mostly company stock. But yer father wanted you to get yer education. That's what himself said to me. And it was right there in the will that you would get your sum in cash when you turned to the age of eighteen."

"Yes, Mother says that money is intact."

Helena crossed herself. "I should hope so."

"Are you telling me that Mother—"

"Believe what you like, lad. Believe in the faeries, if it suits you, and put milk out for 'em so they won't take yer firstborn, like we did in the ole country."

His head was in a swim. Could this be? Had his mother imprisoned him with lies all along?

"Helena, would you mind looking after Eliza for awhile?"

"Mind! It would be all the saints blessing me at once!"

He raced along the dirt roads all the way to the lawyer's office, stirring up a cloud of dust which lodged on his sweat-covered skin. He prayed he wouldn't be too late; he was determined to ferret out the truth.

He had met Mr. Wilson a few times at the house. The lawyer received him warmly.

"I was just closing up, lad. But come in, come in."

"I'm sorry to keep you, but it's important."

"That's all right. How are you, and how're you doing down at the University?"

He was out of breath, and the sweat was pouring down his back. "I'm not in school, Mr. Wilson."

"I'm sorry to hear that. What can I do for you?"

Jorie was so afraid he was out of line; he had to shove his hands in his pockets to keep them from shaking.

"I wonder if I might see a copy of my father's will," he said as strongly as he could.

"I don't see why not. I was surprised you weren't at the reading. Your brothers were there."

When was that? Why hadn't he been told?

"I, I didn't know about it."

Mr. Wilson raised his eyebrows. "That's strange. I thought perhaps you'd gone below to the college."

Jorie shook his head.

"How old are you, lad?"

"Not quite eighteen."

"Well, that could explain it, I suppose. Being a minor, your mother may have decided not to include you. That was her prerogative, of course."

Mr. Wilson fished around in his files and finally produced a folded legal document.

"I can't let you take it, but you're welcome to come back tomorrow and read it."

"Did my father leave me anything?"

"Oh, yes. Same as your brothers, let's see here."

"Mr. Wilson, sir, do you know, at the time of his death, if there were actually funds available, to be dispersed as stated in the will?"

"Yes, of course. Why do you ask?"

"Did he leave my mother enough to live on?"

"If she lives to be one hundred."

Jorie thought his heart would surely give out. "Are you certain?"

"I am. His stock, you see, is doing very well."

Jorie left the lawyer's office in a fury, determined to confront his mother. He tore through town, dodging crowds. Why were there so many people choking the walks and streets? Then he heard it—the sound of drums and horns. The circus parade was coming right down Hancock Street! To avoid them he cut over to Quincy. After three blocks, thinking he'd outrun them by now, he darted up Reservation Street back to Hancock. But they were thicker than ever here. As the hot August dust choked him with its unrelenting blast he bolted through and around bystanders and participants alike, colliding with a clown and practically trampled by the elephant.

Finally reaching the house, he looked wildly about for his mother, first on the ground floor, then upstairs. He burst into her room, but she wasn't there. Retracing his steps he caught sight of her—in his sister's room.

She was on the bed, with only a towel covering her.

He bellowed, "What are you doing in Eliza's room?"

"What's wrong with you? It's the coolest room up here."

"Get up! You've no right in Eliza's room,!" he panted.

"Of course I have. The whole house is mine!"

"Get out! Where are your clothes?"

She looked frightened. "I've just had my bath."

"Get out!"

She rose, grasping the towel in front of her. "Jorie! Are you mad?"

"Everything, it was all a lie! You don't need my money—you've enough to last forever! "

She trembled, and for a moment he thought she might faint.

She stammered, "I had to tell you that to keep you here. Please try to understand, Jorie."

He grabbed her arms and the towel fell to the floor. She tried to pick it up and he kicked it aside.

"Jorie, let go of me!"

He lifted an arm and held it in contracted force ready to strike; finally he willed it to his side, advancing toward her.

"Deceit! That's all it's been. Lies, schemes, deception! Have you ever been honest about anything?" He shook her, pushing her backwards, as he shouted, "Have you?"

"Do you think I enjoyed lying to you? I had no choice!"

She backed into the rocking horse, then fell on it. The picture of his mother's naked body on Eliza's rocking horse was macabre. He pulled her away from it, and pushed her on the bed. She grabbed him, causing him to lose his balance and fall on top of her.

She tried to hold him there. "Jorie, I love you! More than anything! You know that! Come to me, my precious."

Her body twisted against his. Something inside his head was ringing and spinning. Like a snake, her arms coiled around him drawing his head down to her. If he stayed a moment longer the unthinkable would happen.

Suddenly, the ringing stopped and he felt a cord snap. The picture shifted slightly, and he saw her—not a goddess of beauty and power, but a desperate, pathetic human being resorting to anything to hold him in her keep.

Any desire he'd ever had for her vanished.

Carol A Sheldon

As she grasped him ever more tightly, he forcibly uncoupled from her arms and rose.

He picked up her towel and tossed it to her. "Get dressed and get out of this room."

His clothes were wet through with sweat. Exhausted, he went to the back of the house, dipped a bucket in the rain barrel and dumped it over his head. The coolness helped him collect his thoughts.

One thing at a time. Eliza. Yes, she was still at Helena's. He must go get her. Thank God she hadn't been home to witness the terrible debacle in her bedroom.

He used the long walk to try to piece together his mother's deception. Acting, it was all play-acting. The crying over the table with the *worthless* stock certificates. The china she'd *traded* to get the player piano. How she made as though they'd barely have enough to eat if he didn't forfeit *all* of his salary. And her engagement to Mr. Markel, probably cooked up to make her soiree with him seem more respectable. The more he remembered the sicker he got until half way across town he threw up in the ditch.

When he finally reached Helena's street, he could see her on the walk waiting for him.

Eliza ran up to him. "Where were you, Jawie?"

"Daniel, take the child for another walk, will you?"

They left with a jar to collect some polliwogs.

"Tell me lad, what happened to you. Saints be with us, you've a face on you like the deevil drug you over hot coals, and back again."

Only inarticulate noises came out. Finally, the dam broke.

"That's it, lad. Let it out. Let it all out. Faith and Begorrah, you've had a fright."

Much of it—the image of his naked mother, his shame, he couldn't tell her.

Finally he managed to say, "She lied to me, Helena. She fabricated all those stories about having no money just to keep me home."

"I t'ought as much. Aye."

"She admitted—it was to keep me home."

306

"I knew she'd stop you from going one way or the other. It wasn't my business to inquire how."

The tears streamed down his face. "She *lied* to me! Everything she preached about trust and honesty—it was all a charade!"

She looked at him sympathetically. "I think you just grew up today."

He was quiet finally, and Helena brought him a cup of cold tea. When he'd composed himself they walked down to the pond to fetch Eliza. She showed him the polliwogs in the jar.

"Look at my 'wogs, Jawie. They're going to turn into frogs!"

Helena put her hand on his arm as they watched the creatures squirm in the jar. "Everything changes," she mused. "And believe me, sometimes it's for the better."

chapter 29

HE WANTED TO leave the house for good that night, but he had promised to take Izzy to the circus. The next afternoon they joined the throngs entering the big tent outside the village. Her joy at seeing the thrilling feats of the performers made up for missing the parade. But though it tore him apart he knew he must leave her if he were ever to shake off his mother's shackles.

He left the house that night with a few of his belongings and moved in with Phillip and his mother. He would bide his time for three more weeks until his birthday, at which time he'd collect his inheritance and leave for Ann Arbor. At least he no longer had the burden of supporting his mother, nor felt any filial duty to her at all.

Away from Ma, he had a lot of time to think. Perhaps there'd been a kind of victory that night in Eliza's room, after all. He'd finally conquered the perversity that had been his nemesis. A sense of freedom descended on him.

He felt anguish when he thought of Kaarina. He too, had been deceitful. What if she'd known his feelings for his mother? What if she knew him as he actually was? He didn't feel clean enough to be with her, to accept her love. Besides, he was too young to contemplate any serious romance. With Kaarina it could be nothing else. He should go to her, explain why he had to end the relationship.

Two weeks went by before he summoned the courage to see her. He walked around her block twice before he gathered the nerve to approach her porch. Just as he did, he realized she wouldn't be home—she'd be at work! He waited until near the end of the day to go to the book store. He didn't want to make her nervous, so he stood outside by the next shop, and when she left the store, he approached to her.

She was startled, but he tried to offer a friendly smile. They walked side by side for two blocks before either said anything. Finally, he spoke.

"Kaarina, you know you mean a lot to me." It sounded lame. He hurried on. "I'm planning to leave town." That was worse, to spit it out so suddenly.

"Oh," she tried to sound casual. "Are you going back to Ann Arbor?"

"I hope to, yes. As soon as I get my inheritance. In a few weeks. On my birthday."

She waited for more. How could he tell her how unclean he felt. How tangled up he was with his past. How he didn't feel good enough for her. And how he loved her and wanted to be with her always.

He started to reach for her hand, then retracted it. My God, what if she thought he was going to ask her to go with him!

He knew she was looking at him, but he avoided her gaze.

"Kaarina, I think I—"

"Yes?"

"I think we're too young—" he stammered, "to make any plans now."

Her gaze fell to the ground. "You're right, of course."

He turned to her at last, and she looked up at him, then away. He heard a catch in her voice. Every fiber in his being wanted to take her in his arms. Instead, he shoved his hands in his pockets. They continued walking.

A carriage passed, and then the street was quiet. They had not yet reached her house, but she stopped.

"Will you come back, do you think?"

"I, I don't know."

There was nothing more he could say.

"I will never forget you. Minum kaveri," she said.

"Minum kaveri," he repeated. A lump as big as a walnut formed in his throat.

He saw her tears then, as she bit down on the inside of her cheek. All his resolve melted. He took her in his arms and pressed her to his breast. He could feel her heart beating like the little sparrow's who'd been caught in the chimney last winter.

She allowed his embrace for a few moments, and then she pulled away.

"Maybe someday—" he started to say. But she was already gone.

September came and went, and with it his hopes of getting into the fall semester at the University. But he still planned to leave for Ann Arbor after his birthday in October.

He dreaded seeing his mother, but feared if he said nothing, she would be unprepared to give him his inheritance on his birthday. He hadn't been to the house since the night after that terrible scene in Eliza's room. Two weeks before his birthday, he climbed the hill with trepidation.

He found her in the swing on the veranda, eating a cluster of grapes. The vines covered the trellises, and the autumn rains had swelled the Concords to their full ripeness.

He stood several feet from her. "Where's Eliza?"

"With the Stockwell child."

He flicked a mosquito off of his arm.

Her smile was contemptuous. "You still can't kill them, can you?"

"Who are the Stockwells?"

"The family that bought the Kukkonen's place last year."

Well, at least Eliza was allowed friends.

"She goes there almost every day. At least for the time being."

"I've come to tell you that I'm leaving right after my birthday. I'm going back to the University as soon as I get my inheritance." He resisted an impulse to brush away the pesky mosquito trying to land on her face.

She was listening to the drone of the insects. "You know, they never bother me. I rather like the sound they make. Don't they just pinch the music out of the night?"

She sucked the grape from its skin, savoring the sweetness of its flesh, discarding the bitter skin. She plucked another cluster, holding it out to him. "They're more succulent than ever this year."

"No. This is not a social visit. It's an announcement. I'm going back to school."

She laid the grapes in her lap and sat up straight. Jorie watched her mouth move tenuously, carefully choosing her approach.

"Please don't leave me now, Jorie. You can't leave your mother up here in this God-forsaken place, without a man to look after her."

She was still doing it!

"What about Mr. Markel?"

"He's taken up with another widow. Like a vulture, he circles and waits, picks us off at funerals, when we're most vulnerable!"

"You said he wanted to marry you."

"I suppose he got tired of waiting."

Jorie held back a snicker. "Well, I'm sorry. I'm going back to school."

He saw her face harden. A ghoulish smile curled one corner of her mouth. The sunlight filtered through the vine leaves, and for the first time he noticed the lines around her mouth. She picked up the grapes and pinched another from its skin.

"The University of Michigan wants its students to be of up-standing character." His heart froze. *Was she saying what he thought she was?*

"To be plain with you, I am prepared to write them detailing the state of your mind, Jorie. You are mentally unstable, and you will never be admitted. The sheriff can back me up. He was here, you'll recall, the night you broke the door down from *the inside*."

She spat the skin out on the ground, and drew another grape from its shell. "We know about your fiasco climbing the shafthouse! The night watchman saw you, and the sheriff has that on record too. I was compelled to report the bruises you left on my arms the night you went crazy with jealousy over my seeing Mr. Markel, and that in my child's room you stripped me of all covering, and forced upon me shameful behavior no mother should endure."

His gaze shifted to the vines behind her. He knew from swinging on them as a boy how strong they were. In his mind he could see them winding around her neck, ensnaring her in their trap, squeezing and silencing every venomous syllable.

Instead he willed himself to walk away.

Up in the hills he flung himself on the ground, grasping the protruding toes of the beech tree. Howling his rage and despair, he released his energy to the earth, the great mother, who could absorb all his sorrows.

He didn't know which was worse—his dreams of education turning to ashes, or the extent of his mother's betrayal—the collapse of all he'd placed his faith in, his *madonna*.

In the following days he calmed down enough to sort things out. He realized he could probably go to some other college; she couldn't write to them all. But somehow the dream had died, along with something inside. He just wanted to get away. If he could hold on until his birthday.

The national park system interested him as much as anything. He'd take his inheritance, if she hadn't found a way to queer that too, and go out west. Maybe he could even work with John Muir.

In the early evening he found her in the garden gathering the last of the tomatoes before the frost.

"Ma, my birthday's next Thursday. I want you to have the papers ready, or whatever you have to do, so I can go to the bank. Then I'll be leaving."

She turned to him with a little smile. "Perhaps it is time you understood the terms of your father's will."

"Are you going to tell me he didn't leave me anything?"

"Oh, no. He did. But you're making a hasty assumption about *when* you may receive this money."

I knew there'd be something.

"The terms of your father's will state that you shall receive a sum 'upon attaining the age of eighteen, *or at such time that your trustee believes you to have obtained sufficient maturity to manage your inheritance.*' I believe those are the exact words."

"Who is my trustee?"

"Why, your mother, of course."

Everything was spinning in front of him, including the shovel that lay between them. Then he deliberately went numb, for if he didn't, he knew he would strike her.

He walked to the lake, skipped pebbles across the still water, each one disturbing the surface and that which lived below.

He realized he would never get his inheritance. She had always held the high cards, and today she'd played her ace.

He traced over and over the steps she'd taken to ensure his servitude. Ever since he'd been small, training him to be her devoted slave, asking him to sacrifice friends, keeping him so isolated he had none but her as ally and mentor. And when he was fourteen making herself seductive with her nude painting scheme. Posing for him. *But not directly in front of you, Dear—that wouldn't be right!*

He thought of all the tricks and lies she'd employed to keep him home from college. Why? Why was she, whom he had venerated, determined to undermine, sabotage all his dreams? What had he done to cause betrayal of this magnitude? She had even managed to contaminate the first innocent and pure love he had for someone else.

The fact was that according to the wording of the will, not only could she withhold his inheritance as long as she liked; she could have given it to him *before* he was eighteen, if she'd a mind to. There was no financial reason to take him out of school.

But if she thought she could keep him now by withholding the money, she was wrong. He would just leave town. She couldn't prevent that.

He'd promised to stay on the job until the end of the month to cover two stories coming up. Then he would take the train to Chicago, get a job and work there until he had enough money to go west. Until then, he would stay at Phillip's.

She had done her dirty work. There was nothing more she could do to stand in the way of his freedom.

PART III
1900

chapter 30

ON HIS SECOND night in the county jail, an eruption of shouting and cursing from down the hall roused Jorie from a restless sleep. Undersheriff Lockheed was wrestling one of the local trouble-makers into a cell. The turnkey, Hensen, jumped up to help.

Jorie could hear the men scuffling with the prisoner.

"Shit! I didn't do nothing.'"

"Sleep it off, Jimbo."

"What's the charge?"

"Drunk and disorderly, vagrancy."

"Fuck! Nothin' happened. Just a good sportin' fight."

"Get your sorry ass in there before I charge you with somethin' serious."

When they had him secured, Hensen stuck his nose between Jorie's bars. "Looks like you're going to have company tonight—one of the Groden gang. Nasty lot, that. Good luck sleepin'."

For the next hour Jorie lay on his cot listening to the volley of foul language coming from the next cell. At times the kicks on the wall caused plaster to fall off the lath on Jorie's side. Finally, his neighbor passed out in a drunken stupor and Jorie fell back into a fitful sleep.

In the morning Jimbo was raising a ruckus to get out. When Sheriff Foster arrived, he informed the prisoner he was going to be a guest of the county for the rest of the day.

"And when you do get out, you're hot footing it out of town, and taking your whole quintet with you. You got that?"

"Shit! What if I don't?"

"A matured and finished sinner, such as yourself, should know the answer to that."

Earl opened Jorie's cell. "You ready to talk yet, kid?"

Jorie tried to sort out his jumbled thoughts.

"Your boss called, said you'd turned in your resignation a month before—before your mother died. Said you were planning to leave town in a few weeks. What do you have to say about that?"

Earl Foster waited for an explanation. All he got was a puzzled frown.

"Look, I'm running out of patience. You're either being a real smart-ass, or you've gone loony. Whatever it is, I haven't got all month to figure it out. What happened that day in the storm?"

"I don't know."

Earl raised his voice. "You talk now, boy, or you'll talk in court! One way or another!"

Earl Foster counted to ten, turned on his heel and left.

In the afternoon Helena came to see him. During her stay a steady stream of tears coursed down her face.

"I never thought I'd be visiting you in a place like this, lad. I don't believe a word of it. As if it weren't bad enough, you losin' your ma, now they're saying—"

She pulled out a man's handkerchief and blew loudly into it. When she had sufficiently composed herself, she said, "What do you make of it, Jorie? How could they even think—"

Jorie shook his head. "How's Eliza, Helena?"

'She's a frisky one, she is. Up at the crack every day, laughin' and gigglin'." Helena's smiled faded. "It's missin' you, she is. And her ma."

Jorie swallowed hard. "I think she should know, Helena. That Ma's not coming back."

His old nanny's eyes opened wide. "Is it askin' *me* to tell her, you are? That she's...*dead?*"

"If you could see your way to doing it, I'd be mighty grateful."

"Sure and you can't be sayin' that, lad!"

Jorie remained silent as the woman blew her nose again and squirmed in her seat.

"I'll try. With the help of Mary and Jasus, I'll do it." She crossed herself, and Jorie watched the gears move. "I'll explain she died in the storm, which is God's truth, and gone up to heaven, to be with Jasus." She twisted her mouth. "That is what happened, isn't it, Jorie?"

"Yes."

"Then that's what I'll tell her."

The woman wiped her face, then reached down into her basket.

"I brought you some cookies, lad. The kind you were always after me to bake when you were a wee lad."

"How kind you are, Helena."

"Soda cookies with cinnamon and sugar on top."

"I remember."

Helena got up to leave. Jorie started to embrace her, but that set off such a rush of sobs he pulled back.

"Give Eliza lots of hugs for me."

"I will, I will," she managed as she left.

He had assumed the prisoner in the next cell was sleeping while Helena was there. He was wrong.

"Hey, ain't you the guy what left his ma out in the woods to die?"

Jorie was silent.

"I heard about you. Your brother's tellin' everybody he saw you do it." The man waited. "Hey, are you deaf or what? He's sayin' he followed you out there—how you *planted* her in the storm and high-tailed it back to town."

Again the prisoner waited for a response.

"Well, ain't you got nothing' to say?"

"Nope."

"That right? Well, the boys in town do. They're placin' bets on you—whether you done it deliberate or not. Most bettin' you did."

Jorie tried to tune the man out, turned his attention instead to the munching of the termites. But the voice came through anyway.

"If you make it out a here, they'll give you a necktie party fer sure."

The next day Earl brought Jorie his supper. The diner near the jail furnished the inmates' meals, but Earl thought maybe he could loosen Jorie's tongue with something home-cooked. Besides, he felt bad about yelling at him the previous day.

He knew he didn't have to visit the prisoner at all. It wasn't his job. The real reason he was here was that like the itchy rash on his hand, he couldn't leave it alone.

He watched Jorie attack the beef stew with gusto.

"Glad to see you eating, lad. Beginning to think you were set on starving yourself." Jorie said nothing, so he continued. "Do you know who made your dinner?"

"No."

"Mrs. Foster."

Jorie tightened his lip.

"You recall planting carrots with her?"

Jorie barely nodded. He remembered the beef stew and Mrs. Foster insisting he have seconds after all the hard work he'd done in the garden. Then she'd served up the best lemon meringue pie he'd ever tasted.

Tonight there was no pie.

Jorie speared the last carrot and ran the piece of bread around inside the pan to scoop up the rest of the gravy. When he was finished he looked up solemnly at the sheriff.

"Tell Mrs. Foster thank you."

The sheriff nodded. "Look, if I'm going to help you, I got to know what happened, and why."

"I know."

Tell me about this plan to leave town."

"I had planned to, yes."

"Why didn't you tell me?"

"It didn't seem important. I decided I couldn't go. Not after..."

"Why not?"

"My sister. With Ma dead, how could I leave?"

"When did you first decide to take your ma on that ride?"

Jorie frowned. "I'm not sure. Sometime that week, I think."

"Then it wasn't a spur of the moment thing."

"No."

"Why did you want to do this?"

"I've *tried* to remember." Jorie held his head in his hands. "I think she'd been asking me that week to take her for a country ride."

Earl Foster shook his head. "You've had a lot of trouble with your mother. You wanted to have her committed, remember? Why was that?"

Jorie rubbed his face. "I don't know, sir."

"Failing that, did you think the only solution was for her to die?"

Jorie was following a spider's journey along the edge of the floor. "It's getting dark inside my head."

Earl sighed. "Well, when the sun comes out, enlighten me, too." He rose. "I brought you some reading material."

Jorie brightened.

"This is your mama's diary. One of them. I probably shouldn't be letting you have it, but I'm going to. Seems like your mind jumped the track, boy. Maybe reading this will help bring it back."

Jorie was silent.

"You have a go at it, all right?"

Jorie lay back down on his cot.

"Well, I'll leave you to your reading, while there's still some light."

Earl set the parcel on the end of Jorie's cot, and took his leave. He didn't know if he'd done the right thing or not, though he suspected the boy had already read the diaries. Why else were they in his room? And he wasn't sure leaving it would do any good, but it was worth a try.

Jorie stared at the book a long time. It was like a thing alive, waiting, commanding his attention. He'd taken the two diaries from an old trunk in his mother's closet several months ago, but couldn't bring himself to read them.

Now the parcel just sat there, waiting, would wait with infinite patience, until he picked it up. He wanted to hide it—from himself. There was not even a drawer to put it in. Why hadn't he told the sheriff he didn't want it?

When he looked away, the bundle seemed to bore into him with invisible eyes, daring him to open it, daring him not to. Like a cat poised to pounce its prey, it waited silently. For an hour he lay on his cot, resisting the voice: *Go ahead, read it. It's yours now.*

He considered putting it under his bed, but he knew that would be admitting its menacing effect. There was no way to escape it.

Even now, she was defeating him.

With quick darting movements, as though touching hot coals, he loosed the string, gingerly removed the brown paper the sheriff had wrapped it in. The thick volume was closed with a strap and locked. Possessing no implement with which to dislodge the closure, Jorie attacked it. The tired leather put up little resistance, yielded easily to his will. Before him was his mother's hand, younger than the one he knew, but unmistakably hers.

He opened it at random. The brittle, yellow sheets fairly crackled as he turned the pages.

And there she was before him, open and inviting as she'd always been.

February 9, 1888

For many weeks now, it has been most difficult to sleep. Again tonight, after lying awake for hours listening to Thomas's snoring, I left the warmth of the bed, went shivering to the kitchen where a few embers from the stove still gave off heat. Here I took pen to paper, recording my thoughts. It is strange, but somehow when finished, it is as though I have taken a sleeping powder, for then my hand, my head and heart can finally come to rest.

Jorie turned a few pages and read:

I touched Thomas's shoulder gently, ran a finger gently up and down his spine, but he never turned to me. It has been so for several months now.

He snapped the diary shut, tucked it under his thin mattress. This was no business of his—had never been. He would read no more. But like his mother, the balm of sleep did not come.

The turnkey admitted Buck Boyce, and the cell door clanged shut.

"I'm not going to play games with you," the prosecuting attorney told him. "You can save that nonsense for the jury. You and I both know what happened to your mother."

Buck Boyce's hard stare was returned with Jorie's cool, patient one.

"How's my sister?"

"Your sister's fine and dandy and I'm not here to talk about her. Your hearing's coming up, boy, and I want you to give me some real straight answers. You got that?"

"Yes, sir."

"All right, then." Boyce placed his ample behind on the chair and rested his notebook on his belly. He took a pencil from his pocket and flipped open the pad.

"Tell me what you were thinking that day you set out for a joy ride in the blizzard."

"Yes, sir."

"I'm all ears."

"I thought it was a fine day for a ride in the country—blue sky, with a few cumulus clouds, a soft breeze shaking the golden aspen leaves, the smell of autumn fires. Somebody must have been burning a pile of leaves, though it smelled more like hay. You could almost taste the apples in the orchard, but I couldn't say what kind they were. Macintosh, probably."

Bud Boyce snapped his note pad shut. "That's enough of that nonsense. You told the sheriff that a man with a lantern helped you look for your mother."

"Who was he?" Jorie asked.

"You tell me."

"I remember he had huge feet—left much bigger footprints than mine."

The attorney's eyes narrowed. "Yes?"

"But they were covered by the snow faster than we could make new ones."

"Go on."

"It came down so hard I could hardly see my own."

"You lost the big footprints."

Jorie looked up, surprised. "No, my mother's. My mother has very small feet."

When the prosecuting attorney left Jorie wondered what kind of gibberish he'd spouted. It just came out that way—he didn't know why. They'd probably think he was insane. Well, maybe he was.

chapter 31

EARL KNEW CORA didn't like all the time he was spending away from home. She kept reminding him those visits to the jailhouse weren't his job. She didn't understand that he had to. He'd started this ball rolling, and he had to get it sorted out.

"You haven't spent a bit of time at home," she complained one morning. "Even when you *are* here, you're not here, if you get my meaning."

"I do."

"I had a nice mutton roast ready for you last night, fixed up the way you like it, with parsnips and onions. You never came home for supper and never sent word, neither."

"We'll enjoy it tonight, though, won't we?"

She sighed. "It's not the same, warmed over."

"I'm sorry, Cora."

"What's gotten into you? Do you think the world hangs in the balance while the great Earl Foster deliberates this case?"

"That's enough."

"He'll have his hearing, and it will all turn out in the end—however it's supposed to." She softened her voice. "Can't you let go, Earl, a little bit?"

Once more he was on his way to see the lad. Despite her resentment at the time Earl was away, she had wrapped a piece of cornbread. "Take it to the boy."

"I won't be so late. If you behave yourself, we could spend the evening together." He patted her generous fanny.

She pushed him away, but he knew she was pleased.

"Watch your step out there. It's icy. I nearly fell going to the privy."

As he walked across town, a freezing rain descended, adding to the already frigid atmosphere. He could hear the tinkling sound it made hitting the bare elms, encasing them in ice. Tiny pellets stung his eyes; he wound his muffler around as much of his face and neck as he could. He should have taken the buggy, but Bigot didn't like the ice any more than he liked black horses. Shaking as much precipitation as he could from his wraps, he descended the stairs of the courthouse, noting the echo that followed each step in the quiet depths of the building. He found Jorie staring at the ceiling again, probably studying the spider webs.

"Have you had your breakfast?"

"Yes."

"Anything you need?" Earl asked.

"I'd like some books."

"The diary is about all the reading material I can allow you for now." He handed the cornbread to Jorie. "Courtesy of Mrs. Foster."

"That was kind of her."

Jorie ate part of it, wrapped the rest up for later.

"How's Eliza?"

"Mrs. O'Laerty says she's doing fine. Did you read the diary?"

"Some of it. The part about the cemetery."

"The cemetery." Earl snapped the rubber band on his wrist. "She had you keep a punishment journal."

Jorie colored. "How'd you know about that?"

"It's in the second diary."

"Oh."

"How'd you feel about having to keep that journal?"

"I hated it!" Jorie struggled to keep his feelings under control.

"Where is it now?"

Jorie dropped his voice. "I burned it."

"When was that?"

"After...she died."

"Look, lad, the hearing will determine if there's sufficient evidence to bind you over, and if you're sane enough to stand trial. I can't help you, unless you cooperate." Earl waited. "We don't have much time, boy."

"You want me to say I killed my mother."

"We certainly have probable cause. Enough to go to trial. Perhaps the charge will be reduced to manslaughter if you explain to the court *why* you took her out there."

"I don't know! I just don't know, I tell you!"

"What about the inheritance? Did you get your 'sizeable sum'?"

"I...I, no!" Jorie rubbed his sweaty hands on his trousers. "Not yet."

"You must be pretty upset about that."

Jorie turned to face the sheriff. "Yes. But if you think I'd kill for it, you don't know me very well, Mr. Foster."

It was Earl's turn to flush. When he left the courthouse at noon, there was a gathering of citizens on the nearby walk. They carried signs: "Free Jordan Radcliff."

Memories flooded into Jorie's mind like the spring run-off in the hills behind their home, insidiously seeping into the crevices, pooling in the dark recesses of his mind. Ephemeral, like some fairy-tale cupboard that sometimes offered sweet pies and cakes, he might get worms and snakes the next time. He wasn't sure of anything; nothing was as it seemed.

If he could only connect with his starline, he thought he could find the answers, but there were no stars, only clouds.

Sometimes he remembered, no, *felt* all the love he had for his mother, how close they'd been. At these times he absolutely *knew* he'd never harm her.

He tried to sleep. That way he wouldn't be tempted to read the diary. With the sleet beating against the small window, whipped up by sudden gusts of wind, the pane rattled like a madman trying to get in, a demon come to torture him. He slept fitfully off and on all day until the turnkey brought his supper.

Prisoners weren't allowed candles. In another hour it would be too dark to read—if he could just hold out.

He hated his weakness.

The page he opened to was about the silkie stories from Scotland that she told him—how they'd act them out together when he was small.

He is so precious, and oh, so earnest in the parts he plays! A more bonnie lad I could not wish for.

How had those games gone as out of control as a mad dog? What was it that was trying to edge its way into his consciousness?

He turned back to the diary.

August 1, 1888

Jorie awakens frequently with nightmares since that awful business with Walter.

He put the book down and tried to evoke some picture of that time so long ago. He remembered Walter was always trying to frighten or hurt him when they were children.. Somewhere in the back of his mind was a memory of Walter dumping a pile of coal on him...was that why his step-brother had been sent away? The picture was distant and dim, like something in an old family album.

He comes to our bed. Not wanting him to wake Thomas, I pull him to me and quiet his sobs. I am frightened for my boy. I know Thomas will not tolerate his bedwetting for long. My poor lad.

Jorie closed the diary. As the past elbowed its way in, the specter of his father hovered over him. Involuntarily the muscles in his buttocks contracted.

Boys like you have to be punished, do you understand?

"You all right in there?"

From down the hall the night turnkey's voice broke through his reverie. Jorie could hear the night watchman coming toward him, see his lantern swinging at his side.

He covered the diary with his arm, pretended to be sleeping. He heard the lantern clang against the iron door, knew the man was peering in at him.

When the turnkey left he turned on the narrow cot. What else had she to say about his bedwetting? Did she remember it the way he did?

Thomas, drawing Jorie's confession from him over breakfast, looked at this regression as a deliberate act of sloth and defiance, and marched him upstairs.

Jorie closed the book, rammed it under his mattress, and lay on his stomach. The acrid odor of urine from former occupants invaded his nostrils, heightening his memory of those days—his father, the villain, and his mother, the heroine who tried to rescue him. Tossing and turning half the night, finally he fell into another fitful sleep.

He heard the thump, thump, thumping, turned and twisted, trying to escape the blows. They were harder now, and his mother was in the doorway screaming 'Stop!' But his father applied the strap ever more vigorously.

Jorie awoke in a cold sweat, breathing heavily. He flipped over on his back, lay listening. The thumps were coming from the hot water pipes above, which supplied steam heat to the building. He was drenched in sweat and out of breath. He sat on the edge of his cot and tried to rein in his wits.

When he'd managed to calm himself, he attempted once again to mine the truth. What was it he wouldn't let himself see? Had he really committed this most outrageous of crimes? It seemed sometimes he had, and others he hadn't. Every time he thought he was close to the truth, a veil would descend and he could see no more.

With another unruly drunk in the next cell kicking the wall, plaster again fell on Jorie's side. Maybe he could draw with it. The walls were light green, or used to be. One had a barred door, the opposite a small barred window. He chose the one with nothing to mar its surface, except a lot of boot prints.

He didn't want to think about what kind of picture he'd make. He'd just let his hand move where it wanted to. Perhaps the picture would tell him something.

He drew until it was too dark to see. But there was barely anything visible; the plaster was not a good medium.

The storm had stopped. Light from the streetlight found its way through the cell window, casting its eerie glow below. Shadows from the window bars pushed their way to the pool of light on the stone floor, surrounding him. The bars of imprisonment were everywhere.

chapter 32

EARL SCRATCHED HIS hand and turned the page. In the second diary he was reading the account of the night Jorie broke the door down and Catherine called him over.

Poor Earl Foster is not the brightest light, but he was a comfort to me last night. And I believe he convinced Jorie that he should remain at home and take care of us.

Humph! Not the brightest light! Well, he'd known she didn't have any particular regard for him, but this was putting it plainly.

She ended with: *I shall have to be clever to think of ways to make my Jorie stay. Those to whom you give your love have no right to abandon you. This is where he belongs, and I'll do whatever I must to keep him here.*

He dabbed at the blood on his hand, wondering if he'd done the right thing, persuading the boy to stay with his mother. He knew Thomas would have liked to see him at the University, but if there wasn't any money...

He continued reading. Her tales got more and more bizarre. He could hardly believe she'd had an affair with an itinerant worker. Did Thomas know about this surveyor? Maybe he had his own secrets. There was that Redson woman he'd seen him with a couple of times. He wondered how many other people in Hancock had been unfaithful to their wives or husbands.

If he thought he was being invasive before to read her diary, he felt downright shameless now, almost as though he'd walked right into the bedroom and watched. The things she talked about doing with this Chester fellow sounded like they were right out of one of those scandalous books the boys in school passed around. *The Illicit Loves of Lacy Loomis* came to mind. They were embarrassing to read, but had excited him too. He couldn't help wondering what it would be like if he were to attempt that sort of thing with Cora. The thought of turning her over his knee pleasured him immensely. He could just see her plump, round rump turning rosy beneath his hand. Then they'd have a good laugh, and maybe she'd let him take her from behind...

But that was ridiculous; she'd think he'd gone plum loony.

He set his prurient interests aside and brought his thoughts back to the diary. There was this Catholic business. Something else he hadn't known about. That's where the rosary came into the picture. This Father Dumas—he wasn't like any priest Earl had ever heard of. *Perhaps it's your conscience bothering you, not the actual act.* Words to that effect. Well, wouldn't we all be Catholics if the priests were so easy on us!

There were other words in the diary that wouldn't go away. After she gave up her lover, she wrote, *I have made a great sacrifice. I intend to reap its rewards!*

What did she mean by that?

Earl finished the second diary and dropped it off for Jorie before going home. All this talk about the *Golden Bubble*, whatever that was. Something so private Jorie wasn't allowed to tell anybody. He wasn't even allowed to have friends.

Her ideas about penance and sacrifice—making it sound so sacred and noble for him to give things up. The way she thought about punishment gave him the creeps.

Catherine MacGaurin had fallen off her pedestal.

But so far there was nothing to tie these two diaries to her death. He couldn't help feeling there must be a third one someplace. Catherine had written regularly, and had filled the whole of the second diary two years ago. He doubted she'd have given up this practice just because the book was filled. If there was another diary, it could be important, especially if it were up to date. Perhaps the incident which precipitated her demise would be in it. There were too many secrets in the shadows yet to be uncovered. So far, the diaries were his best lead.

He had gone through every drawer in Catherine's dresser and armoire, searching for false bottoms. He'd rummaged around the desk downstairs, and Jorie's room as well. He'd looked in the pantry, under rugs, mattresses, and loose floorboards. But an investigation of the Radcliff home turned up no further diary. Maybe Jorie had burned that too.

The judge was getting impatient.

"How long you plan to keep him in the jug without a hearing?"

"I'm trying to gather information. It takes time, and patience."

"Three more days. That's all I give you, Foster. The hearing will be on Friday."

Earl hadn't been able to sleep well ever since this thing began, and his psoriasis had left ugly red patches on his body. He had started a fireball rolling that he couldn't stop. With sleep again eluding him, he rose early and made his own breakfast.

He'd pretty much exhausted ideas on how to get Jorie to open up. Yesterday he'd thought that maybe if he shared some of his feelings with the boy, some of the mistakes he'd made as a young man, the lad might start to thaw. He even told him about the shivaree he and some chaps had staged on his parents' wedding night. He knew getting someone to open up when they wanted to clam up wasn't his strong suit. He'd never been able to get Cora to talk when she didn't want to. It didn't work with Jorie either.

Today he had another plan. Maybe it was a mean trick, or maybe it wouldn't cause any reaction at all. But he'd packed Jorie's lunch himself, with a purpose in mind, and started off to work.

At six o'clock, November skies had not allowed even a sliver of light to break the night. He walked from one gaslight to the next, watching his step in the dark stretches between, feeling the uneven surface of slippery slush beneath his feet. Earl sighed; the good citizens of Hancock had voted against electric streetlights. At least it wasn't as cold as it had been. He grabbed a handful of snow. Good packing, the kind they liked to make iceballs with when he was a kid. He held it to the back of his hand until it was numb enough to stop the itching.

He passed the houses all in a row, occasionally seeing a light in one, hearing a baby cry in another. Did each have its own dark secret carefully hidden from view?

He stood back in shock as he entered the cell. Somehow Jorie had gotten hold of some coal and drawn a ghastly mural in heavy black. Two walls were covered, and he was still at it. They looked like the workings of a madman.

Earl's knee-jerk reaction was that the boy was defacing public property, but his second thought stopped him short. Maybe he'd reveal something through his drawing that he couldn't otherwise express. Besides, it would be a good excuse to give these filthy cells a fresh coat of paint, once Jorie was out of here.

An ominous chill went through him as he tried to interpret Jorie's scribbles. People—he guessed that's what they were. Some lay prone, but in another section, they were climbing all over each other, trying to get to the top of a mountain. On closer look, most had tails. When they reached the top, they raced to jump off the cliff like a bunch of lemmings. He wasn't an expert on lunacy, but he knew enough to tell that these scenes represented a very troubled soul.

Jorie threw down a scrap of coal and picked up a bigger chunk.

Earl cleared his throat. "I see you've been hard at work."

Jorie didn't answer.

"Who gave you the coal?

"The night turnkey."

"What's your picture about?"

"I think it speaks for itself."

Jorie had read that statement in a book about some artist who would never explain his work; it seemed somehow useful now. He stood back and surveyed the scene himself.

"Over here," he said pointing to one corner, "it gets kind of messy."

Earl thought the whole thing a mess.

"Doesn't looking at this give you nightmares?"

"No. When I sleep my eyes are closed. The pictures that give me nightmares come from the *inside.*"

Jorie threw down the piece of coal and dropped on his cot.

In the silence Earl studied the wall, trying to decipher its meaning. He saw only someone's dismal, tormented view of humanity.

"Have you been reading the diary?"

"I open the same book, but each time the story's different. That ever happen to you, Sheriff?"

"You mean the diary?"

Jorie sat up. "No, the book in my head! The book of *my* life."

"Tell me about that."

"That's it—the story's different every time. The characters change, I mean they're the same ones, but they're *different.*"

"How different?"

"Good, then evil, then good again. It's a plan to make me go mad."

"Whose plan?"

"The demons." His voice was rising.

"What demons, lad?"

"In here, in my head! They won't leave me alone!"

"Maybe they would if you let the whole story come out, Jorie. It's too hard, holding it all inside. You haven't enough fingers to plug all the dikes."

Jorie buried his head in his hands. Earl waited a few more moments, but nothing more was forthcoming. He opened the lunch pail, spread the food for Jorie on a napkin, and placed it on the cot.

Jorie took his hands away from his face, glanced at the food. Suddenly the color left his face. The odor riveted his attention; it was loathsome, unmistakable. At the same time he started shaking. With unexpected force, he hurled the odious object across the room, where it splattered and bounced off the wall. With quick rejoinder, he followed it, bouncing off the wall himself.

Earl heard the plaster crack and the lath splinter, as termites scrambled for new lodgings.

"Limburger! You know I hate it! You can't make me swallow that. I will not!"

He picked it up flat in his hand and smeared it over the wall, over his drawing.

Earl watched with mounting alarm, as the boy's past erupted in a torrent.

"Take off this blindfold!" Jorie tore at his face. "Take it off!"

Earl grabbed him by the arm and pushed him down on the cot. "That was a long time ago, Jorie. There's no blindfold, nothing like that now!"

"I hate her! I tell you I hate her! She, she—" He was grabbing for breath in large, uneven gulps.

Earl's senses reeled with triumph and dismay. He'd just tapped the mother lode of Jorie's troubled mind.

"Did you ever want to kill your mother, Jorie?"

He was panting. "No! No. *Yes!*"

"*Did* you kill her?"

"I don't know!"

"Think hard, Jorie. Did you take your ma out there to die?"

Earl waited, listening to the gradual cessation of the painful sobs. Like a train coming to a halt, each revolution was a little slower, less powerful than the last.

"What are you hiding, boy? Was there some terrible thing you had to stop her from doing, at all costs?"

"I don't know! I would tell you if I did!"

"Do you *want* to know?"

His fists were clenched. "Yes, yes, I have to know!"

Finally, exhausted, Jorie fell back on his cot. Earl put his blanket over him, and sat beside him, distressed that he'd provoked this explosion. But it had served some purpose.

Earl's attention returned to the tortured drawing, trying to make sense of it. Perhaps some small detail would give a clue. In one part he saw two lovers floating upwards in the sky, surrounded by a ring of stars and the moon. It was the only happy thing Earl could find in this agonized depiction of the boy's mind. Maybe it was the girl he'd brought to the John Muir lecture. In another he saw what could only be his mother lying prone under snow, with more snow falling. Although it gave no clue as to whether foul play was involved, it did indicate Jorie had some awareness of what had happened. *At least at the moment he'd drawn it.*

Something far down in one corner caught his eye. He took a closer look. In small, but unmistakably clear formations, surrounded by scribbles and smudged spots, were two figures, each was on a cross. There were tiny initials under each—'J' under one, and 'I' under the other.

The 'J' could be for Jesus. Then again, it could be for *Jorie*. But what was the 'I'?

chapter 33

JORIE COULD NOT stop reading the second diary.

He will come to see punishment as an expression of my devotion, as its sting will be tempered with soft caresses and my words of love. And he will understand that sacrifice is an expression of his love for me.

Sometimes, reading her accounts of them, scenes would spring to life as clearly as the day they happened. Others he couldn't recall at all.

Nights under the stars, teaching Mummy the names of the constellations.

Nights under the stars, Mummy teaching him the redemptive powers of punishment:

She'd held him close, rocking him, humming to him. "You must have no secrets from me, Jorie. When you've done something wrong or that you think might be wrong, write it in your journal, and let Mummy decide if you need penance. Do you understand?"

"Yes."

She'd kissed his forehead.

"What will leave you if Mummy punishes you?"

"The guilty feeling "

"And what will take its place?"

"The peaceful, clean feeling."

What do you have to do for that to happen?"

"Surrender to the punishment completely."

"Are you ready, my Darling?"

Jesus! She'd been his confessor. She'd made him actually want it, ask for it! It made him cringe with shame, just to remember. And how much better he'd felt afterward—just like she'd said. My God, how twisted it all had been.

"And what kind of chastisement do you think would be appropriate?"

"I don't know."

"Find a solution."

"Should I make a switch?"

"Oh, Jorie, a switch again? Does my little lamb have such a dearth of imagination? Think of something else, for heaven's sake."

Not only had she insisted that he confess his offenses, but she was as particular of his expression of them as she was of his behavior, often criticizing him for faulty grammar or vague detail.

"What do you mean by 'the whack'? Did it feel like a sting or a thud?"

He had honed his writing skills working in his discipline journal.

Overcome by a firestorm of emotions, Jorie slammed the diary shut and added his boot print to the others on the wall. No wonder she didn't want him to have any other friends! He might reveal their secrets, their bloody *Golden Bubble*. Or he might find out about their lives—their *freedom!* He had worshipped her, and she was a monster!

That evening Earl came to his cell with an extra bounce in his step. "I brought you something to read. And it's not a diary. They called me from the post office and wanted to know what to do with your mail. I said I'd come and get it. Guess what they had."

Jorie sat up eagerly. Earl handed him a package. The return address read *Journal of Modern Poetry.* Inside the package he found five copies of the fall issue. He picked up one and scanned the Table of Contents. And there it was—*The Intruder, by Jordan Radcliff.*

He looked up with the first hint of pleasure Earl had seen on his face in weeks.

"Looks like you got yourself published, kid."

Jorie handed the sheriff a copy.

"What page?"

"Seventeen."

They both found the poem. Earl said, "Will you read it to me?"

Jorie stood up. He wasn't sure why—maybe because in school he'd always had to when it was his turn to recite.

He cleared his throat. "It's called *The Intruder*. It doesn't rhyme or anything. It's the new 'free verse' style."

Earl nodded, waited. Finally, Jorie began.

Arriving before anything else, and after all these years,
Still, you loiter on the dark side of my mind,
Fill its crevices with sadness and pain, rage and guilt.
I know you only by your sounds, your low grunts and wails
That drag me from serenity.
Familiar, unwanted tenant, I'm following your vein—

His voice broke. He hadn't read it in so long, he'd forgotten how revealing, how *naked* it was. He sat down and closed his eyes. It was so quiet, the sound of water dripping from a pipe was all that reached his ears.

Suddenly, he heard the sheriff's voice:

Familiar, unwanted tenant, I'm following the vein,
Searching for the mother-lode. I want to take you by surprise,
Grasp you, make you look at me, talk to me,
Tell me who you truly are.
Come out! Come out of hiding! Tell me what you want.
I demand to see you in the light, where I will look you
Straight in the eye and have a good laugh,
Come out and dance with me. I will love you to death!
And then, I will be free.

When the sheriff had finished, Jorie's eyes were still closed, squeezing back the tears.

Earl came over and embraced him. Jorie finally pulled away. If he didn't, he was afraid he'd bawl like a baby.

They sat quietly while Jorie looked at the other verses, or pretended to.

"When did you write this, Jorie?"

"A couple of years ago."

Earl figured he'd learned more about the clock-works of this kid through his poem than by any conversation they'd had so far. What kind of hell had the boy been living in? And for how long? But there was also a kind of a bright ending to the piece.

The sheriff had meant to tell Jorie that the preliminary hearing was the day after tomorrow at nine o'clock. But after the poem, he couldn't say any more.

His attention traveled to the corner of the wall with the two crosses. 'J' and 'I'. He felt it was the one thing in this horrendous drawing that might offer up some answers. But what did the 'I' signify? Was it *Isis*, Catherine's middle name?

Maybe.

Jorie looked out the window and saw the snow falling again. Some of it landed on the sill, reminding him of home. The snow he'd used to cool his passions, the guilt he'd felt for having them. During the night the clouds blew away, leaving the sky clear for the first time since he'd been in jail. He could see the Pleiades. With the Sisters in sight he tried once again to connect with his starline. Bringing all his powers to focus, he was, finally, able to get the line straight. No longer did the veils of illusion, like the chimney smoke swirling around the window, provide a barrier to reality. For the moment they were gone, and nothing was left but the truth. He stopped resisting it.

He'd taken his mother out in the storm to die.

Gradually, he remembered with painful clarity the sequence of events that led to the planning and carrying out of his crime. But *why* had he done it? Even her deceit and trickery didn't explain it.

He could have just left town.

He found himself facing a truth that omitted any mitigating motive for his actions. He felt like the most depraved of souls.

There was no penance harsh enough to absolve him. No string of beads or repetitive prayers would offer pardon.

Forgive me. Please forgive me!

But he knew it was too much to ask.

He thought of how she'd tried to protect him from his father, made his punishments more bearable by the stories she'd woven, and the salve she'd used to soothe and heal. She'd threatened to leave Papa if he didn't stop the whippings.

He took out her picture, looked at her lovely face, and held it to his breast.

Once after seeing the opera *Othello* in the new Kerridge Theatre, she had come home and told him the story. *"Oh, Jorie, isn't it just too sad, that a man could love a woman so, and yet there be such misunderstanding that he could kill her, and she be innocent?"*

Pervasive feelings of guilt worsened. The pressure in his brain was building up, as his recriminations took up more and more space. He clutched his head. The internal frenzy mounted to such a maniacal pitch that all he could do was knock his head against the wall until the throbbing forced him to lie down, and the demons left him alone for a spell.

Arthur Johnson came the next day.

Jorie could only look at the floor. How humiliating it was to have the person who'd always been so kind to him see him in his present state.

"Good of you to come, Doctor," he mumbled.

"How are you doing, Jorie? Are they treating you all right?"

"Yes."

There was a pause. The doctor handed him a jar.

"What's this?"

"A sarsaparilla I thought you might enjoy."

Jorie took the drink and smiled shyly at the doctor. "Thank you." His finger traced the rim of the container.

"I have to be frank with you. I've been appointed by the court to determine—your state of mind."

Jorie took a drink from the jar.

"Whether I'm sane or not, you mean."

"Yes, precisely." The doctor looked at him kindly. "So let's just talk."

Doctor Johnson started reminiscing about days gone by, the animated discussions of biology they'd had in his room. He could make anyone feel at ease, and Jorie thawed somewhat.

"Sometimes I pretended to be sicker than I was, just to get a visit from you."

"I suspected as much." The doctor chuckled.

The doctor had told him, all those years ago, that he could be anything he wanted to be—a scientist, or a writer. "What are your plans now, son? Have you decided on a career yet?"

"I couldn't get a career as a street cleaner after what happened."

"Let's talk about that."

"It seems like such a long time ago."

The doctor checked his notes. "Your mother died two weeks ago."

"Seems longer."

"I suppose it does."

"How long have I been in here?"

"Five days. I'd like to hear the whole story, whatever you remember."

Jorie said nothing.

"Look, keep in mind that I'm not against you, son. And I'm neither judge nor jury. So anything you say that will assist me in my task will be of benefit to you."

Jorie nodded.

"Did you grasp what I said?"

"Yes, sir."

"Tell me about you and your mother."

The question surprised Jorie. "I love her—loved. I still love her."

"Did you ever get angry with her?"

"Enough to kill her? That's what you think, isn't it?"

"I don't know what happened. Remember, I want to hear your story. It won't go on the record, I promise. My task here is to see if you're coherent, can comprehend our discussion, so I can aid in your defense. As your *physician* anything you tell me is confidential."

The doctor waited.

"You trust me, son, don't you?"

Jorie wanted to pour out all his guilt and pain to the doctor. Maybe with the doctor's help he could finally unravel the truth.

But could he trust anyone?

chapter 34

As Earl walked across the bridge toward home, the wind was so strong it almost blew him over. The omnibus lumbered by, throwing bits of snow and dung in its wake.

There was something besides his psoriasis that kept itching at him ever since he learned of Catherine's fate. Earl had based his first suspicions of foul play on Jorie's earlier clash with his mother. But that suggested that if he'd murdered her, it would have been an act of rage, and he would have been devastated with remorse. But it hadn't happened that way. If it was murder, he had planned it, had bided his time for the right weather conditions to fit his scheme. And that didn't set with his picture of Jorie Radcliff at all. There was a missing piece. There *had* to be.

Well, there wasn't much more time to get a handle on this thing. The hearing was tomorrow.

His mind flashed back to Jorie's tortured picture, and the corner with the two crosses. There was something about that. I and J. J and I. Suddenly he *knew*. It hit him with the force of a blow and turned him to ice. *What was it Jorie called his little sister? Izzy? He called her Izzy!*

God Almighty! What secrets still lay buried?

Helena looked frightened when Earl Foster appeared at her door.

"Is there something wrong, Sheriff?"

"I'd like to make a thorough check of Jorie's room, if it's all right with you."

She swallowed. "Of course, sir. Right this way."

She led him upstairs to the tiny spare room. Plain and tidy, with little furniture, it wouldn't take long to find what he was looking for, if it was there.

Helena stood nervously rolling up the hem of her apron as he conducted his search.

He looked in the armoire, which still held some of Jorie's clothes, and checked the drawer at the bottom. Then he got on his knees, looked under the bed. As he started to raise the mattress Eliza burst into the room.

"What are you doing, mister?"

"Oh, looking for something I thought I might find here."

"Is it a book? I found a book when my ball rolled under Jawie's bed."

Earl looked at the child, and back to the woman, whose face had gone the color of paste.

"I gave it to Henna," Eliza explained.

The woman burst into tears.

"Oh, help me, Jasus, I didn't mean no harm."

Earl got to his feet. "Take it easy, Mrs. O'Laerty."

"But sure, and I have'na been meself lately."

"Where is it now?"

"If you'll jes wait a bit, please."

She scurried off, and returned with something wrapped in a pillow case.

"I wanted to do the right thing by it. After all, it was Mrs. Radcliff's."

She could only be talking about one thing.

"I t'ought of bringing it to you earlier, but, well, a diary's private, isn't it? Didn't I know I couldn't keep it, and did'na want to. But it wasn't anybody else's either—Sweet muther of Jasus, I don't know what Jorie was doin' with it. And didn't it just sit there the whole time starin' at me, darin' me to do *somethin'*."

She crossed herself, then looked up in sudden consternation. "Begod and bejasus, you don't think I *read* it, do you? Truth be known, I can hardly read a'tall."

Carol A Sheldon

Earl could hardly keep from grabbing it out of her arms .

"Did I commit a crime, Mr. Foster, not bringing it to you, straight away?"

"No, Mrs. O'Laerty, you did what you thought was right."

A great relief came over the woman's face.

"How long have you known about this diary?"

"How long? It was on Monday last, sir, the child brought it to me."

"And now, ma'am, will you give it to me?"

She looked as though she'd forgotten what she was holding. "Oh, yes, sir. To be sure."

She thrust it into his waiting awaiting arms.

chapter 35

JORIE SAT ALONE in his cell, obsessed with what he had done. He was convinced that he'd ended his mother's life to break her hold on him.

But it hadn't worked. He was more obsessed with her now than he'd ever been. She just wouldn't get out of his head.

For many nights now, with sleep unavailable, he'd searched to find a solution to his unbearable anguish. It didn't matter what they said in that courtroom. He had become his own judge. The verdict was clear. Only his death would silence the jury of demons that taunted him. *You have no right to live!* It wasn't that he wanted to die; he just couldn't go on living. Sobbing into his mattress, he wept for all the love he'd had for her, and all the hatred too. And he wept that the only solution he could find for himself, was to die.

But at least then, maybe his internal judge would leave him alone. Hopefully, some sweet oblivion. Yes, that was the answer.

He tried not to think about hell and how he might be eternally damned. Maybe none of that was true, anyway. *Dona nobis pacem.*

With the decision made, the demons seemed satisfied, receded to the furthest recesses of his mind. At last a certain peace enfolded him.

He removed the sheet from the bed.

As he finished reading the third diary, Earl looked up from the last page Catherine had penned, to discover it was already approaching morning. The black of night had thinned to grey. He hadn't been to bed at all. Today was the hearing!

In all his career he had never encountered anything as depraved and deranged as what he'd just read in Catherine Radcliff's diary. He hadn't known her at all; only thought he had.

He got up and walked to the privy. Had he actually read it, or was it the perverse stuff of his own dreams?

He went back to the book, flipped through the pages again, his eyes lighting on certain passages:

May 4, 1900

Perhaps I should give up on my own writing altogether, and devote myself to furthering his career. He is so talented, and I can help him a great deal! I cannot bear to dwell on the possibility that next year he may leave me, perhaps forever. It is to him my heart belongs, for we are two of a kind, and dip our quills in the same well.

But it was what followed that turned his stomach. In late summer she was on another tack.

"August 15, 1900

If Jorie leaves me, I still have my little Eliza. What a ready disciple she is. Already she asks to make sacrifices and happily submits to my loving discipline!

"August 29, 1900

When she is five, I will give her a ritual for the initiate. I will dress her all in white and prepare her for what's to come, so that she will understand the importance of the vows she is to take. What pleasure I will have creating these vows! Each year new ones will be added. After her initiation she will be allowed no contact with others."

"September 3, 1900

I am teaching Eliza to speak the French language, and following her initiation that will be the only tongue she will be allowed to use. Soon she will forget English. I will school her at home and her education will be entirely under my control. We can hardly wait. But such sanctified events must be heralded by periods of agonizing anticipation!

"September 7, 1900

Perhaps I will tell people that Eliza is mute. She will not be allowed to speak to anyone except me, and then at certain times only, when spoken to.

In any case after a time she will not understand what others say. I will rid this house of all books printed in English and purchase many in the French language.

September 8, 1900

She will be my little dress-up doll, my lady-in-waiting, my acolyte. Even her thoughts will be under my domain. Perhaps I will invent a new language that only she and I will understand. In this way, she will of necessity turn to me for everything."

He scanned the remaining pages, caught fragments: *'acts of sacrifice,' 'an exciting experiment.' 'In time she will not be able to distinguish pleasure from pain.' 'If our Lord could wear a crown of thorns..."*

Earl's palms were all sweaty. What a diseased mind she'd had. He wondered how she'd come to be that way. To think of your children as globs of clay that you could form into anything you please, however damaging. With Thomas's death, there was no one to rein in this wildest of mares!

All the pieces were coming together.

Now he understood why Jorie had sought to have her committed. When he failed, the lad had seen no other recourse but the one he had taken. This most vile of mothers had to be stopped.

That the mystery had finally revealed itself to him was cold comfort. He carried the diary to the shed, and concealed it behind some old harness pieces. It felt heavier than when he'd first held it.

Earl had never before questioned the meaning of justice. If you broke the law, you paid the consequences. Simple.

He'd been zealous in law enforcement ever since that time in school when his family lost their home and farm to some real estate swindle. Earl spent his graduation day loading their furniture onto the wagon. It had taken the life out of his father, years before he died.

When he'd first suspected Jorie, there wasn't any doubt in his mind that as much as he liked the boy, if he were guilty he should be brought to justice, and that was that. Justice and the law—they were one and the same.

But Catherine had betrayed her son and was set on a course to destroy her daughter. She had tricked Jorie into staying home from college on the grounds they had no money. No wonder he'd pushed her around upstairs! It wasn't anything like what she'd implied. He felt tremendous anger boil up inside.

She involved *me* in her dirty scheme!

Find a way to save Jorie!

He had to catch McKinney before the hearing. He had to get it postponed, if he could. It was vitally important that he help the kid. He'd gotten him into this mess-'o-mackerel; he'd have to get him out.

Despite his taste for drama, George McKinney was a fair man. But what would he consider fair in this case? Did Earl dare tell the judge about the diary? It would almost prove Jorie's guilt. George might be sympathetic, but he couldn't be expected to disregard the law.

And Earl couldn't overlook the power of the prosecuting attorney. He wondered how much investigation Buck had done on this case. Buck Boyce had a history of relying on others to provide the necessary evidence for a conviction. Come to think of it, most of the cases he'd won were pretty cut and dried—lethal fights in barrooms, a runaway horse that trampled a child. All with plenty of witnesses.

Earl walked to work, again guided by one gaslight to the next. His psoriasis was blaming him, it seemed, for this sorry state of affairs.

As he entered the courthouse he knew it was too early to find George. He went downstairs, passed the night turnkey sleeping on his chair, grabbed the key off the hook, and continued toward the prisoner's cell.

From the hall Earl could see Jorie using his mother's pearls like a rosary. With each bead he said, "Holy Mary, mother of God, pray for us sinners now and at our hour of death."

Earl stepped inside the cell. "Don't let me stop you."

Jorie put the beads in his pocket.

Earl picked up the spoon and stirred the contents in the untouched bowl. "Can't say as I blame you—some sort of gruel out of 'Hansel and Gretel'. He tried to break Jorie's solemnity. "Who mixed up your poison today?"

"Yes." Jorie stated.

"Yes, what?"

Jorie swallowed. "Haven't you been trying to get me to say it? Don't you want to know?"

Not now. Earl wanted time to freeze. But he could not stop the words coming from Jorie Radcliff's mouth.

"I killed her. I took her to the forest to die."

The long-awaited confession came so easily it was as though Earl had leaned hard against a door he didn't expect to give, only to have it unexpectedly swing open landing him on his ass.

He let out a low moan. "You're upset over all that's happened, and you feel responsible."

"I killed her."

"You took her out on a day when there was going to be a blizzard. Bad judgment perhaps, but not murder."

"On purpose."

Earl was starting to sweat. He had to have time to think. Something that hadn't fully registered when he first came in a moment ago suddenly leaped into sharp focus. He looked around the room.

"Where's your bedsheet?"

Jorie didn't answer.

"Come on—where is it?" Earl pushed Jorie aside, pulled the blankets back, discovered strips of cloth tied into a noose.

He glanced at the steam pipes above. "What did you plan to do with this?"

"Isn't it obvious?"

"What the hell for?" the sheriff yelled. "The sentence can't be any more than *Life!*"

"That's just it."

"What in tarnation is that supposed to mean?"

"I committed murder. I can't live with that."

"Well, for now, you'll have to." Earl dug at his hand. "Listen, everything depends on the hearing this morning. If you stick to this story, they're going to try you for sure, and if that happens you won't have the chance of a fly in a pail of milk."

The only response was a slight nod from Jorie.

Earl took a deep breath. The hearing was about to start. Maybe he could talk George into holding it without Jorie.

He bundled up the makeshift noose and stuffed it inside his coat. He was about to wake the jail keeper when he thought better of it; the less anybody knew about this, the better.

He locked the cell and darted up the stairs two at a time.

George McKinney was not in the building. Earl sat on the bench in the hall and looked at the big clock on the wall. Eight-thirty, too early. He waited several minutes, tried to calm himself. Suddenly he remembered the wad of cloth under his coat. What to do with it? He ran to his office, and stuffed the rags in his filing cabinet. Lockheed was there.

"What are you doing here? You're supposed to be over at the court for the hearing."

"Now?"

"Yes, *now*, dammit."

"Sorry, sir, I thought—"

"Never mind. Go."

Incompetence, all around him. He missed old Flint, the best deputy he'd had. But Flint had retired early with the French pox.

By the time he got back to the court it was eight-forty-five. Would the judge never come? The itching was out of control. He blotted the blood on his hand from the scratching. He'd like to go outside and get some more snow, but he might miss the judge.

He wondered if there was anything else in the cell that Jorie could use to do himself in. No, he didn't think so.

He heard footsteps on the stairs and waited anxiously. Buck Boyce—the last person he wanted to see right now.

"Morning," the prosecuting attorney said, seating himself beside Earl.

"Morning, Buck." He hoped Boyce couldn't see how anxious he was.

"Nice to see the sun, finally. Beautiful day."

Was it? Earl hadn't noticed.

Boyce was in a good mood. "Interesting little drama we have here. Yup, this case is shaping up nicely."

"Depends on how things go today."

"Not much question, it'll go to trial."

Earl was reminded of a passage from "Julius Caesar" he'd had to memorize in school. It seemed to apply here: *Yon Cassius hath a lean and hungry look.*

"Guess you'd like to see that happen."

"Hey, you're the one that started this. You going soft on me?"

"I don't have a lot to go on, Buck. Do you?"

Buck stared at Earl in amazement. "Well, what the hell did you drag me into this for? I was counting on you—"

George McKinney strode down the hall and entered his private chambers.

Earl rose. "Always count your *own* chickens, Buck. Not somebody else's." He excused himself and tapped on the judge's door.

"Come in, come in."

The judge was lighting up his first cigar of the day. "No poker game, tonight, Foster. Got company."

"That's fine with me." Earl didn't waste any time. "Does the accused have to be present for the hearing, George?"

"You know he does."

"Aren't there any exceptions?"

"Not in my court. Why?"

Did he dare tell the judge?

Earl watched the ash grow on the judge's cigar. He swallowed hard. No, he couldn't tell anyone about the confession, or the diaries. If it was known what was in them, Jorie's motive would be clear; he'd be tried for sure, and the outcome would serve no one.

"The kid's real upset. He's been throwing up."

"Bring his chamber pot."

Earl shook his head.

"Come on, Earl, you gotta do better than that."

Earl asked again, "Does Jorie have to be present?"

"Yes, dammit." The ash dropped on his desk. The judge swept it off. "Look, I don't like this thing any better than you do. What have you got up your sleeve?"

"You don't have to *ask* him anything, do you?"

Judge McKinney let out an exasperated sigh and spun in his swivel chair. His eyes narrowed, and by the look of him, Earl thought maybe he'd guessed the truth. The pigment Earl had thought was permanently imbedded in George's face had vanished.

"We have to do this by the book, Earl. I can't make a mockery of the courts of Michigan."

"Of course not.'"

Finally, he said quietly, "At least his name. I have to ask him to identify himself."

The sheriff wanted to thank his friend but knew it might suggest the judge had done something irregular.

"I hope you know what you're doing, Foster."

Earl hoped so, too. He sincerely did.

Suddenly George stood up. "Get the prisoner."

chapter 36

EARL DESCENDED THE stairs one more time. The jail keeper was still asleep. He found Jorie lying on his back, his hands beneath his head, staring at the ceiling. Or maybe it was the steam pipes that still held his interest.

"You're going to have to come with me to the courtroom now. I don't want you to say anything in there."

Jorie continued to stare at the ceiling.

"The judge won't ask you anything, and you won't say anything but your name. You got that? Let's go."

The hall outside the second floor courtroom was the same shade of green as the cells below, but had not endured the abuse, and had, in fact, been given a fresh coat of paint two years ago.

On this morning it was crowded with people who had something to say about Jorie or Catherine Radcliff, and hoped Judge McKinney would call them in to speak their piece. Undersheriff Sam Lockheed stood sentry at the door.

"I gotta get in there. I'm a witness, see?"

Earl recognized the voice.

"They'll want to know what I have to say. She was my step-mother."

"Have you been summoned?"

"What I got to say's important."

Lockheed stood his ground. "No one's allowed in unless they were summoned by the court."

Earl heard curses, as Jorie's half-brother was turned away.

The corridor was crowded with people who had nothing better to do. Gawkers, Earl called them. But only a handful of people were allowed in the courtroom. He was glad to see that Mrs. O'Laerty was one of them.

Earl took a seat beside the prisoner. Pray God they could get this over with quickly and Jorie would hold his tongue.

George McKinney brought the gavel down hard and all were quiet.

"This court will come to order. As this is a hearing, and not a trial, the proceedings will be handled somewhat informally. Let me remind all present that our sole objective here is to determine whether there is sufficient evidence of foul play to bind the prisoner over for trial."

Earl caught the word *evidence*. He was sure Boyce wouldn't like that. Ordinarily, the burden of proof was pretty low to go to trial. Earl recalled other times when George would say sufficient 'reason' to go to trial.

"The prisoner will please state his name for the record."

Earl nudged him, and Jorie stood.

"Jordan Radcliff."

"The court will now entertain the arguments."

Earl pulled on Jorie's sleeve and the boy sat down.

When asked to give his report for the record, Earl stated that although originally he'd thought there might be some foul play involved, upon further investigation, he didn't believe there was.

"And what caused you to do such a turn-about?" the judge inquired.

Earl swallowed hard. He'd have to eat humble pie if he expected George to accept this reversal.

"Well, your honor, initially, due to the unusual circumstances of the deceased's death, I thought a hearing was in order. I guess I jumped the gun—there just isn't enough to go on. I lay it to my own concern over the deceased that I started on that course, which I now regret. I had known Mrs. Radcliff since our school days, and erroneously thought I was representing her best interests in requesting a hearing."

Earl rubbed his sweaty hands together and picked at a sore. He hated to grovel, especially before George McKinney. And he knew what he'd said was as far from the truth as poor rock was from copper.

"Have you anything to say as a character witness for the defendant, Mr. Foster?"

"I've known Jorie a long time. He worked in our garden one summer. I found him to be honest, agreeable and hard-working."

"You liked him."

"Yes, I liked him."

"What about the hostility between mother and son?"

"Your honor, in my opinion—" Buck spoke out.

"I was addressing the sheriff." McKinney turned back to Earl. "There was, as I recall, some incident of violence in the prisoner's past."

George wasn't making it easy. Earl tried to recall if he'd ever told George anything about Catherine's coming to him with tales of violence. Well, he might have, *before* her death. He hesitated, refrained from wiping the sweat he could feel running down his neck.

"I do not believe the accused ever hurt his mother." He glanced at Jorie, who seemed not to be in the room at all. "If kicking the door in, when he found out his dreams of going back to college were going up in smoke—yes, he was violent on that occasion—with the door."

"Mr. Foster, do you have any evidence that the accused might have been involved in the demise of his mother?"

The rubber band snapped once too often, broke.

Evidence? He turned the word over in his mind. *He had no actual proof.* "No, your honor, I do not."

The judge turned to the prosecuting attorney.

"Mr. Boyce, you submitted the petition for a hearing. Could you state your reasons, please?"

Buck Boyce gave Earl a withering look. "It was on the insistence of our esteemed sheriff, your honor," he said sarcastically, "who beseeched me to do so."

"Please tell the court, Mr. Boyce, what purpose, if any, you have for proceeding with this case."

Earl could almost see the anger surge in Buck's arms and ride up his neck. Buck Boyce was stymied. He looked at Earl as though he'd been stabbed in the back.

"Mr. Foster stated he preferred to keep the exact reasons for calling this hearing to himself."

"I asked if *you* have any objective in pursuing the matter?"

Buck straightened his collar. "It seems evident, your honor, that anyone with even a modicum of common sense wouldn't take their mother on a pleasure outing with a blizzard on the way. That is, unless, he had planned some dastardly deed." He paused to let this sink in.

"Go on," urged the judge.

"That fact in itself, sir, would appear to be sufficient cause to bind the prisoner over for trial."

"Do you have anything else?"

Earl watched Buck swallow, move his lips, and stammer, "Not at this time, your honor."

The sheriff let out a long, slow breath.

George McKinney questioned the examining physician.

"Dr. Johnson, how did you find the prisoner's state of mind?"

Arthur cleared his throat. "I found him cooperative, if somewhat bewildered. His distress at the death of his mother was apparent in his manner, his general state and his heartfelt tears. If the accused is in a precarious mental state, it is temporary, having been brought on by the passing of his mother and his inability to save her."

"Then you see no reason to appoint a lunacy commission?"

"No, your honor."

"In your considered judgment, Doctor, would you say the prisoner capable of comprehending the proceedings of this court?"

"Yes, sir."

Well, Earl thought, if they didn't plead insanity, his only chance was to get the case thrown out altogether.

"And capable of assisting in his own defense, should this case go to trial?" the judge continued.

"Yes, sir."

"As the family physician, do you have anything to add regarding Jordan Radcliff's character?"

Doctor Johnson cleared his throat again. "I have known the defendant since he was a young boy. I have always found him an eager student and a tender lad who wouldn't harm a butterfly."

Jorie took the pearls out of his pocket, and fingered them under the table. Somehow their smooth, round orbs were comforting. He had little interest in the machinations of the law; it was his internal jury he had to answer to, and in this public place he could not hold court.

He turned his attention to the ocean where the oysters came from, the flaw—the grain of sand that made the beautiful tumescence inside. Could flaws in humans ever lead to something greater, he wondered?

"For the record then, Doctor, you judge him 'sane'."

"I do," replied the doctor.

Jorie caught the last, wondered if it were true. He'd thought about what he'd say all the way to the courtroom and during the proceedings. He knew he could speak up whether the judge called on him or not. He also knew if he confessed in court he'd be sent to prison, and they probably wouldn't give him any more bed sheets. *If I want to die, there are a hundred ways to do it on the outside, probably none on the inside.*

He turned his head to the window, where the sun had disappeared and another Lake Superior storm was sending tiny pebbles of sleet against the panes. Little pebbles were hitting against the solid wall of his resolve, too. Trying to put a chink in it.

Buck Boyce interjected, "The accused agreed to tell me everything, but not until I brought his mother in." He turned to collect chuckles of appreciation, gathered none.

"Perhaps he was putting you on, Mr. Boyce," the judge said.

McKinney called on Mrs. O'Laerty. "It is my understanding that you worked for Mrs. Radcliff for several years."

"Aye, sir."

"And what was your relationship to the accused?"

"I was there the day he was born, I was. I saw the boy grow up. A kindhearted lad, loved his mum ever so dearly. She and him was that close, they were."

"Did you ever observe any arguments between them?"

"No, sir, never. He was a very obedient lad, mind you, always doin' just what he was told." She twisted her handkerchief. "And after his pa passed, he stayed home to support her, he was that devoted to her."

"Did you ever detect any signs of violence in the accused?"

"Oh, Lord, no! Himself wouldn't hurt a single crayture, not never."

"Thank you, Mrs. O'Laerty."

"Does *anyone* have anything further to add to their testimony?"

Earl looked at Doc Johnson, who was shaking his head.

"Your honor?" It was Buck Boyce.

"Yes, counselor?"

"I would like to raise the issue of Radcliff's sanity. Based on my talk with him, I submit that the accused *is* insane, and a lunacy commission should be appointed to—"

"Mr. Radcliff is not on trial for lunacy. Let me remind you that the examining physician found him sane."

Earl held his breath.

"Then, as ruling magistrate in this court—"

Just as it looked as though they might be home free, something caught the judge's eye. Earl followed the turn of his head toward the door. Undersheriff Lockheed, approached the bench and whispered something to the judge.

"Show him in."

chapter 37

EARL'S HEART SANK. What could interfere now, delay the outcome of this hearing? He didn't know how long Jorie would stay silent. He felt droplets of sweat run down his face. If the lawyer Olsen decided to show up—he didn't want to think about it.

Lockheed held the door for a man Earl had never seen before. He was clutching a burlap bag to his chest, and Earl thought he looked like he hadn't bathed in a year.

Could this be...

The woodsman stepped forward a few feet, stood with his back to the judge, searching for someone.

"Approach the bench."

The man turned around, stared blankly at the judge.

"Come here," McKinney beckoned him. "Please give the court your full name."

"Colin Trethaway. Hain't got no middle name."

"State your purpose."

"I can't read, but a neighbor told me you was lookin' for the man who 'elped a young fellow in the snow storm we 'ad a few weeks back, t' find his ma." He paused, wiped his nose on his sleeve. "I'm yer man."

I knew it!

Colin Trethaway looked around the room, spotted Jorie. "That's 'im!"

Earl watched Jorie, who was studying the man's face.

"We never found her, though. I 'ad t' git 'ome before I froze." He sniffled some more. "I 'eard she died."

"Jorie Radcliff, do you recognize this man?" the judge asked.

Jorie squinted, considered the man's countenance while Earl held his breath.

"It's difficult to tell. It was snowing hard, I couldn't catch his features."

Earl suppressed a sigh of frustration. For God's sake, what would this man be doing here if he *hadn't* been the one to help him in the storm? This was a sheer stroke of luck, and Jorie was not biting.

The man walked toward Jorie. "Well, hit's me, boy, don't y' know me?"

"That's enough, Mr. Trethaway. Do you have anything else to say before this court?"

Trethaway reached into his bag. "I brought this." He took a rusty lantern out of the bag, and held it up for all to see. "Evidence." He looked as though he'd just pulled a rabbit out of a hat.

The judge concealed a smile. "Thank you. In your opinion, Mr. Trethaway, the person whom you've identified was sincerely trying to find his way back to rescue his mother?"

"Yes, sir. 'E was hall upset cuz 'e'd lost 'is way. Didna have no lantern, and his ma, she was back in the woods and couldna walk no more. I was 'eaded for 'ome in my wagon, when 'e come upon me an' asked fer 'elp. I wanted t' git on 'ome, but what's a God-fearin' man to do? Don't the Good Book say, 'Do hunto hothers as ye would 'ave—"

"Yes, thank you. Your testimony has been most helpful. You may leave now."

Colin Trethaway held the lantern up again. "Will you be wantin' this? Reckon I could spare it fer a few days, if you could git it back t' me. 'Hit cost me a day's work t' come down 'ere."

"No, you can take it with you."

Trethaway remained, shifted his weight from one foot to the other, wiped his runny nose on his sleeve.

The judge said again, "You are dismissed."

The man looked at Joric for help, then back at the judge. "Well, hain't there no reward?"

"For what, Mr. Trethaway?"

"Well, fer, fer..." he blustered some more, then mumbled, "I'll be jiggered," and left the room.

When Trethaway left, Earl wanted to jump up and down. At least that part of Jorie's story was corroborated. He could breathe a little easier.

Earl thought he caught a glance from George McKinney that suggested relief. Then the judge released a small chuckle. This seemed to give permission to the others, and a collective release of tension came forth in chortles and titters. From all, that is, but Boyce and Jorie.

McKinney went on. "As I was saying, before the interruption, as ruling magistrate in this court, finding insufficient reason to proceed toward trial, I will close this case. But not before I admonish those present to proceed with greater diligence in the future before petitioning this court with unsubstantial cases that do not merit the expenditure of taxpayers' money or the magistrate's time."

The judge paused. "I now declare this case closed."

He brought the gavel down swiftly. Mrs. O'Laerty tried to give Jorie an encouraging smile, but he wouldn't raise his eyes. She turned slowly and left.

Earl could hear the buzzing in the corridor, as folks who had waited for the outcome of the hearing voiced their reaction. Cheers that the case was not going to trial outnumbered those of complaints. But some were disappointed: Public murder trials were considered real good entertainment.

The room emptied quickly, as did the corridors. Earl called Lockheed over and told him he was taking some time off, and told his assistant to take over.

Jorie and Earl were the only ones left. They sat with their hands in their laps, Jorie looking out the window. The lad didn't seem in any hurry to leave. It was so quiet, Earl thought, you could hear a person change their mind.

He said, "You can go now, Jorie. You're free."

Jorie turned slowly toward him. "Free of what?"

"Free to leave."

"Do you know anything about the prisons of the mind, Mr. Foster?"

Oh, yes, I do!

He put his hand on the boy's knee.

"As I said, you're free to go anywhere, but I'd like you to stay with Mrs. Foster and me for a few days. We have a spare room."

Jorie didn't seem to be listening. But he didn't put up any resistance, either, as the sheriff led him downstairs, across the bridge, and over to Hancock.

By the time Earl got home with Jorie, he felt he'd done a day's work, and it was only eleven-thirty. He was glad there was no game tonight. He'd have to keep an eye on Jorie.

He got the boy to eat a little soup, to take a good soak and scrub in the copper tub. Then he showed him to his room.

"He's going to sleep," he told Cora. "At least I *think* he is."

He told his amazed wife how Jorie was fixing to hang himself that morning. "We have to keep a careful eye on him."

"It's a good job the window in that room sticks," Cora said. "He couldn't get it open without making a lot of noise."

"And there aren't any exposed pipes on the ceiling, either, thank God."

For the next few days Earl watched over Jorie like a newborn. They played cribbage, talked about the forecast of a long, hard winter, and went on walks in the evening. Daytime attracted too much attention. All the time Jorie held a neutral countenance.

Sometimes on these walks, Earl tried to get Jorie to talk about his mother's death. If they could discuss it, maybe he could help Jorie begin to forgive himself.

"Look, kid, I know why you wanted to take your life, but—"

"Don't you understand? *I killed my mother!* Ask the doctor. I told him all about it."

"You told Doctor Johnson? When?"

"In jail, when he came to see me."

"Put away."

"Did Mummy make you give them up?"

"No. It's a sacafice. I was very good today. I didn't have any supper."

Jorie's stomach turned over.

"Mummy loves me now. We have the *Golden Bubble*, Jawie. Just the two of us."

My God, she was doing it again!

"She's teaching me to speak French. And then we won't need English at all. Comprenee vous, Jawie?"

A kind of fire was rising from the base of his spine. "What else does she make you do?"

"Sometimes I'm not allowed to speak all day long. I must stay in my room."

Suddenly her hand shot to her mouth. "I'm not supposed to tell, Jawie!." She started to cry. "Now I'm going to get in trouble!"

Jorie held his little sister against his breast and comforted the child. He could feel her little heart beating like a small frightened bird.

When he went downstairs his mother was in the kitchen.

"You've come back." She missed the fire in his eyes. "I knew you couldn't stay away. Sit down, and I'll fix you something."

"No, *you* sit down. I have something to say to you." He took a deep breath. "You cannot start in on Eliza the way you did with me. It's wrong!"

"What are you talking about?"

"Sacrifice and the *Golden Bubble*—all of *that*."

"It never did you any harm."

"It's got to stop!"

"Oh, you hush your mouth. She likes it. Don't you remember how you loved it? She was made for surrender, Jorie, even more than you. She has the temperament for it."

"It's *damaging*! You *will* stop!"

She laughed. "And how are you going to make me?"

"I'll take her away from here!"

Catherine laughed. "You'd be caught and put in prison. And what could you do for her from there?"

"I'll report you—to the authorities!"

"Who would believe you? It's *you* who has a record of violent and unstable behavior."

"What you're doing is *not normal,* Mother. Don't you understand?"

"No, Jorie. It's you who must understand. She's my child, and I'll raise her as I choose. It's every parent's right—"

"It's evil! Before I leave—"

"You're not going anywhere. I have you for life. Don't you know that yet?"

She said it with the smugness of someone who had just played her trump card. Taking a hairpin from her hair, she gathered and twisted the rogue tendrils that lay against her back, pushed them up and fastened them securely with the pin.

"You cut your teeth on me," she smiled. "If you won't remain for me, you'll stay for Eliza."

He studied her small delicate neck. How easy it would be to squeeze the life out of her there on the spot. His hands clenched and unclenched, while she stared at him with that Mona Lisa look. Finally, he turned and strode out before he did the unthinkable.

He had to get Eliza away from her.

He remembered type-setting an article a couple of months ago about a boy in Red Jacket who'd been severely beaten by his parents over a period of time. The teacher had reported it, but the deputy said there was no provision which entitled the law to intervene. He was quoted as saying, "We don't take children away from their parents."

The boy had died.

What hope was there for getting Eliza away from her mother? He'd have to find a *solution.*

The next day he went to see a lawyer in Dollar Bay. He didn't know Mr. Olsen, and he didn't think the man knew his family either.

In obvious pain the old attorney seated himself on the swivel chair, cleared a space in the center of his desk, and brought out a fresh piece of paper. He dipped his pen in the inkwell, brushed back a lock of thinning grey hair and looked up.

"And what can I do for you, my lad?"

Jorie said, "Could you tell me, sir, the procedure for declaring a person insane?"

"Insane? To what purpose?"

"Well, so that...they would be put away." He could hardly believe he'd said it.

"Committed."

"Yes."

"Who is 'they'?"

He wet his lips, felt the sweat on his brow. "My mother."

The lawyer's eyes narrowed suspiciously. "On what grounds?"

"I'd rather not say."

"Then I can't help you."

"Well, that would come later. I'm just trying to get a feel for the procedure, how difficult it would be."

"I'll tell you this much, lad, you'd have to have a lot of evidence, witnesses to back up your testimony. Including her doctor."

"Thank you for your time, sir."

He paid the lawyer on the spot and left the office in frustration.

Witnesses. He had none. He thought of Doctor Johnson, who had attended him through so many illnesses, had braved the winter nights to bring medicine for him when he was ill. The doctor who'd visited him so often the year he was kept from school because of the Scarlet Fever scare. Could he trust him with this unspeakable story? Would *he* be willing to talk to his mother, convince her that what she was doing with Eliza was wrong? And if he couldn't persuade her to change her ways, would he be willing to have her *committed?* It didn't seem possible. But still, he would try.

The doctor listened sympathetically, but was clearly uncomfortable. He shook his head, said he'd make a poor witness, never having known Catherine to behave in any harmful way to her children. He suggested Jorie get his mind focused on his studies, and assured him he would keep this conversation to himself.

It would be just as useless to talk to the sheriff. He could think of no legal way out of this quandary.

What if he kidnapped Eliza and took her out west with him? His mother's derisive taunt came back to him: *You'd be caught and put in prison. And what could you do for her from there?* With each plan he found fault.

He must find a solution.

When he could think of no other, though every fiber fought against it, he started scheming how he would end his mother's life. The images would play in his head, no matter how he resisted. In one scenario he would start playing games with her again. He would suggest *Blindfold and Taste*. Only this time it would be she who would have to guess what food or drink he gave her. And after offering her a bit of cake and perhaps a taste of honey, he would give her poison, mixed in a sweet drink. If he had to, he'd force her to down it.

He dismissed this idea. The cause of her death would be obvious. Whatever happened to him, he couldn't leave Eliza alone with a legacy of scandal.

Perhaps a boating accident in Portage Lake.

His mother must think that all was well again between them. He'd have to move back to the house. Yes, she'd have to trust him, as he'd trusted her so many times. He packed his things up from Phillip's and returned to the hill. This done, he started playing the piano again, even cards with her. He was eating humble pie, but his larger objective made it bearable.

His mother reveled in triumph. He could see it in her face.

The sound of Cora Foster's voice broke through Jorie's reverie. It was time to eat.

Of course! How could he have forgotten the reason he'd stopped his mother's life? Why had his demons filtered out the reason for his act?

Jorie put his head down and cried. Anguished sobs and splintered memories collided in a new version of all that had occurred.

When the storm had passed, gradually, another kind of feeling began to take root in Jorie's senses. His self-condemnation was there, droning away in the background, but it didn't come with such fiery spikes now. It began to melt. He took quiet pleasure in the plain fare of hearty meals Cora Foster brought him, and her husband's unrelenting vigil.

The ordinary became exceptional, and healing.

He was still appalled by what he'd done, but looking back he still didn't see an alternative that would have saved Eliza. Could he live with what he'd done? *Every day?* He didn't know.

The next morning when Mr. Foster tried to talk to him, Jorie didn't resist. He poured out the whole story of that night in Eliza's room and what followed. It felt good to wrench these secrets from their hiding place, place them in the open within the safety of these walls.

"Do you believe me—about what she planned to do with Eliza?"

The sheriff nodded. "It was all in the last diary."

Jorie looked up, surprised.

Earl wanted to unravel this last knot. "You said you didn't read this diary—"

"I never read any of her diaries before you brought them to me."

Earl tried to figure this out. As if on cue, his elbow started itching. "You had two of them in your closet."

"But I didn't read them. I just...couldn't"

"And the third you took to Mrs. O'Laerty's. It spelled out—"

"I found it at the house the day before you took me in."

"But you didn't read it?"

"I was going to—the night you arrested me."

"How come you didn't read the first two, but you were going to read the last one?"

"I didn't want to re-live all that old pain between Ma and me that had to be in the earlier diaries. But after that night in Eliza's room, I thought maybe Ma had written her plans for Izzy in her last book. It seemed very important to get a hold of it. I thought if I could bring that part to you as evidence, maybe you could stop her. Then I wouldn't have to..."

Jorie knew his lips were starting to quiver. He blew his nose to conceal his feelings. "I searched everywhere, every chance I got. I knew it had to be there someplace. Finally, I couldn't wait any longer."

"How did you even know the diary existed?"

"Because I *made* it for her. And I knew she was using it. But even...*afterwards,* when I moved into the O'Laerty's I couldn't find it. I went back twice before I finally discovered it."

"Where was it?"

"At the bottom of a box of toys in Eliza's closet."

Earl stirred his tea, removed a leaf floating on top. "Why didn't you tell me where it was?"

"It was too late. I'd, I'd already..." he stuttered and stopped. He took a deep breath. "And then my mind—Everything was just erased"...His voice trailed off.

It was getting cool in the room. Mr. Foster got up and put more wood on the fire.

There was a long silence, while the two listened to the popping of the pitch as the flame licked the pine and maple. Slowly, the tension between them seemed to float up the chimney with the smoke.

Jorie looked out at the storm clouds gathering in the north. Almost December, there would be no more here-today-and-gone-tomorrow weather; winter was preparing to ensnare the whole of Copperdom in its clutches for the long haul.

His thoughts traveled back to the first storm of the season. The prison bars of his mind had dissolved enough to allow him to look at that last afternoon with his mother just as it was:

It was nearing the end of October; the days were definitely getting cooler and shorter. It wouldn't be long before the snows. He had a new plan, but it depended entirely on the weather. Each day apprehension mounted in his belly as he waited for the forecast. Since he worked at the *News,* it was easy enough to get.

Early on the morning of the twenty-second of October, he learned that a snow storm was coming in from Lake Superior, and should hit sometime late afternoon.

But so far it was still a crisp and sunny day. After work he didn't go to bed as usual. Instead, trying to sound casual, he said to his mother, "Ma, it's such a beautiful day I thought you might enjoy a ride in the country."

"Now?" She was clearly surprised.

"When it warms up a bit. Perhaps after lunch."

"Yes, I'd like that, Jorie."

"Where's Eliza?"

"She's at Stockwells. We can fetch her at dinnertime."

If she hadn't been at the neighbors', he was going to suggest they take her there. Something about the ride being too cold for her. Ma might refuse, but he didn't think so. She liked it better with just the two of them.

They had their noon meal. Then Jorie went to the stable to hitch up. Familiar smells assaulted his nostrils, reminding him of that day long ago when she'd made him stay naked, spread-eagle on the stone. He shuddered to think of that happening to Eliza.

He wasn't at all sure his idea would work. If it didn't he'd have to think of something else. But even now he could feel the temperature dropping.

He brought the buggy round to the house, helped his mother in, and spread the fur lap robe across her knees. They headed down to the main road, and followed it up the hill past the mine and north out into the country. To the far west he could see dark clouds forming, but his mother didn't seem to notice. It was still sunny.

She was chatting merrily, as though they were on good terms again, and all was forgiven. She seemed excited, like a schoolgirl being taken for an outing by her beau.

"I've started a new sweater for you, Jorie. You've outgrown your old ones. This one will be blue. Will you like that? It will bring out the color of your eyes."

He turned east onto a side road. The clouds were behind them, but the snow was not far off. He hoped he could get her on the trail before it started.

"Where are you taking me? Is it to be a surprise?"

"Just a pretty road I discovered. Then if you're up to it, there's a lovely footpath through the forest."

He continued on, watching the skies. Timing was everything. If the snow started too soon, they'd have to go back. If it was late, she'd be cold and want to go home before they left the buggy.

Finally, he turned onto an old lumbering road that veered north.

"It's beautiful, Jorie. I've never been back in here. Look at the maples—gorgeous colors. They're still holding their leaves. Are you looking, Jorie?"

"Yes." He looked but didn't see.

"And the oaks, of course. They always do—through the whole winter. Strange, how they cling so, those brown leaves, when their life is over."

He swallowed hard.

"It reminds me of the time when you were about eight, and we were somewhere in a forest. We pretended I was Titania, queen of the faeries, and you came to save me from the leprechauns. " She turned to him. "Do you remember?"

"Yes."

"You idolized me. I could do no wrong in your eyes." She squeezed his hand.

He wished she'd stop this kind of talk.

"Can't you say something, Jorie?"

"I reckon all boys feel that way about their mums at that age," he managed.

"Oh, but we were different. We had a world into which no other could tread. And that made our bond very unique."

It certainly did.

He drove on about a half a mile, stopped the horse, and helped her out of the buggy.

"Let's go down this trail."

The blue sky was almost gone, and the clouds were gathering quickly. They walked for about twenty minutes. Twice the trail split and each time he took the path to the left.

His gaze went skyward. The first large, lazy flakes were descending slowly. He licked one off his lip.

"It's starting to snow, Jorie. We should turn around."

"It won't last. We'll be all right."

Soon it was coming down fast, turning serious.

"Jorie, we have to get back!"

They turned around and walked until the trail split.

"Which way did we come?"

"This way."

They pushed on. Finally his mother said, "I'm sure we didn't come this far. Are you certain we're going in the right direction?"

"No. Perhaps it was this way." He led her onto another path.

"It's coming down so fast! I'm frightened!"

Walking became more difficult. The snow fell so thickly they could barely see in front of them. Unseen branches tore at their sleeves and caught in their hair.

He could hear her gasping for breath, as her steps lagged.

"I can't go much farther. I'm slipping, Jorie!"

"Take my arm."

"Do you know where we are?"

"I think so."

"I believe we're lost!"

She clung tightly to his arm except where the path was too narrow to pass two abreast. Then she would let go, and fall behind for a few steps.

Suddenly she slipped and fell, letting out a shrill shriek. He turned to see her on the ground grasping her ankle. He knelt beside her.

"It's my ankle."

She held it with her hand, rocking back and forth.

"Do you think you can walk on it?"

She tried, soon crumpled to the ground.

"Here, I'll put some snow on it, to keep the swelling down."

He packed her ankle with snow and made a pillow of leaves for her. "Lie down, Mother. Rest."

He helped her to a reclining position. She held her arms up to him and he bent to her. The snow was pouring down now, sticking to her lashes and whitening her hair. How old it made her look! How frail!

"Jorie, you can't stay here! Go on ahead, find the path. Then come back for me."

"Yes, all right."

"Go!"

He could see she was in pain and afraid, but she smiled bravely. "I may die, here. What will my poor Jorie do without his mummy?"

"Just rest, Mother."

"I've always loved you, more than anyone, Jorie."

He brushed the snow from her face, kissed her on the cheek. He knew if he stayed a moment longer, he would lose his resolve.

"Go, Jorie. You must hurry."

The hooting of an owl reverberated through the woods, answered by the cackle of a crow. He stood, turned quickly toward the path obliterated now by the silence of the falling snow. Leaving her there was the hardest thing he'd ever done. He had never loved her more.

chapter 38

ARTHUR JOHNSON CAME to the Foster house to check on his patient. When he was leaving, Earl walked down the steps with him.

"He finally broke last night. He told me everything," Earl confided to his friend.

Arthur sighed. "He told me as well. In his cell."

For the second time Earl felt a pang of jealousy. How hard he'd tried to get Jorie to confide in him. Arthur sees him once and the lad spills all.

"Do you believe it, Earl—Catherine's plans for her daughter?"

"Oh, yes! It's all laid out in her diary like a blueprint."

The doctor removed his hat, pushed a gnarled hand through his white hair, and replaced the hat, all the time his lips working. Earl knew he was fixing to say something. He watched the doctor work up to it.

Finally Arthur spoke. "You see, the boy came to me *before*... her death. He told me some story about the perverse designs she had for his little sister. He asked for my help in getting his mother committed, to protect the child."

Earl was stunned.

Arthur rubbed his forehead. "I refused. Frankly, I thought... The boy has a wild imagination, you know, Earl. Believes he receives guidance from his starline...The things he told me that day were just too bizarre for me to believe."

Arthur looked at the ground, then raised his head suddenly. For a brief moment Earl got a glimpse of the torment behind his friend's faded brown eyes.

"I didn't even try to talk to Catherine." The doctor nodded good-bye, turned abruptly and walked away.

Earl stood watching his comrade climb into his buggy and drive off. He felt a certain bond with the old man now. Perhaps the yoke of guilt would be a little easier to bear.

The judge had cancelled two poker games. Another Friday had rolled around, and tonight the game was on.

Jorie had been with Earl for two weeks and had shown no signs of doing himself in, or running away. Earl figured it was safe to leave him.

The seed of a plan was sprouting in his mind, but it depended on his getting the other *Aces* to agree.

He wouldn't walk tonight. He'd take the buggy, just in case he could pull off his scheme. Bigot would just have to put up with it.

When he arrived, the usual props were in place—*Matilda* and the cards and chips, though no one seemed eager to begin. He could hear the argument in force.

Boyce sat with his arms crossed, nursing his wound over the way the hearing had turned out. The judge was blowing halos of smoke above his head.

"I was hoping you'd have calmed down during our little hiatus. Cheer up, Buck, there'll be other cases. Maybe some actual trials for you to win." He smiled at Boyce. "Or lose."

"This one was hot, and you let it slip away."

Doc Johnson looked uncomfortable.

George asked, "Anyone like some beer? Iva's special brew."

"I'm talking to you, McKinney! I think you let this one get away!"

"I'll have one," the doctor said.

"Comin' up." George left the room.

Buck Boyce couldn't contain himself. He stood up. "Holy shit! The old man's retiring, doesn't want to bother with another trial."

"Calm yourself," the doctor advised. "You'll have your asthma trouble back."

Turning his wrath on Earl, Buck said, "I blame you, Foster. You had it in the palm of your hand." He was pacing back and forth now. "I know you had enough on the boy to bring him to justice. Then you just spread your fingers and let it all slip through. What the hell's going on?"

"It was never more than a notion in the first place, Buck. A sort of feeling. As I said in court—"

"I don't give a damn what you said in court. What the hell happened to make you go back on yourself?"

"Just didn't hold up. Wasn't enough to go on."

"Bullshit!"

George came back with a pitcher and glasses in time to quip, "Buck, you'd kick if you were hanged with a new rope."

As Arthur picked up his beer, Buck picked up the deck of cards, shuffling them crazily.

Earl was itching to get on with his real business. He wiped his mouth, in preparation of what he had to say.

"This pot of gold, we have here—"

"Gold?" the judge laughed.

"All right. Guess they're mostly coppers. This pot of copper—*Matilda*, is getting mighty heavy. I was wondering if we couldn't put her to some use."

Buck's eyes narrowed. "What are you getting at?"

"Are you saying what I think you are?" George asked.

"I'd like to see the Radcliff boy get out of town, make a new start."

"Well, if that don't beat all," Boyce tossed the deck of cards in the air.

"What are we saving her for? The Second Coming?" Earl wet his lips. "I realize Jorie will get his inheritance," Earl said. "But it will have to go through probate, and that will take time."

"Up to six months," the judge said.

"He can't survive in this town that long."

"Why's that?" Arthur said.

379

Carol A Sheldon

"Likely to be a lynching, from what I hear. His stepbrother, the Groden Gang, and their friend. I don't want to take a chance."

Earl knew the good folks of Houghton County didn't assume Jorie was guilty. Many thought it was an unfortunate accident—at worst, a case of poor judgment. But gangsters and hooligans were spreading rumors like poisonous gas around town. They would think it was sportin' fun to take the law into their own hands and make Jorie dance.

Well, boys, what do you say?" Earl held his breath.

With clenched teeth Buck spat, "Not on your life."

"I think it's time we gave the little lady up for a good cause," George said.

"I would like that very much," Arthur concurred.

Best thing for all of us, Earl thought.

The judge said, "Three 'yeas' and one 'nay'." He looked at the sheriff.

Earl spoke slowly, and with an authority he didn't feel. "The way I figure, if someone doesn't want to support this cause, he could withdraw his share of the winnings from the pot."

"We don't even know how much that would be! Never kept track," Buck said.

Earl was prepared for this. "True. That might pose a problem. Guess he'd have to estimate what he'd won over ten years or so. Of course, some of us did better than others."

"Jesus, Foster."

"And don't forget, a good deal of *Matilda* came from young Radcliff's father." Earl stopped to let this sink in. "But the rest of us would accept a fair estimate, wouldn't we? A matter of honor."

"Right," Arthur said.

Earl looked at the others. "So, if you're with me—"

"Hold on here." Buck leaned forward. "I say whoever wins the game can do whatever he wants with *Matilda*."

"All of her?" the doctor asked.

"All of her," Buck said.

Earl felt the perspiration pop. That wasn't the pact he'd hoped to get.

380

George pushed a little smoke in Buck's direction. "Our prosecuting attorney here, would probably use it to finance his campaign. Am I right?"

Buck waved the smoke away.

"All right. Fair enough," the judge said.

The doctor agreed.

"It's a deal." Earl spoke with a confidence he didn't feel.

"Ante up." The doctor dealt the first hand. "You betting, George?"

"One." The judge pushed a chip toward the middle of the table.

"Earl?"

"I'm in."

Arthur turned to Buck. "What are you going to do?"

"Submit a petition for another hearing." The prosecuting attorney was still bristling. "And I'll give my reasons to the paper."

"And what might they be?"

Buck straightened his tie. "You'll see."

"You had your hour in court. It's a little late to be thinking about doing your homework," McKinney said.

"It would look mighty strange if you refused to grant a hearing on the request of the prosecuting attorney, George."

George blew another halo of smoke. "And it might look peculiar if the retiring judge didn't support you in your upcoming campaign, boy." George bestowed a benevolent smile on the prosecuting attorney.

Earl reveled in a moment of victory, hearing Boyce called by the name usually reserved for him.

After Earl and Arthur folded, Buck and George were head to head; Buck won the hand with a flush. Pleased with his win, he seemed pacified for the moment.

It was ten minutes to ten, only time for one more hand, and Earl didn't know if he was ahead or behind. He studied the loose pile of chips in Buck's corner, and tried once again to figure the amount. He knew they had to be pretty close, but he wasn't sure *how* close. He wished for once he wasn't so orderly, hadn't stacked his up in neat piles of ten for everyone to calculate so easily.

Buck gathered in the cards, started shuffling the deck, "I've got a proposal of my own."

"Put it on the table," said George.

"Since this is a farewell party for *Matilda* here, what do you say we raise the stakes for the last hand?"

"To what?" Earl asked.

"A nickel." Buck slapped the deck down on the table.

From a penny? Earl knew he couldn't afford it, and he suspected Boyce knew it, too. He hadn't even been able to buy Cora the new stove she wanted. He broke out in a sweat, which he was sure gave Buck immense satisfaction.

"Maybe not everyone can manage the increase," offered the doctor, not looking at anyone in particular.

"Let's do it," Earl said finally, with an unaccustomed reckless-ness.

The others agreed. Buck pursed his lips and studied Earl. He picked up the cards and began shuffling again, his eyes still on the sheriff.

Earl felt uncomfortable, couldn't resist scratching his elbow. "Well, let's get on with it."

"That's just fine with me," said Buck. "Cut, Arthur. Let's keep the game honest."

Earl was dealt almost nothing of value—one king and little else. Nevertheless when it was his turn, he matched George's bet of one.

Even before the draw, Buck bet two.

He's trying to squeeze me out, Earl knew.

"How many cards?" Buck turned to Arthur.

"Two."

"Same here," said George.

Earl could feel the perspiration trickling down his back. "Three."

"Three it is."

Buck took one. "Let the betting begin," he said.

Earl picked up his cards. Another *king.* Well, at least he had a pair! He'd had better; he couldn't take the pot with what he held if Buck wasn't bluffing. It didn't help, either, having to bet before Buck.

Arthur bet one. George matched him.

Earl could feel his sphincter muscles tighten. "Two," he said.

"Here's your two and one to raise," Buck said.

Arthur and George both folded. That left Earl head to head with Buck, and it was his turn.

Earl couldn't forget how high the stakes were: *Five times what they usually were! He* was doing some other figuring. How much did he have in his bank account? Would he be able to cover the losses and pay the rent? What would Cora say if he landed on his ass?

"Quit stalling, Foster."

Earl pushed a chip forward, looked at Buck, and added a second.

George was leaning back in his chair, enjoying the playoffs.

"I'll see your bluff," called Buck.

Earl raised one bushy eyebrow. "That'll cost you."

Buck pushed his chip forward. Earl held his breath as he turned up his kings.

A brief shake of Buck's head told Earl his opponent could not best him. With a poker player's discipline, he resisted an urge to cry out in elation.

But it was only the *hand.* The pot would go to the one who had the highest winnings for the night.

When they were finished with the game, he watched as Buck finally stacked his chips. It was going to be close. But even before the last of the prosecutor's chips were stacked, it was plain to see Earl had won. This time he didn't try to hide his elation.

"I did it! Yes." His eyes filled with joy.

"I couldn't be happier," the doctor added.

"Well done, boy," George beamed at him.

This time the 'boy' didn't bother him. He'd won! He'd won *Matilda!*

Buck rose. "Can't help wondering what nefarious plot you've cooked up—involving the Radcliff kid."

Without further ado, Buck Boyce took his leave.

"Poor loser," Arthur said.

"He'll get over it. He can't afford not to." George laughed heartily. As he began to scoop the cards in, the ash from his cigar dropped on them. Earl reached for the ashtray, picked up the cards that held the ashes and dumped them in the tray. As he did, he saw their faces—the ones George had folded with. Two deuces and three eights. *A full house!*

He looked at George, who only held his eye briefly. George could have taken the hand, but not the night. He'd tossed it in to throw the game to Earl. Without that last winning hand, Earl would surely have lost to Buck.

He could say nothing, nor would George want him to.

When he left the McKinney home that night, the doctor helped him heave the heavy load into the buggy, and gave him a handshake he wouldn't soon forget. Earl climbed into the buggy. Well worth hitching up that night. He wouldn't have been able to waltz *Matilda* all the way home in his arms.

chapter 39

THE NEXT MORNING Jorie could hear Mr. Foster scurrying around. The sheriff seemed excited, said he had some errands to run, and told Jorie to *be there* when he got back. At noon, he'd returned, went out again, coming home about two.

Finally Mr. Foster said, "I want to show you something. Get your coat."

They bundled in wool jackets and mufflers.

As they stepped outside Jorie took a deep breath. It was not yet dark. If he did decide to live, how in the world would he fit back into the community? Gossip was rampant and everybody seemed to know him now. The thought of being watched daily by judging eyes was unbearable.

They walked several blocks through downtown Hancock. It was about four o'clock, already darkening; lights from the shops provided the only cheer in the quiet streets. Earl led him through the back streets, then down toward the lake. Jorie wondered again where they were going, but it didn't matter.

Descending the steep grade of Tezcuco Street was a challenge. During the last two days, the snow had started to melt, then descending temperatures had caused it to freeze. Frozen boot prints, like fossils, were imbedded in the solid surface, making it difficult and dangerous to navigate.

Just then the sheriff lost his balance on the ice and started to fall. Jorie caught him, righting him just in time.

"Thanks, thanks. I would have gone down for sure." He laughed, embarrassed. "Mrs. Foster would not take kindly to nursing me through broken bones."

They reached the train station. The sheriff opened the door and ushered Jorie inside.

"What are we doing here?"

"Good a place as any to warm ourselves. Let's get some hot tea."

They walked toward the empty end of the station where refreshments were sold.

The tea came. Jorie sat with his hands in his lap. Earl wiped his spoon carefully with his napkin and added milk and sugar. He stirred the contents of his cup slowly.

Jorie picked up his cup and blew on the tea.

Earl finally began. "Listen to me, son. I know how guilty you feel. But you can't afford to indulge in penance. Not that kind. I know all about the sort of education you got at your mother's knee—large doses of suffering leading to absolution. Well, this time, you're just going to have to live with what you did." He took a gulp of his tea. "And find a way to forgive yourself." He looked down at his cup. "I think you'll discover more than enough suffering on that road to satisfy the heartiest of appetites."

Jorie recognized for the first time that Mr. Foster must be suffering too. The sheriff knew everything, and had kept it all out of the court to protect him. This gentle man had worked unstintingly in his behalf.

He wet his own lips. "I, I want to thank you, and Mrs. Foster too, for everything—I don't deserve it."

"We think you do."

Jorie picked up his cup, drank the tea. He wished the sheriff would change the subject. He couldn't help thinking there was something else up Mr. Foster's sleeve.

He asked again, "What are we doing here?"

"I was just getting to that." Earl cleared his throat. "Your friends have taken up a collection for you—"

Jorie started to object, and Earl put up a hand to stop him.

"Rather, one we have accumulated over the years—we didn't actually know to what purpose." Earl smiled. "Now we know."

He pulled a money bag from his coat and placed it on the table. Jorie stared in amazement.

"This was not decided on a sudden impulse. Careful thought went into it."

"I can't take it."

"It's a loan."

The word 'Who?' formed on Jorie's lips.

"You don't need to know who the involved parties are. Just that there are people in this town who want to help you, Jorie. They ask only that you stay alive. If not for your sake, then for your sister's."

A lump started to form in Jorie's throat. *Everyone didn't despise him.*

"We have a ticket for you to go out west. To grow up a little, and allow this thing to die down. Let the land heal you. Give your pain to the mountains and the rivers. Then, in time, when you're ready, you can come back, see your sister again."

Jorie started to say again, "I can't—"

The sheriff almost rose out of his seat. "How long will you allow folly to hold you from your dreams? Besides," he added, calming himself, "this money is an investment in you, Jorie, We know you're clever, and you can make something of yourself. So we expect you to come back here one day and pay off your debt." Mr. Foster folded his hands. "It's a matter of honor."

Overcome with emotion, Jorie managed to say, "What's to become of Eliza—now?"

"Mrs. O'Laerty petitioned the court for custody of the child. I see no reason why her request would be denied. I trust this meets with your approval?"

Jorie could only nod. The feelings that churned and tumbled inside him were too complex to understand. They were rolling over him, intermingling in convergent waves. At least he was *feeling* again.

"I collected your things this afternoon at O'Laerty's. Your suitcases are waiting in a locker. The train leaves at four o'clock."

"Train? *Today?*" It was all coming too fast.

"Yes. I packed your clothing, a few books, and your sketch pad. Here's the sum we have for you." Mr. Foster pushed the bag across the table. "Perhaps not as sizeable as your father meant you to have. We'll get the ball rolling on that, too. But for now, this will give you a start."

Jorie could only swallow.

"There's about a hundred fifty dollars there."

Mr. Foster placed the ticket in front of him. "This will take you to Chicago, and there you'll change trains to Denver, then—"

The door opened, ushering in the elated shriek of a little girl.

"Jawie!" the child squealed.

Eliza came running up to him, with Helena on her heels. He swooped her up in his arms, buried his head in her chestnut curls. Tears filled, then overflowed their banks.

She gave him a quizzical look. "Why are you crying?"

"Your brother's about to leave on a long journey, Eliza."

She looked frightened and pulled back.

"Are you going away to die like Mummy did?"

He pulled her to him. "No, Izzy, I'm not going to die."

"Promise?"

He looked at Earl. "Promise."

"Where are you going?"

"Out west."

"May I go with you? S'il vous plait?"

Jorie's stomach turned. Maybe he'd saved her just in time.

"Not this time, Izzy. I want you to stay here and be very happy with Henna."

"Will you come back?"

Jorie took her small face between his hands, and pushed out the words, "I will, and I'll write to you every week."

Jorie closed his eyes, and held Eliza closer. For one precious moment, all he knew was the sweet breath of his little sister. Then he said, "I can't thank you enough, Helena."

The Irish woman wiped her eyes. "Oh, be gone with you, now."

Earl stood up. "I'll get your traveling cases."

The party headed for the platform, with Eliza in Jorie's arms. When the train announced its advent with long, piercing whistles, he reluctantly handed his sister over to Helena and picked up his bags. He gave Izzy one more kiss and looked at Earl, unable to speak.

"Say hello to Mr. Muir for me, kid."

Jorie returned the grin. For the first time he felt a kind of peace. And maybe, even something close to hope.

EPILOGUE

IT'S BEEN A year and a half since we put Jorie on the train to go out west. He kept his promise and wrote to his little sister—not every week, but almost. I reckon I'd find out from Helena what he was up to out west. Seems he met up with John Muir and was working with him. Sometimes I got to read his letters when Izzy showed them to me. Of course, since these notes were written to his little sister, there was nothing sad or depressing in them. Whether he was as cheerful as he made out, I don't know.

One day I got a letter from him addressed to me. There was a note for twenty dollars in it, a partial return of the loan, he wrote, and there would be more. He said he wanted to live up to the trust I and the unknown others had put in him. He said that the tranquility and vastness of the mountains instilled a sense of peace in him, and that the beauty of the open land was a refreshing tonic. "I am finally appreciating the life I have, and want to give you credit for saving me to live it." Well, that brought on a tear or two.

He went on to say he'd written a few letters for Mr. Muir to send back to Washington, asking that some of this land be put aside for national parks for future generations to enjoy. He said we needed to do this before it was all gobbled up and consumed by the onslaught of buying and building.

Then in a post script he asked me if Kaarina had married. When I replied that she had not and frequently asked if I'd heard from him, he wrote to say that when he came back to visit Eliza, if she were still available, he'd like to ask her to join him out west. He didn't know if she'd like living in the rough conditions out there. Maybe he could build a cabin for them. And she might enjoy putting a woman's touch to it.

He said he wasn't sure any of this would ever happen, but would I give her my best wishes. I sent him her address. He got the point and they began corresponding.

The last I heard he was coming back to Michigan to see his little sister this summer and I hope, for God's sake, to propose to that lovely girl he left behind.

Earl Foster
May 12, 1901

Made in the USA
Charleston, SC
19 August 2011